Thunder in Paradise

Satan's Last Storm

Thunder in Paradise
Satan's Last Storm

Jonathan R. Cash

ш
WHITAKER
HOUSE

THUNDER IN PARADISE: SATAN'S LAST STORM

For interviews and speaking engagements, contact Jonathan Cash at:
In the Sky Ministries
P. O. Box 15770
Chesapeake, Virginia 23328-5770
Phone: 757.546.3313
E-mail: intheskyministries@juno.com
Web site: www.theageoftheantichrist.com

ISBN: 0-88368-656-2
Printed in the United States of America
© 2001 by Jonathan Cash

Whitaker House
30 Hunt Valley Circle
New Kensington, PA 15068

Library of Congress Cataloging-in-Publication Data

Cash, Jonathan R., 1965–
     Thunder in paradise : Satan's last storm / by Jonathan Cash.
          p. cm.
     ISBN 0-88368-656-2 (pbk. : alk. paper)
     1. Spiritual warfare—Fiction. 2. End of the world—Fiction.
     3. Good and evil—Fiction. 4. Devil—Fiction. I. Title.
     PS3553.A79373 T48 2001
     813'.54—dc21
                                        2001002808

2 3 4 5 6 7 8 9 10 11 12 13 / 08 07 06 05 04 03 02 01

Dedication

This book is dedicated to every person who longs to see the face of God and who recognizes the authority of Scripture. There is great debate among theologians about who will live during the Millennium and who will go straight to heaven. Whether you live during this blessed time or not, it is my desire to whet your appetite for the things of God and to give you a greater desire to see heaven in all of its glory.

I also dedicate this book to my two children, Christina and Caleb. I pray that I will always be a father who imitates his heavenly Father in heaven.

Foreword

This book is my attempt to create a plausible story about the Millennium. The Bible speaks little of this period, but it does say that it will happen. Revelation 20 offers the best picture of this spectacular yet unusual epoch. Several passages from the Old Testament prophets are also used to form this tale, but I have taken great liberty to fill in the gaps that the Bible leaves untold. The structure and outline of *Thunder in Paradise* is biblically accurate, yet the day-to-day details and the characters are fictitious. My prayer is that, after reading this book, readers will not only have a greater understanding of Bible prophecies surrounding the Millennium, but also have a closer walk with the King of the universe.

—Jonathan R. Cash

Contents

One

The Great Leap

The young man whistled softly, trying to calm his racing heart. He forced himself to stroll casually down the boulevard, but his eyes darted to and fro as he neared his target.

Solomon glanced at the mountain peaks rising above the quaint northern Russian town of twenty thousand in which he lived. He experienced the same pang of longing he had felt for some time. He wanted nothing more than to get beyond those mountains to some faraway place.

"Good evening, Solomon," smiled Anne Margaret, a lady who belonged to his church.

Solomon jumped. "Uh, good...good evening, Ms. Margaret."

She stopped in Solomon's path. He wanted to walk around her but didn't want to appear suspicious.

"Are you okay, Solomon?" Solomon groaned inwardly, but he smiled and touched her lightly on the arm.

"I'm fine, Ms. Margaret. I just didn't get a lot of sleep last night. I was reading one of my favorite history books about World War II. Wow, that was one cool time!"

She shook her head. "Well, Solomon, I'm afraid I don't share your enthusiasm for war. I happened to live through the Battle of Armageddon, and I didn't find anything 'cool' about it. It was devastating."

Ms. Margaret looked intently at him for a moment. "History is important, son, but remember, it's *His* story. We must concentrate on Jesus."

11

Solomon forced another smile.

"I've read my history over and over again. I'm sure Armageddon was pretty frightening. A week doesn't go by at my house without my parents reminiscing about the Stone Age."

Her spirit sensed something foreign, something almost evil. It wasn't Solomon's words; it was an air, an attitude. His demeanor conjured up some very bad memories that were over 999 years old.

"Remember, Solomon, we don't know what we will face in just a few weeks. Armageddon may not seem like a distant memory then."

Solomon started to walk away. "Well, I guess I'll be seeing you on Sunday..."

"Tell your parents hello," Ms. Margaret called as he sprinted away.

"You bet."

Solomon was annoyed at what Ms. Margaret had said. It was only weeks away from the year 1000. All his life, he had heard that at the turn of the Millennium the Devil would be released for a final showdown with God. His parents, his teachers—even Allison, the girl to whom he had been engaged—were preparing as if it were the end of the world.

Solomon had settled on a more realistic explanation for the supposed coming of the Devil. It was all a bunch of hogwash designed to scare the younger generation into blindly obeying Jesus. Life would continue as usual, as it had for hundreds of years, and he was restless for something new.

He had tried to tell his parents and Allison about his doubts, but they didn't want to listen to his "lack of faith." Lately, however, a small but growing number of the youngest generation had begun to resist Jesus and His daily *Word*. Solomon counted himself among those who were beginning to resent the world they lived in, feeling as if they were being told how to think and what to do.

The only adventures his family had ever taken were vacations to Jerusalem in order to worship the Lord. He was eighteen years old, and he wanted to experience something different in life. He didn't share the interests of most of his friends at school, and though he had tried to fit in, he felt he had nothing in common with them. He didn't know how to explain his feelings of intellectual and spiritual unrest.

His love was ancient history, especially twentieth- and twenty-first-century history leading up to the Great Tribulation. He could spend days reading and studying about the way life used to be and not even notice that he was hungry. He consumed history like a glutton devours food.

As the sun's light faded in the west, stars brightened the evening sky. Solomon stopped a block away from the three-story building that housed Thompson's Gravity Vehicles. He leaned against a lamppost, pulled out a newspaper from his knapsack, and pretended to read the latest edition of *The Word of Jesus*. The paper was published daily, and everybody was highly encouraged to study the King's words. The millions of people who had survived the Great Tribulation, and those in heaven who had been chosen by Jesus to return to earth for the Millennium, absorbed every word as if their lives depended on it.

He looked up from the newspaper and saw no one in sight. Everybody was home for family time, something Jesus preached about on an all-too-regular basis, he thought grimly. Solomon slowly walked toward Thompson's store. The showroom filled the entire first floor of the building. His hands began to sweat as he lusted over the "Meteor," the latest air bike model—considered the crème de la crème. Almost every teenager in northern Russia wanted one, and almost every parent had already said no.

"I want you to rely on Jesus for everything, and to know the difference between wants and needs," his father had said yesterday. "I'm not going to buy it for you, and I don't want you spending your money on the latest fads. That kind of lifestyle will corrupt you!"

He sighed. How he wished he could burn that memory into ashes! He had feigned compliance to his parents, but in reality he rejected their beliefs. Something was changing deep inside him about which he understood little. It made him feel strong, in control, powerful, even respected.

As the Meteor glowed in the light of the street lamp, Solomon thought it was the most beautiful thing on the face of the earth. He pictured himself rocketing around the countryside like a racecar driver in the old Indy 500. Everybody would want to be like him or at least be seen with him. The Meteor seemed to beckon him through the window.

"The fastest bike on the market!" read the sticker. "Zero to 250 mph in six seconds. Maximum speed, 500 mph. Try the *Meteor Experience* today. It's like riding on the back of a shooting star."

As Solomon gazed at the vehicle, a dark spirit hovered nearby. His black wings flapped methodically against the breeze. As the venomous spirit neared Solomon, his rigid claws slowly opened. A megawatt smile covered his face; his teeth dripped with anticipatory drool.

Solomon's mouth dried as he examined the glass-enclosed structure. The showroom could be seen from the street. How could he steal the Meteor and not be caught? He strolled nonchalantly around the side of the building.

Bright headlights greeted him.

"What are you doing away from your family? It's almost nine at night," shouted a police officer.

Solomon's heart jumped.

"Is that you, Bill?" Solomon asked, shading his eyes. He quickly recovered his composure and smiled between gritted teeth.

The spotlight died on the state gravity vehicle. Bill Larkson hopped off its seat and approached him. He looked relieved to see Solomon. Bill was the town's popular chief of police. He was 5 feet, 11 inches, and as he walked toward Solomon, Solomon realized for the first time that he had grown almost as tall as Bill.

"Solomon Action? Your dad told me you like to wander around at night. I thought at first you were one of those rebellious youths from the East. You should be more careful about staying out so late," he added with concern.

Solomon forced himself to ignore the warmth in Bill's voice. He tacked what he hoped was a benign expression on his face. Bill was his neighbor and Allison's father. He had an easy laugh and had been a good friend for years. It was practically impossible not to like him—unless, of course, you were attempting to break the law.

Solomon patted Bill on the back and laughed too loudly.

"Oh, man, you caught me red-handed. I was going to rob that bank over there, take your daughter hostage, head for Jerusalem, and overthrow the city."

Bill grew uneasy. Solomon hadn't been acting like himself for weeks. What's going on with you, Solomon? he thought. This is a dangerous time for you to start drifting away from God. Aloud he said, "Don't be joking about that stuff. I know you young men have never experienced Jesus on the same level as those who survived the Great Tribulation, but you must—"

Solomon rolled his eyes. "Come on, Bill! I'm just having some fun. You old-timers don't know how to laugh anymore!"

Bill relaxed a little and chuckled. Then he placed a hand on Solomon's shoulder, and his eyes grew serious.

"Are you really all right?"

"Sure." Bill looked down at Solomon's hands, which were shaking. Solomon quickly hid them from view and popped another smile on his face. Bill frowned but attributed Solomon's behavior to youth.

He really wanted to ask Solomon why he had broken his daughter's heart, why one minute she was everything to him, and the next, she was nothing. He wanted to, but he didn't.

The demon shadowing Solomon grumbled at Bill under his putrid breath, "Go back to your wife and daughter. I have some real work to do here for my master."

"You'd better be moving along now, son," Bill said. "Your parents love you, and they'll be wondering where you are."

Solomon turned as if to leave. Then he stopped and saluted Bill.

"Thank you, sir, for looking out for my welfare. See ya later!"

Bill shook his head, then jumped on his air bike and headed north toward the town center, disappearing from view.

Solomon was alone at last. He made up his mind to do what he felt like doing. He sprinted to the nearest window, grabbed a towel from his knapsack, wrapped it around his fist, and smashed a window. No alarm sounded. Solomon grinned as he carefully climbed through the open window.

"People are so trusting nowadays."

The demon smiled. He would do anything to capture Solomon's soul.

Solomon moved toward the coveted prize. His eyes feasted on the machine as his hand caressed its black seat. "Oh, baby, you are so beautiful. You are mine, all mine."

He heard a soft cackling sound from the direction of the shattered window, and he lunged under a counter. He held his breath and felt his heart pummeling his chest. Had it been his imagination? He closed his eyes and tried a prayer. "I deserve this cycle," whispered Solomon. He clenched his fist toward the marble floor, then raised it toward the sky. "Prove Your love, Jesus. If You really want my heart, let me get away with this."

He waited several more minutes without hearing anything out of the ordinary. Spotting a case of keys behind the counter, he cautiously moved toward it. There were at least a dozen keys, all unmarked. He grabbed them with both hands and ran toward the prize, ducking behind it. He knew that if somebody were to come along the sidewalk in front of the showroom, it wouldn't be hard to spot him. But he didn't care now. His hand trembled as he placed the key near the hole.

Solomon squinted through the darkness. "Come on, baby, fit...fit..."

The tip of the key touched the metal near the keyhole. He slowly moved it toward the hole. The key hit its mark.

"Bingo!"

Suddenly, he jerked his head to the left. Was that a shadow? The muscles in his face froze, but his eyes darted back and forth, scanning the sidewalk outside.

The Great Leap

The demon lurking nearby laughed. "Foolish human!"

He wrapped his invisible wings completely around Solomon's body, his fangs within inches of the boy's skull.

"Probably only a dog," Solomon said with relief.

He didn't have time to waste. He was missed at home, and he knew his snoopy neighbor Bill would conveniently drop by to see how the family was doing. Solomon was a good liar, yet every deception had its limits. He mounted the gravity cycle as if it were a wild stallion ready for a fight.

He stared at the large, glowing red button near the speedometer, his eyes fixated on seven small letters encircling the top of the button. They spelled g-r-a-v-i-t-y. His right hand moved excitedly toward the hypnotizing light.

At that moment, sharp yet undetectable teeth penetrated Solomon's flesh. The demon screamed in ecstasy as his teeth sank deeper into Solomon's soul and then penetrated his heart. The sinister spirit entrenched himself within the naïve boy. Solomon noticed only a sense of inner strength, a feeling that he was right no matter what anybody else said, even Jesus Christ Himself.

"Nobody is going to tell me what to do."

"Good boy, Solomon," encouraged the demon.

Solomon placed his index finger on the booster switch. "As they used to say, 'You only live once,'" snickered Solomon as he tensed his body for the jolt.

"Don't move!" cried a familiar voice from the other side of the building.

Solomon pounced on the button. The machine instantly reared several feet off the ground.

"Don't make me shoot."

The light shining from the man's gun blinded him for a moment. Solomon slapped at the throttle. The machine rocketed toward the window. A gunshot of spiraling light knocked Solomon off the bike inches from the window. The Meteor kept going, crashed through the glass, flew through the air, and ran straight into the town clock. It crashed to the ground in a dirt-splitting thud. Twirling streaks of light encapsulated Solomon, suspending him just inches above the glass–coated floor. The man approached him with caution. Then his eyes grew wide.

"Solomon!" gasped Bill Larkson, shock registering in his voice.

Allison stared at her reflection in the mirror. She puckered her petite lips, then pressed them together for a moment and released them. She looked down at the open cedar chest below the mirror and spotted a pink bow. *His* favorite bow. She caressed it fondly. Corralling her long, brown hair, she made a ponytail, tied a bright bow around it, and went back to scrutinizing her appearance.

"What's wrong with me?" Allison deliberated. She held her breath for a long time as she studied herself, then suddenly let out a deep sigh.

"I think I'm at least attractive. I have a good personality. I'm fun to be with—and, most importantly, I love the Lord. What more does Solomon want?" She pulled her ponytail up near the top of her head and moved her face to the right and to the left, examining her profile. Closing her eyes, she let her hair fall back down again.

In truth, Allison was beautiful. She had soft, wavy brown hair, strikingly blue eyes, high cheekbones, and almost translucent skin. A child of the millennial age, she was tall and slender and had never experienced sickness, disease, or death. She also had never known deep sadness—until recently.

An obedient child, and now, an elegant young lady, Allison was cheerful and outgoing. She had easily accepted the world into which she had been born and felt love and gratitude to the Lord and to her parents, with whom she shared a warm, close relationship.

Intelligent and curious about the natural world, she had immediately been drawn to Solomon and his quick mind. As little children, they had eagerly explored the world around them, enjoying a special kinship with the animals that roamed peacefully in the forested area close by. They had spent hours hiking in the surrounding mountains and valleys, always wanting to learn more about God's amazing creation. As they grew older, they shared a fascination for science and history.

Allison knew there were others who sought her company, but she was happy with Solomon. She liked to talk with him about the books he had been reading and to see his eyes light up as he talked about the history of the world in the twenty-first century. When she studied history, she looked at the destruction of the Antichrist and the imprisonment of the Devil as one more reason to thank God for all He had done in creating a perfect world for them to live in.

She had thought Solomon felt the same. In fact, she and Solomon had grown so close that becoming engaged seemed to be the natural next step in their relationship. She had felt so sure that they were meant to be together. So what had happened? What had changed?

She remembered their last conversation.

"I don't see life the way you do, Allison. You just accept things the way they are. Don't you want anything different from what you have?"

"I don't know what you mean!"

"Don't you want freedom?"

"Freedom? I have freedom!"

He shook his head. "Not that kind of freedom. I mean freedom to do your own thing!"

Her heart sank into her stomach. She muttered softly. "You mean freedom to...to disobey Jesus?"

Solomon started to respond, then stopped. He stared at her for a long time, then exploded.

"I'm just tired of the same old stuff!"

Staring at the wall, she quietly asked, "Solomon, is it me you're bored with?" She paused. "Or is it Jesus?"

"Allison, dinner's ready," called her mother.

As she turned away from the mirror, a tear slipped from her eye and dropped to the carpet.

"Be right there, Mom."

———————

Ken Action glanced at his watch for the hundredth time in the past hour. He shook his head in disbelief.

"I just don't get it."

His wife managed a fleeting smile. She knew that Ken and Solomon were having their differences, but she tried to keep a positive attitude. She ran a hand through her long brunette hair. Emily was a pretty woman with a slender, petite frame. Her upbeat, outgoing nature had won Ken over many years before.

"Ken, don't worry. Solomon will be home soon. You know he loves being outside at nighttime."

She sympathetically watched as her husband struggled with his thoughts.

Ken was both alarmed and angry. "Why is he always wandering around at night?" he wondered out loud. "Is he hiding something? Is he starting to get tempted by the demons that are sure to start attacking at Satan's release?"

He vented to Emily. "You know we've told him to be home by eight." He was getting heated. "Solomon's not obeying us anymore! He was so good when he was younger. Jesus meant so much to him. Now, it's like—" He clenched his fists. "It's like something has gotten into him, something that brings back memories I'd rather forget."

Ken closed his eyes. He was six feet tall and able bodied. He felt confident at handling most things, but tonight he felt weak and vulnerable. Emily clutched his hand as she moved closer to him on the loveseat. She had never seen him like this before. She was hurting as much as he was, but she was trying to be strong for him.

"Don't do this to yourself, Ken." Emily caressed his neck. "You have been one fantastic dad and spiritual leader of this family. You have nothing to regret. You have always been there for him—and you've always been there for me."

Ken jumped to his feet, looked at his watch, and nervously walked toward the window.

"All those trips to Jerusalem to visit King Jesus. How could anybody see the Lord in person and not give his whole heart to Him?" His eyes scouted the landscape.

Emily got up and moved toward Ken. "It's just a phase Solomon is going through. He'll snap out of it soon, I'm sure." She stood behind him and put her arms around his waist; she softly rubbed her forehead against his neck. "Have some faith, honey. Maybe he's with Allison."

The Great Leap

Ken turned from the night and faced his wife of 999 years. "Allison's home with her parents. She knows how to act." He took a deep breath and sighed, his body exhausted from worry. "I know Allison adores him, but she's one smart cookie. She knows there's something wrong, too. I have faith in Jesus," Ken hesitated as his wife's eyes grabbed at his heart, "but I'm not so sure about Solomon."

His fears for his son's salvation had been growing. He turned back toward the window. The darkness of the night seemed to drain his hope. "Two weeks from now, Satan is going to be set free." He shook his head as he peered into the shadows. "I'm afraid that Solomon is not ready."

Ken and Emily turned from the window. A ray of light reflected off a mirror in the room.

"It's Solomon!" Ken said, as he ran toward the door. Emily followed him onto the front porch.

A gravity vehicle slowly cut through the air as it approached their home.

"It's Bill!" exclaimed Ken as he and Emily hurried to meet the cycle. As their eyes adjusted to the darkness, they recognized their son, sitting handcuffed on the back of the machine.

"Solomon, what have you done?" cried Emily. She wanted to run to his side, but Ken tightened his grip on her hand.

"Solomon, tell us what happened," he said firmly.

The boy stared at the ground without a hint of emotion. How he wished he hadn't gotten caught. Facing his parents was the hardest thing he had ever had to do.

Bill climbed off the police vehicle and slowly helped Solomon do the same. Bill sadly stared at the teenager as he directed Solomon toward his parents.

"Ken, Emily," sighed Bill. He struggled for a sympathetic way to break the news. "Solomon wasn't stargazing tonight."

Ken continued holding Emily's hand as they walked toward their son. "Solomon," began Ken, "don't make Bill tell us."

Solomon raised his face toward his parents. Their pain appeared excruciating. He glanced at his mother as he spoke.

"Guys, I, uh..." He began to shake his head violently. "All I wanted was that G.V. that I've been asking for, begging for, since last year." He kicked his foot against the earth. "You can afford it. I even offered to pay for it myself, and you wouldn't let me buy it. I'm sick of being treated like a child. I don't know what got into me tonight. I just had to have the Meteor—even if I had to steal it!"

"Ken and Emily," interrupted Bill, "I'm sure you know stealing is a very serious offense. The fact that we are friends cannot interfere with the justice system."

Ken broke from Emily and approached his son. Solomon refused to look his way. The boy turned his head to the side.

"Son, are you ashamed, or are you just mad that you got caught?" tested Ken.

Emily began to weep as she read the answer on his face.

"Solomon, you know the law of Jesus," sobbed the brokenhearted mother. "I can't believe you would do something like this!"

Ken turned toward Bill, who was fighting back tears.

"Can we keep him here tonight?"

Bill grimaced as he swallowed the lump in his throat. "This type of evil must be addressed with the utmost severity." He mumbled to himself as he looked away, "I don't know how I'm going to break this news to Allison."

Emily interrupted him as Solomon's face turned gray. "He's just a boy, Bill! You can pick him up tomorrow morning if you must, but please let him stay here tonight."

She couldn't bear to think about the son she had borne sitting in a jail cell for even one night.

She tried to hug him, but Bill pulled him away. "Ken, you need to take Emily right now. My hands are tied. He must stay overnight in the detention center."

"No, Bill, you can't do this," cried Emily as Ken restrained her. Ken peered into Solomon's eyes. His gaze was not returned.

"Bill, do what you must." He wrapped his arms around Emily's quivering body. "Solomon, we love you." He began to fight his emotions. "Solomon, what about Jesus? You know Him, don't you, son?"

Solomon burst forth in wild passion.

"I went to the altar at church! I know Him all too well!"

Solomon tried to pull away from Bill. Ken quickly helped restrain him. Emily dropped to her knees as she saw the torment within her son.

"Take him away, please," said Emily as she tried to gather her emotions. Solomon looked scared and shocked as he heard his mom say those words. Ken bent down and embraced Emily as Bill guided Solomon onto the gravity bike. Solomon had to choke back the tears as Bill checked the cuffs. The reality of the situation had hit all of them.

"Mom, Dad," whimpered Solomon as Bill climbed aboard the bike.

Ken and Emily clutched each other silently as they stared at their son. Words were useless as Solomon's downcast face turned away from them. Only the sound of crickets filled the deafening void, until the state gravity vehicle took off, carrying their son to jail. As Bill drove off into the night, he wondered how he would break the news to Allison.

Two

Gathering Clouds

Ken helped Emily up from the grass. Neither knew what to say. The image of her son in handcuffs was engraved in Emily's mind. She couldn't shake it as they slowly walked toward the empty house.

Ken stopped near the steps to the porch. He couldn't believe this was happening to his boy. He wished this were just a dream, a nightmare that he could awaken from at any moment. He sighed as he realized that life wasn't going to be easy anymore. His tear-filled eyes gazed deeply into Emily's pale face.

"We've got to trust Jesus," Ken reminded her. Emily dried her eyes with the back of her hand. The boy she had borne, had breast-fed, had nurtured, was a felon. It was horrible. "You've been a great mother, Emily." He cupped her cheeks in the palms of his hands as he tried to reassure her. "Jesus will get through to him." Ken softly chuckled. "I was more hardheaded than Solomon before I got saved. If He can get through my hard skull, He can get through to Solomon."

Emily cheered up a bit. "Let's try to get some sleep."

"I'll meet you in the bedroom in a couple of minutes." Ken gently pulled away from his bride. "I need some time to think things over."

Emily took the cue. "Don't be long."

Ken strolled down a well-beaten path to the frog pond at the edge of the woods. The night air was crisp but not cold. He sighed as he thought about his son. Solomon was beginning to remind him of himself when he was young and foolish. Ken had grown up in a time before the Second Coming of Christ, a time when evil was the way of the world. His father had been a hypocrite, and his mother was always making excuses for her husband's ways. Ken closed his eyes. He knew deep down that Solomon didn't have an easy excuse for rejecting the Lord. He knew that Emily and he were godly parents, but with their son's latest actions, he was tempted to blame himself.

He took a deep breath as he tried to figure out what had gone wrong. "Maybe I work too much? That can't be it." His responsibilities at the university took him from home only thirty hours a week. "How ironic. I'm supposed to be good at teaching communication skills, and I can't even talk to my own son anymore."

A Siberian tiger met him along the path.

"Hey, boy." Ken ran his fingers through the tame beast's colorful coat. "Sometimes I wish I had your kind of life—no cares or concerns."

Life in the Millennium was paradise compared to life during the Great Tribulation and the time leading up to it. Everybody had a job and received enough money to live a comfortable life. Jesus ran the economy and the government, and they hummed along like perfectly tuned machines. Nobody was hungry, there was no war, and most people treated their neighbors as they themselves wanted to be treated. Sin was nearly absent on the earth. This was paradise, yet over the past couple of years, thorns had begun popping up out of nowhere. Jesus had warned His people to expect this kind of unrest before Satan's release, but it still wasn't easy to swallow, especially when the weed was in your own backyard.

The slim but muscular cat stared at Ken. It was as if the tiger knew what Ken was going through. It followed him to the edge of the pond where Ken dropped to the ground in exhaustion.

He loved this spot. It was his favorite place in the world, barring Jerusalem. When Jesus placed him in Northern Russia, his first reaction was, "You're sending me to Siberia!" Ken chuckled at the thought. The Millennium's weather patterns were perfect for everybody except for meteorologists who loved storms. The earth's temperature from pole to pole was seventy-seven degrees twenty-four hours a day, seven days a week. Rain was not needed because springs of water bubbled up from beneath the surface, feeding the crops and watering the rivers.

Northern Russia was a great place to live, thought Ken, and a great place to raise a family. He moaned at the thought of the word *family.*

Ken gazed at the pond; its water was as pure as a glacier stream. Fish frolicked in all corners. The tiger licked his hand as Ken's eyes slowly closed. The sounds of paradise faded as a past war filled the screen of his mind. The Battle of Armageddon began to replay in Ken's mind...

The Devil lunged toward Christ. His claws were only inches from Christ's face when he was blinded by the glory of the Lord.

"Guilty!" judged Jesus.

"You overgrown, judgmental—" shrieked Lucifer.

"Quiet!" ordered Jesus as a flaming sword gushed from His mouth. Satan was surrounded by an unbreakable force field. Christ motioned for the False Prophet to join him. The imposter's eyes filled with fear as he suddenly found himself joined at the hip with the Devil himself.

Blasphemy, Satan's highest-ranking demonic general, couldn't control himself any longer. He rocketed toward the Messiah with reckless passion. The archangel Michael darted toward the demon, only to be stopped by a gesture from the King. Jesus pointed His nail-scarred hand toward the demon general.

"You have no right to—" spat Blasphemy as a tornado-like vacuum of pure light captured him.

Ken was suspended above the town as the battle raged. His jaw dropped open as he saw the Devil, Blasphemy, and the False Prophet squirm in Jesus' noose. Their combined, absolute evil shocked Ken.

"Come out of him," ordered Jesus as He pointed toward the Devil.

The Devil had taken complete control of the Antichrist's body. Jesus was separating them for eternity. Satan's spirit body peeled away from the Antichrist. The light cascading from the finger of Jesus glued the False Prophet and the Antichrist together for eternity.

"You will pay!" screeched the two as they tried to free themselves in vain.

Ken heard a loud crash coming from below his feet. A monstrous earthquake began to wreck the remains of Jerusalem. The penetrating eyes of the Lord remained fixated on the two.

"You coward," spouted the Antichrist, "fight fairly! Let us out of this dog's net!"

Jesus turned His flaming eyes to a vacant part of the city. Ken began to shake as a quarter mile chunk of earth crashed inward toward the bowels of hell. Troops from the Antichrist's army, along with Chinese militia from the East, panicked as the earth swallowed some of them whole. Ken closed his eyes. The blackness of the crater was darker than anything he had ever seen. What he tried to mask with his eyes shocked his spirit. The evil was palpable.

The Antichrist and False Prophet were busy vomiting accusations toward Jesus. They didn't see their eternal grave waiting for them. Orange and purple flames crawled toward the top of the great abyss. The flames appeared purposeful, as if they were an army marching toward conquest.

"Satan, Blasphemy, help us, you cowards," huffed the Antichrist as his feet reacted to the first flare of divine wrath.

Neither could offer help. They were tied with the light of Christ. Jesus' stern demeanor alarmed the four. They had never seen this side of Christ before. When Jesus spoke, they were silenced.

"You have tried to destroy My kingdom. You have attempted to destroy the people I love." His words were like daggers to their hearts. "You have deceived the nations. You have mistaken My mercy for weakness."

The flames from the pit of hell spiraled around them. They screamed in anguish. The Devil and Blasphemy turned their heads. For the first time in thousands of years, they feared a wrathful God.

"Guilty of high treason," pronounced Jesus as the flames swept them downward.

Ken opened one eye. The hole closed around them as their faint screams followed them. Jesus turned toward the Devil. Millions of angels and humans watched in horror as Satan took one last stab.

"Jesus," smiled Satan, trying another ploy, "we are brothers. The Bible says to love your brother as you love yourself. You cannot be righteous if You don't love from Your heart."

Jesus didn't flinch. He stared at the Devil without any sign of emotion. He raised His nail-scarred hands toward him.

"You did this to Me. You are not My brother. My Word says in Revelation 22:15, 'Outside are dogs and sorcerers and sexually immoral and murderers and idolaters, and whoever loves and practices a lie.'"

Satan laughed as a haunted expression crept on his face.

"That's Your interpretation, Brother," Satan smirked. "Sounds like You are setting Yourself up to be judge above Your Father."

Jesus countered, "John 5:26–27 says, 'For as the Father has life in Himself, so He has granted the Son to have life in Himself, and has given Him authority to execute judgment also, because He is the Son of Man.'"

Satan sneered, "It's just like You to quote Yourself and claim You're something special."

Jesus ignored the Devil as He turned His eyes toward the earth. With a nod of His head, He opened the eyes of the troops infesting the planet below. Tens of millions of them suddenly saw Jesus in the sky. They turned their laser guns toward the King of the universe.

"Get Him," screamed the commander of the Antichrist's army.

A double-edged sword shot from the mouth of Jesus as their arsenal of weapons were unleashed against Him—all to no avail. The sword of the Lord slammed into the earth only feet from the commander.

"Missed," mocked the Devil as he struggled to break free.

The silver sword, which was stuck in a rock, began to glow red. The commander reached for it, and a blinding light flashed from the weapon. He writhed in agony as his body began to melt. His tongue rotted in his mouth as he choked on his bloodied vomit. The troops began to scatter as they saw their leader's flesh drip onto the ground. The plague quickly spread like a flood. Hundreds of fleeing men near the commander were smitten in like fashion. Panic spread like wildfire as an invisible plague consumed the men.

"You call this love?" belched Satan as thousands more were destroyed.

Sorrow filled the Lord as millions began to thrash about in anguish. The troops of heaven covered their eyes and ears. Ken sobbed.

"They chose your way over My Father's way," thundered Jesus as He blast a burst of light at the Devil. His mouth was instantly welded shut.

The Devil remained silent. His worst nightmare could not be shut out. His body was immobile; his eyes were forced open, yet his spirit remained stubbornly closed.

Millions of men lay dead in the Valley of Jehoshaphat. The Lord's sword continued to glow a deep shade of red. Without mercy, the plague attacked the remaining troops. Not a soul survived. Blood ran like a river. Ken tried to shake the image from his memory as he watched Jesus move toward the Devil. All of creation watched as the King confronted Satan.

"I created you as the most beautiful of the angels. I gave you more than you could have imagined, yet you craved more. How you have fallen, O morning star! You weakened the nations. You said in your heart, 'I will ascend into heaven. I will exalt my throne above the stars of God; I will also sit on the mount of the congregation. I will ascend above the heights of the clouds; I will be like the Most High.'"

Jesus slowly circled the Devil as He spoke. Blasphemy wisely resisted comment. Satan was powerless. He couldn't move a muscle, not even his mouth.

"Your pride has been your downfall. You are guilty of twisting My Word, guilty of destroying My people, and guilty of leading the great rebellion of angels. You are hereby sentenced to one thousand years to an abyss of darkness."

Jesus raised His hands toward the heavens. A black hole appeared on the eastern horizon. As it cascaded toward the earth, the hole appeared to envelop the atmosphere. Within seconds, it covered the entire sky. The moon seemed to turn bloodred as the black hole absorbed its light. The blackness began to implode and rocket in Satan's direction. Blasphemy sneered as he watched his overbearing boss get the ax.

"People of My kingdom," announced Christ, "evil never wins. I am the Creator of the universe, and I set the laws. Obey Me, and it will go well with you. Love Me with your whole heart, soul, and spirit."

The resurrected saints, who had followed Jesus from heaven, bowed to their Maker. Ken, along with those who were not killed during the Tribulation, sang a hymn of deliverance.

"'Great and marvelous are Your works, Lord God Almighty! Just and true are Your ways, O King of the saints! Who shall not fear You, O Lord, and glorify Your name? For You alone are holy.'"

The black hole continued to shrink and encompass the Devil. The archangel Michael appeared from within the darkness. He held a key in his right hand and a great chain in his left. The earth began to shake fiercely. Boulders of granite shot to the sky as the dark blob slammed into the earth, dragging the Devil toward his dungeon. Michael tightened the chain around the Devil's neck. Resistance was futile. The saints continued to sing as they focused on Jesus.

"'All nations shall come and worship before You, for Your judgments have been manifested. You are righteous, O Lord, the One who is and who was and who is to be, because You have judged these things. For they have shed the blood of saints and prophets, and You have given them blood to drink. For it is their just due. Even so, Lord God Almighty, true and righteous are Your judgments.'"

Blasphemy managed to cover his ears. He recalled this hymn from the sixteenth chapter of the book of Revelation. Praise for God was more than his calloused heart could handle. He shivered as he watched the earth swallow Satan whole. The Devil and Michael were transported through the crust of the earth and into the hot core in a matter of seconds. Michael locked him in the abyss. Satan only hissed as the archangel fled away.

Blasphemy howled uncontrollably. The worship ceased as Christ approached the demon. Not a voice stirred as the last of the deceivers prepared for his sentence. Blasphemy frantically scanned the horizon. He was waiting for reinforcements, or maybe a miracle.

"I repent of my..." Blasphemy paused to clear his throat, as he choked out the lie. "I repent of my wicked and despicable ways."

Jesus remained silent. He x-rayed the demon's heart as Blasphemy grinned at the Master of the universe.

"Forgive me for my...my backsliding. I accept You as my own, personal, one and only Lord and Sav—"

Jesus sealed his mouth closed.

"I have examined your heart, have weighed your repentance, and you come up lacking," judged Christ. "You are a fake!"

Jesus waved both hands in the air as if He were shaking the dust from a carpet. The spiritual phony was knocked off his feet and tossed toward another galaxy at the speed of light.

"I will return," bellowed Blasphemy as he and his false repentance disappeared into outer darkness.

Jesus turned and stared at the sun. Ken could see an angel standing in its midst.

The angel cried in a loud voice to all the birds flying in midair, "Come, gather together for the Great Supper of God, so that you may eat the flesh of kings, generals, and mighty men, of horses and their riders, and the flesh of all people, free and slave, small and great."

Ken turned away as millions of birds flocked toward the human carnage littering the valley. The birds gorged themselves on the human debris. The blood in the valley was nearly five feet deep. Jesus gazed on the ghastly battlefield beneath His feet. Tears rolled down His cheeks.

"I desire that none perish, no not one!" thundered the Lord.

Gathering Clouds

Ken was sweating profusely as he relived the Battle of Battles. A fawn came over, cuddled on his lap, and began to lick his face. He smiled as the baby deer rubbed its head against his neck.

"Hey, little guy," smiled Ken. He caressed its fur as he cast the cobwebs from his mind. "Sometimes I wish we could change places," chuckled Ken. "You don't have a care in the world."

The fawn's appetite for salt could not be quenched. Ken gently pushed the animal away.

"Go find a tiger to romp with," joked Ken.

Ken surveyed the mountain in the distance. He thought about his first wife, Tina Marie. She loved mountains, picnics, life—even him. He remembered the Antichrist's police pulling her from the window and how he was powerless to save her. He thanked God, though, that wasn't his last memory. As he strolled along the well-beaten path toward home, he recalled that contagious smile of hers that had greeted him at the beginning of the Millennium. He was in the New Jerusalem worshipping the King when she had appeared out of nowhere and tapped him on the back.

"You were my hero, Ken Action!" said Tina Marie.

Ken nearly fainted when he heard her soft voice. He instantly turned around and lunged at her for one of her famous hugs.

"No, Ken. You can't touch me," sputtered Tina as she jumped backward.

Ken was shaking as he stared at his lost love.

"Tina Marie, it's so good to see you! What...what's wrong?" stammered Ken as he moved toward her. Each of his steps forward was met with her stepping backward. "I've missed you so much. Why are you moving away?"

Tina raised her hands in front of her heavenly body. "Ken, I have a resurrected body now." She glanced at him before turning her eyes toward the Lord.

Ken seemed drained of emotion as he peered at his earthly wife.

"Your body has been renewed but not resurrected," explained Tina Marie. "It would be like an angel trying to marry a human."

"I tried to save you, Tina Marie, I really did. You have to believe me," began Ken.

Tina quickly stopped him. She slowly retreated toward the grand temple at the center of the city.

"I will always love you, Ken," beamed Tina Marie. "You are a brave warrior for our Lord and King, and you will make your new wife very, very happy."

"Wait," shouted Ken as Tina floated away.

One of the apostles stepped in front of him. Ken's tears were as a torrent.

"Trust in Jesus," said the apostle Peter.

Ken's thoughts returned to the present as he walked under a weeping willow tree near the edge of the path. His memories felt so real that it seemed like they had all happened yesterday. He breathed deeply and glanced toward the bedroom window. Emily was brushing her hair. His heart was comforted.

"Trust in Jesus," Ken said softly.

———————

Solomon's back ached as he lay on the hard, lumpy bed. It was midnight, and he couldn't sleep. The jail cell was hardly the size of his smallest closet. He stared at the concrete ceiling as he rapped his fist against the metal bunk. His mind was running in circles.

This wasn't in his master plan. All he had wanted was a thrill; instead, he had felt the iron rod of justice. It wasn't fair, and someone was going to pay! He glanced toward Bill, who had dozed off on the other side of the titanium bars.

"Hey, Bill," shouted the boy nearly at the top of his lungs.

The shout so startled Bill that he nearly fell from his reclining swivel chair. He rubbed his eyes and shook his head in disbelief. He wanted to help Solomon, but...

"Solomon, what's gotten into you?"

"This rock that you call a bed," answered Solomon. "Why don't you let me go? Nobody has to know a thing."

Bill frowned. "Son, why can't you understand the fact that Jesus is my King, and He sees and knows everything?

You are asking me to disobey my Master and Savior. Have you asked Him into your heart, Solomon?"

The soft tapping on the metal frame of the bunk began to get louder as anger churned below the surface.

"Don't you old folks get it?" fumed Solomon. "I have gone to the altar in my parents' church at least a dozen times." He didn't notice his knuckles bruising. "I did what they said, followed all the stupid rules, but it just didn't work for me."

Solomon lunged off the cot toward Bill. His hands quickly turned white as he gripped the bars with all his might. Solomon's lifelong neighbor slowly backpedaled toward the door. It wasn't the physical danger that he feared, but the more dangerous, contagious spiritual cancer plaguing Solomon. Bill remained silent.

The invisible demon emerged from the ceiling, his eyes wide with excitement. He eyed his dinner in the jail cell.

"It's time to have some fun!" he hissed, the words flowing off his tongue like rotten honey.

"I'm not a bad person," fired back Solomon. "We simply have a difference of opinion about religion. Whatever happened to freedom of religion, freedom of speech, and freedom of privacy?"

Bill turned away from the young, confused rebel and glanced at the full moon. "King Jesus, help me to be a light to Solomon," he whispered in prayer.

Solomon's attitude soured further.

"Why are you talking to that window? Why don't you face me like a real man? You can't answer my questions about Jesus, or that overbearing vice-regent of His, David. It doesn't make sense, and you know it, don't you?"

Righteous anger spread across Bill's face. He walked to within an arm's distance of the bars.

"Solomon Action, Jesus has given you everything that you have. This heavenly, peaceful world; the animals you love; the beautiful home you live in; your godly parents—all these are gifts from Jesus."

Bill shook his head as he headed for the door. "I'm going home to my wife and daughter."

Solomon thought about Allison for a fleeting moment. "You can't leave me alone in this hole," yelled Solomon as he pounded his fists against the cell bars.

Bill slowly turned around and stared at the thief. His heart ached. Solomon's eyes began to water.

"You are the first person I've had to arrest in my thousand years on this job."

Solomon's eyes dropped to the ground. Bill slowly opened the jailhouse door.

"No, Solomon, you won't be alone."

Bill closed the door and locked it. The clicking sound of the lock jarred something inside Solomon. He looked toward heaven and started to shake.

He began to think. What have I done? What got into me? His thoughts turned to his history class and all the "exciting" things that happened before Christ took over the world. His love of history was beginning to control him; he wanted to live his life in a different time. Oh, how he wanted to travel back in time and live life when one's every move wasn't monitored by Jerusalem.

He shook his head and sighed. He was confused. Less than a year ago, his life had been perfect, but something had happened that he couldn't put his finger on. Something seemed to push him away from the people he loved, yet he didn't know what or who or why.

Bill drove his gravity vehicle slower than usual as he headed for home. How was he going to break the news to Allison? Would this be the final straw for her? Would she stop trying to change Solomon and move on with her life? Bill sighed at the thought of her misplaced commitment.

He steered the supersonic machine into the garage. The sound of the opening door brought Allison and his wife Gail running out the front door.

"Dad, what's going on? You've never been this late for dinner. Mom wouldn't tell me what you told her on the phone." Allison's face was filled with worry.

Bill grimaced as he avoided eye contact with his daughter. He shut off the machine and looked around the garage.

"This place needs a good cleaning."

Allison jumped in his face. "Dad!"

Bill nodded as he walked toward the door to the house. "Okay, honey. You deserve to know the truth." He glanced at Gail before he spoke again. She turned away and closed her eyes. He walked to the kitchen table and sat down. Allison quickly followed him. She sat down across the table and stared at him, her heart racing with concern.

Bill sighed. "It's Solomon. I arrested him tonight for breaking and entering—and stealing."

Allison appeared statue-like. His words seemed to bounce off her like arrows off armor.

Her father continued. "He's in jail, honey. I'm sorry. There wasn't anything else I could do."

Those words pierced her heart. In shock, she silently arose and walked toward her room. If she were wise, she would have told herself that this was the final straw, but she was in love, and love didn't always make sense. Allison took a deep breath as she walked into her lonely room. She walked to the window and looked toward town. She missed Solomon immensely, at least the old Solomon. Where had he gone? She needed to fix things, but she didn't know how.

———————

Emily stared blankly into the giant oval mirror as she stroked her long brown hair with a brush. Her thin face seemed lifeless as she sighed. Part of her felt dead, like somebody had taken a piece of her and squashed it into a million pieces. She didn't notice Ken open the door to their bedroom.

"How you doing, honey?" Ken asked as he walked toward his wife.

Her eyes remained fixated on the mirror, though she wasn't looking at herself.

"Our boy is in prison!"

Emily began to weep. Ken rushed to her side.

"It's going to be okay, Emily," sighed Ken as she collapsed in his arms. "He's not saved!" sobbed Emily. "What did we do wrong?"

Ken anchored her in his grasp as he forced her to face him. Emily kept trying to turn away from him as her grief overwhelmed her.

"You have been a wonderful mother. Stop beating yourself up." She cried harder. Ken lovingly pressed her head against his chest. "Calm down, honey, please. Solomon will make the right decision. I promise."

Emily managed to lift her head out of his tear-stained shirt. She sniffled uncontrollably as she placed her index finger on his bottom lip. Ken forced a smile as he stared into her reddened, hazel eyes.

"When's he coming home?"

Ken's smile disappeared. He turned toward the pair of windows facing east.

"I don't know," he replied softly as he tightened his hold on his wife. He wanted to believe that Solomon would come around, but was that faith or blind hope? Would their son continue to fall for the Devil's trickery?

Allison couldn't believe what she was doing. She wasn't directly disobeying her father, yet she knew he wouldn't approve. Would her parents notice that she was gone, or the open window that she had forgotten to close? She cared, but she was bent on seeing Solomon one more time, alone, one on one. She had to have some answers, or she would go crazy.

She placed the metallic card against the sensor to the jailhouse door. The light flickered green, and the lock pulled away. The sound jarred Solomon from his sleep. He opened his eyes and turned toward the door, thinking that he would see Bill.

Allison stood next to the door and gulped. She didn't know what to say and wasn't sure if she should even be there. When Solomon's eyes met hers, she knew she had made a mistake.

"Breaking the law, I see." Solomon spoke in a monotone. "Maybe you should join me in my international, intergalactic crime spree."

Allison took a step forward, then stopped. She shook her head in grief and said, "Solomon, Dad had no choice in the matter, and you know that! What's gotten into you anyway? Last week, you broke our engagement for absolutely no reason at all and—"

"I gave you my reasons," interrupted Solomon, "and you didn't like them. Can't help you there." His face turned hard and distant.

Allison closed her eyes. She started to cry but stopped herself. She needed to be strong.

"Wanting to have your own way is hardly a mature reason, Solomon!" Her voice quickly escalated out of control. "You would rather be reading one of those blasted history books about war than spending time with me."

She clenched her fists to her side as Solomon turned his face away from hers. "Solomon, you are obsessed with the past and the war between good and evil. What you don't seem to understand is that you are fighting your own battle. If you would just surrender to Jesus and follow Him, you would..." She lowered her voice as she approached his cell. "Solomon, the present and the future are in front of you. Even if you don't want to be with me, please give your heart to the Lord."

He turned toward her, his divided heart refusing to budge.

"You want me to be someone I'm not, Allison. I can't become a Christian just because you want me to. I have to know for myself that the Devil is real and that Jesus is who He says He is."

"Solomon, you have an unhealthy interest in evil, and it's beginning to control you. You've got to ask for the Lord's help and forgiveness before it's too late."

Solomon jumped out of his bed and paced the floor.

"Don't start preaching, Allison. I get enough of it from my parents and at church."

Allison wanted to say the right thing, but she didn't know what the right thing was for Solomon. He was distant, and his hardness made him seem like a stranger.

"Just answer me one thing, okay?"

Solomon glanced her way, but refused to make eye contact. He grunted, "Okay."

"Did I do something wrong?"

Solomon's eyes dropped to the ground. He said nothing. Allison waited for what seemed like hours, but was only a few minutes. She closed her eyes and turned around.

"Well, then, I think I'd better get home before..." Her tears took over as she hurried through the door.

Solomon fell on the bed. He pulled his fingers through his hair and cursed himself for letting her go.

Three

Sour Fruit

Satan glared into the darkness with vengeance. The last living being he had seen was the archangel Michael nearly one thousand years ago. It seemed like an eternity to him. All he could do was ponder the past, try to forget his present, and hope for the future. Flames from the pit of hell swiped at his flesh. Alone and tired, he still refused to give up on his future dream of godhood. Like clockwork, a scream of agony radiated from within him.

"I will destroy every hint of that ruthless dictator. Just wait," Lucifer boasted. "Thirteen days and the world will be mine!"

Logic mattered little to this fallen angel. He claimed not to believe a word of the Bible, yet he had been counting the days since his imprisonment. He tried not to think about the passing time too much, but the book of Revelation said that he would be released after one thousand years. Was it a literal thousand years or some arbitrary number that could mean anything? He hissed to himself as he remembered his days of power and all of the times that he had deceived the nations. Maybe it wasn't a literal thousand years. What if it didn't mean anything? He was counting down the days, nevertheless. Even if the number was symbolic, impossible to interpret correctly, he fed on the hope of his soon release.

"Christ," screamed Satan, "You are a sniveling do-gooder—always obeying Your Father. I will escape these chains and prove once and for all what those humans really want. They want me, my ways, and independence from Your overbearing meddling. You may think that You have won, but most will side with me!"

The deadly silence from heaven encouraged the Devil. Dark red lightning flashed against the canopy of night. A burst of untamed energy missed him by inches. The Devil laughed in delight.

"I will never fear You, my Maker and Master," mocked Lucifer.

"Wake up, boy," called Bill as he unlocked the door to Solomon's holding cell. "You have an appointment with the King!"

Solomon grunted as he turned over on his stomach. The light of day annoyed him.

"Go find some real criminals to nab," mumbled the boy as he yanked the thin covers over his head.

Bill stared at him for a moment, torn over how to treat the young man whom he had recently thought would be his son-in-law. He decided to mete out justice blindly.

"This is not a democracy!" returned Bill. "Your mommy and daddy aren't going to hold breakfast for you and wait on you hand and foot."

Bill grabbed Solomon's arm and pulled him over onto his back.

"You've got five minutes. If you're not dressed, I'll take you to Jerusalem half naked."

Solomon stared at him with a "Bill, it's me" expression on his face.

Just then, Ken and Emily rushed into the jail. Bill had called them an hour earlier to give them an opportunity to see their son.

"This guy's not acting like your son," frowned Bill as he greeted his neighbors.

"Thank you for calling us, Bill," Ken said as he shook his neighbor's hand. Ken looked over at Solomon and grimaced. "How's he doing with all this?"

Bill watched Solomon, who was dressing at a snail's pace.

"Unfortunately, his attitude stinks to high heaven, if you want to know the truth. This isn't the boy I've known as he was growing up, and it's not the young man Allison was crazy about marrying."

Emily could only glance at her son. He seemed distant and different from the boy she had raised. She had been up all night praying over the situation, and now she hoped that the Lord would help her keep her composure.

"Can we take him home with us?" asked Ken.

Solomon acted as if he were deaf. He showed no emotional reaction at all.

Bill seemed taken aback by the question.

"I'm sorry, but I thought you understood the procedure for these matters."

"How would we know that?" asked Ken. "When's the last time our boy, or for that matter anybody we know, broke the law? It just doesn't happen."

Bill scratched his head and stared at Ken. He avoided direct eye contact with Emily but felt her penetrating stare.

"Folks, Solomon broke the law. He committed a felony. Justice in the Millennium is very different from what you remember way back when. I had this same conversation this morning with Allison. I've never seen her beg so hard for something in her life, but I wouldn't let her see him. Rules are rules—period."

Emily clutched Ken's hand as she again tried unsuccessfully to see into Solomon eyes. It was obvious that he was ashamed to look at her. She was close to losing the battle to control her emotions.

Solomon badly wanted to melt into his mother's embrace, but pride held him back.

"You guys haven't been living under a rock these past thousand years. The Word clearly says that 'He shall rule them with a rod of iron.'"

"What are you telling us, Bill?" exclaimed Emily as she turned to confront him both with her words and her physical presence.

Bill glanced at the floor and sighed deeply. Ken grabbed Emily from behind.

"Whoa, honey," soothed Ken.

Ken wanted to grab Solomon, too, and run—run far away and hide, talk, and make him into his little boy again. But time has a way of stealing your youth and your children's youth. Ken had to be the rock, even though he felt like a sponge.

Solomon sneaked a look at his mother as he bent to tie his shoes. It was impossible to read his thoughts.

"Bill, you're upsetting Emily," responded Ken. "Just tell us what's going to happen. We're all grown-ups here."

Emily's heart felt like it had been put through a meat grinder. She had never known this kind of pain in her life.

Bill's eyes tracked Solomon's every move as he broke the news.

"Solomon and I are headed to Jerusalem." Emily silently placed her quivering hands over her mouth. "One of the twelve apostles or even Vice-Regent David himself will be his judge." Ken supported Emily while Solomon stood and stared at the floor. "It's quite possible he will receive years of detention and rehabilitation for what he has done."

Solomon's eyes widened. He shot a look at Bill that could melt metal.

"Years of detention!" He began to shake. "Mom, I'm sorry. I just wanted to have some fun." Emily moved toward Solomon but was stopped by Bill. "You guys wouldn't buy it for me and wouldn't let me spend my own money. Why? Why did this have to happen?" cried Solomon as Ken restrained Emily as well.

Solomon dropped on the bed and began to cry. With years of hard labor in prison facing him, Solomon's pride crumbled.

"Ken, you and Emily need to go home. You will hear from me after the sentence is announced."

"Solomon, we love you, honey. Do the right thing, Solomon," wailed Emily.

"Son, be a man and accept the consequences of your actions. We will be waiting for you with open arms," said Ken.

Solomon stared at his parents as Bill whisked him off the bed and into handcuffs. Bill glanced at Ken and Emily.

"Go now. I'll call."

For the first time in his life, Bill hated his job. These people were like family to him, and it took all of his courage to follow the rules. It wasn't always easy to obey Jesus, even in the Millennium, thought Bill.

Bill gently guided Solomon toward the door. Emily and Ken quickly exited the jail. They stopped near their air vehicle and turned toward Solomon as he was placed on the police cruiser. Emily managed a smile as she waved at her baby. Ken gritted his teeth as he nodded. As Bill started the atomic engine, Solomon glanced their way. His heart beat erratically as the engine ignited. Their eyes met. Those few moments seemed like an eternity. In spite of his disobedience, the bond of love between them was strong. Time and distance could not dissolve it. A lump the size of a chunk of coal lodged itself in his throat. Emily blew him a kiss. Solomon turned his head away as he broke into tears. His heart shattered as the air cruiser headed south.

A black viper hiding in a cloud above the jail snickered his approval. His nose snorted contemptuously as he watched Solomon being carted away. His triangular-shaped, ragged wings shoved the air downward. As he flew into the heavens, he shouted, "Satan is king!"

The Actions' guardian angels responded. Timothy, the senior-ranking angel, scoured the sky above them.

"Did you hear that?" he yelped, his heart racing with adrenaline. It had been hundreds of years since encountering a demon, and he had thought it wouldn't happen until Satan's release.

Daniel, his sidekick and the more excitable of the two, shoved his sword high over his head.

"You bet I did!" His eyes were moving so fast that he was having trouble seeing anything well.

Timothy motioned to Daniel to join him. They followed Bill and Solomon as they skimmed along the surface of the earth at nearly two hundred miles an hour. Timothy and Daniel had been with Ken Action since the Great Tribulation more than one thousand years ago. Neither angel was particularly large or muscular, yet they were wiser than their serpent counterparts. Their petite frames reached five feet. They looked like young human adults except for their wings, which were larger than their bodies. Both angels had blondish hair. Their eyes were twice the size of a human's, their ears were also rather large, and their mouths were smaller than their mortal counterparts.

The peace of the Millennium overjoyed them. The demons were disorganized and running scared, and their supreme commander, Satan, was locked away somewhere inside the planet. Nobody knew where, but rumors were plentiful. Blasphemy, the five-star general from the Great Tribulation, also was missing in action. He was the number two demon in charge, and most of his comrades in crime remembered Jesus shooting him into the far reaches of outer space. Everybody figured he was history.

Timothy and Daniel enjoyed the peace and tranquility of the time, yet their trigger fingers were getting a bit itchy. It had been nearly six hundred years since a few drunken demons had dared to attack their position, but they knew that things would change since the time of Satan's release was at hand.

"Are you sure we should follow Solomon to Jerusalem?" asked Daniel.

Timothy didn't hesitate. "Absolutely! Maybe if we had been on guard more, we could have helped Solomon handle his temptations."

Daniel didn't pay attention to Timothy's response. Instead, he blindly nodded and began flying around upside down. He was always doing stuff that irked Timothy.

"Stop goofing around. You know we are only days away from Satan's last hurrah." Timothy yanked his silver sword from underneath his gold robe. He snared the tip of his buddy's sash and pulled him in.

"Okay. I get the point, angel," responded Daniel.

Timothy shadowed Solomon's vehicle as it continued southward toward the Holy City.

"Ken and Emily will be fine at the homestead. Solomon is in a heap of trouble. His salvation is in jeopardy!"

Solomon barely noticed the passing landscape. As the clock ticked forward, his heart slid backward. He blamed everybody but himself for the trouble he was in. He was hopelessly divided in heart and mind, unwilling and unable to take responsibility for his actions.

"How much longer?" asked Solomon.

"About two more hours. You need a bathroom break or something?" inquired Bill as he stared forward. He couldn't help thinking of Allison and how this was going to affect her.

"Yeah, in a couple of minutes," responded Solomon. "How far are we from Jerusalem?"

"Four hundred miles, give or take some."

"Is there security all around here?"

Bill was puzzled. "What's with all the questions? Planning on escaping?" he kidded.

"Yeah, man, just call me Jesse Solomon James."

Timothy was getting uneasy as they neared a tall mountain range. It was impossible to see the other side, and he didn't like the way the conversation was going down below.

"Daniel, fly ahead and scout out the next valley. Get that sword of yours in plain view."

"Angel, I can't wait for some action!" grinned Daniel as he exploded toward the blue horizon.

Timothy stared at Solomon. He sighed as he remembered the old Solomon, the young man who had swept Allison off her feet and loved her with purity and passion.

Blasphemy stretched out on a meteor billions of miles from planet Earth, his thorny body limp with exhaustion. He had been searching in vain for his way back home. He had no maps, no compass, and no inkling where home was located. Every planet looked the same, every moon lifeless and meaningless, and every meteor a distraction. The space rock that Blasphemy occupied was rocketing around a distant star known only to God. It was flying at over one hundred thousand miles an hour, but it might as well have been at a standstill. Any wrong movement could take him further from his calling, his rightful position of authority over the demons of planet Earth.

He found it impossible to forget what Jesus had done to him. Outer darkness took on an entirely new meaning to Blasphemy. The demon had been alone for nearly ten centuries. Loneliness was a greater curse than he could have possibly imagined.

"Is this hell?" pondered Blasphemy as he sat upright on the shooting star. "Is this it? Will I ever see a fellow demon again?" He wondered if Satan had it any better.

Suddenly, a black speck appeared against the backdrop of a large star. Blasphemy zoned in on it like a dog eyeing a choice steak. "Could it be?" wondered the demon. "No! I don't believe it."

Gail softly rubbed her coffee cup with her finger as she pondered the murky liquid inside. She didn't know what to say to Allison, so she just listened.

"Do you remember when Solomon and I were ten years old?" asked Allison, sipping her hot chocolate.

Gail nodded and smiled.

"It's like Solomon and I were brother and sister." She closed her eyes, struggling with the joy and pain that her memories created. "He would pick wildflowers from our garden and put them in our mailbox." She laughed. "By the time I got them, they were dead, and he could never figure out why."

Allison looked at her mother with a rare, serious expression.

"Do you think I'm crazy for holding on to hope?"

Her mother placed her hand on Allison's and smiled. "Hope is a wonderful thing, honey. I just don't know if placing your faith on the notion that he's going to change is wise or not."

Allison's hand began to shake, causing her drink to splash onto the saucer and table. Neither moved to clean up the mess. Allison sighed as more memories forced their way into her mind. Her mother saw what was happening and tried to divert Allison's thoughts.

"You have a solo tonight in church. I bet you're excited."

Allison slowly stood up and walked toward the front door.

"Not if Solomon won't be there."

Emily lay in her bed crying. It had been seven hours since she had said good-bye to Solomon. Ken tried to mask his hurt and confusion by keeping busy. He had cleaned feverishly throughout their twenty-six-room mansion. Now he quietly tiptoed into the heavily shaded room and sat on the corner of the bed. He gently rubbed Emily's leg.

"Honey, there's some bread in the brick oven. It's hot and buttery and has your name on it."

Emily slid the covers from her reddened face. The depressed expression on her face didn't need words. Emily's mind was traveling in circles, desperately trying to uncover the reasons behind Solomon's actions. She looked at Ken and sighed. She loved him, but sometimes his comedic ways annoyed her, especially when they were ill timed.

"I've swept just about every molecule of dust from this entire house. Want to join me in taking care of the rest of the town?" joked Ken as he lightly shook the sheets.

She attempted to giggle but a sob escaped instead.

"Do you remember when Solomon began to walk?" started Emily. Ken couldn't handle that memory right now. There was work to be done, somewhere out there. Emily placed a hand over her mouth. Was she laughing or crying? "Remember? He fell flat on his face in the flower garden."

Ken's heart throbbed with pain. Memories were sometimes a double-edged sword. He desperately tried to maintain his composure, but the battle was already lost.

"Do you remember his first trip to Jerusalem?" lamented Ken as the tears burst forth. Emily scooted closer to Ken and grabbed at his hand.

"Yes, I remember," began Emily. "I'll never forget his calling David, 'Jesus,' to his face! I thought David was going to fall off his throne."

"And how about the freshman prom?" continued Ken. "Solomon and Allison looked so good together. I said they were a match made in heaven. I thought for sure they would marry someday, but..." He thought about Allison. "She must be hurting right now."

Minutes turned into hours. The memories flooded their minds. Silence followed as the couple watched the daylight fade. They were unable to share what was in their hearts. How could they reminisce about the past when the present was biting at their heels? How could they be happy when their beloved son was falling from grace?

A burst of energy once again energized Ken. He jumped off the bed and yanked the covers from Emily.

"Let's go worship Jesus in Jerusalem!" exclaimed Ken.

Life returned to Emily. She rushed toward the closet.

"What a great idea! Just think, we may even happen to bump into Solomon."

———————

"That bathroom break is sounding real good right now," said Solomon as he held his stomach.

Bill glanced in the rearview mirror. Solomon was hunkered over, acting as if he were about to have a baby.

"Don't you think you can hold it?"

Solomon moaned as he contorted his face in all directions.

"That answers that," sighed Bill as he looked for the nearest town. They were approaching one of the largest mountain chains in the area. "There's nothing until we get to the other side of those," pointed Bill. "I think there's something just on the other side, though. Can't guarantee anything, but we'll see in a couple of minutes."

The cruiser effortlessly climbed up the periphery of the peak. Bill eyed Solomon with suspicion. Solomon was quite the actor sometimes, thought Bill. He remembered the times he had caught Solomon and Allison swimming in the lake at night and Solomon's straight-faced excuse that they both were sleepwalking at the same time and had accidentally fallen into the water.

Meanwhile, Daniel returned from his scouting mission. He saluted Timothy.

"Nothing exciting in those parts, sir," said Daniel as he clicked his heels like a marine in training. "Whoever that demon was, he's long gone."

Timothy returned a worried smile. They were closely following Solomon to the top of the mountain, then down the other side. Nothing seemed out of the ordinary.

"There she is," pointed Bill as a small town appeared in the valley below. "Hold on, son. We'll be there soon enough."

As the police cruiser neared the tiny town near the Israeli border, Solomon groaned in pain.

"Hurry up."

Timothy watched Solomon with interest. He quickly scanned the outskirts of town.

"Solomon is acting strangely," reacted Timothy.

"What's strange about having to go to the bathroom?" asked Daniel as he scratched at one of his wings.

Timothy had had more experience with humans than Daniel, and he knew something was up. When Bill wasn't watching Solomon, the boy would suddenly appear normal, except for his eyes, which twitched all over creation.

Bill abruptly stopped the air cruiser outside a rundown pub. Several teenagers who were seated on the porch watched with uncanny interest. Solomon quickly disembarked and waved his shackled hands in the air.

"Bill, would you please take these cuffs off?"

Bill glanced at the young men and then at Solomon.

"I don't think so, Solomon."

The boy quickly dropped on his knees and grunted. The teens nearby smiled.

"Have some heart, man!" begged Solomon.

Bill shook his head, pulled the keys from his belt, and moved to his side.

"You've got five minutes, son."

Solomon continued to gasp in pain as Bill unlocked the cuffs. Bill frowned as he watched Solomon run toward the door.

"Don't do anything you'll regret," he whispered to himself.

Timothy's gut kept talking to him, yet he couldn't figure out what it was saying. He flew over to the teenage boys to see what they were mumbling about.

"Let's go have some fun!" whispered Denny, the older of the two.

Solomon glanced at the two rough-looking boys as he hurried into the men's room. Both smiled at him as if they were his best friends. Solomon quickly ran inside, forgetting their bizarre behavior. Bill took a seat on the edge of his air vehicle and casually watched the boys walk away.

Timothy tailed Denny and his younger friend, Cleveland.

"Say something, guys!" vented Timothy as he motioned for Daniel to accompany Solomon. Daniel raced into the restroom, looked around for anything suspicious, and hastily flew back into the weakened sunlight.

"Nothing there, Timothy."

Timothy's stomach was churning like a runaway washing machine. He couldn't see the evil, but he could feel it and smell it.

Denny and Cleveland stopped about thirty yards away from Bill. They were directly behind him, out of his sight and mind. Bill stared at the entrance to the pub. He glanced at his watch and shook his head.

"What are they doing?" mumbled Timothy to himself.

With his sword drawn, Daniel rushed to Bill's side and scanned the sky. Bill bent forward to stretch some tight muscles inflamed by the long trip. The two boys suddenly sprinted toward him.

"They're rushing him," screamed Daniel.

Timothy brandished his dagger in the air and flew quickly toward the commotion.

"Secure your position, Daniel!" shouted Timothy as he inspected the airspace around them.

Bill heard footsteps. As he turned around, Denny dove over the air bike and tackled him at the shoulders. Cleveland ran around the other side and sat on his neck. Bill tried to free himself, but the boys were too strong. Denny grabbed the communication device from Bill's belt and pretended to talk into it.

"Headquarters, we have an old man here who is having trouble talking," mocked Denny. "I think it would be best to put him out of his misery. Over."

Bill was horrified. They used an extra pair of handcuffs to bind him and tied his feet with some rope. As he tried to speak, Denny shoved a dirty rag in his mouth. The boy kicked the officer in the gut and laughed.

"I've been wanting to hog-tie one of you pigs for a long time. Man, it feels good."

Timothy and Daniel floated above the crime scene.

"Do you see anything?" asked Timothy

"No, sir, but I feel awful sorry for poor Bill."

"Don't watch, angel!" warned Timothy. "The demons want to distract you with that fight. Then they will pounce on you like buzzard meat."

Solomon stood at the sink and glanced toward the window connected to the back of the building. He could escape right now and then...and then what? Run from the law and never see his parents or Allison again? He gritted his teeth as his eyes stared at the bait. He knew what the right thing was, but what did he want? He sighed because he was scared and confused and mad and...and because he would do the right thing, and he wasn't at all happy about it. Solomon casually walked out of the restroom and glanced up and down the deserted street. He didn't immediately notice Bill's predicament. Denny strutted toward him with a broadcaster's smile. His cocky attitude made Solomon feel at ease. Solomon glanced at the air bike but didn't see Bill on it.

"Hey, dude, what's going on?" Solomon could see Cleveland on the ground near the bike, but he couldn't tell what was happening.

"Brother, we had a little business to take care of." Denny put his hand up for the typical high-five greeting.

"Where's Bill?" asked Solomon as he tried to look around Denny.

Denny slowly moved to the side as he pointed toward his roadkill. Solomon was stunned.

"Whoa, man! This is too much!" stammered Solomon. He ran toward Bill.

Cleveland quickly stood up and blocked Solomon's access to Bill. Denny grabbed Solomon's arm.

"Now, let's just think straight for a minute," began Denny with a smug tone in his voice. "This thug was going to deliver you to a kangaroo court. You would be unfairly sentenced to months or years of hard labor, and worse yet, be forced to attend their religious services."

Solomon looked at Bill. Bill's eyes were telling Solomon to do the right thing.

Timothy and Daniel began screaming at him, "Say no to them. Say no to them." They couldn't believe there were no demons taunting these two ruthless boys, yet they knew it didn't take a demon to make a person do evil things—only a heart that was separated from God.

"What's your name?" asked Cleveland.

"Solomon." His divided heart was obvious. He couldn't take his eyes off Bill.

"I'm Cleveland, and that ugly one over there is Denny." Denny punched his younger friend in the arm with all his force. "Wimp. Is that all you got?"

Solomon smiled. Denny shook his head.

"We just got out of one of their 'schools,' as they like to call them," complained Cleveland. "Two years of hard labor." Cleveland showed him the calluses on both hands. "Can you believe this? The gall of those people."

He glanced over at Bill and then looked sternly at Solomon. "You know what we did?" Solomon quietly shook his head no. "We refused to go to church with our parents!" Cleveland was nodding his head violently up and down. "That's right, partner. We didn't go, so we were branded criminals in need of rehabilitation."

Solomon knew deep inside it wasn't the act of snubbing church that made them into criminals, but the wholesale defiance of the King of the land. He conveniently forgot what he knew and focused on what he wanted.

Denny saw a vehicle approaching. He jumped on the air cycle and motioned for Cleveland.

"Come on, man. Let's get out of here!"

Cleveland ran toward the getaway vehicle. Solomon glanced toward Bill. He began to shake.

"You coming with us, man?" shouted Denny as Cleveland hopped on board. "It's now or never."

Solomon mouthed the word *sorry* to Bill as his feet dragged him away. Timothy and Daniel couldn't get to Solomon in time. His heart was hardening by the second.

"Yee-haw!" yelled Denny as Solomon climbed aboard.

The slowly approaching air vehicle began to pick up speed.

"It's a cop!" shouted Solomon.

"Hang on, guys," roared Denny. The air vehicle accelerated toward the east. "I've never driven one of these things before." The police cruiser wobbled all over the place.

"Watch out for that tree," yelled Solomon. Denny yanked upward on the controls as the boys closed their eyes. Solomon looked toward town. "There's someone following us," yelled Solomon as he reached for the seatbelt.

"It's the cops, man!" bellowed Cleveland as he followed Solomon's example.

Blasphemy stood at attention as the spirit approached the meteor. His dark, stout body stood over ten feet tall; his wingspan was a staggering thirty feet. Long, coarse nails protruded nearly six inches from his paws and were capable of ghastly deeds. He had been alone too long and was eager to even the score with God Almighty. His kingly stance made the visitor somewhat uneasy.

"Sir, I have been searching for you for nine hundred years," began the first lieutenant demon, Zeus. The spirit dropped on his knees and bowed.

Blasphemy smirked at the show of humility. "Who told you to search for me, lieutenant?"

"Nobody, sir! The forces of evil are in total disarray. Satan is in jail, and you, sir, were given the royal boot into..."

Blasphemy lunged at Zeus. He grabbed him by the neck and lifted him off the ground. Zeus gagged.

"Jesus didn't give me the royal boot, son." Blasphemy smiled. "Who told you that?"

Zeus knew how to play the game. He had seen Blasphemy kicked into the outer darkness with his own two eyes, yet if the boss said it didn't happen, it didn't. Truth was not an important part of demonic vocabulary. Blasphemy dropped him on the rock and howled in the direction of a nearby moon.

"Sir, I figured you were lost in the outer darkness, and I have mapped my entire voyage."

Blasphemy smiled at the demon's blind loyalty.

"Lieutenant, you never saw Jesus and me together. That is a fantasy. I have been on an extended vacation and am ready to return to conquer my planet."

"Sir, may I accompany you back to Earth? It would be an honor."

"No, you can't! You are not worthy to be seen with royalty."

"Yes, sir. I understand, general." The demon saluted and began to fly away. Blasphemy suddenly realized his predicament. He didn't know where he was.

"Wait, captain!" Zeus immediately did a U-turn.

"Sir, I'm sorry to correct you, but I'm a lieutenant." He quickly returned to his knees.

"No, Zeus, you have been promoted!" Blasphemy placed his oversized paw around his new companion's neck. Zeus looked confused. "Any demon that can find me in the vastness of outer space deserves some recognition. You lead, my demon. This is a great test for you. If you make it back without my help, the title of major is yours."

Zeus saluted Blasphemy.

"Sir, my best estimate is three days, maybe four."

Blasphemy followed Zeus as they rocketed through the night.

"Sir, permission to speak freely?"

"What is it?" growled Blasphemy.

"There are rumors circulating in the ranks, at least what's left of them, that Satan will be released one thousand years after the Battle of Armageddon." Blasphemy seemed irritated. "Sir, by my calculations, that's only a couple of weeks away."

Blasphemy was stunned. Had he been out of service for that long? He knew the Holy Scriptures by heart, yet he refused to believe them.

"I will hear no more talk about this. The Battle of Armageddon never occurred. You understand me?"

"Yes, sir."

Blasphemy began to crunch numbers in his head. The time was short, and the work was plenty.

"Captain Zeus, pick up your speed. There is work to be done."

"Can't you go any faster?" asked Emily as she tied her hair back.

"We'll be there in less than an hour," responded Ken. "You want to get there in one piece, right?"

"Yes, honey, but what if we miss Solomon?"

Ken ignored the question as his eyes feasted on the stately mountain peaks in view. He had never gotten used to the beauty of the millennial kingdom. He couldn't remember the last time he had seen a weed or a thorn. The mountains reminded him of the Lord's majesty and His promises about the future kingdom of heaven.

"See over there," pointed Ken. "That's the last chain of mountains before we hit the Israeli border."

The five-hour trip was beginning to take its toll on Emily. It had given her time to think about things she wanted to forget. As the air cruiser reached the pinnacle of the mountain, Emily's eyes caught a glimpse of the other side.

"Ken, let's take a five-minute break at that town. Got some girl business to do."

Ken smiled as he glanced at his watch, then at his wife.

"Thought you were in a huge rush."

"Hush your mouth, Ken Action," smiled Emily. "A woman's got to do what a woman's got to do. Don't argue. Just obey!"

He liked it when she was spunky. Ken revved the engine to one hundred percent power as the ten-foot-long cruiser sped down the large mountain.

"Whee!" squealed Ken as the air rushed by with increased force.

Ken had never fully matured. He loved a good thrill ride, and he was the number one fan of the world's largest roller-coaster park outside Paris. He couldn't help but think of the best of them—the one named "Monster." It had a top speed of two hundred miles an hour, had fourteen loops, and a track that was nearly twenty miles long. Jesus wanted His people to have fun, as long as they thanked Him for it.

She lightly tapped Ken on the shoulder. "Slow down, or we won't get anywhere in one piece."

Ken smiled as the cruiser entered the dusty town. The couple saw a group of people gathered on the side of the street near an old pub. He slowed the vehicle and squinted to see through the crowd.

"Let's check this out," suggested Ken as he stopped within thirty yards of the commotion. "Why don't you run to the little lady's room, and I'll figure out what's going on."

"No way," said Emily as she jumped off the cruiser.

"I thought you had to..."

"I can wait." Emily rushed to the edge of the crowd and tried to gently push her way to the front. Ken tried to follow her, but his size held him back. Seconds later, Emily screamed.

"Ken, it's Bill!"

He pushed a few people aside and ran toward his neighbor and friend.

Bill held a bag of ice on his left side, and a bruise was beginning to form on his right cheek. Ken looked at Bill and feared the worst. He tried to pull Emily away, but she refused. She had to know the truth, no matter what.

"What happened, Bill?" panted Ken.

"Are you all right?" added Emily as she gently hugged him.

Bill remained silent as he stared at the couple. He tried to speak, but shook his head instead. He didn't want to tell them, but what choice did he have?

"Where's Solomon?" asked Emily, not sure if she really wanted to know the answer.

Bill stared at her for what seemed like hours. He was carefully choosing his words, which was making her antsy.

"Emily, Ken, Solomon did not do this to me."

"Oh, thank God," sighed Emily as she hugged Ken.

"Wait a minute, guys," started Bill. "Solomon didn't do this, but he took off with the thugs who did." Bill grimaced, not at the physical pain, but at the thought of having to tell Allison. Two down and one to go, he thought.

Emily began to bitterly weep as she clutched Ken with all her might. Ken closed his eyes and prayed silently.

"Lord Jesus, please forgive him."

The teenagers recklessly maneuvered the air cruiser into a narrow canyon and ignored the rocks and tall trees that protruded in all directions. The police officer was hot on their tails. Timothy and Daniel followed, but the boys didn't seem interested in prayer.

"This is Ted in sector Alpha."

"What do you have out there?" responded a dispatcher in Jerusalem.

"Three boys on a stolen police cruiser. Looks like they beat one of our own pretty bad. Need backup ASAP." Ted turned on his three-dimensional radar screen designed to automatically direct the vehicle through tight topography.

"I've never had so much fun in my life," shouted Denny as he slung the cruiser to the right.

Solomon was less enthusiastic. He kept eyeing their rear. They couldn't shake the tracker.

"Hey, man, he's gaining on us. Why don't we give ourselves up? This isn't looking good."

Denny yelled at Solomon. "If you're not with us, you're against us."

Cleveland tried to ease the tension. "Hey, guys, calm down. Let's have some fun. Remember what we told you about those camps, Solomon. You're going to end up there either way—"

"Unless, of course," Denny interrupted, "we don't get caught."

Solomon didn't have time to think or react. If he had, he would have jumped off and prayed for grace.

Denny changed tactics. "Hang on, warriors!" The air cruiser turned its nose straight up and quickly climbed in altitude. Soon they were over ten thousand feet in the air. The officer had stopped. The boys began to gag and cough. They were running out of oxygen.

"Go down, down, now!" wheezed Solomon.

Cleveland agreed. "Listen to him, Denny. This thing runs on air; if there's no air, we'll fall."

As the words left his mouth, the engine began to sputter. Denny mumbled an expletive as he leveled the machine. He stared at the flashing red lights on the dash.

"What's going on?" His eyes were wild with anxiety. "Oh, no! We're going to die!" Denny lost consciousness.

Solomon didn't want to die. He knew he would go to hell without Jesus. He thought about praying.

Cleveland, who was seated directly behind Denny, pushed against him with all his might. Denny's body collapsed forward, sending the machine spiraling downward.

"Keep your head," barked Solomon as he held on to Cleveland for dear life. "Dear God, save us!"

"Did you hear that?" asked Daniel. A shot of energy entered his body.

"Sure did, angel," replied Timothy. Timothy grabbed onto the back of the tumbling vehicle as Daniel steadied the front.

Solomon's desperate plea had energized the angels in the nick of time.

"Let's stop this thing from spinning first," yelled Timothy. His wings flapped rapidly as he pushed against the power of the spin. Daniel followed his example.

"Pull up, pull up," yelled Cleveland. He desperately tried to reach the handlebars, but the eighty-degree dive made it impossible to move. Denny opened his eyes as Cleveland started hitting him on the back.

"Wake up! Pull up!"

Denny gasped for air as he yanked upward on the handlebars. The air cruiser slowly responded as it neared a dirt cliff.

"We're going to hit!" screamed Solomon as he dug his face into Cleveland's sweating back. "Help us, God."

Another burst of supernatural energy shot through the angels' veins.

"One, two, three, now," said Timothy as the two spirits turned the vehicle away from the mountain.

A tip of a tree brushed Solomon's foot. He looked toward heaven. Timothy and Daniel did a corny victory dance around the boys.

"Park this thing," shouted Cleveland.

Denny eased up on the accelerator and examined the countryside below. The near bout with death didn't seem to faze him. He cursed the name of Jesus in jest, while Cleveland took credit for their survival. It took Solomon less than a minute to forget the prayer that had saved them.

"Smooth driving, dude," smiled Solomon as he reached over Cleveland to pat Denny on the back.

Denny smirked. "Did you see that move right at the end? Last second stuff, man. I love it!"

Five miles north of the Israeli border, the officer continued to search for the boys. He had lost them in the clouds after his radar malfunctioned.

They're probably dead, thought the officer. He probed the horizon as a surgeon would search for cancer. A bird squawked overhead. He sighed. "Lord, why would these youngsters rebel against You? They have their health, peace, prosperity, and Your presence on the earth, yet they refuse to believe in You."

He shook his head as he grabbed his communicator. "Headquarters, I've lost them. Permission to abandon the search. Over." He waited for a response. He was tired.

"Permission granted," responded a female voice in Jerusalem. "Go get some sleep. We'll handle things from this end."

Meanwhile, Denny slowly maneuvered the air cruiser into a large cavern the size of a football field. The thirty-foot ceiling gave him plenty of room as he parked the machine several hundred feet inside.

"Gentleman, we are fugitives now," began Denny as he cracked his knuckles. "Solomon, you sure you want to hang out with a couple of bad boys?"

Solomon eyed Denny as he considered his options. What choice did he have now? Surely he would be blamed as an accomplice if he turned himself in. How could he turn back now? He tried to blot out Allison's face from his memory.

Cleveland patted him on the head as if he were a dog.

"You're going to be a good boy and keep your mouth shut, aren't you?"

Solomon pushed a heavy fist into Cleveland's chest, then turned and threatened Denny. "I suggest you learn some manners," countered Solomon.

Cleveland was bent over trying to catch his breath when he began to laugh loudly. "Solomon, you're one of us." He reached his hand toward Solomon. "Come on, shake it, man. You have guts. I like that."

Solomon slowly moved forward to meet Cleveland. The boys stared at each other with distrust. Denny watched as they shook hands. Then he followed Cleveland's example.

"Welcome to the team, Solomon," congratulated Denny.

Solomon smiled for a fleeting moment. He thought about the Three Musketeers. He would be the third one. He was now part of a team. It felt good—well, at least it kind of did.

Denny winked at Cleveland.

"What was that?" responded Solomon.

"Oh, nothing."

"Guys, if you're planning on pulling a fast one on me, let me know now so I can beat you silly."

"Listen, man," began Cleveland, "Denny has a slight temper. He, uh, well, he doesn't get over things too quickly."

"What's that supposed to mean?" asked Solomon.

Denny smirked as Cleveland talked. "It means you're part of the team, but watch your back."

The country church was packed for the evening recital. Glancing around the sanctuary, Gail stared forward at her daughter. Allison was in her best dress, but not in her best mood. Gail could see the pain on her daughter's face as she stood in the choir, waiting for the music minister's cue.

The pastor shook a few hands as he entered the church from the rear. He quickly noticed Gail. He nodded to her, letting her know he understood what her family was going through. The news was especially difficult on the pastor, knowing the spiritual authority the Lord had entrusted to him in regard to Solomon.

"Tonight we've come to worship Jesus," announced the pastor, raising his hands into the air. "Allison Larkson will be singing a solo tonight, and we all are looking forward to hearing that beautiful voice of hers."

Allison didn't hear much of what he said. She stared at the back wall of the sanctuary, avoiding any form of eye contact with her family, friends, or neighbors. Everybody knew what had happened to Solomon, but nobody dared to bring it up to her. She felt trapped by her love for him, unable and unwilling to give up hope that he would repent. She was convinced that somehow she could do something to help. She pictured Solomon in jail, thinking about her and wondering why he was so foolish to give up on their love.

Suddenly, she heard her name announced. She walked toward the microphone and forced herself to smile. As she sang from her heart, her love for Jesus and Solomon grew.

Four

The Iron Rod of Justice

Captain Zeus was traveling close to the speed of light. Blasphemy silently followed him as they dodged space debris at every turn.

"Sir, the brightening star in the distance is our sun," pointed out Zeus. He glanced toward Blasphemy for his approval.

"Well done, captain." Blasphemy slowly closed the distance between the two of them. "What's our E.T.A.?"

"Less than two hours, sir."

Blasphemy rushed toward the demon. He grabbed him by the wings and slowly crushed them in his paws.

"What are you doing?" screamed the demon before the extreme pain made him black out.

Blasphemy stole the map out of the demon's inner pocket. With Zeus's wings inoperable, Blasphemy picked him up and kicked him into the outer darkness. He smirked at the sight of the limp body careening into space.

"I don't need some low-life demon suggesting I'm not his god. Imagine his thinking I needed help finding my way home!"

Blasphemy's chest swelled as he drew closer to Earth. It had been a long time, too long, he thought. He missed tempting humans and ordering demons around at whim. His eyes turned dark as he thought of Satan and of God's prophecy. It was a perfect opportunity to take control, to set himself up above the stars, to sit on the great assembly, to be king of the universe!

The air cruiser glided over the sparkling city of Jerusalem. Ken and Emily could never get enough of this striking city brought into existence by God alone. The buildings were not built by human hands, but had been created in the mind of God. They had spontaneously appeared at the beginning of the Millennium.

The city was six miles in circumference, but the suburbs extended dozens of miles in all directions. It was the worship capital of the world and was filled with the light of the Lord.

"There's the temple," pointed Emily as Ken slowly descended to a gold landing strip near the center of town.

In spite of the beauty of the city, their mood was heavy since meeting with Bill. Worry sought to dominate their thoughts during the remainder of their trip, but both responded by rebuking it with prayer. Their vehicle landed and the apostle Peter was there to meet them.

"Blessings, my friends," smiled Peter as he helped Emily off the cruiser.

"Peter! What are you doing here?" Ken's surprise was visible.

Tears rolled down Emily's cheeks. "Is it Solomon? Have you found him?" She couldn't read any clue from Peter's face.

"Is he okay?" begged Emily. She began to whimper. "Is he...," she choked, "is he dead?"

Ken steadied his wife as they watched Peter's every move. Ken was ready for anything, or almost anything.

Peter placed his hand on her shoulder, then turned toward Ken. "Emily, Ken, your son is fine, physically."

They breathed a sigh of relief, yet were bothered by that last word.

"What do you mean by that?" asked Ken as the apostle motioned for them to follow him.

"Please, folks, it would be better if we talked about this in my chamber in the temple."

Ken and Emily stayed close together as they walked down a golden boulevard outside the temple. It was the longest walk of their life. Emily wondered why Peter was making them wait for any news of their son. Every time they mentioned Solomon, Peter asked them to think of Jesus. Minutes later, they walked into the outer court of the temple. When they reached the temple court, Emily realized Peter was trying to teach her patience.

"My chamber is located in that building over there," pointed the apostle.

Emily's eyes feasted on the beauty of the marble blocks glistening in the sunlight. They were perfectly shaped rectangles with a silver composite cementing them together.

They walked under a massive canopy of hand-carved marble supported by seven, seventy-foot columns. Once inside the building, they could sense the awesome presence of God. The hallway walls glittered with a ruby-like stone that scattered light in all directions.

Peter directed them into his meeting room. Four wooden chairs encircled a bubbling fountain, which seemed to spring up from the center of the floor. A man with red hair and an unassuming build was on his knees in prayer. His back was to them as they entered the room.

"Who's that?" whispered Emily.

Ken seemed confused as Peter motioned for them to sit. Neither could make out the man's face, which was hidden. They heard him praying out loud.

"Jesus, I worship You, O Lord and King." The voice seemed familiar, but Ken couldn't identify the speaker. Peter fell to his knees. Ken and Emily instantly followed his example. "We pray as one that Solomon Action would love You as Lord and Savior." Ken and Emily broke down. "Grant Ken and Emily peace as they struggle with their son's ill-fated decision. In Your name we pray, amen."

The ruddy-faced man slowly lifted his head from between his knees. Ken and Emily remained on the floor weeping. He moved toward them and embraced the grieving couple.

"May our Father bless you in your time of suffering," offered the man. As they lifted their heads, they nearly collapsed at the sight of his face.

"King David!" murmured Ken.

David smiled at them. He could feel their pain, and he wanted to do everything within his power to help. David was second in command of the kingdom. He ruled the world under the watchful eye of Jesus. He was one in spirit, mind, and heart with the Lord, similar to Jesus' relationship with His Father.

Emily tried to lift herself off the stone floor, but crumpled in anguish. Ken tenderly helped her to her feet.

"We need to talk, Ken and Emily," said David. "The future of your son is at stake."

The following day, the boys remained in the cavern. Water buildup from the ceiling occasionally dripped on them, shattering their edgy nerves.

"I'm fed up with this dungeon," complained Denny. "I say we get on that machine and head for the nearest tropical island."

Denny, the taller of the two friends, had a big chip on his shoulder. The nineteen-year-old had jet-black hair, a large nose, and a big mouth that liked to talk and be heard. He had grown up with godly parents, good moral friends, and townspeople who followed the teachings of the Lord. Like all the children of the Millennium, he was an only child. He had been born during the three-year window that Jesus had given for procreation, which had ended sixteen years ago.

He was part of a new generation that was a test for humanity. Would young people growing up in a perfect environment choose Jesus? Unfortunately, not all of them did. Many adults tried to figure out why these youngsters were rejecting the King of the universe. Nobody had a firm answer, but the best one was pride. It seemed to sprout up in their hearts like a renegade weed on a mission to infect good crops. Denny didn't know why he hated Jesus, but he did—and vehemently!

Cleveland, who was seated on a small damp rock, was tossing stones toward the dark side of the cave. He was smaller and plumper than Denny and had reddish blond hair covering his head. His hatred for Jesus was somewhat less than Denny's, yet it was enough to keep him on the wrong path. Cleveland tended to be a follower. Sadly, he had chosen Denny as his guide.

"Listen, Denny. We're dead meat if we leave this cave. Every cop on the face of this demented planet has a picture of us."

Solomon played peacemaker. "Come on, guys. There's got to be a smart way we can get out of here without being detected."

Unseen to the boys, a demon named Fester entered the cave. He was four feet tall, with stubby arms. A tattoo of a flame stood out on his left forearm. He was the same demon that had been influencing Solomon for the past several months. When he saw the angels, he slowly backed away and hissed his disapproval. Timothy and Daniel, who were lounging on a rock near the boys, were exchanging war stories from the Great Tribulation.

"Do you remember that time when I did that triple back flip reverse sword move on that ugly demon?" asked Daniel, grinning as he relived the thrill.

Timothy sniffed the air. "Yeah, I can almost smell that nasty demon now." He opened his eyes and stared at Daniel.

Fester hid behind a rock. He wanted to avoid a fight. He glared at the boys and began to salivate. It had been so long since he had possessed anyone. He would give anything for the chance to feel human blood coursing through his system again.

"The way I see it," began Denny, "we're dead in a couple of weeks if we don't get some food." He opened his mouth, awaiting a drop of water from the ceiling. "And we can't sit here all day with our mouths cocked open, hoping we will get enough water to survive on."

"You're giving us the problem and not the solution," responded Solomon. He stood up and stretched. Denny stared at Solomon angrily. He didn't like to be corrected. "I say we head to my parents' house on foot. It would take us a while to get there, but at least we would have a chance of making it," Solomon suggested.

Cleveland mocked him with a well-timed laugh. "If you think I'm going to walk thousands of miles on foot, only to be met by Christ's police force at your front door, then you're out of your mind."

Fester began jumping from rock to rock as he neared the boys. Daniel and Timothy were still in their own dreamland as the demon approached. In a few seconds, he was within range of Denny's spirit.

"Solomon is a plant," whispered the demon. "Don't trust him. Kill him before it's too late."

Denny's stare intensified. "Why do you want to take us to your parents' house?" His tone made Solomon uneasy.

"My mom and dad are cool. They believe in forgiveness. They would never turn us in."

Cleveland's spirit picked up on Fester's message. He stood and slowly advanced toward Solomon. Denny moved to Cleveland's side as both boys pressed in on Solomon.

"If your parents are so cool," questioned Cleveland, "then why didn't they stop that cop from taking you away? You said he was a neighbor and a good friend."

Solomon began to slowly back away toward the dark side of the cave. He shook his head in fear. Solomon stumbled on the wet rock as the light grew dimmer. What he couldn't see on their faces, he could sense in their spirits. Something possessed them.

Timothy and Daniel jumped to their feet and drew their swords.

"What's going on?" asked Daniel as he watched the boys.

"That smell was real," whispered Timothy. "I think we have a rat in here." He flew toward the entrance of the cave. "Hold your ground, Daniel. I'm going to start looking under some rocks."

Fester slid his plump body in between a large rock and the side of the cavern. He said nothing as Timothy flew directly overhead. Timothy glanced downward but didn't appear to see him. He flew to the entrance of the cave and turned around.

"It's just our imagination. There's nothing here."

Daniel sliced the damp air with his sword. "Too bad. I was hoping for some action."

Cleveland and Denny edged closer to Solomon. A large boulder stopped Solomon's backward escape.

"Come on, guys," began Solomon, "I'm a felon, too." He tried to relax in hopes that they would follow his example. "I don't want to get caught. I love my freedom."

The two were within an arm's length of Solomon when they stopped. Cleveland glanced at Denny, obviously waiting for him to take the lead. Denny stared at Solomon.

"So you have an illogical and stupid emotional connection to your mommy," began Denny. "I don't fault you for that." He jammed his pointer finger angrily into Solomon's chest. "Just don't let your 'touching' relationship with Mom cloud your wits."

Timothy quickly flew to Daniel's side. Fester didn't budge. Timothy took his sword and pointed toward a rock about thirty feet away. Daniel appeared puzzled. Timothy slowly spelled out a word with his sword, talking all the while in an effort to cover his real intentions.

"Wasn't it a pretty day today?" asked Timothy as he spelled the letter "d."

"Sure was, big angel," responded Daniel as he closely followed the sword's movements.

"Should be a great one tomorrow, too," continued Timothy. The letter "e" followed. "With the temperature around seventy-five, it should be great flying weather." His sword had carved out an "m" and an "o."

A titanic smile flashed on Daniel's face. He didn't need the last letter.

"Hey, Timothy, I say we leave the cave right now and go have some fun with some flight maneuvers."

"Sounds like a plan to me," grinned Timothy as he headed toward the light.

Fester snickered to himself as he watched the angels move overhead and away.

Solomon was backed into a corner. "Listen, man. I love my parents, but I obviously disagree with them about this Jesus stuff." He eyed his new "friends." "What do you guys think we should do? You know their radar will pick up that cruiser anywhere in the world."

Fester slowly crawled from the cubbyhole behind the rock and tiptoed toward the boys. Daniel and Timothy were outside the entrance to the grotto.

"On three, we scare that demon out of his dark, prickly skin," directed Timothy.

"Kill him while you have the chance!" whispered Fester, encouraging Denny to take an evil course of action.

A demonic glare possessed Denny's face. "I'm not so sure we can trust this guy. So what, so he tried to steal something. Just a teenage prank if you ask me. He's not in our league."

"You might be right," started Cleveland as he moved closer to Solomon. "What if he's working for the police? We don't need him. He can only hurt us."

Fester was having a ball. His demon wings were flapping feverishly against the rock. "Finish the job. Be a man," he urged. Denny picked up a large rock. Cleveland hesitated, but then followed Denny's lead.

"Slam!" shouted Timothy as he sliced a chunk out of Fester's wing.

"Boom!" yelled Daniel as he body-slammed the dark spirit.

"Whoa, whoa! Truce—I give up," groaned Fester.

"Not in this lifetime," hollered Timothy. He smashed his forearm into the demon's head. "Your tempting days are over."

Fester lay motionless on the cavern floor. Timothy saw the rocks in the boys' hands.

"Do what you can while I hold him down," Timothy directed Daniel.

"Come on, guys. Let's just relax here," stuttered Solomon. "We're a team. This will get us nowhere." Solomon didn't want to die this way, in the middle of a dark cave. Would Allison know how he had died? He would never have the chance to tell her he was sorry for the stupid things he had said.

Denny held a five-pound rock in his hand. Fester's message was ringing in his mind. He cocked his arm back.

"Don't do it," screamed Daniel at the top of his lungs.

"Tell God we said hey," laughed Denny as the rock hurled toward Solomon.

He tried to duck, but the stone grazed the right side of his forehead. Blood began to trickle down his cheek. Without a trace of emotion, Denny readied his next rock.

"No!" cried Timothy.

Solomon was dazed. The blood was flowing into his eye, obscuring his sight. "Allison," mumbled Solomon as the light began to fade.

"You are trash!" screamed Denny.

The last thing Solomon remembered was the crazed expression on Denny's face. Everything turned dark. Was he asleep or...or dead? He could hear their voices blaring in his mind but didn't know if they were real or if this was all a nightmare.

He sighed, "Jesus, help me."

"Allison, where are you going?" asked Gail from the table as she and Bill ate breakfast.

"I'm going for a walk on the mountain. I need to clear my head." Allison flashed a brief smile at them before walking toward the door.

"How about breakfast?" suggested her worried mother.

"I'll grab an apple from the tree." She quickly exited the house and jogged toward the large hill adjacent to her home. She stopped at the apple tree near the base of the hill. Reaching her hand toward an apple, she thought about Eve and the enticing beauty of the fruit. The Holy Spirit seemed to encompass her as she stared at the apple. She smiled as the Spirit spoke to her heart.

"Solomon is that apple. Stay clear of him right now, for he can only lead you astray. Just continue to pray for his salvation."

As Allison looked at the apple, it suddenly fell from her hand. She gazed toward heaven and sighed.

"Oh, I get it. You want me to entrust him to Your care."

The sun's warmth comforted her as she walked away from the tree. She wanted to go to Jerusalem to be by Solomon's side, to hold him and never let go. But she wanted Jesus more, and as she climbed the steep, green terrain, her heart gradually regained its peace. Minutes later, Allison sat on the ridge. She took her shoes off, removed the band holding her hair, picked a wildflower, and held it closely to her chest.

"Jesus, help me to be wise. You are my first priority. I've always believed Your Spirit brought Solomon and me together, but now, I'm confused, hurt, sad. If You want me to let go of him for a time, then so be it. I'll trust you to bring us back together, if that is in Your will."

Suddenly, what seemed like a thousand-pound weight fell off her shoulders. Instead of speaking Solomon's name, she joyfully whispered, "Jesus, I love You."

———————

Blasphemy felt like a new demon as the blue-green planet came into full view. He stared at the Earth and began to drool.

"The time has come for some divine justice—Blasphemy style," mused the demon as he increased his speed. "First I'll take out Satan, then Jesus, and finally the Father." His ambition was higher than his intellect.

Suddenly, a flicker of light flashed in his face. Seconds later, a sword crashed into his left side. A sharp, razor-like pain throttled his body. He quickly drew his sword and flew in a circle.

"You're not what you used to be," thundered a distant voice.

Blasphemy shook as he peered into the darkness. "Must be a friend of mine," shouted Blasphemy. "Come out and fight like a demon."

A pair of black wings floated ceremoniously from behind Blasphemy. A large, foreboding demon shot toward him. Blasphemy dove out of the way.

"A thousand years is a long time. You must be rusty!" echoed the deep voice.

"Are you foolish enough to challenge the great one?" retorted Blasphemy as he captured a glimpse of the intruder.

The demon slowly appeared from the darkness with his sword held high in the air. He was nearly ten feet tall with dark, prickly fur covering everything but his face. The hideous, disfigured spirit moved closer. Blasphemy's face brightened.

"Is that you, General Ruse?"

"Yes. Are you surprised?"

"Of course not," responded Blasphemy. "Treachery is one of your most admirable qualities."

General Ruse had been one of six generals directly beneath Blasphemy during the time preceding the millennial kingdom. His territory extended from China to Russia. Since Satan's capture and Blasphemy's judgment, General Ruse was one of six demons that had tried to replace Satan and his iron rule. He never succeeded. None of them was strong enough or wise enough to rule over the demons. None of them captured the respect or the fear of the dark underworld.

Ruse pointed his sword toward Blasphemy. "I figure if I have your head on a stick, the other demons will fear me. Then I will rule the world and rid it of Jesus and His sidekick, David." Immediately, the general wanted to take that last statement back. His impulsive tongue always seemed to hurt him. With his entire hand out on the table, he tried to make the best of it.

"Would you like to cooperate now and lay down your arms?"

Blasphemy laughed. "Quite impressive, Ruse. The only flaw in your logic is staring you in the face!"

Blasphemy lunged at Ruse with reckless passion. Ruse held his own as their swords clashed into each other. The demonic scuffle lasted several minutes and appeared to be a draw.

"Jesus is King!" trumpeted a piercing voice.

The demons stopped fighting.

"Who's there?" asked Blasphemy.

"Identify yourself," ordered Ruse.

The archangel Michael appeared from above. The heavily armored angel slowly floated downward. His sword was not drawn, to the surprise of the demons.

"Blasphemy and Ruse," began Michael, "your days are numbered."

The radiant angel was muscular in frame but gentle in spirit. His robe glittered with golden dust. He disliked confronting these demons. God had always given him a short stick with the demonic generals. He knew he could destroy them at any moment, but his trust in God prevented him from acting on his military impulses. He knew that God wanted these demons around to test the saints and to refine them into pure gold through trials and tribulations.

"Your boss will be released shortly. If I were you, I would stop bickering among yourselves and get ready for the wrath of the Great Dragon."

Blasphemy spit toward the archangel. "Why would you come all this way to tell us that?"

General Ruse exploded toward the archangel with his sword leading the way. Michael instantly pulled his own sword into view. General Ruse took a quick swipe at Michael, but missed when the archangel jumped to the side. Instead, the archangel's dagger pierced the demon's side.

"Ah, glad you're taking care of my light work," seethed Blasphemy.

With a gaping hole in his side, General Ruse fled toward Earth. He had been humiliated, and he hated that feeling more than any other. It only made him hate Michael, and the Lord, even more.

Michael looked at Blasphemy. "Blasphemy, your master has been locked and chained for nearly one thousand years. The time is coming when you and he will be banished for eternity."

Michael slowly floated upward. Intense hatred welled up inside the demon as he watched God's servant disappear.

"You might have won this battle, Michael, but we will win the war!"

David's appearance was striking. He was handsome and looked to be in his thirties. He had the bearing of a king, yet he was humble. David was seated near Ken and Emily with Peter on the other side of the central fountain. His hands were resting in his lap as he interviewed Ken and Emily.

"I know this is going to be hard on you, but I must ask you these questions. Did either one of you notice any signs that Solomon was contemplating such an act of disobedience?"

They looked at each other thoughtfully, then turned to David. "Solomon was always a good boy," began Ken. "He always obeyed us growing up. He seemed to enjoy church and traveling to Jerusalem to worship Jesus." Ken shook his head in disbelief. "It's like one minute he had the heart of a Mother Theresa, and the next he was acting like Jesse James." Ken paused as he tried to pinpoint when Solomon's attitude had soured. "I remember how persistent he was when it came to that air cruiser." David and Peter listened intently. "And yet, Solomon didn't seem to get irritated when we told him no. He seemed to blow it off like it wasn't a big deal."

David moved forward in his seat. "Emily, did you sense any changes in his attitude?"

"Now that you mention it, yes, sometimes—especially in the past couple of months. Even though he obeyed us, it seemed like he was fighting an internal conflict. Outwardly, he did as we asked, but it was like he was just going through the motions. Does that make any sense at all?" She wiped her eyes with Ken's handkerchief. "I guess I just chalked it up to the natural process of growing up and becoming independent."

Ken knew what Emily was talking about. He remembered a rebellious look he had seen at times on Solomon's face. It would disappear almost as soon as it came. It was so subtle that they had overlooked it. He closed his eyes and shook his head. Maybe they had known something was wrong, but just hadn't wanted to deal with it. It was easier to deny a problem than to confront it.

"King David, she's right," added Ken. "His attitude did seem to shift somewhat. I can't put my finger on the exact time it started, but there was something going on."

"Do you believe Solomon is a born-again Christian?" asked David. The blunt question caught the couple off guard.

Ken and Emily were silent. The tension in the room seemed to grow. Emily wanted to say yes, but she couldn't because she wasn't sure, or maybe she was sure and didn't like the answer.

"I know this isn't easy, Emily," Peter said kindly, "but we have been receiving numerous reports of teenage rebellion all around the world—particularly in your area of Russia. For one thousand years, only a few, sporadic cases like this have cropped up among your generation. Peace and safety, love and joy, have been the mainstays of the kingdom. But now," he paused as he battled his emotions, "now this generation is...." He shook his head as his eyes glazed over. His heartbreak was evident. "This generation is in trouble." Peter knew the prophecies that disobedience would occur even during ideal situations. They all knew that truth. But now they were living it, and it wasn't easy.

Ken couldn't believe he was sitting with the apostle Peter and King David talking about his wayward son. How he wished he could be with them worshipping the Lord, talking about their lives during Bible days, and picking their brains about the nature of good and evil. He leaned back in his chair as David continued.

"Remember the Garden of Eden. Adam and Eve sinned even though perfection existed. God walked in their midst, yet they fell. And even though Israel was set free from Pharaoh, the Israelites rebelled in the desert. There is only one way to respond to this kind of defiance. That is why the Scriptures say, 'He shall rule them with a rod of iron.'"

"What are you going to do to Solomon?" asked Emily, who was only half paying attention to David's words. She was focused on what was going to happen to her son.

"He will stand before me and give an account for his foolishness," replied Peter.

"Then what?" asked Ken.

"Then he will pay a heavy price for his sin." Emily's emotions began to splinter. The apostle raised his hand into the air. "Calm down, Emily. It will be just and fair. We must return to the original question." He glanced at Vice-Regent David.

"Is Solomon born again, or is he playing a religious masquerade?" asked David again.

"He's gone forward to the altar at least a dozen times in the past five or six years," answered Emily. "I always assumed he was a Christian, but, come on, one act of disobedience doesn't make somebody a sinner, does it?" Emily knew her theology was on quicksand. She knew Solomon's repeated acts of profession were one of the red flags they had buried.

"Honey, they know that," interrupted Ken. "That's why they want to know about his attitude. He could be sinning in his heart all day, but not necessarily showing it on the outside."

"That's right, Ken," agreed Peter. "You could compare it to an iceberg. Only a tiny percentage of an iceberg is above water. Most of it is below the surface. Sin is the same way. It begins in the heart. That's hard to see, but occasionally— or often—it will reveal itself in a person's actions."

Emily's fear and frustration were obvious as she exclaimed, "I don't need a theology lesson here. I just want to know what's going to happen to my baby." She paused to catch her breath. Emily glanced out the window and stared at the happy people strolling through the temple area. She regretted her quick words. Her eyes began to fill with tears as she turned back to David and Peter. She knew she was in the wrong.

"I'm sorry." She shook her head slowly, weakened by her emotions.

They smiled at her. It was tough losing your son to sin, and their empathy for her showed.

"I want to be there for the trial."

David and Peter stood.

"I'm sorry, but that isn't possible," Peter stated gently but firmly. "Go home and pray for your son, and for his salvation."

Cleveland's hand began to quiver against the weight of the stone. He just couldn't make himself throw it.

"Get it over with," shrieked Denny as he pushed Cleveland from behind. "Come on. Nobody will know a thing."

"Drop it now!" screeched a voice from a loudspeaker outside the cave. "You're under arrest."

Cleveland instantly dropped the weapon and looked at Denny. The boys put their hands over their heads and turned toward the voice. A dozen agents from the apostles' police force were pointing laser guns at them.

"Keep your hands over your heads and slowly walk toward us," ordered the leader of the company.

"All right!" shouted Timothy as he celebrated with Daniel.

Daniel stood atop Fester. "You demons just never learn that evil doesn't pay."

"It's not what it looks like," offered Denny as he walked toward the light.

"Save your excuses for the apostles," answered the head officer, Will Bunding. He walked farther into the cavern ahead of the rest of the team, each wearing white uniforms with the words *King Jesus* woven on their shirt sleeves. "Don't make any sudden moves." He spotted Solomon. "Sam, Karen, someone is injured. Get over there and see what you can do."

Denny and Cleveland were shaking as they neared Officer Bunding. They knew it was over and what was coming. They would probably spend the rest of their lives in prison working the fields. Denny glanced at Cleveland and growled. Cleveland closed his eyes in shame. He thought about his age of innocence, the times in his youth when he had played with his young friends and enjoyed hanging out with his parents. It all seemed so long ago, like it had happened to someone else. He looked at the drops of Solomon's blood that were splattered on his and Denny's clothes.

"Now, drop to your knees and place your hands behind your heads." The ranking police officer stopped about ten feet from the boys, his weapon pointed directly at them. "Arrest them."

"Brilliant move, Cleveland," snapped Denny as one of the officers cuffed his hands and his feet.

Cleveland didn't respond. He sighed as he looked at Denny and then at Solomon.

"If you boys want to live a life of crime, you need to get a bit smarter," said Captain Bunding as he lowered his weapon. "Didn't you even consider trashing the police cruiser?" He walked to the unit, opened up the engine compartment, and pulled out a small box. "This sent us a very precise signal. We knew where you were and what you were saying."

Denny and Cleveland stared at the hard muddy floor.

"Solomon was right," whispered Denny under his breath. Cleveland didn't hear him, but he already knew what his friend had said. Denny was getting madder by the second and felt like exploding.

Captain Bunding glanced at Solomon, then immediately turned to stare intently into Denny's and Cleveland's eyes. "You boys may bypass one of the apostles and go straight to Vice-Regent David."

The police medics wiped the blood from Solomon's eyes. Solomon was semiconscious. He tried to open his eyes.

"Mom, my, my head. It hurts." Solomon started to breathe erratically. "Allison, sing that song to me again." He lost consciousness.

Will Bunding watched Solomon close his eyes. "You boys better pray to God he makes it."

Neither boy had the wisdom or courage to take the officer's advice. The medics examined the lesion on Solomon's head with a sonic device, then dressed the wound.

"It doesn't appear to be too serious. I don't know why he passed out, but it looks like he will be okay," said the lead medic.

"Get him to Jerusalem," ordered Captain Bunding. He looked at Denny and Cleveland. "I want you two," pointing to the guards standing nearby, "to ride in the back with these boys. If they make any kind of offensive threat, you know what to do."

Blasphemy shook off Michael's words as he entered Earth's airspace. A few low-ranking demons nearly flew into themselves when they recognized their lost leader. He happily sneered at their theatrics, craving the attention that he had sorely missed.

"There's a mandatory meeting at the Dead Sea at six o'clock this evening. Spread the word," hissed Blasphemy as he sped toward Jerusalem. Minutes later, he arrived at the Holy City. There wasn't a demon in sight. Millions of angels patrolled the atmosphere. Blasphemy hid behind a cloud so he wouldn't be detected.

Cowards, thought the demon. He didn't like what he saw. This was far different from what he had expected. To think that he had to hide from the do-gooders was almost more than his evil spirit could take. As he inspected the city, he didn't recognize anything. The buildings were new, built of a material he wasn't familiar with. The temple was made of gold, with the highest-ranking angels guarding the four corners.

"Demon alert!" yelled an angel.

Blasphemy foolishly chased the angel. Hundreds of sword-carrying angels were on him like fleas on a dog. He was surrounded and instantly recognized. For the first time in a millennia, he felt fear, real fear that numbed his stomach.

"It's Blasphemy. He's back," alerted an astute general.

Blasphemy hissed violently as the throng of angels closed in on his position. He quickly looked around him. There still wasn't a demon in view. Suddenly, a flashing sword shot down from the sky. General Ruse appeared out of thin air and began cutting a hole to his freedom. Blasphemy began to breathe a little easier. He certainly wasn't going to refuse the charity.

"What do you think you're doing?" happily yelled Blasphemy as General Ruse's sword knocked back a dozen angels.

"Saving your sorry skin," gasped Ruse.

"Cease fire, angels!" ordered the commander.

The demons stared at the angels, not knowing what to think. The angels literally stopped in mid-fight.

Blasphemy and Ruse looked at each other, then did what came naturally to them: They began to mock their opponents.

"Thank you for the warm welcome, my fellow angels," laughed Blasphemy. "Obviously, you're smarter than I thought. Messing with me can be hazardous to your health."

The angels stared at him as if he were some wild animal. Blasphemy ignored them as he glared at Jerusalem. Suddenly, he felt the intensity of a penetrating look. It was Jesus! The Lord's iron gaze seemed to drain him of his power. He was scared, but tried not to show it.

"Let's get out of here," gulped Blasphemy.

———

The one-hour trip seemed to take forever. Denny and Cleveland were chained and secured in the back of a police cruiser. Out of deference to Solomon's wounds, he was not handcuffed, but two highly armed guards watched over the three young men.

"How can you boys spit in our King's face like this?" asked the younger guard, Bruce Deal. They ignored him as they stared at their chains. "King Jesus has proven His love and devotion to you, yet you mock Him by your actions."

The elder guard, Calvin Mann, interrupted him. "Bruce, you've got to understand this. These boys know who Jesus is in their heads. They simply reject Him in their hearts. They want to do their own thing."

Solomon, now fully conscious, had the headache of his lifetime. He tried to block out the guard's words. He knew they were true, terribly true, but he seemed set on a course that made it impossible to repent or change his ways.

"Entering Jerusalem airspace," announced a female voice from the front of the cruiser. The boys looked at the passing houses through the back window. Cleveland noticed a home that resembled his. It brought back memories that he quickly tried to repress.

"How long do you think they will get?" asked Bruce.

"They may not see the light of day for a long time," figured Calvin as he glanced at the boys. His statement seemed to incite Denny.

"If Jesus is such a great King, then why did He allow the Battle of Armageddon to destroy so many people? I know my history, cop."

The elder officer shook his head in disbelief. The police cruiser began to slow as it neared the temple area. The guards stood as the vehicle stopped. They grabbed the boys by the arm and helped them down the steps of the wagon.

"You blame our King and Lord for the failings of the Devil," responded Calvin.

Denny spit on the ground near the guard's feet. "Fairy tales, if you ask me. If I can't see the Devil, I don't believe in him. Sounds like Jesus just likes to pass the buck to an imaginary character. It makes it convenient for Him to blame bad things on somebody else."

The boys were led in chains to a court building near the center of town. Hundreds of people gawked at them as they marched down the main artery. The sight of chained criminals in the sin-free city was rare. All of them avoided eye contact with the people. For Denny, it wasn't that he felt shame; it was the joy and peace in their eyes that annoyed him.

"When you reach that door," directed the older guard, "you will stop and drop on your knees."

The justice building was seven stories tall, oval shaped, with seven columns surrounding the smooth marble shell. The top of the building had a gold sword reaching toward the heavens, symbolic of the Messianic justice of Jesus.

A man whom the boys didn't recognize appeared at the main door. He wore a white robe and a golden crown. Solomon was the first to obey as he fell to the ground. The younger guard gently nudged Denny's and Cleveland's shoulders. The boys grumbled under their breath as they joined Solomon on the ground. A trumpet sounded from inside the building as the man with the crown stopped in front of the criminals. Denny and Cleveland seemed disinterested in the proceedings, but Solomon appeared to be sniffling as he stared into the eyes of the apostle.

"You three boys have been charged with multiple felonies," began the apostle Peter as thousands began to gather around the scene. "How do you plead?"

One could hear only the sound of shuffling feet as the citizens of Jerusalem flocked to the proceedings. Denny and Cleveland were angry and defiant.

"Who gave you the right to judge?" ridiculed Denny as Cleveland nodded his approval.

The apostle Peter showed no emotion as he walked toward Denny. He kept his hands behind his back as he began to speak. "The King of the universe has entrusted me, the eleven other apostles, and, of course, Vice-Regent David, to judge truthfully, fairly, and without bias."

"Who gave Him the right?" retorted Denny.

Solomon appeared perplexed by their bold cockiness. He dropped his head to the earth as a sign of guilt and humility.

"God the Father gave King Jesus that right. He also lovingly gave you the right to choose Him or reject Him."

"Who gave God the Father the right to judge?" continued Denny. The citizens surrounding him were astonished at his insolence. "God gave Himself the right to judge."

Denny began to breathe heavily. "Then I give myself the right to do what I want—when I want."

Solomon could not believe his ears. The blasphemy spouting from Denny's mouth shocked everyone.

"Your trial is set for ten o'clock tomorrow morning," announced Peter. "Vice-Regent David will preside as judge. You may take up your opinions with him."

The two guards quickly guided the boys toward their holding cells inside the justice building. They could hear hundreds of people praying as they entered the structure.

Denny watched Solomon as they continued their trek down a hallway.

"We should have killed you when we had the chance," mumbled Denny outside the hearing range of the guard.

"Crying is a sign of weakness," Cleveland retorted. "You'll be one of them before you know it."

Solomon smiled slyly. He had to stay in their good graces. "I don't think so," whispered Solomon. "I just know how to act when I'm caught."

Blasphemy eyed General Ruse with suspicion.

"You don't expect me to believe that you saved me out of the goodness of your heart, do you?"

General Ruse eyed his nemesis. "There is no goodness in my heart." Ruse grabbed his sword and began to rub his finger carefully across the blade. "Satan wants a piece of you when he is released."

As the two generals stood on a mountain overlooking China, they didn't realize they were being spied on. An aide to the archangel Michael was hiding behind a boulder.

"So he wants a piece of the great one, does he?" mocked Blasphemy. He pulled his sword into view and pointed it toward General Ruse. "Sounds like you've been talking to that loser." He edged his way toward the general. "Sounds like he had you doing his dirty work for him. Am I right, General Ruse?"

Blasphemy hurled his razor-sharp sword toward Ruse's large head. Ruse ducked and dove toward Blasphemy with his sword leading the charge. Blasphemy jumped out of the way with only a millisecond to spare. He jumped on General Ruse and held him on the ground.

"You will submit to my authority. Satan is no longer the boss of this planet. Any questions?"

Ruse stared defiantly into Blasphemy's eyes. "I have millions of demons that follow my every whim," lied the general. "It would benefit you greatly if you treated me with a little more respect."

"I respect nobody but myself, General Ruse." Blasphemy lowered his face to within inches of his opponent's. "I will be watching you like a hawk in the coming days. One wrong move, and I will pulverize you and your so-called supporters."

Their holding cells were dark and lonely. It was midnight, and the boys couldn't sleep. They were in separate but adjoining cells. Solomon couldn't get comfortable on the flimsy mattress covering the metal cot. To top things off, his head was still pounding. He glanced at Denny, who was staring at the white ceiling.

"Where are your mom and dad?"

Denny rolled over and looked at Solomon. Cleveland had his face stuffed in the pillow.

"They actually live near your hometown."

"Why did you reject Jesus? Were your folks hypocrites?"

"I'm not sure what that word means anymore," began Denny. He closed his eyes as he spoke. "My parents treated me fine, I guess. Sometimes they were rough on me, and the older I got, the harder they were. I finally decided that I had had enough, and I ran away." His eyes were glassy and distant. "Sometimes they seemed to treat my friends better than me."

"What do you mean?"

Denny sighed as he wiggled his body, trying to find a comfortable spot in the lumpy mattress. "I don't know if I can put my finger on it. They always seemed to compliment everybody but me when it came to different things. Our house was like the community playground, and everybody congregated there." He stopped talking and started mumbling. "It's not that I was doing stuff wrong. I just wasn't doing things as well as I could have. Know what I mean?"

Timothy and Daniel rushed into the room. They had followed Ken and Emily back home and then had flown at top speed back to guard Solomon. They sat on the floor and listened.

"Yeah, only too well," responded Solomon as he frowned at the thought. "Sounds like my parents. They said they loved me unconditionally, but if they spotted even a hint of what they considered to be a bad attitude, their love would disappear. Then I'd have to endure another one of their lectures."

Cleveland pulled away from the crumpled pillow. "Sounds way too familiar to me. My whole neighborhood was a bunch of saints, and I was always the stray sheep in my town, you know, laughing in church, not obeying one hundred percent of the time."

Solomon laughed out of frustration. "They kept insisting that I trust Jesus with all my heart, and I kept telling them I did. But I'm not sure I even know what He wants from me, or even who He really is."

"It's plain to me that this entire thing is one huge charade," observed Denny as he sat up in his bed. "If Jesus wants my entire heart, why doesn't He just take it?"

The boys agreed as they looked back and forth at each other. Denny and Cleveland were beginning to trust Solomon. Their conversation continued for several more hours.

"What's happening with them?" asked Daniel.

"They're turning sour," responded Timothy.

"I don't see any demons around. They're not being tempted, so how can they go bad?"

"You don't need a demon to tempt you, only a heart that's not fully devoted to God. The demons can't really affect you until you give them the right of passage. Kind of like a fish in water. Without water, the fish dies. Without the evil already lurking in their hearts, the demons are powerless. They can go only where darkness already exists."

Daniel began to pace around the room. "So what you are telling me is that we are powerless to stop this?"

Timothy nodded his head. "We can't control their hearts. We can only fight off the demons."

"My biggest problem," vented Denny, "was with my father. He always seemed to criticize my work around the house, but would make glowing comments about kids who weren't even his own flesh and blood."

Cleveland turned and looked at Solomon. "Do you have a girl back home?"

"No," answered Solomon as a picture of Allison formed in his mind. "Well, I used to, but we," he paused and tried to forget, "we just grew apart." The pain in his voice was quite apparent.

"Whoa," teased Cleveland, "you've got it bad for her."

"Shut up!"

"You shut up!" yelled Denny as he flung himself against his pillow.

Solomon forced himself not to think about Allison. It was too painful, and even he didn't know why. He was running from something he didn't understand—or maybe he did, but was too afraid to admit it.

Silence followed as each boy began to doze off. They were bonding in a way they had never done with their families, causing Timothy to begin a theological discourse of sorts.

"This is just amazing, Daniel. Don't you hear what they're saying?" Daniel stared at Timothy with confusion on his face. "Don't you remember Cain and Abel? Why did the murder take place? One had his sacrifice accepted by God, but the other didn't! The root of the problem is jealousy and pride. Thousands of years later, during the peaceful years of the Millennium, a subtle evil springs not from demons, but from the depraved heart of man." He began to pace the room like it was on fire. "This is incredible!"

Daniel didn't seem to get it. "Take a break. I'm exhausted, and you're making my brain hurt."

Timothy tried to calm down but to no avail. He was wound tighter than a Texas tornado.

"I'll see you a little later. I'm going to take a stroll through Jerusalem and bounce this idea off some higher-ranking angels."

"Whatever," mumbled Daniel as he snuggled himself into the corner of Solomon's bed.

Five

The Trial

Birds were singing and the sun was shining as nearly one hundred friends and family filed into the small country church. The sight of Solomon sporting a full-length white tuxedo mesmerized Allison as her father escorted her down the aisle. Her future husband's winsome smile was intoxicating as she reached for his hand and they turned to face the preacher.

As the pastor spoke about the duties of love and a life-long commitment, her eyes were fastened on Solomon. The warmth of his strong hand in hers sent shivers down her spine. Every time he squeezed her hand, her heart skipped a beat. Her soul was finally at peace; her first love had come home to her, pledging with a pure heart a lifetime of love.

Suddenly, the church filled with a heavy fog. She could hear the distant voice of the preacher asking Solomon if he would fulfill his vows. Everything was in slow motion as she watched Solomon's lips begin to move.

He's going to say it, he's going to say it, she thought as the fog thickened and the sounds faded.

"I do. I do. I do," she murmured as beads of perspiration trickled down her back. A blinding light flashed, a loud explosion followed, and blaring voices filled the air. She sat up, looked around her room as if it were part of a nightmare, then slumped back down on her bed.

"I want to go back," she moaned, her hand searching for the jarring alarm clock, her heart in a distant land of make-believe. Allison stared at Solomon's picture on the wall.

"We've got to get you saved, rebel boy," said Allison, her face turning resolute, almost soldier-like. Even if they weren't to be together, Allison knew she couldn't stop praying for Solomon.

The day dawned bright in Jerusalem, and the sun cast long shadows against the historic city. Every morning at sunrise, millions of residents would congregate around the throne of Jesus to hear a word from the King. It was televised around the world and practically everybody tuned in to hear a fresh word, a life-giving anointing from Jesus. Nobody went to work until after His sermon. As the masses returned to their homes, the three boys were awakened.

"A little sleep, a little slumber, and poverty will overtake you!" announced a young guard.

Solomon, Cleveland, and Denny covered their heads.

"One more hour," pleaded Cleveland as he plopped the pillow over his head.

"You're not at home, men. You have five minutes to get ready to meet the King."

"I'll pass," groaned Cleveland, exhausted from a restless night's sleep.

The guard pushed a button on his belt. "I need backup immediately," reported the guard to his boss. Seconds later, two burly, middle-aged men were by his side. The young guard opened Cleveland's cell door first. He yanked the covers from Cleveland's half-naked body and tossed a black robe in his face.

"Don't fight the system, young man. Put this on, now."

Cleveland noisily exhaled as he stretched his tight back. He groggily donned the robe.

The young man moved to Solomon's cell. Solomon was sitting up in his bed.

"Glad to see you're feeling better. Looks like your attitude has improved, too," voiced the man as he threw a black robe onto the bottom of Solomon's bed.

Solomon grunted softly. "Hard to sleep on a lumpy rock." He closely watched the guard, who appeared to be happy and at peace with the world. I'm stuck in this hole, thought Solomon, as he buried his face in his hands.

The sentry stared at him for a second. "Jail is not supposed to be enjoyable."

He proceeded to Denny's holding cell. He lobbed the black gown toward the sleeping teenager.

"Get moving, kid."

There was no response. He edged closer to Denny as the others watched. He nudged the boy's arm with a nightstick. "It's time to get up and face the judge."

Denny didn't budge. He wasn't really tired; he was just being ornery. The guard lifted the sheet from him with his stick and discarded it on the floor. They could see Denny's back moving up and down.

"You're already in a lot of trouble. Don't make things worse. I can see you breathing."

"Come on, Denny. Just get up and get it over with," urged Cleveland. He knew Denny's lack of cooperation would only make matters worse for all of them.

The two husky guards began to clear their throats.

"Don't do anything stupid," said Solomon as he rubbed the muscles in his neck.

The young guard moved closer to Denny. Denny's head was completely hidden under the pillow. The guard placed his face within inches of Denny's head.

"Boo!" shouted Denny at the top of his lungs. He burst out laughing.

The guard nearly had a heart attack. He ran out of the cell, shaking his head furiously. "That was not funny, not the least bit funny. They will hear about this," he growled. Solomon and Cleveland were trying to hold back their laughter when one of the elder guards tossed a dose of reality their way.

"Jesus is monitoring everything you say, everything you do, everything you think."

Their laughter died.

Thousands of demons were flying around the Dead Sea, excited that Blasphemy was back from the dead. At the meeting the night before, every spirit with a ranking of colonel or better was commanded to be present first thing this morning to receive his orders. To miss this meeting would mean certain death. Blasphemy was nowhere to be found as the clock ticked past ten.

The demons were not accustomed to seeing this body of water surging with life. They had always enjoyed this spot for its heat, dryness, and death. Since the beginning of the Millennium, Jesus had rejuvenated the earth from the original curse of "thorns and thistles." It irritated the demons to see life where once there had been only death. They hated the beauty of planet Earth with its abundant animal and plant life, ideal weather, and nearly perfect people. They hated to see humans filled with joy and giving God the credit for it. The demons abhorred Jesus and His government based on truth and justice.

General Ruse was on the front row of the flock when he looked at his watch for the tenth time in less than a minute. He whispered something to his neighbor, a three-star general named Fright.

"How can Blasphemy lead this great nation when he can't keep his own rules? Hypocrisy, if you ask me," criticized Ruse. He was searching for powerful allies.

"Blasphemy has always liked to make a grand entrance," retorted General Fright. "Take a pill and relax. You had your chance to rule." Fright's honesty was not welcome. "We had privates doing their own thing when you were in charge. You never used fear to your advantage."

General Ruse was livid. How dared that demon speak to him that way? It wasn't his fault that the demons wouldn't obey him when he was in charge. He watched Blasphemy zoom across the horizon with his sword held high. The demons applauded with all their might as he landed in front of the herd. Ruse growled under his breath. Blasphemy paraded around for a bit as the demons screamed accolades. The large demon chucked his sword in the air. The silver dagger traveled several hundred feet high, then began dropping toward the crowd. General Ruse angrily watched the sword drop directly toward him. He lunged to the right at the last second. The sword landed in the exact spot where Ruse had been.

"Good shot," muttered Blasphemy as he raised his paws into the air.

General Ruse stared hotly at the demon. Blasphemy ignored him as he gazed on his loyal subjects. Blasphemy knew how to handle treasonous demons; he'd had plenty of practice with treason himself.

"Fellow demons, as you all know, our fearless leader Satan has been captured by the enemy. He has instructed me to lead us to a bright and glorious future, to stand up against the forces of humility, and to bring our kingdom of strength, vigor, and self-determination to fruition."

It had been one thousand years since the demons had been united. The throng of spirits cheered and hissed at every pause.

"Secure your sectors, work together, and lean on your fellow brothers. A kingdom divided cannot stand." Blasphemy pranced all around with his paws behind his back, as if he were a college professor. "I am your greatest hope for victory. Satan is gone forever. Avenge his death and win the war!"

General Ruse interrupted Blasphemy. He quickly shot above the mob.

"There are rumors that Satan is close to breaking out of prison. Please address that, O great one."

Blasphemy forced a smile as he glared at Ruse. Blasphemy wanted to kick Ruse straight into the fires of hell. He had no choice but to do what he did best—in other words, lie.

"Those rumors are not true. The Bible says he will be released after one thousand years. If that were true, he would be out in the next couple of days, if my calculations are correct."

Sporadic conversation erupted. Blasphemy had to think of something quickly.

He raised his sword in the air. "Do you believe one of your own or the driveling Bible?"

Pride filled the crowd as the demons cheered their new leader. They trusted Blasphemy because of his command position under Satan, but beneath it all, they were still loyal to the Devil.

"Blasphemy, Blasphemy, Blasphemy!" they chanted.

Solomon, Denny, and Cleveland were chained at the hands and ankles as they shuffled down the hallway of justice. Each wore a black robe with a hood covering his head. Without shoes or socks, the chains began to rub against their ankles. Two guards were in front, and two more at their rear as they headed for David's throne.

An intense light shone from the end of the corridor. As they neared the entrance to the throne room, Solomon began to get the shakes.

I'm not ready for this, thought Solomon. He began to tremble all over as the light hurt his eyes. He wanted to be a kid again, innocent, with all his life before him. When he thought about his future, all he could see was pain and suffering. Hope was gone, and paradise was lost.

"What's the deal with the light?" complained Denny as he tried to shield his eyes.

"I don't know," squinted Cleveland.

As they entered David's throne room, they rubbed their half-blinded eyes. The square room was fashioned in pure gold from the roof to the floor. No furniture, no pictures, nothing adorned the room except an impressive white throne measuring seven feet high and three feet wide. Vice-Regent David was seated on the throne with several people surrounding him. The guards stopped at the entrance and removed their sandals.

"What are you doing that for?" asked Solomon.

"This is holy ground," responded the elder guard.

The guards moved forward several more feet, then dropped to their knees. The boys wisely did the same. Solomon quickly recognized one of the men near David as the apostle Peter. His jaw dropped open when the other turned toward them.

"Jesus," gasped Cleveland as he stared at His face.

The Trial

King Jesus' eyes flamed like fire; they were piercing yet compassionate. Several golden crowns, intertwined in a majestic design, rested on His head. On the lower third of His white robe, red blotches resembling blood were dramatic reminders of the ultimate sacrifice Jesus had made. The boys read these words emblazoned on the robe over His pierced side: "King of Kings and Lord of Lords."

"Please stand and move toward me," ordered David as Jesus looked on.

The guards remained near the entrance. For once, Denny, Cleveland, and Solomon didn't hesitate to obey. They stood and took short awkward steps as they struggled with their chains. Denny and Solomon couldn't look at King Jesus. Cleveland, though, stared straight into His eyes as if hypnotized by His Majesty. The boys were within seven feet of Jesus when David spoke.

"Stop there, and remain standing, please."

A basin of water miraculously appeared in the hands of Jesus. He moved toward the boys with the meekness of a lamb. All eyes were fastened on the King of the universe. The silence was deafening as Jesus stopped in front of the boys. He looked at Solomon. Solomon could only return the glance for a few seconds before guilt forced his eyes away. Jesus turned toward Cleveland. The close proximity of his Creator instantly broke him. Cleveland wept and bowed his head. Jesus moved to Denny. Denny defiantly glared into Christ's eyes. He felt as if every ounce of his being was being scrutinized and dissected. A rush of adrenaline flooded his body. Jesus moved His eyes toward the basin. He lowered Himself to His knees in front of the boys and placed His nail-scarred hands in the container. Their eyes shadowed Him as He began to wring out the excess water from a piece of cloth.

"Humility, young men, is the greatest trait one can possess," began Jesus in a soft yet authoritative tone. Still on His knees, He moved toward Denny's feet. "Humility teaches that you are not the center of the universe, that you should consider others before yourself."

The King's strong hands reached toward Denny's feet. Denny began to shake uncontrollably as the Lord's steady hands placed the wet cloth against his dirty feet. Denny wanted to speak but couldn't.

"I died on an old rugged cross for your sins, Denny. My love for you is real. I gave My life for you so that you could be washed clean and spend eternity with Me in a new heaven."

As Jesus methodically moved the wet rag across his feet, Denny attempted to form a complete sentence.

"I'm not worthy of this," struggled Denny. "Stop."

Jesus paused and looked up at Denny. "If I do not wash you, you can have no part of My kingdom."

Denny's lips moved without words. He shook his head. "No...No..."

Jesus immediately stopped the washing. I don't get it, thought Denny. I don't understand. Why is He doing this to me? Kings don't do this. Jesus read his mind and sighed before moving toward Cleveland. Cleveland backed away as he stared at Jesus. The Lord moved forward toward him.

"Your sins separate you from God's goodness." Jesus placed the damp rag into the water, wrung it out, and moved it toward Cleveland's feet. Cleveland remained still as the King tenderly cleaned his feet. "You must give up your sinful ways to be My disciple. Repent and worship Me, and you will live."

Cleveland didn't know how to respond. He turned and looked at Denny as Jesus finished the washing. Denny shook his head in disbelief. Cleveland looked at Jesus and whispered, "I wish I could, but I can't change."

Jesus stared at him intently. "You can't change yourself. You must want to change and allow Me to do it."

Cleveland's heart was on the verge of something he didn't understand. He understood partially, but not fully. His heart was still sitting on the fence.

Jesus turned from him and moved to kneel in front of Solomon. Solomon didn't know how to act as the King placed the moist towel on his right foot. He tried to close his eyes but felt mesmerized by the moment.

The Trial

"I and the Father are One. There is no greater authority in heaven or on earth than Us." Jesus carefully moved the cloth around the steel chains binding his feet. "I want your entire heart, soul, and mind. I am a jealous God, and I will not take your second best. No one can serve two masters."

Solomon's heart sputtered as it tried to grasp the meaning of Jesus' words and actions. His childhood flashed before him: His father teaching him to ride a bike, his mother reading bedtime stories, images of Allison reading her Bible, the preacher pleading at the pulpit for people to repent of hidden sins, and the moment only weeks ago when he had told Allison that they were finished as a couple. Emotions surfaced momentarily, each one fleeing as quickly as it came.

"Do you believe I came to save you from your sins?" asked Jesus point-blank. "Do you believe that I'm the only way to peace and joy?"

Solomon took his eyes off Jesus and looked at his friends. The confusion and fear in their eyes helped in his answer. He figured he believed, sure, but not enough to obey Him the way his parents did. Solomon was influenced by his peers who said they believed in Jesus—most of the time. Jesus immediately sensed his lack of faith. He returned the cloth to the basin, which suddenly disappeared from sight. Jesus rose to His feet. His look of peace and tranquility was replaced with righteous anger.

"My servant David, whom I love, will follow up." The Lord's face suddenly began to shine as bright as the sun. His body began to lift toward the seventy-foot ceiling. He began to recite from the book of Revelation: "Blessed are those who do His commandments, that they may have the right to the Tree of Life, and may enter through the gates into the city. But outside are dogs and sorcerers and sexually immoral and murderers and idolaters, and whoever loves and practices a lie.'" Seconds later, the King vanished above their heads.

The boys were frozen in place, unable to move or speak. Jesus numbed their minds; their hearts were moved but not shaken. Pride and sin held them captive, and only the grace of God and their true desire to seek Him would free them from the darkness.

Ken was lying in bed with Emily. The entire night was a blur to them. The sun had been up for hours, yet they felt like they had been up for days. Ken leaned his arm against Emily and tried to smile.

"Come on, honey. Let's get up and try to be happy."

She frowned at the thought. "You can make me get up, but you can't make me be happy."

Ken moved to the other side of the bed to confront her despairing spirit. "Listen, honey. We need to go on with our lives." He made a funny face at her in an effort to cheer her up.

"Your stupid humor is not working this time, Ken Action," vented Emily as she pushed him away. He fell on the floor with a thud. She quickly moved to peek over the edge of the bed. "I didn't mean to push you that hard," she apologized.

Ken was lying on the floor as if he were a bearskin rug. He was staring at the ceiling with his mouth hanging wide open. Emily's fog lifted as she began to laugh. Ken began to rub the back of his head. He looked toward her and grimaced.

"So it takes physical and psychological pain on my part to cheer you up." Ken pulled himself off the floor and shook his head. Crawling on all fours, he moved to the edge of the bed and slowly lifted his head toward hers. "This is where the rubber meets the road, honey." He kissed her lightly on the lips. "Having faith during the good times is easy. It's during times of testing that the fruit is squeezed from us. Let's be faithful."

Emily stared at him. She knew he was right. She smiled, a rare thing indeed! She was getting caught up in the moment, encouraged by her husband's faith.

"So what do we do now?"

"I know what we don't do, and that is panic. This depression is not from God, so we can't give in to it."

The Trial

The satellite phone began to ring.

"Don't answer it," said Ken.

Emily jumped out of the bed and ran toward the communicator. "It might be news of your son," rebuked Emily.

Ken stood and looked out the large picture window. He was preaching faith to his wife, yet he was simply trying to forget. He wanted to grab Solomon and take him over his knee. He took a deep breath. Solomon was too old for that. He didn't need their preaching; he needed their prayers.

"Hello." Emily listened carefully to the voice on the other end of the line.

Ken pretended he wasn't listening as his eyes stared blankly into the yard.

"How long do we have?"

Emily began to change her clothes while trying to listen intently.

"He did what?"

Ken couldn't take it anymore. He flew to her side and tried to listen in on the conversation.

"I don't know if you two will get to see him or not, but I would get here as soon as possible," said the voice from Jerusalem. "Pray for him."

The conversation ended. Emily looked at Ken as she haphazardly slid into a cotton dress. Ken was standing there with his hands in the air.

"Come on. Don't play this game with me. What did they say?"

Emily hurried into her shoes as she watched Ken squirm. The hundred-pound weight wrapped around her neck dropped to the ground. She was free and smiled as she spoke. "King Jesus washed Solomon's feet."

Amazed, Ken froze. "King Jesus washed our son's feet?"

She rushed toward the door. "We might get to see him after the trial. Just think," she paused as her hope grew, "maybe Solomon gave his heart to the Lord this time."

"How about Allison? Should we call her?"

Emily stopped for a moment. "No, I don't think we should tell her anything yet. He's already broken her heart once. She doesn't need anymore pain if this isn't for real."

Vice-Regent David sat on his throne and eyed the boys. The apostle Peter stood by his side. Solomon, Denny, and Cleveland didn't know what to expect. They were hoping to go home, but they knew that was wishful thinking. Their concept of grace was cheap and distorted.

"Please step forward," ordered David.

The young men shuffled forward. It was impossible for them to move quickly with the chains allowing only eight-inch steps. The security guards disappeared through the rear exit. They were alone with David and Peter. When they reached the first step, David raised his hand in the air.

"Stop." David stood up and began to pace back and forth in front of the throne chair. He remained silent as he occasionally glanced at them. Peter whispered something to him. "Yes, good idea," responded David. He stopped and faced the young criminals.

"What is your reaction to our Lord and King washing your feet?"

The boys were puzzled by the question. They looked at each other, each hoping the other one would be the spokesman. Denny knew he would stick his foot in his mouth, so he looked at Cleveland, who immediately turned to Solomon. Cleveland didn't like the limelight, at least not in this setting. As David and Peter looked on, the pressure to answer was immense. Solomon looked at Cleveland and gulped some air. He swallowed hard as his eyes turned toward his judges. Heartbeats quickened as Solomon took a half step forward.

"King Jesus was showing us the proper way to live. He was teaching us to have humility in all our actions." Solomon's words surprised Denny and Cleveland. "Jesus wants us to give up our wills and follow Him with unending devotion." The analysis stunned Peter and David. "He showed us that our criminal activity is forgiven by Him and that He wants us to go and sin no more."

David smiled. He was pleasantly surprised, yet he knew words didn't mean anything without a willing, obedient heart.

"That's quite an observation, Mr. Action," David said as he watched for Peter's reaction. "Denny, would you like to add to his thoughts?" asked David.

The Trial

Denny grudgingly stepped forward as he grinned at Solomon. There was something in that smirk that didn't sit well with Peter. Denny cleared his throat as if he were about to embark on the greatest speech of his life.

"Vice-Regent David, apostle Peter, and the many angels watching in the shadows, I humbly submit my intense sorrow and repentance for the ungodly acts that I have committed." Denny's thumbs were twitching as he tried to look at his judges. He thought of himself as a classy liar. His pride pushed him into believing that he could make anybody believe anything, anytime.

Timothy and Daniel hid their heads under their wings as Denny began to lay it on thicker than molasses.

"King Jesus could have sent us off for the rest of our lives to that awful detention camp, but He didn't. He washed our feet in hopes that we would change our criminal ways and become active, wholesome members of His great society."

"I think we fully understand what's on your heart," Peter said as he looked to David for direction.

David rubbed his chin as he thought. "Peter, let him continue." Peter nodded at Denny.

"Thank you, your excellency," beamed Denny. "I know the Bible quite well, and I remember the final supper."

"That's the Last Supper," corrected David.

"Uh, yes, of course, sir. Modesty and meekness will make us into better people, and I give my word today as a changed man that crime is in my sordid past and a bright and glorious future awaits me as I walk anew in my Christian life."

Solomon hid his face as he shook his head in amazement. "You should have been a politician," whispered Solomon.

"Would you like to address the court again, Solomon?" asked David, annoyed by the interruption.

"My apologies, sir."

David frowned as Denny continued. "Also, I would like to add that—"

David tossed his hands into the air. "I think we have an excellent feel for what's in your heart, young man." David motioned for him to return to the lineup.

"Cleveland, can you offer us something different from what we've heard thus far?"

Cleveland took a large gulp of air as he stepped forward. "I am sorry for the things that I have done, and I know Jesus was trying to show me mercy."

David and Peter were not listening to his words as much as observing his actions.

"Are you sorry because you have hurt Jesus, or because you were caught?" tested Peter.

The question puzzled Cleveland.

"I'm not, uh, I'm not sure what you mean."

Solomon and Denny did. They watched Cleveland panic.

Peter frowned as he glanced at David.

"That's all, son," observed Peter. "I think you answered the question."

Cleveland relaxed a bit. He thought that he had curried some favor. Timothy and Daniel were hovering over the armrests of the throne. Both of them were shaking their heads in astonishment. They realized the boys actually thought they could fake their way into heaven, or at least out of that camp.

"How do you think they are doing?" asked Daniel.

"They could probably fool a regular judge and jury," figured Timothy, "but I'm sure Peter and David can smell the fishiness of their repentance acts from a mile away."

"Of course, I'm sorry, I, uh, I mean, that we were caught." Cleveland scratched his head. "It's never fun to get in trouble and all that stuff."

"Thank you, that will be all," said David.

"But I haven't gotten to the repentance part of—"

"That will be enough," said David in a calm tone. He moved back to his seat and began to confer with Peter for several minutes.

The teenagers were quite proud of themselves. They were looking at each other, trying to keep straight faces. Confident in their efforts to save themselves from punishment, they felt like bursting into laughter at the con jobs they had just pulled. Solomon turned away from his compatriots, only to encounter David's wrath.

The Trial

Blasphemy took a wide detour around Jerusalem. The angels controlled a perimeter of seven miles around the city. Blasphemy grazed the outer limit of that boundary as he searched for weaknesses in the angels' armor. A lone demon appeared in front of him.

"Sir, I have information you may be interested in," said the demon as he saluted sharply.

"What's your name?"

"Fester, sir."

Blasphemy looked him over. "Quite impressive, young demon. How is it that you have the courage to be so close to the enemy?"

"Sir, I fear nobody but you."

Blasphemy laughed so hard that his stomach began to ache. "Well, what do you have for me?" He believed the demon; his insatiable need for flattery was a weakness he didn't recognize in himself.

"Sir, rumors are flying that you are itching for revenge." Fester waited for Blasphemy to respond, but he didn't. "Well, sir, there's a young man in Jerusalem who is standing before Vice-Regent David right now." Fester paused again.

Blasphemy was not a patient demon. "Don't play games with me. Tell me who it is."

"Sir, his name is Solomon, Solomon Action." Fester smiled, hoping for a figurative pat on the head.

Boiling drool began to seep from Blasphemy's mouth. He recognized that last name very well. His hands began to sweat as he contemplated the evil possibilities.

Vice-Regent David paced back and forth in front of the boys. His hands were behind his back as he contemplated their judgment. He didn't enjoy punishing this younger generation, yet he knew their short-term pain was worth it if it led to their repentance. As he watched their expressions, he was reminded of actors in a play.

"You boys sound like you were fine citizens of our Lord's kingdom. What went wrong?" He directed his attention at Solomon. "Stealing is a felony. Add to that running from the law. I've heard such wonderful things about your parents—and Allison is a jewel. Yet you have broken all their hearts. How could you forsake the teachings of your youth?"

Solomon stared at him. How did David know about Allison or about his parents? He felt like a caged rat that was being watched twenty-four hours a day. Solomon avoided the reference to Allison and responded to what was closest to his heart—his desire for his own way. "I thought that my parents should have let me have that gravity machine, sir," Solomon said in a defiant tone.

David turned his attention to Denny and Cleveland. "You two were together in my training camp east of town. You both have been taught how to live, but you have spit in the Lord's face."

"Vice-Regent David, we really are sorry," said Cleveland.

David began to walk down the seven steps of his throne. "You are sorry that you got caught. Worldly sorrow will never please Jesus."

"Sir," began Denny, "this will not happen again."

Denny wanted to say, "We will never get caught again." David instantly saw through his attempted deception. David reached the bottom of the stairs, and as the apostle Peter looked on, he walked to within an arm's distance of the boys.

"Denny, you will serve a life sentence of hard labor."

Denny's heart nearly stopped beating.

"But, I—"

"Silence," David commanded. "You didn't learn your lesson the first time. This time you assaulted a police officer for the fun of it. You eluded authorities, almost wound up killing another person, and you led Solomon into sins he never imagined he would commit."

Denny's face hardened. He wanted David's head on a platter. He wanted revenge, long and sweet revenge. Nothing would quench that evil thirst.

Vice-Regent David faced Cleveland. "Your speech was touching, son." Cleveland smiled. "The only thing wrong with it was that you didn't mean it." Cleveland's smile instantly withered. "A person can understand something in his head but not grasp it with his heart. I pray that your time in camp will help you to understand this truth in an intimate way. Your judgment: a life sentence until the end of days."

Cleveland looked at Denny. Horror and pain stained his face as reality clouded his senses. He couldn't believe his life was essentially over. Freedom would now be a memory, a fleeting recollection that would add to his torment. Denny nodded his head as if to say, "Don't worry. I've got a plan."

David ignored them as he turned the iron rod of justice on Solomon. "It appears to me that you want to be just like your friends."

Solomon remained silent as he avoided eye contact with everybody. He didn't like the way things were going, but surely, he thought, life in prison was too severe a punishment for his crimes. He was a first-time offender, influenced by two persuasive criminals.

"I understand that this is your first offense and that you have not been charged with attempted murder."

Solomon sighed in relief.

"However," began David, "stealing is serious, and avoiding the police simply paints a picture of what is really in your heart." Solomon's eyes suddenly widened. "I've been most distressed about your attitude and your belief that you can con your way out of trouble. You cannot fake repentance in this court, Solomon."

Solomon swallowed hard as he stared at David's feet. He couldn't think, and he didn't want to. He wanted to crawl into a corner and hide. Allison and his parents were right. He knew in his heart that he needed to repent, yet he refused to surrender his will.

"Since your actions speak for your heart, it is quite evident that you want to be like Denny and Cleveland; therefore, you will get to spend much time with them." David paused to gauge Solomon's soul. Anger began to slowly surface on Solomon's face. "You, too, will stay in prison until Satan's release!"

Allison stared out the window as Ken and Emily raced away on their gravity machine. Her hands began to sweat as she thought of Solomon. Was he in trouble? Was he hurt? Did they sentence him to life? She paced around the room, wondering what to do. Allison glanced at the pen on her desk. She sat down and began writing Solomon a letter from her heart.

"Dearest Solomon, I'll be praying..." She stopped writing and started crying. Balling up the note, she threw it in the trash can.

Allison looked at her Bible and knew where her hope could be restored. She opened the pages and began to read.

Ken and Emily were halfway to Jerusalem when the air cruiser sped past a field of daisies. With the vehicle on autopilot, Ken began staring at the flowers. They reminded him of the day of regeneration. He remembered it as if it were yesterday; the entire earth had been recreated and made new. The thistles covering many plants were gone, and every weed was thrown into the fire. New species of plants and animals, long since extinct, reappeared in glorious form. It was the Lord's gift to those who had trusted in Him, to those who had taken up their crosses and followed Him. He closed his eyes as he held Emily's hand. As she slept, Ken's memory began to replay moment by moment that day that had occurred almost a thousand years ago.

Jesus Christ had finished His forty-five day judgment of the saints as alluded to in the twelfth chapter of the book of Daniel. The earth was a vast wasteland. Earthquakes had turned cities into garbage dumps. The most majestic of mountain chains had crumbled like sandcastles at the seashore. Fire had ravaged entire forests, grasslands, and cities.

Before Judgment began, the Lord wanted each of the saints to understand the dreadful consequences of sin. With the Millennium around the corner, Jesus wanted to solidify their allegiance to Him. He knew that there would still be free will during the upcoming thousand years.

The Trial

Ken sighed as he thought about Solomon. He opened his eyes to check the gauges. A mountain covered in cedars approached. He closed his eyes again, and his thoughts returned to Judgment Day.

Jesus was sitting on the most beautiful throne that anyone could ever have imagined. Standing at the front of the line to be judged, all Ken could do was stare at the beauty of the Lord. Then, suddenly, it happened.

"Ken Action," thundered Jesus as His gaze reached inside Ken's soul.

Ken rushed forward and bowed. He dropped on his knees and looked up at the King. This was it, he thought. All those years, all that pain and suffering, everything coming down to this singular moment in time. The feeling was indescribable.

Jesus' eyes penetrated his spirit, inspecting every particle of his being. Ken's heart raced inside him, yet he was at peace.

"Well done, good and faithful servant. Come and enter My rest."

The air cruiser jarred him from the past. A strong wind riding up the mountain was creating some turbulence, but it wasn't enough to awaken Emily. Ken closed his eyes again. He tried to remember everything Jesus had said to him. His mind returned to thoughts of the rebirth of the world.

After the Great Judgment, the Lord gathered the Christians and instructed them to hover over Jerusalem.

"Remain in place, children" began the Lord, "and I will grant you what I gave to My first children, Adam and Eve."

Jesus raised His hands into the air and prayed. "Father, erase the curse on this earth. Create a heaven on earth." The Lord clasped His hands together. Every Christian watched as a concentrated ball of white light began pushing against His hands. Jesus slowly moved His arms outward, releasing the expanding white light in all directions. At first, the light moved slowly. Within seconds, its speed increased dramatically. A low, bass-like sound radiated from the light as it began to crash into the earth. Ken covered his eyes to protect them from the intensity of the rays. In less than a minute, the sound passed, and he could once again hear birds singing against the backdrop of a cascading waterfall.

Jesus had miraculously restored the Earth's poisoned atmosphere to its original Garden-of-Eden composition. The pure, life-giving air, enriched with its high moisture content, provided a protective canopy that allowed people to live indefinitely.

The wall of divine light encircled the globe in less than a minute. Earth and its creatures were instantly healed. Ken slowly dropped his arms. He descended from the sky and was placed feet first on the new earth. His countenance brightened as he looked around. The green grass was perfectly manicured, as if he were on a high-priced golf course. He ran toward a single rose blooming near a rock. As he sniffed it, he realized there were no thorns on it. The fragrance was like nothing he had ever experienced. As he ran his fingers up and down the stem of the rose, an oversized butterfly caught his eye. He rushed toward it like an excited toddler learning to run.

"Come here, buddy," said Ken as he neared the purple and blue insect. The butterfly turned and flew toward him. "That's right," Ken encouraged. The ten-inch-long creature had a wingspan of nearly two feet. Ken stuck his arm out and watched the millennial insect land. The butterfly didn't fear him. Ken glanced over at a sparkling waterfall several hundred feet away. He gently nudged the butterfly off his arm and sprinted toward the brook. The water was pure and clear, and its color was a shade of silver that he had never encountered before. He reached down and tested the liquid with his fingers. The water was warm and inviting. Several others were near the banks of the stream.

"Let's jump in," proposed one of them as he grinned at Ken.

"Beat you to it," yelled Ken, diving headfirst into the deepest part of the creek.

"Ken," called Emily. She started gently shaking his shoulder.

"What..." said Ken as tried to hold on to the blissful dream.

"Wake up, Ken. We're here."

She didn't know what he was thinking about; her concern was seeing their son.

Jerusalem glittered like a treasure chest of precious stones. Ken turned off the autopilot and steered the cruiser toward the center of town. The judicial building appeared on the horizon.

"Where do we go first?" asked Emily.

"We'll go to the apostle Peter's court. Maybe Solomon will still be there," figured Ken.

"But they told us we couldn't go to the trial."

"He didn't say we couldn't see him afterward."

Emily smiled at the thought of seeing Solomon, holding him like a baby, and whispering in his ear that everything was going to be fine. As the air cruiser neared the building, Ken and Emily saw a crowd of hundreds, perhaps thousands, of people waiting outside.

"What's going on?" wondered Emily.

Ken looked around as they landed. He grimaced at the thought of Solomon's having to endure public humiliation, but he didn't dare speak his thoughts to Emily.

Vice-Regent David was visibly upset as he exited the throne room. The false repentance of the boys reminded him of the lukewarm state of the church before Christ established His reign on the earth. The apostle Peter was slowly pacing back and forth in front of the teenagers with the same thoughts disrupting his spirit.

"What's he going to do?" asked Daniel.

"I've got a feeling you're going to hear a hellfire and brimstone sermon that will knock your socks off," replied Timothy as he studied Peter's face.

The teenagers' faces were downcast, not because of their sins, but because of the penalty.

"Look at me," ordered Peter.

The boys forced their eyes upward while their heads remained down. None of them believed in Satan's imminent release, so to be sentenced to a life of hard labor was more than they could handle.

"You are depressed because you have lost your freedom. You feel badly because you won't get to have fun anymore. You'll miss your friends, and maybe your parents somewhat." Peter took a deep breath as he sighed. "Jesus' kingdom is based on truth, justice, and righteousness. You have received what you deserve. All three of you have been running from God since your adolescence. When you sin, you hide and blame others. You have even blamed God Himself."

Solomon glanced at Denny and Cleveland. How he wished he had never met them. If only he had said no when they were escaping.

"You three are just like your ancestral grandparents of long ago. Adam and Eve didn't agree with God's commandment not to eat from the Tree of Knowledge of Good and Evil. Eve gave in to the serpent and disobeyed, and Adam followed, just as you boys have done. Instead of owning up to their sin, they decided to hide from God."

Peter's voice was getting louder and more passionate by the second. Solomon, Denny, and Cleveland had never heard such zealous preaching before.

"You steal a police cruiser to run and hide. You are willing to assault one of my men to shove your evil under a rock. What is hidden will come out into the light. Every knee will bow and every tongue will confess that Jesus Christ is Lord."

Peter reached for his Bible on the steps of the throne. He turned to the book of Genesis, chapter three.

The boys wanted to put their hands over their ears. The last thing they wanted was to be stuck here with one of Jesus' "cronies" lecturing them. They had just been sentenced to something worse than death by their standards. They felt they deserved to be left alone.

Peter cleared his throat and began to read. "'Then the man said, "The woman whom You gave to be with me, she gave me of the tree, and I ate." And the LORD God said to the woman, "What is this you have done?" The woman said, "The serpent deceived me, and I ate."'"

The Trial

Peter placed the Bible back on the steps. The boys appeared bewildered by the story. The Word of God had always confused them. Peter sensed their spiritual immaturity.

"Instead of taking responsibility for her actions, Eve blamed the serpent." Peter stood in front of Solomon. "Solomon, who are you blaming for this mess you have created? I'm sure you believe your parents are at fault, and, of course, Denny and Cleveland have their share of the blame."

Solomon's head began to spin. Peter's logic seemed to short-circuit all his available alibis.

"Think about the Scripture, Mr. Action. Adam blamed Eve and then had the guts to accuse God of causing his sin. Adam said, 'The woman whom You gave to be with me, she gave me of the tree.'"

Peter didn't wait for Solomon's response. He rushed toward Denny and moved to within inches of his face.

"Are you blaming God for your sin? Or maybe you are just angry at God that you were caught red-handed."

Denny tried to mumble some kind of excuse. "My father used to—"

"Quiet!" ordered Peter firmly.

Denny's lips kept moving, but his voice stopped. He loathed God for allowing him to be born, to experience such humiliation at the hands of those who claimed they loved him.

The apostle quickly moved to Cleveland. Cleveland did not return the fierce look confronting him. He was unable to show any kind of emotion.

"Your sins are a burden to God. You have no excuse for your wayward actions. Jesus has given you a perfect world in which to live. He is with you on the earth to guide you and teach you right from wrong. The time before the Millennium was chaotic and wicked, yet people loved the Lord without seeing Him. You are just like Adam. In the Garden of Eden, he disobeyed the Lord to His face and blamed everybody but himself."

Peter paused as he observed each of the boys. Their dejected appearance saddened him.

"You gentlemen have a choice. Love Jesus or hate Him. Remember, there is no middle ground. A decision for Christ doesn't automatically turn out to be a lifelong commitment to Him. Repentance is necessary, and holiness must be your goal. Your punishment is just and fair and will provide the right amount of time to gauge your hearts."

A trumpet blew outside the courthouse as the boys were escorted from the judgment chamber. Peter remained behind to pray for their souls. Ken and Emily fought their way to the front of the crowd.

"Why are all these people here?" asked Emily as she strained to see inside the building. She would have given her next hundred meals just to catch a glimpse of her son.

"Maybe Jesus is still in there," hoped Ken as he tried to see around several heads in the crowd.

Denny was the first to exit into the courtyard. Cleveland and Solomon followed.

"Who's that?" asked Emily.

"Must be one of those boys that Solomon was with."

"He's rough-looking," Emily observed. She was desperately trying to see behind Denny who was a head taller than Solomon.

Solomon squinted as the sun blazed overhead. When he saw the crowd, he lowered his head in shame.

"Solomon!" cried Emily. She was too far away to be heard. Suddenly, the crowd began to drop to their knees. Ken and Emily looked around at the saints.

"Get on your knees," said Ken as he tugged on her sleeve. "Jesus must be coming!"

The apostle Peter appeared from the building. He motioned for the guards to stop the prisoners. Solomon couldn't look anybody in the face as he was forced to stand at the center of the crowd in his black robe. Denny seemed to enjoy the attention while Cleveland kept his eyes tightly closed.

"People of Jerusalem, this is a somber time in our Holy City," began Peter. "The iron rod of justice has fallen on these three young men. They have been convicted of numerous crimes against our civilization and our Lord. They

114

stand before you condemned to a lifetime of heavy labor. Pray that they will allow our Lord to save their souls."

The scene was more than Emily could handle. Her sobs echoed throughout the crowd. Her boy, the baby who had been formed in her womb, the toddler who had learned to walk in their garden, was now standing in the Holy City condemned before the world.

"Mother," whispered Solomon as he looked in her direction. He couldn't bear seeing her hurt or watching his father unable to comfort her.

Ken grabbed Emily's arm. "Wait."

Emily couldn't take her eyes off her son. She reached out for him. "I'm here, honey."

Peter closed his eyes and prayed. "God of our fathers, open their eyes to Your love for them. Though You bruise the body, You save the soul. Discipline them in righteousness. Keep them from evil." Peter could hear Emily's sobs. "Give hope to their families. Remind them that You are in control and will do what's best. In the precious name of Jesus, we pray. Amen."

Peter glanced at Solomon, then turned to Ken and Emily. "Go to your home and pray unceasingly for the boys. People of Jerusalem, pray for their families."

The crowd quickly dispersed. A few near Ken and Emily hugged them before leaving. Peter walked over to them.

"You may see him for a moment."

"Didn't he accept Jesus as his Savior?" asked Emily, sobbing.

Peter looked at her. He wanted to sugarcoat the truth for her, but he didn't. "No, none of the boys did."

Emily shook her head in disbelief. Ken was crushed.

"Didn't Jesus wash their feet?" asked Ken.

"Yes, He did. It was obvious they were touched by His display of humility, yet they refused to truly repent of their actions." Peter placed his hands on their shoulders. "Don't ask any more hard questions that you don't want answered. Go say good-bye to your boy. Remember, he'll have a much better chance of accepting Jesus in prison than where he's been."

She nodded and quickly ran toward Solomon with Ken directly behind her. Solomon cried silently as his mother approached.

"I'm so sorry, Mom," whimpered Solomon as Emily embraced him with all her might.

"It's going to be okay," she said as she caressed his face with her hands. "Solomon, you need to do the right thing." Solomon looked toward Peter. She pulled him back. "Don't be bitter at them. They want what's best for your soul, and so do I! They are doing the right thing. They are obeying Jesus." Her face turned stern. "Don't turn away from Him. You will lose, Solomon!" She held his face tightly. "Solomon, I see it in your face. Stop!"

Solomon pulled away. "I'm a grown man, Mother. You need to let me live my own life."

Ken pulled Emily away. "Solomon, you know right from wrong," added Ken. "And you're right. You are a man now. It's up to you to make the right decision." He reached out to his son. Solomon looked at the ground as he hugged his father.

"I love you, Dad. Take care of Mom while I'm gone. Tell Allison I'm sorry for leading her on."

Emily stood on her tiptoes as she hugged him one more time. Solomon slowly pulled away from her and quickly gave her one of those looks that said, "Don't say it, Mom. I know."

Peter nodded at the head guard.

"Let's go, boys. You have a debt to pay," the guard told them as he led them away.

Cleveland and Denny frowned at Solomon's parents and began to move toward the prison truck. Solomon followed them. He took one final glimpse at his parents as they waved. The apostle Peter stood by the entrance to the truck. He closely watched Solomon as he turned away from his parents' view. A smirk crept on Solomon's face as he nudged Denny from behind. The apostle silently prayed for Ken and Emily as he saw their hope fade.

Six

The Slow Road to Hell

King Jesus walked along the Jordan River, enjoying the gentle westerly breeze. Apple, pear, and fig trees lined the banks of the water's edge. Wildflowers dotted the landscape, and songbirds sang a tune of redemption. A solitary bear quenched its thirst in the refreshing waters. As it turned to look at Jesus, a peaceful expression covered its face. Then it lumbered off into the forest.

"King Jesus, You wanted to see me?" asked a voice behind Him.

Jesus turned and faced David. "Yes, My son, I did." Jesus appeared sorrowful as He invited David to follow Him.

"Lord, what brings this sadness to Your spirit?"

Jesus slowly walked along the bank without answering David's question. Staring toward Jerusalem, He shook His head.

"The time is at hand, David." He looked at His vice-regent as a father would look at his only son. "It's very difficult to share My heart on this matter."

"What matter do You speak of?" asked David with a confused expression.

"I speak of evil, My son. We know My Father has determined to allow Satan his freedom for a time, and now that time is at hand."

David saw a doe staring at them from behind a flowering bush.

"When I ruled Israel, I always wondered what the Garden of Eden must have been like. I've never understood how anyone could fall in such a perfect environment."

Jesus nodded as if He agreed with David. "The seductiveness of evil is well-documented throughout the ages. You need to be prepared for the final assault from the Enemy."

David stared into his Lord's loving eyes. "How long are You going to allow the Devil to roam freely?"

"He will have six days to prove his case once and for all."

Then Jesus surprised David by changing the subject. "Tell Me, My son, why did you allow Bathsheba to tempt you?"

A look of shame spread across David's face. He knew he was forgiven, yet he wished he could take the entire sordid story and change the outcome. He had broken God's heart by his carelessness. The painful history was known by saints and sinners alike, and now Jesus was bringing it up at a time when Satan was about to be loosed.

"Lord, I guess I started taking You for granted. I became careless in my faith." He sighed. "I even refused to go out with my men to fight Your battles."

"David, why did you kill her husband? Did you think that I wouldn't notice, or that I wouldn't care?"

David said nothing as he pondered his past. It was never easy to think about these things.

"Did you believe that you deserved her and that breaking My commandments would be acceptable because of who you were?"

David looked into the Lord's eyes. "Jesus, I don't have an answer for You. One sin led to another, which led to further transgressions. It was a slippery slope that was almost impossible to stop once I had begun to slide."

"Yes, David, I understand, but can you identify the catalyst that caused you to begin to lose your first love?"

A large oak tree captured David's attention. It was strong, mighty, and unbending. It seemed to reach nearly to heaven. His awe of this grand tree provided the answer that he already knew in his heart.

"Pride," David said quietly as he turned his eyes toward Jesus.

"You should have been a Hollywood star," laughed Denny as he patted Solomon on the back.

"Me? What about you? 'I'm not worthy. Please, stop, O Master of the universe!' That was classic." Solomon was half serious, half joking. He wanted them to be his friends.

Cleveland quietly smiled at their shenanigans. He seemed distant, as if he were in deep thought. He couldn't get the image of Jesus out of his head.

Denny patted his long-time friend briskly on the back. "Come on, man. Cheer up. This isn't going to be that bad. We'll be with guys like us. We'll have fun."

Cleveland ignored Denny's misplaced enthusiasm.

"What's gotten into you?" scolded Denny. "Either you're depressed or you're doing some heavy-duty thinking." He paused and smiled sideways at Solomon. "And I know that you've never had a deep thought in your life, so what's up?" When Denny was nervous, he liked to insult people in a strangely humorous way.

Cleveland couldn't put his thoughts or feelings into words. He shook his head. "Just leave me alone, and give me some time. I'll be fine."

Solomon looked at Denny and then burst into nervous laughter. "Sounds like the guy needs some alone time to manage his feelings," teased Solomon.

"You didn't let Jesus get to you, did you?" questioned Denny with a look of horror on his face.

Cleveland painfully tried to erase the memory of the foot-washing incident. He couldn't forget the look in Jesus' eyes. It was as if He said, "I love you for who you are, no matter what you have done."

Cleveland tried to shake off the impact Jesus had made on him and give them what they wanted. "You guys are nuts. I'm just going to miss my freedom, that's all. I have a right to be a little depressed, don't you think?"

Realizing the truth of Cleveland's words, Solomon's mood quickly darkened. "What's this place going to be like?"

"Lots of sweat and work," began Denny, "very little free time, and church every day."

Solomon pretended to go into shock. "Whoa, I could handle the long hours of work," he said, seeking their approval, "but church every day might drive me to the insane asylum!"

The three boys laughed. Solomon jumped out of his seat and banged against the titanium wall separating them from the guards.

"How long before we get to paradise?" yelled Solomon as he watched his friends' faces.

The truck began to slow.

"Now you've done it," vented Cleveland with a scowl on his face. "You're new at this, so you might as well learn your lesson now."

"What lesson?" asked Solomon, trying to conceal his nervousness.

Denny stood up and patted him on the back. "They don't take any junk from the prisoners in these camps." He spoke in a conspiratorial whisper. "They will severely punish you for the slightest infraction of their stupid rules," he lied.

The truck had stopped moving. They could hear at least three if not four men outside the vehicle. Solomon wasn't feeling so cocky anymore. Now I've done it, he thought. What if they dropped him off in the middle of nowhere and never came back?

"Why didn't you guys warn me?" whined Solomon as he fought back his rising nausea.

"Best lessons are learned by the school of hard knocks," laughed Denny as he watched Solomon tremble with fear.

The truck door suddenly opened. A tough-looking security guard in his mid-forties poked his head inside.

"Okay, boys, you have five minutes to do the necessities before we're back on the road."

Solomon looked at his friends with disgust. "You two are lying sacks of..."

"Cool your jets," laughed Denny. "They don't always punish you when you expect it. They may come to you in the middle of the night next week and slam you for today's 'transgression.'"

The Slow Road to Hell

The guards closely watched the boys as they stepped out of the truck. The land was dry and wild. It was the only spot on the newly created planet that resembled the former Earth. Jesus had left this wilderness barren to correct and reprove those who consistently sinned against Him.

"Is this hell?" Solomon asked one of the burly guards.

The guard chuckled. "No, son. This is heaven compared to the real hell. You're here so you won't go there."

His statement confused Solomon. He didn't understand the concept of a real hell, though he had heard his preacher describe it repeatedly. He figured religion was a crutch for some people, a fantasy designed to help them cope. If it worked for them, then fine. Solomon followed Denny and Cleveland to the restroom.

"I hope you two don't try to pull any fast ones this time," voiced Solomon as they walked through the door.

Denny looked at Cleveland and smiled. He was making Solomon uneasy.

"It's not impossible to escape from these watchdogs," said Denny.

Cleveland grimaced as he looked away from Denny. "Solomon, if I were you, I would play it straight. It's a no-win situation and a no-brainer. Keep yourself clean, and maybe one day you'll see your family again."

"What's wrong with you, Cleveland? Let's live life and go for the gusto!" spouted Denny as he eyed the teen suspiciously. "You know we have a life sentence; we will never see our families again!"

His words cut deeply into Solomon's softening heart. Hope seemed very distant, but not completely gone—at least, not yet.

"I'm with you, Denny," assured Cleveland, "but I'm tired of fighting the authorities."

Denny smirked as he left the bathroom. Cleveland and Solomon followed as they neared the transport vehicle. One of the guards was in the front seat of the truck, while the other two were standing at the back.

"We should be there in less than an hour," the guard on the left informed them.

"Thanks, man," said Denny as he noticed the strap of the stun gun in the locked position.

He glanced at the other guard who was holding his gun loosely in his left hand. He was talking to his comrade, not paying much attention to the boys. Denny gave a subtle thumbs-up signal. Solomon was confused by the gesture, but Cleveland was all too familiar with Denny's body language.

"He's going to do something really stupid," whispered Cleveland to Solomon.

"What are you talking about?" asked Solomon just as Denny dove headfirst for the laser gun.

The surprised security officer tried to back away as Denny's large frame collided with his. Cursing Denny's stupidity, Cleveland jumped the other guard, who was reaching for his gun. Solomon didn't know what to do. Everything began to move in slow motion.

"Go for the guy in the front," howled Denny.

As Denny and Cleveland battled with the men in the back, Solomon foolishly decided to sprint toward the front of the truck as Denny had directed. He reached the closed door of the cab. Panting heavily, he crouched beneath the window. It appeared to him that he was out of view of the man in front. Solomon could hear loud grunting and groaning from the rear of the unit. Slowly, he reached toward the control pad for the door. Suddenly the door to the cab flung open, knocking Solomon to the ground. The husky guard jumped out of the cab, holding his laser gun with both hands. Solomon was flat on the ground, dazed and bleeding from his nose.

"You rebels would be dangerous if you had some common sense," said the sentry. Seeing that Solomon was in no shape to be a threat, he ran to help his colleagues.

Denny was on top of his captor with his hands tightly around the guard's neck.

"You pigs think you know it all," spouted Denny as he glanced over at Cleveland.

Cleveland was covered in blood as he stood meekly over the prostrate guard.

"I think I killed him." Cleveland appeared mummy-like as he stared at his bloodstained hands. He began to feel dizzy, like some force field was draining him of all his energy.

"Don't sweat it, Cleveland," called Denny as he spat an obscenity.

"Move and die," barked the guard behind Cleveland and Denny. "Put your hands in the air, step back, and don't make any sudden movements."

Cleveland backed away from the hemorrhaging guard. Denny held tightly to his man as he glanced over his shoulder.

"I'll kill him," threatened Denny in a possessed tone.

The guard stared Denny down as his gun pointed directly at Denny's chest. Denny grinned at the armed guard as he squeezed the other man's neck even tighter.

"I mean it," growled the guard. He had never shot anybody in his life, and he was praying that this time wouldn't be the first.

"It's over, Denny. Give it up," said Cleveland as he dropped on his knees with his hands on his head.

"Be smart like your buddy," voiced the guard. His trigger finger was twitching. "Come on, boy. Don't make me hurt you."

A rare smile emerged on Blasphemy's long, crude face. Fester saluted him as he slowly stepped away.

"Thank you, sir, for the opportunity to serve you," said Fester.

"How did you know about my deep hatred for Ken Action?" inquired Blasphemy.

"Sir, you apparently don't remember, but I served under you during the Great Tribulation. I know what Ken Action did and how he was the catalyst to the downfall of the Antichrist's kingdom. A person that high up in the government should have been tortured unmercifully for his treasonous acts. I share the same feelings toward him as you do, sir,

123

and, may I add," he stumbled a moment, "I have admired you from a distance and agree that your ways are far superior to Satan's."

Blasphemy was hanging on his every word. Nothing is better to a demon than unadulterated praise.

"Go on," said the general.

Fester's heart began to race. "I love your purity of purpose, how you are willing to do good, so that evil might prosper. I read the Bible every day so that I can twist it more effectively."

Blasphemy patted the demon on the back.

"Well done, good and faithful servant. For your service and your obvious wisdom, you will be my left-hand demon. You, Fester, will be by my side from this moment forward."

Fester hissed with joy. "Thank you, sir. What is our first mission?"

"To find Ken Action's son, Solomon." A sinister expression came to life. "We don't want to leave anything to chance. We want to be sure he joins our team."

Fester nodded his head. Brainwashing was his favorite hobby.

"Blasphemy, sir, I know exactly where he is."

The general was impressed. "Time is crucial. Show me the way."

"Pride is the most seductive form of evil. It can come on a person during his greatest spiritual victories," enlightened Jesus.

David was listening intently to the Lord.

"Satan discovered he was the most beautiful, powerful angel ever created. Unfortunately, that knowledge swelled his head, and he fell from grace. But, David, I want to go deeper than this. Do you understand when pride begins?"

"Lord, I've wrestled with that question since I was a flesh and blood human trying to lead Israel."

Jesus smiled. "David, pride begins the moment you take your eyes off Me. The second you believe you can do

124

any good on your own is the moment that pride starts. Few humans grasp this simple truth. I washed those boys' feet to demonstrate humility. Sadly, humility and meekness cannot be understood by proud individuals. It is foolishness to them."

David looked at the imposing oak tree again. "Lord, Satan had to know the moment that You created him that he was the mightiest angel ever formed. When did this temptation to exalt himself above You hit him?"

"The mind and the spirit are separate entities that function both individually and collectively; they are intricately linked together. Lucifer's mind knew what I gave him, and that knowledge was not sin. It was when his spirit and his soul took that information and twisted it that sin swept him away like a torrent."

Jesus lifted His finger in the air as if He were making a major declaration. "It was when his mind told him that he *deserved* to be the greatest angel. It was when he decided that I had chosen him for that position not because I wanted to, but because it was My duty to bless him for his prominence. See, David, he never considered the fact that I was the Potter and he was the clay. I created him to serve Me, but he decided to serve himself instead."

"So why are You allowing Satan to be freed? Haven't you proven Your point by now?"

Jesus looked toward heaven. "When I completely destroy heaven and earth with fire, you will have your answer." He paused and then said, "Prepare for war, David."

————

Solomon lifted himself off the dusty ground. He could hear loud talking from behind the truck. He wiped the blood from his head and stumbled toward the voices.

"This is your last chance. Let go of him, or I will shoot."

The guard seemed to mean business, but Denny still heard fear in his voice. Denny maintained the pressure on his captor's neck. He saw Solomon behind the guard slowly moving toward him. He tried to communicate with him with his eyes without letting the guard know.

Solomon rubbed his aching head as he assessed the situation. He was tired of fighting the Lord—tired of the trouble and the hurt he was causing to those back home. He wanted to pay the price for his actions and be left alone. Cleveland followed him with his eyes. He slowly shook his head, urging Solomon not to make things worse.

The guard began to edge closer to Denny. He didn't notice Solomon behind him. Denny mocked him for his cowardice.

"You don't have the guts to use that thing. Give it to a real man, and I'll show you how—"

A blast of light rocketed from the gun. The force knocked Denny ten feet backward. Muscle spasms surged through his flesh as he lay on the ground, writhing in pain. Solomon was within jumping distance of the guard and for a moment entertained a very foolish idea. The patrolman's hands began to shake violently as he watched Denny suffer. He had never had to inflict pain on anyone, and his emotions were getting the best of him. His eye caught a shadow near his left side. He jumped to face Solomon and accidentally dropped his gun.

Solomon saw the gun and hesitated. Not another chance to do something stupid, he sighed.

"Sir, I'm sorry," said Solomon as he fell to his knees and placed his hands on his head.

Cleveland and the guard both breathed a sigh of relief.

"You two boys try to help your friend. I'll see what I can do with my guys." He grabbed the gun and pointed it away from them. "But be slow and careful. One smart decision doesn't make you saints."

The guard watched them carefully as they ran to Denny's side. Cleveland rapped him on the cheek.

"Wake up, man. Come on, wake up!" shouted Cleveland as Solomon checked the pulse in Denny's neck.

This wasn't supposed to happen, thought Cleveland. He was in the middle of hell, condemned for what he felt was an eternity, and now he was watching his childhood friend die.

"His heart's beating!" yelled Solomon. He placed his ear against Denny's chest. "He's breathing, but it sounds kind of shallow."

"Oh, Lord, don't let him die," prayed Cleveland.

Solomon closed his eyes. "Forgive him, Jesus."

The guard kept the boys in view as he examined the more seriously injured of his partners.

"Sam, are you okay?" Sam tried to move.

"Yeah, I think so, I just lost my breath for a moment." He slowly pulled himself upright and grabbed his head. A large puddle of blood stained the ground underneath him, but the injury was not as serious as it had first appeared. He looked at Solomon and Cleveland standing over Denny. "You boys made a good decision in surrendering. You saved yourself from a whole lot of trouble."

"Have a seat, and I'll check on Toby." He hurried to Denny's victim. "Toby, how's your neck?"

He placed his hand on Toby's neck and slowly rubbed it. "Does this hurt?"

"Not too bad." Toby tried to get up. "I think it's just bruised." He stumbled as he stood on both feet.

"What are we going to do with them?" asked the uninjured guard, directing the question to his boss, who was still sitting on the ground.

His superior officer scratched his head. Dried blood stuck to his hand. "We're going to tie them hand and foot and never trust them again." He grimaced, "We'll let Grizzly take care of them."

Cleveland and Solomon frowned at his words. Their divided hearts always seemed to fall on the side of sin.

The guard walked over to them as they hovered over Denny, who was slowly coming back to consciousness.

The senior guard placed his laser gun near the back of their necks. "Gentlemen, welcome to hell on earth."

The next day dawned bright and inviting outside the Action household. Inside a dark cloud of despair hung over

Ken and Emily. Emily paused to brush her hair out of her eyes as she stoically washed the dishes. Just then Ken walked into the room after taking a morning walk around their lake. He saw his spouse's face and quickly prepared himself for a bumpy ride. It had been a long time since he'd seen her like this, and he was clueless as to how to handle the situation.

"Why are you washing the dishes? What's wrong with the machine?" Ken tried to wrap his arms around her, but she squirmed away.

"I need to keep myself busy. I can't stop thinking about Solomon mixed up with those thugs. They're going to destroy him." She gently placed a saucer on the edge of the counter, avoiding eye contact at all costs. "You know that Solomon was very impressionable as a child." She glanced at the empty sink, then started pulling clean dishes from the cupboard.

Ken bit his tongue as he watched her routine. "That was a good thing, Emily. We raised him right, and he will follow through with our teaching in the end."

Emily's back remained toward Ken as she scrubbed the already clean dishes. "I hope you're right. That has been my prayer, but remember, Ken," she took a long pause before turning to face him, "Solomon is still impressionable, and he is with two boys we know nothing about—except that they have criminal records." Emily frowned. Her imagination was racing wildly, filling her mind with all sorts of horrible scenarios. She tried without success to shake off the feeling of impending doom.

Ken kissed her forehead and rubbed her arms as he forced her to make eye contact. "You, my dear, need a break." His eyes began to sparkle. "Pack your bags. We are going on the vacation of a lifetime."

Emily was mystified by his logic. She abruptly turned around and started drying coffee cups. Now she wasn't just sad; she was mad! Her husband had better explain himself. She was steaming hot.

"I'll never understand you, Ken Action. Our son is going through Hades right now, and you want to go on A VACATION!"

Ken muttered something under his breath, an unwise move he couldn't help.

"That's so selfish!" Emily's voice raised in pitch and volume as she increased her cleaning pace.

Ken sighed. He wondered why he hadn't figured out her hot buttons after nearly a thousand years of marriage. He edged closer without touching her.

"Emily, we don't need to go through torment just because our son is." He prayed for peace in his family. He heard a soft whimper escape from her mouth. Ken took a step forward as he continued his silent prayer. Suddenly, she turned and fell into his arms, crying uncontrollably. Ken held on to her quivering body.

"We need to move on," whispered Ken as he kissed her on the ear.

"It's all my fault," she sobbed with a muffled voice.

He grabbed her with both hands and forced her to look him in the eyes. "No, it's not." His words were slow and steady. "Come on, Emily. He's practically a grown man."

She grabbed a stack of tissues. "You didn't carry him in your body. I have an attachment to him that you'll never understand," she blurted out between sobs.

Ken was having trouble understanding her words as well as her feelings. "Emily, honey, that's just your emotions talking." Oops, thought Ken. Bad move.

She cried harder as she tried to pull away. "Just leave me alone!"

———————

A hundred yards away, inside the Larkson's home, Allison and her mother were in the midst of an intimate conversation. Allison could open up to her mother as if she were one of her teenaged friends.

"Do you think Solomon meant it?" asked Gail as she sat on the corner of Allison's canopied bed.

"Mom, that's what gets me. I'm not sure why he did it. I can still see the look on his face; it was like there were two Solomons there, and the Evil One won out."

Gail gazed at her daughter. If only she could take the pain away from Allison and transfer it to herself.

"Honey, I'm sure that's exactly what's happening with Solomon. The Bible calls it being double minded."

Allison sighed. "Then why does the sinful side of him always seem to win out lately?"

Gail glanced at the bed cover and straightened a few wrinkles. "He's making the wrong choices, and all we can do for him now is pray."

"I know that, Mom." She closed her eyes, took a deep breath, then exhaled slowly. "It's just so hard to only pray for him. Isn't there anything else I can do, you know, like grab a heavy pot and knock him on the head?"

Her mother laughed as she took her daughter's hand. "Trust me on this one, honey. Men can be unbelievably stubborn." She shook her head as she thought of her husband Bill. "Your dad can be hardheaded sometimes. He was especially so when he was younger."

Allison smiled. "Got some dirt on Dad? Maybe that will make me feel better." Her curious yet innocent expression made her mother laugh.

"You ever tell your father I told you this, and it's curtains for you. Understand, young lady?"

Allison saluted her mother, a mock-serious expression suddenly covering her face.

"How dumb do I look, Mom? Come on. Just spit it out."

Gail went to the open door and shut it.

"Allison, your father used to frustrate me so much when you were a baby." Gail paused to gather her thoughts.

"Would you believe that he absolutely refused to change your diapers?"

"Why?" asked Allison, somewhat surprised.

Gail shook her head. "He would never level with me. If I asked him to do it, he always had an excuse why he couldn't. He always had something important to do right at that moment. I would finally give up and do it myself."

"So do you know why now?"

"No!" answered her mother. "He claims he doesn't remember details the way I do. Can you believe that?"

Allison frowned as she thought about Solomon. She mumbled, "Yeah," and turned her gaze toward the open window.

Gail gently placed her hand on Allison's knee.

"Honey, give Solomon some time to think. Give him some room to breathe, and he'll come around."

Allison stared at her mother and grinned. A spark of hope flickered in her heart.

A trumpet blast soared through the heavens with a ferocity that hadn't been heard since the Battle of Armageddon.

"Whoa, what was that?" reacted Daniel as the sound nearly knocked him out of the air.

Timothy shot into the sky like a bottle rocket. "I've been waiting to hear that sound my whole life!" His excitement was contagious.

"Get down here and tell me what you're talking about," yelled Daniel.

Timothy took his time landing. He loved to string along his best friend. He playfully looked around as if he were alone and was looking for somebody to talk to.

"Tell me now or face the consequences!" Daniel called, half jokingly.

"Have a seat up here," Timothy said as he pointed to the top of a tree, "and I will give you the best news of your life."

A second later, Daniel was seated with his hands folded in his lap. He was pretending to be patient, yet his acting skills were horrible, to say the least. Timothy slowly and methodically flew toward the cedar tree. He landed near the angel and leisurely faced him.

"Have you ever had a dream where—" began Timothy. Daniel jumped in his face.

"Tell me NOW!" yelled the angel.

"The Lord is going to..." he paused as he stared at Daniel with a sense of wonder and excitement, "Let's go, angel." He started flapping his wings. "The meeting of our lives starts in ten minutes over Jerusalem."

Blasphemy's bloodshot eyes opened wide. He and Fester took a nosedive toward their target. Their spirit bodies cut through the wind as if it didn't exist.

"Sir, permission to sift them like wheat?" asked Fester as he trailed behind Blasphemy.

"Don't touch them until I give the approval," hissed Blasphemy. He was a control freak. His eyes caught a glimpse of the truck carrying Solomon. His spirit sizzled with exhilaration. "My eyes have seen my salvation! Revenge will be sweet."

Within seconds, the demons were standing on top of the truck. Fester was possessed with feral fury as he stared at Blasphemy. How he loved to pounce on, demean, and destroy humans. Fester resembled an alcoholic lusting over a drink. Blasphemy stared at him with indignation.

"Get yourself under control, demon." He placed the tip of his long, bony finger near Fester's elongated chin. "A spirit must control his emotions to be an effective agent of evil." Blasphemy smiled and tilted his neck, as if to say, I'm all-wise, and you're one blithering fool.

Fester wisely remained mute as he stared at the boys. Black goose bumps the size of marbles appeared on the less hairy part of his wings.

"This is my prey, understand?" directed Blasphemy, fiercely staring at the demon.

Fester silently nodded in obedience. He abhorred orders, yet it was fear that prompted his obedience, not loyalty or any form of goodness. Blasphemy dove through the metal ceiling, landing on all fours among the three dejected teenagers.

Denny was tied hand and foot with metal irons that were secured to the inside of the cab. The hair on his arms stood on end as Blasphemy neared him.

"You guys feel that?" asked Denny.

Solomon frowned as he glanced up at him.

"Denny, no more games," Cleveland pleaded wearily. "You have single-handedly ruined my life and Solomon's. Enough is enough."

Blasphemy decided to test the waters. He jumped into Denny's body without any human resistance. He wore him like a mink coat; bodily possession was his favorite pastime. Denny gulped as if he had swallowed a pound of Los Angeles' finest mid-summer, smog-filled air. Solomon did a double take.

"Denny, that's not funny."

Cleveland opened his eyes. "Denny, quit being stupid."

Denny's pupils had enlarged almost to the size of quarters. Surrounding the dark pupils was a blazing yellow color. Denny's breathing was heavy and erratic.

"Boo!" bawled Denny as a sinister smile overtook his face.

Fester laughed as Blasphemy jumped out of Denny. "Pretty tame stuff, if you ask me."

Blasphemy dove into Solomon. Solomon began clawing at his stomach and chest.

"Ah, man, not you, too," sighed Cleveland. His nightmare was only getting worse. He cursed the day he was born.

The demon struggled with Solomon for several seconds before winning the battle. Solomon's hands tensed, and his jaw quivered.

"Something is HERE," whimpered Solomon in a strange, foreign tone.

Cleveland pushed his body against the unforgiving, metal wall. "It's a demon, man! We're going to die!"

Fester could not control himself. He lunged toward Cleveland as he screamed with all his strength. "Die, coward!"

"No!" screamed Blasphemy, coming out of Solomon and diving toward Fester. Blasphemy stopped him in the nick of time.

"You have a lot to learn about obedience," howled Blasphemy as he smacked Fester repeatedly.

The boys were screaming for their lives as they punched at the air, trying to fight their unseen attackers.

"Get him off me!" yelped Solomon.

"Stop the truck!" barked Denny as he dug his nails into his arm.

"They're going crazy," hollered Cleveland. "Get me out of here!"

The truck instantly stopped, and the heavily armed guards sprinted around to the back doors. As they slowly opened the doors, each stuck the nozzle of his gun inside.

"Don't move," shouted the leader as he looked inside. He quickly lowered his gun to his side.

Solomon and Denny were semiconscious; their bodies were limp against the force of the chains. Their eyes were bloodred, and their cheeks were swollen and blotchy. Numerous three-to-six-inch knife cuts were evident on their slashed clothes and bodies. The guards' eyes turned to Cleveland, who was trembling visibly. Cleveland appeared unharmed physically, yet emotionally he looked as if he had been through an earthquake.

The head guard spoke directly to Cleveland.

"Can you tell me what happened here?"

Cleveland stared blankly in his direction. Solomon and Denny were moaning softly as they reached their arms toward the guards.

"I know you boys didn't do this to each other. You can't even reach one another." The head guard hesitated. He wanted to help, but wisdom and experience told him otherwise. "Did you do this to yourselves? I don't get it." He shook his head.

"Help," whispered Solomon. His eyes connected with the guard's.

The head guard raced to the front of the truck and grabbed a medical kit. Seconds later he reappeared.

"Son, we'll be at camp in less than fifteen minutes. You boys use the bandages to dress your wounds. I'll call ahead for a doctor to meet us when we arrive."

He tossed a key toward Cleveland.

"This will unlock the chains, but I warn you—don't try any funny business."

The guard slowly shut the door as he glanced at the other officers.

"They're either brilliant con artists, or they've just been attacked by one nasty demon."

Blasphemy smirked. He loved human attention. He stared deeply into Fester's spirit.

"Lesson learned," Fester acknowledged meekly.

"Go take a shot at those guards," ordered Blasphemy.

Without a lick of thought, Fester leaped toward the smallest of the men. A flash of light exploded around the man, knocking Fester and Blasphemy violently backward. Several dozen swords appeared out of the illumination, each pointing directly at the demons.

"Where are they? Who are they?" panicked Fester as his sword was stolen from its scabbard.

"Stay back," yelled Blasphemy as he strained to see through the spiritual fog bank. He yanked his sword into the air. "Don't even think about messing with me!"

Suddenly, something knocked the dagger from his hand. Blasphemy instantly retreated toward his weapon. Fester wisely followed him away from the light.

"I'll find out who you are, and you will pay, and pay dearly at that," threatened the demon general as he and Fester escaped.

———————

Ken was running out of ideas. He had tried every rational and not-so-rational idea to help Emily regain her normally upbeat, positive attitude. In his mind, a vacation would be a perfect way to clear their minds and put things into perspective. It had been several hours since the fiasco in the kitchen. Ken had one more idea.

Emily was in the living room reading her Bible. He sneaked in on his hands and knees and cautiously approached the sofa from behind. He could hear her soft breathing as she read the Word of God. He was going for broke.

He slowly moved one hand, then one knee, toward the side of the couch. It has to be perfect, thought Ken. Emily closed her eyes as she meditated on God's Word. Ken silently crept around the front of the sofa and crouched under her feet, which were resting on the coffee table. Rolling onto his back, he placed his hands over his mouth.

"Whoosh," voiced Ken with a steady tone. He was trying to sound like the ocean, but was failing miserably.

Emily didn't hear him at first. Ken picked up the volume a notch. She cracked open one eye and looked toward the ground. Emily wondered what he was up to, but she had learned to expect anything and everything from her man. She contained her smile, waiting to see what he would do next.

"Whoosh...," bellowed Ken at a higher, more noticeable level.

Emily pulled her hands into her body as if she were settling in for a mid-afternoon nap. Since reading the Bible, she felt like a new woman.

"Whoosh...," roared Ken. Instead of producing soft and peaceful waters, he sounded more like a hurricane. He sighed loudly and contorted his face. She was intentionally making this difficult, he figured.

Emily could barely restrain her laughter. Ken was being Ken, which usually caused her to chuckle. He heaved a breath and squirmed away from under her feet. He snaked his way behind the sofa, stood up, and glanced at her sleeping face. Ken shook his head as he turned to leave. Emily began to moan softly as she pretended to wake up. She stretched her arms into the air, pretending not to see him. Suddenly, she reached back for him and gave him her most vivacious smile.

"I can be packed in an hour," beamed Emily.

Ken exhaled noisily as he ran his fingers through his hair. As he headed toward the bedroom, he mumbled something under his breath that Emily couldn't quite hear.

Seven

The Rod of Discipline

imothy and Daniel scanned the angelic crowd, looking for long-lost friends. They loved these meetings with a passion. It was like a high-tech pep rally with supernatural overtones. Hundreds of millions of angels were floating in the air seven miles above Jerusalem.

"There's the Lord," signaled Timothy, pointing toward the grand city below. A hush fell over the congregation of spirits.

The angels bowed as Jesus moved with elegance and ease toward the center of the assembly. A light, whiter than snow, shone from His body in all directions.

"Angels of righteousness," the Lord's voice thundered throughout the audience, "I thank you for your loyal support all these years. Your service and deeds have been noted and will be rewarded."

Jesus paused to look at His subjects and friends. Many of the angels were overcome with emotion as His eyes met theirs.

"This is a day like no other. Today, many of you will be assigned a new duty."

Daniel was about to burst. The hand he used for sword fights was twitching fiercely. More than any other angel, he wanted to be chosen for battle.

"One half of you will be assigned earth duty. For a short period of time, you will walk in human form, yet retain all the powers you have as angels."

Looking at each other in delight, the angels began to cheer. Daniel was having trouble controlling his wings; they were vibrating so quickly that he couldn't keep himself from shooting above the crowd. Timothy grabbed him and sighed.

"Try to control yourself, angel. Show some respect."

Timothy smiled nervously as he stared at the Lord.

Jesus placed His hand in the air, and silence quickly followed the divine gesture.

"Evil's final grasp for power is approaching from the east. Each of you will be assigned a human who has not accepted my Kingship in his or her life. Preach the Word valiantly, be courageous in and out of season, and understand that the souls of millions of young people hang in the balance."

Jesus lifted both His hands high over His head as He gazed toward heaven. "May it be so," commanded the Lord.

A wind of dazzling light flared from the sky and quickly rained down upon the congregation. Daniel's eyes tracked its path as a dog eyes food dropped from the dinner table. The mass of energy separated into streaking drops of elongated light. The rainbow-colored light bounced off select angels, immediately transforming their angelic spirits into human bodies. Several angels near Timothy and Daniel were miraculously changed in the twinkling of an eye. Their human bodies floated toward Jerusalem like an autumn leaf falling from its branch.

It appeared as if an intense meteor shower was pelting the earth. Millions of residents of the New Jerusalem were out on the streets. Most were on their knees in holy fear. Thousands upon thousands of human bodies slowly floated out of the sky and landed within the city limits.

The light drops had hit neither Timothy nor Daniel. Both could see the end of the light show on the horizon. Their hands were clutched to their chests, as if in prayer.

"Come on, light," shouted Daniel as he pointed to his forehead. "Hit me right here, right between the eyes."

Timothy ignored his buddy as he tracked a purple streak of light that was racing toward them. Daniel slowly moved his body to the left, then the right, in an attempt to help the selection process along.

138

"Stop that, Daniel," said Timothy as he briefly noticed his shenanigans. "The Lord is choosing, and He doesn't need your help."

The band of light appeared to be heading toward Daniel.

"Yes!" shouted Daniel. He closed his eyes and hoisted his arms into the air. "Take me away!"

Suddenly, the light veered from him and crashed into Timothy. The light wrapped around his body. His wings were suddenly transformed into muscular shoulders, and his sword changed into a Bible. His excitement waned when he saw Daniel, with his arms open to the sky and his jaw quivering. Timothy began falling toward the ground. He had to think of something quick. He couldn't believe that he had been chosen. The look on Daniel's face, though, melted his heart. How he wished that Daniel had been chosen over him.

"Daniel."

The younger angel folded his wings over his broken heart. Part of him, though, wanted to share in his friend's joy.

"I know, brother," sniffled Daniel. "I'll be by your side to help you out."

Timothy stared at his companion as the distance between them increased. It was as if a long chapter in his life was ending, a chapter of brotherhood and joy, of laughter and sharing, of war and peace. He reached toward Daniel with an outstretched arm.

"Fight the good fight. I love you."

A lonesome tear dropped from Daniel's eye, and a lump the size of a bullfrog swelled in his throat.

"You'll always be like a brother to me," cried Daniel as he watched Timothy glide toward earth. He swallowed hard and looked toward the sky.

"I'm on my own," thought Daniel, "and I must be prepared to meet the challenges that are ahead." His chest began to swell as he glanced one last time at Timothy falling toward Jerusalem. He looked at Jesus, who was gliding toward His earthly throne. Daniel took a deep breath as a light illuminated his heart. This was his chance to prove his angelhood. The Lord didn't want him to depend on Timothy any longer. Jesus was going to put him through the valley so that he could make it to the top of the mountain. He would rely on the Lord.

The truck rounded the corner of the barren wilderness road. Dust shot in all directions as the tires sliced through the dry earth. Vultures squawked their disapproval as the humans violated their turf. Cacti littered the side of the road, a testimony of God's displeasure over sin. This slice of earth was the Lord's way of giving unrepentant people a little taste of the wasteland called hell.

The truck slowly came to a halt. The boys looked at each other without saying a word. The pain from their wounds didn't compare with the fear of living in prison the rest of their lives. Cleveland was angry with himself for his foolishness, Solomon was angry at Denny, and Denny was angry with God. They heard the doors from the front of truck slam shut. The guards were gabbing about looking forward to some home-cooked dinners. Seconds later, the back doors opened, and light flooded them.

"Gentlemen," smiled the head officer, "welcome home."

He glanced at their cuts and abrasions.

"You boys had quite a fight back there. How did you get out of your chains?"

The head guard spoke. "I let them out, sir." He looked at the boys and shook his head. "They were chained when this happened. I can't figure it out. I let them out so that they could dress their wounds."

The officer bit his lower lip as he thought. He turned to speak to the medics at his side. "You can have them in a few minutes. They should be fine for now."

A dozen armed security personnel from the camp waited to greet the boys. The husky, six-foot, six-inch warden in blue jeans and a white tee shirt climbed into the back of the truck. An intimidating look filled his face as he scrutinized the boys. He glanced back toward the three guards.

"You guys let these youngsters take you down?"

He chuckled for a moment before his face turned stormy. Solomon took a step forward and stretched his sore muscles. The warden pushed him backward.

"Solomon Action," mouthed the guard in a stern tone, "welcome to your worst nightmare." He reached down and grabbed Solomon's hands. The warden rubbed his rough fingers over the palms of Solomon's hands. "Just as I thought." He sighed as he glanced toward the fields. "You are absolutely of no use to me." He released Solomon's hands. "Not a single callous. I bet you haven't done a lick of real work in your life."

Solomon was about to speak, but Cleveland wisely shook his head in the negative.

"You have something to say?" The warden eyed Cleveland suspiciously.

"No, sir. I'm sorry, sir."

Satisfied with that response, the warden turned his attention to Denny.

"Don't I know you?" he asked. Denny gulped as he lowered his head.

"Look at me, son." Denny slowly lifted his head without raising his eyes. The warden shook his head and sighed. "What do you know. Look at this, gentlemen." He grabbed Denny by the arm. "You would think one visit to this camp would be enough," the warden said sadly. He dropped Denny's arm and stared into his eyes. He was hoping to see some sorrow for his sins, but all he saw was defiance and anger. "I thought three years would have knocked some sense into you."

The warden's name was Grizzly. Nobody knew his last name or anything else much about him. The prisoners didn't like him, but he was respected. His job was to discipline them with the "iron rod" of the Lord, without going overboard. They were here to be punished and to be rehabilitated.

The warden did a quick about-face and stared at Solomon and Cleveland. His glare could have melted metal; it certainly scorched their hearts. Grizzly started rubbing the top of his teeth with the tip of his tongue. Those close to him knew that was his way of thinking. The silence was deafening.

"Cleveland, front and center," ordered Grizzly.

Cleveland rushed out of the truck in record time. He stood within an arm's length of the warden. Cleveland knew the warden wanted complete obedience, and he tried to comply.

Grizzly moved closer to him. Cleveland was scared. He tried to hide it, but he couldn't.

"What's wrong, son?"

The warden tilted his head back and studied Cleveland's eyes.

"Go ahead. Let's hear it. To what do I owe the pleasure of your company again?"

Cleveland licked his lips nervously. He knew not to keep the warden waiting too long.

"Sir, I have no excuse. I didn't learn my lesson the first time."

The warden's upper lip twitched a bit as he stared at Cleveland and pondered his fate.

"Hopefully you will learn your lesson the second time around."

"Yes, sir. I'll certainly try." Cleveland breathed a sigh of relief as the warden turned his attention to Solomon.

"Get out of that truck, now," barked the warden as the other guards looked on.

Solomon promptly obeyed the man. He climbed down from the truck and stood at attention in front of him. He recalled reading history books about marine boot camp. He had never imagined in his worst nightmares that he would be living through a real-life version of it. He loved history and had dreamed about traveling back in time to before the Millennium—but not here, not as a prisoner. In some ways, it was partly his love of history and his fascination with the more brutal episodes in it that had landed him here.

Grizzly greeted him with a scowl.

"Looks like you've gotten yourself involved with some bad young men." He glanced at Denny and Cleveland. "Do you have anything to say for yourself?"

Solomon's cheeks began to flush a little. "No, sir," responded Solomon in a deep tone.

Grizzly smiled. "That's good to know. At least you're not starting out making excuses. Hopefully we can help you see the light."

"Yes, sir," Solomon gulped.

Grizzly watched Solomon's hand rise over his head. "What is it?"

"Sir, is it true that we have to work twelve-to-fourteen-hour days? I've heard rumors that—"

Grizzly interrupted, his tone somewhat threatening. "Solomon, don't question the way I run this camp. You are the prisoner, and I'm the boss. Do you understand me, son?"

Solomon swallowed hard and answered, "Yes, sir."

"So we have a boy who thinks he knows it all." Grizzly began circling around Solomon like a vulture. "The rules are not good enough for you? I'm not God, but I'm the closest thing to Him in here. I am responsible for keeping you alive. You don't eat without my approval. You don't sleep without my good graces. You don't wake up unless you are told to. Bathroom breaks are considered heaven here. Do you understand me, son?"

Solomon nodded his affirmation.

"I can't hear you, Solomon. You got a problem with your mouth?"

"I understand, sir," Solomon answered with as much strength as he could muster.

Grizzly's demeanor suddenly shifted dramatically. He patted one of the guards on the back. His tone was gentleman-like.

"Get them some medical attention and food, and make sure they make the church service tonight."

Tiger Stith, the senior guard under Grizzly, addressed the boys.

"Get yourselves moving! I warn you. Keep your noses clean," he paused for effect, "or else!"

Solomon nervously looked at Denny and Cleveland as they marched alongside the medics toward the hospital. The hopeless expressions on their faces spoke to him. Did he want to be like them? What was he doing here? He missed his parents. He missed his home. He really missed Allison.

Allison took a deep breath, staring at the pen and paper on her desk. She glanced around her room.

"This place needs a major cleaning," she said to no one in particular. Allison started picking some stray socks off the floor when her eyes wandered back to the desk.

"I can't do it," Allison mumbled, looking back at the floor.

"Allison," called her mother from downstairs. "I'm going to the grocery store. Do you need anything?"

Her eyes were pulled back toward the pen and paper. If she wrote the letter, she feared Solomon would not respond. Maybe it was better not to try at all.

"Allison!" hollered Gail, now walking up the steps.

"Oh, I'm sorry, Mom," she said as her mother entered the room. "No, I don't need anything. I'm fine." Allison glanced at the desk for the hundredth time.

Gail noticed her struggle. "You're not fine, honey. Just do it and get it over with." She nodded toward the desk. "It's better to seek love and not find it than to never try. You'll never forgive yourself if you don't."

A cursory smile hit Allison's face.

"Thanks, Mom. I love you. You always seem to know just what to say." She kissed her mom and moved toward the desk. As Gail began walking down the stairs, she called back, "You don't have to wear your heart on your sleeve, though."

Allison sat at the desk chair and reflected on her mom's advice. She picked up the pen and pulled the paper near her.

"Dear Solomon, I hope this letter cheers you up some. I know that life in that camp can't be easy, but I'm sure you'll make it, with God's help. I will be praying for you constantly." Her pen stopped; she couldn't go further. How much do I tell him? Will he be offended if the letter is too casual? Will he be turned off if I reveal my feelings too much? She sighed. The muscles in her hand seemed frozen by fear. The roadblock led her to pray.

"Jesus, I feel pretty pitiful right now, like a desperate little girl hoping for a love that may never return." She took a deep gulp of air. "Please guide my hand—and my heart. Amen."

She opened her eyes and felt her heart and mind fill with God-given words.

"Solomon, I feel bad about the way I reacted before. I should have known you needed your space without your having to tell me. God has a funny way of working sometimes, because you have your space now." She shook her head, erasing that last sentence. "Since you have your space now, I want you to know that I will be here for you whenever you need me. I know they don't let you call out, but they do accept letters. I know you can write back, so I hope to hear from you soon. Mom and Dad say hello, and, Solomon, Dad came to your defense when the authorities from Jerusalem questioned him. He told them you didn't lay a hand on him. Anyway, I'll write back soon, maybe every day, so you will have something to look forward to. I miss you. Allison."

Her hand shook as she signed her name. The pen dropped and rolled to the floor. She stared at it; her body was limp from too much emotion, and her heart was heavy with despair. Life in prison...life in prison...life in prison... echoed in her mind. She trusted in the Lord, but her chances for a lifetime with Solomon seemed remote, nearly hopeless, almost impossible.

———————

Ken sipped on pure cranberry juice as he looked out over the Mediterranean seashore. He watched as a row of palm trees swayed against the sea breeze. Several doves flew overhead as music played softly in the background. The tropical paradise numbed his memories, at least for a time. He turned to Emily, who was resting comfortably on a lounge chair. Ken could see the pain etched on her face. He silently prayed for her as he started on plan number two to cheer up his wife.

"This is the life." He reached for his darkly shaded sunglasses and smoothly placed them on his face. "The sun, the sand, the trees—everything about this says, 'Come to me, ba-aa-by.'"

Emily politely smiled at Ken's juvenile communication skills.

"Don't think you are the one who persuaded me to come," she told him. Solomon came to mind. She sighed as her eyes looked longingly toward Jerusalem.

Ken placed his hand over his heart, as he appeared to be slightly offended.

"Hey, did I say that? I never said any such thing."

Ken's response pulled her back. He was watching her like a hawk, doing everything in his power to make her happy.

"It's not what you said; it's your attitude, man of my dreams."

Ken flexed his muscles and took a sip of his beverage. He could see Solomon on her heart and hoped his "juvenile" antics would distract her at least for a while.

"My attitude is just fine. You see things my way, and that makes me very happy indeed."

Emily stood to her feet. "Let's take a walk on the beach."

Ken rolled his eyes and groaned loudly.

"Ah, I just started to gel with this chair. Give it a while, and I'll take you up on your offer."

Emily grabbed him by the ear and pulled.

"It wasn't an offer; it was a command. Move it, buddy," joked Emily as she towed him away. Emily thought of Solomon again, but this time, Jesus' face appeared in her mind. Her heart relaxed. Ken's silent prayers were working.

As the couple walked the sparkling white beach, creatures of every type made them feel at home. Several seagulls landed on their shoulders, wanting to be stroked; a dolphin beached itself so that it could be petted; and several wolves from the surrounding hills rushed to the beach for a game of chase.

Emily began shaking her head as she sighed. "I just can't believe Satan is only days away from attacking Jerusalem."

Ken looked out on the quiet sea.

"Yeah, I know. I remember a long time ago when Jesus started talking about it. I thought *we* would be fighting it out with the Devil." He breathed a sigh of relief. "When Jesus told us that the only thing we needed to do was to pray for the younger generation, it was kind of a letdown."

"Jesus is trying to teach us that He's in total control," responded Emily.

Ken smiled.

"That's sometimes a hard lesson to learn—even here in this perfect world."

Emily squeezed his hand.

"I'm glad we're here," admitted Emily as she rubbed the head of one of the gray wolves. She stared lovingly into Ken's concealed eyes. "Take off those glasses, please."

Ken placed them into his pocket.

"Come on," he called, as he started sprinting toward the aquamarine water. "Let's take a dip."

Emily hesitated. Ken hit the water in full stride.

"Come on, honey," he encouraged. "It's room temperature."

She casually jogged toward him as he dove into the ultra clean waters of the Mediterranean.

"Be careful, Ken," called Emily as she slowed her pace. "You don't know how deep the water is."

"Thanks, Mom," responded Ken as he performed a fancy backstroke for her eyes.

Suddenly, Ken wanted to kick himself. Don't use the "M" word, not now, he thought. One look at Emily was all it took. He saw immediately that thoughts of Solomon were possessing her face, her mind, and her heart. Then all of sudden, she was back.

"You're such a show-off." She placed her toes in the water.

Ken smiled happily. Wow, he thought, she can change her moods instantly from night to day. "Come on, stop being a chicken." Ken was weaving in and out of the water like a fish.

Emily inched toward him. Ken couldn't take it any longer. He raced toward her, splashing about like a man ready to drown.

"Don't you dare do what I think you want to do, Ken Action," said Emily as she started to back away from the animal she called her husband.

"You've got to learn to have some fun, Emily."

"I mean it, Ken. Leave me alone!"

Her objection was soon drowned. Ken picked her up and ran toward the deep water. He raised her shaking body over his head and dropped her into the water. When she surfaced, Ken covered her with kisses. Her anger turned to joy as she pushed her wet hair behind her ears.

"I guess I can't complain about having a boring husband," figured Emily as she punched Ken on the shoulder.

Ken splashed some water toward her, as a gesture of love, of course.

"Do you remember that time we went swimming in the Dead Sea?" asked Ken.

"How can I forget," reminisced Emily. "It was two weeks before our marriage ceremony, and the ever-so-bright Ken Action decides to dive into water that was about, uh," Emily thought for a moment.

"It was four feet, seven inches deep, dear," responded Ken in a slightly irritable tone.

Emily smiled as the real story came to mind. "That would be one foot, seven inches. The bump on your head was four feet, seven inches." Emily shook her head. "You always seem to mix those numbers up."

Ken's face suddenly turned pale. His distant look caught her off guard.

"What's gotten into you?"

Ken thought for a moment. He appeared to be struggling with a memory. He lowered his body into the water so that only his head was visible.

"Ken, what is it? This isn't like you."

"I know, honey. I guess with what's going on with Solomon and everything, and our being at this resort, it brought to mind that time when we almost ruined our wedding."

Emily's face suddenly mimicked Ken's. A storm cloud descended upon the couple, choking away their paradise.

"It wasn't your fault, Ken."

"Oh, yes, it was. My life would have been over with."

———————

Timothy stood on both feet as he gazed at the temple in Jerusalem. He moved his shoulders back and forth, trying to get used to not having wings.

"What's it like?" asked Daniel who was hovering overhead. He was a little jealous, but he had promised himself that he wouldn't show it.

"Kind of strange. I want to walk, but I don't know how."

"Wish I had your problem," sighed Daniel as his wings fluttered against the breeze.

Timothy glanced at his buddy and sighed. He knew Daniel was taking it pretty hard.

Timothy watched several angels near him begin to walk. Seconds later, one of them began to jog, then to run.

"Just do it, angel," prodded Daniel.

"Easier said than done." Timothy glanced down at his feet. "This is really weird." He tried lifting one of his legs with his hand.

"No, not that way," directed Daniel. "Just lift your leg and move it forward."

Timothy glanced up at Daniel. "Listen, buddy. This isn't as easy as it looks. Let me do it my way." One of the transformed angels started leaping in the air and yelping out loud. Timothy watched his foot as he lifted it off the ground. "Come on, move."

Minutes later, he was comfortably walking on his own. He noticed several dozen ex-angels congregating a hundred yards away.

"Let's go check it out," said Daniel.

"Sounds good," observed Timothy. "Maybe they will know our next move."

Timothy started trotting toward the group.

"Hey, angel, this is fun, but taxing. Flying is a lot easier."

Daniel sighed at what might have been. Suddenly, his eyes caught a glimpse of Jesus on His throne in the center of town.

"Thousands of people are gathering around Jesus," observed Daniel. "I think He's going to give the marching orders Himself."

They noticed a group of men starting to move toward Jesus. Minutes later, millions of ex-angels, who now had human bodies, gathered around the King. The atmosphere was electric and charismatic. Jesus stood, which brought immediate silence.

"As you know from My Holy Word, Satan is soon to be released. He will attempt to manipulate and distort everything that is holy and true. Millions of young people born in the last twenty years have not accepted Me as their King or their Lord. Your job is to witness to them about Me. Tell them that you are angels. Preach to them about the coming judgment. Help them to understand their need for true repentance of the heart. Also, encourage My people to stay the course. Make sure they understand that Satan's time on earth will be very short. I don't want robots following Me because they have to, but human beings choosing Me out of love and commitment. Be strong and courageous. Fight for the spiritual lives of these young people. Be brave soldiers, and your reward in the new heaven and new earth will be great."

The crowd cheered loudly as Jesus sat back on His white throne. Daniel and Timothy looked at each other with a new sense of purpose and excitement.

"I'm going to be your backup out there," voiced Daniel as he began looking for enemy spirits. He was happy again. His excitement level shot sky-high as he thought about fighting the demons. He would have to take the lead now, instead of relying on Timothy.

"Thanks, pal. I'm going to need you to be at your best for this mission. Understand?"

"Yeah, this is going to be as big as the Battle of Armageddon."

Timothy turned his eyes to the north.

"No doubt."

"So what's our next move?" asked Daniel.

"I need to talk to Ken and Emily. They need encouragement. I don't want their concern for Solomon causing them to lose faith."

Satan peered into the darkness. His mind was working overtime, formulating strategy and counter-strategy against his lifelong enemy. How much time would he have? How many humans would he be able to tempt? What was their spiritual condition? Did he need to twist God's words, try to discredit them, or simply try to erase them from the face of the earth?

A baleful, vindictive smirk surfaced from his dark heart. It was all too perfect. He knew the human population was inexperienced with the finer points of evil. Angels were rusty from a thousand years of inactivity, and demons were restless and excited about the return of their fearless leader.

Satan spit volcanic saliva toward heaven.

"You underestimate me, Jesus, and because of that, Your plan will fail." Satan wanted to claw at the air, but his body was still in limbo. "You think this jail proves that You have all the power, but You are wrong," screamed the Dark One. "I could have resisted You and won, but I knew the greatest victory for my divine forces of evil would be now, at the height of Your kingdom."

Satan's chest bulged as his heart did the same.

"Remember the Cross, Jesus? My greatest victory turned out to be my worst defeat. And now, I promise You, Your greatest victory will turn out to be Your most humiliating, disastrous defeat."

A bolt of lightning suddenly burned past the Devil's overly bloated head, missing him only by inches.

Satan snickered at the Lord's response.

"Don't like the truth?" seethed the Devil.

Another blast of lightning flashed across the sky; this one missed him by less than an inch. He gulped and said nothing.

His dream was the worst kind of nightmare. It started with a pure, deep, almost holy kind of sleep. This divine feeling of rest was interrupted by a loud, bodacious trumpet blast of biblical proportions. An earsplitting scream jolted him awake.

"Get up and get moving," roared Grizzly as he placed his mouth near Solomon's ear.

Solomon yelped as he fell off the bunk bed. Grizzly picked him up and placed him on his feet.

"It's time for you to pay your debt to society and clean up your life. You've got five minutes to be outside. I've heard you like history, so I hope you've read about military boot camp."

Solomon's tired muscles reacted in fear as he jumped up from the floor and ran toward his locker. A glimpse of Grizzly was enough to motivate him.

"You two get moving."

Denny and Cleveland wisely remained quiet as they dashed toward their lockers. Grizzly marched out of the barracks.

"What happens if someone crosses that guy?" asked Solomon as he frantically buttoned his uniform.

Denny wasn't moving as quickly. "He's a big blowhard, if you ask me."

Cleveland had little expression on his face as he tied his shoes in a double knot. He glanced at Solomon with worry overtaking his face.

"Solomon, don't cross that man." He stared at the wall, as if recalling some painful memory. "He will win every time."

"Is it all an act?" asked Solomon as he swiped at the wrinkles in his shirt.

Denny didn't try to mask his venom.

"You bet it is, Solomon." A hateful gaze materialized. "The man is only making up for being a wimp in his childhood. He used to get beat up on by the girls."

Solomon wondered about Denny; his hatred for the system and Jesus was so far out there. Solomon couldn't help but wonder what had made Denny so bitter.

Cleveland finished dressing. He draped his arm around Solomon's back and accompanied him to the door. He hoped Solomon trusted him. Something inside him was telling him to take care of Solomon, to take him under his wings and protect him.

"Solomon, keep your nose clean." He looked at Denny and shook his head. "Don't let his rotten attitude rub off on you. I'm telling you, Grizzly can read your mind."

Denny followed closely behind them. As they left the barracks, the cold early morning air seemed to flow right through their thin, dark uniforms.

"What time is it?" whispered Solomon to Cleveland as Grizzly's eyes met his.

"It's four in the morning, Mr. Action," quietly spoke the warden. Grizzly's expression appeared pleasant.

Solomon was surprised by Grizzly's civil reaction.

"Thank you, sir," said Solomon with a kind of buddy-to-buddy tone.

Grizzly marched over to Solomon, who was standing at attention with Denny and Cleveland. That pleasant expression of his began to make Solomon uneasy. The warden's smile turned downward. Then his cheeks began to fill.

"I want fifty push-ups, now," ordered Grizzly.

Solomon hit the ground. Grizzly's growl echoed against the night sky as Solomon pushed himself to his limit.

Solomon was quickly tiring as he counted out loud. "Thirty-one, thirty-two…"

Grizzly watched the sweat flow down Solomon's half-frozen cheeks. He wished he didn't have to be so hard on the boys, yet he knew they needed tough love. It was the only way to break their wills and save their souls.

"Thirty-five," moaned Solomon as he pushed against the dirt with all his might. His arms refused to hold his weight, and he dropped on his heaving stomach.

Grizzly looked toward Cleveland and Denny, watching for a spark of rebellion. Their blank expressions seemed to appease him, for the moment. He grabbed Solomon and lifted him off the ground.

"Obviously you are severely out of shape. Every morning you will begin the day, right here in front of us, doing push-ups until you make it to fifty."

Solomon wiped the tear-moistened dust from his cheeks as he moved back into the lineup. He was hurting inside and out. Solomon had loved reading war stories, and military life had enthused him, but no more. This wasn't fun at all; it was painful, disgusting, and grueling.

Grizzly placed his hands stiffly behind his back and began to pace in front of the boys.

"Until further notice, you will wake at four in the morning." The warden stopped in front of Denny. The vapor chugging from Grizzly's mouth passed across Denny's face. "From four in the morning until eight at night, you will work."

Cleveland closed his eyes and appeared to be praying. Grizzly halted his pacing in front of him.

"Son, if you had done that in the first place, you wouldn't be here now." The warden's smile dimmed as he began to pace again. "Prayer is a very good thing, gentlemen. You will need much of it in the future, and to help things along, I will offer a reprieve of sorts to your schedule."

The Rod of Discipline

The warden turned toward a small building about a hundred feet away. The wooden shack was neat, but modest. A wooden cross stood atop the one-story church. The warden called out, "Paul," and a short man dressed in a white robe appeared at the church door. Clutching a well-used Bible in both hands, he slowly walked toward the group.

"Boys, this is Pastor Paul, and he will be your spiritual counselor in the future."

The pastor moved over the well-trodden ground near Grizzly. He slowly lifted his eyes into the air, continuing to grip the Bible tightly in his hands. Paul was 5 feet, 5 inches tall with sandy brown hair and hazel eyes. He was humble but tough. A brilliant preacher, he gave all the glory to his Lord and King, Jesus Christ. The greatest thrill in his life was seeing youngsters come to know the Lord.

"Young men," began the pastor, "the Word of God says that Jesus will rule His kingdom with an iron rod." He glanced toward Grizzly and quietly sighed. "This is your iron rod, gentlemen."

Grizzly showed little emotion. Both men knew that the warden always tried to balance that "iron rod" with the Lord's compassion.

"You will graciously be allowed three meals per day, along with a church service at exactly eight in the evening." The pastor's face turned stern but loving. "Your attendance is not optional, young men. It is mandatory. Please do not miss even one service because Grizzly has been given strict orders from Jesus to punish that type of rebellion with the utmost severity. Remember, the entire purpose of your stay here is to clean up your life and understand what life can be like with Jesus—and without Him."

The tough-looking warden crossed his arms as he stared the teenagers down. Solomon gulped in fear.

"Gentlemen," continued Pastor Paul, "I love the Lord with all of my heart. My desire is to see you saved from your sins." He gently opened his frayed Bible to the book of First John, chapter one. "If we say that we have fellowship with Him, and walk in darkness, we lie and do not practice the truth. But if we walk in the light as He is in the light, we have fellowship with one another, and the blood of Jesus Christ His Son cleanses us from all sin.'" He closed the Bible and glanced at Grizzly, who was nodding in agreement.

"Boys, there are two sides to our Lord: His unconditional love for us that we call His grace," he paused to gauge the boy's attitudes, "and His righteous jealousy and anger brought about by our sins." He closed his eyes for a moment and caressed his Bible. "My prayer is that you will choose His grace," he lifted the Bible toward them, "over His wrath," said the pastor as he looked at Grizzly.

Ken sat in the sand as Emily rested her head in his lap. He gently curled the wet strands of her hair around his fingers. He smiled as he looked down at the sand, which, thanks to Emily's shenanigans, was now burying his feet. He bent to tenderly kiss the top of her head as he gently caressed her damp shoulders.

"I can't stop thinking about that trip," sighed Ken, stopping his fingers at the memory.

"Why do you want to dredge up that stuff?" She sat up and turned to face him. She didn't want to think about that part of their past, especially not now that Solomon was in trouble.

"I'm sorry, honey, but we need to talk about it," replied Ken. He looked Emily squarely in the face. "I know this is way in the past, but I need to get something off my chest."

Emily appeared concerned, but she was confused by his persistence. "Well, okay. What is it that's bothering you?"

Ken shifted his position in the sand. He blushed as he stared into her puzzled eyes. He started to talk, but suddenly stopped. Emily shook her head at his theatrics. He tried again.

"I've repented for my mistake and have apologized to the Lord, but," he paused for many seconds before he mustered the courage to continue, "but I've never sincerely apologized to you for that evening before we got married."

The Rod of Discipline

She breathed deeply, gently touching his cheek with her hand. Now she understood; it all made sense. She smiled nervously, "It takes two to tango."

A surge of energy seemed to overtake Ken. One would think that by now Emily would be able to predict his enthusiastic outbursts, but she couldn't.

"Don't you get it, Emily? We didn't sin, but we came so very close." Ken looked at her with unbridled anticipation.

Emily nodded her head, waiting for something that made some sort of sense. Ken was fidgeting as he spoke.

"Solomon did sin against God, but I believe he is so very close to repenting. Just like we were close to sinning, but didn't, Solomon is close to repenting, but hasn't yet."

Emily was staring at her husband with a "Is that the brilliant thought you've been trying to express?" kind of look. Ken shook off her gaze as he rattled on in his thinking.

"I believe we need to pray harder than ever. Honey, he's so close to repenting, just as we were close to sinning. He just needs that extra oomph to push him over the edge."

Emily began to picture what he was saying.

"But, Ken, we already know that prayer is our only hope with Solomon. So what's all the excitement about?"

It was like Emily had knocked all the air out of Ken. His enthusiasm weakened as a result.

"I thought the Lord had just given me a brilliant theological metaphor relating to our family," complained Ken as he got up and began walking toward the hotel, "and then you shoot me down in flames."

Emily was not accustomed to Ken's once-a-year bout with emotional sensitivity. She loved to see it, yet it came at the strangest times. She ran after him as she spoke.

"You're right, Ken. We need to pray, as the Word says, 'unceasingly.'" She placed her arm around him and hugged him as they walked.

Ken's mood shifted again. "Do you remember our wedding?"

Emily giggled, her eyes glittering against the setting sun. "How could I forget? The wedding cake down my dress was uncouth and barbarian."

157

"Come on, honey. I told you that I tripped," replied Ken innocently.

Emily shook her head and said, "That excuse is as lame now as when you concocted it. Save it for Judgment Day!"

———————

Blasphemy carefully scrutinized the enemy positions around the camp. Everything had to be just right for his "divine" plan to succeed. His black, stiff eyebrows arched as his eyes widened at the sight of the angels' headquarters located on top of the church.

"As predictable as ever," mocked the general as he squinted into his laser binoculars.

"Why don't we just get it over with and attack now?" asked Fester as he cracked his knuckles in Blasphemy's ears.

"Because, you fool!" He whacked Fester upside the head. "Agents of evil must be wise. We must know the strengths and weaknesses of our enemy."

Fester sizzled with anger. He wanted to smack Blasphemy into the sun, but he knew he didn't have a chance. He changed his tactics.

"That explains why we've been losing since we lost you and Satan." Fester knew how far flattery would get him.

"You're wise beyond your rank, demon." Blasphemy moved the binoculars to scan the area around the church. His black wings flickered with anticipation. "Ah, there are the boys."

Fester heard a swarm of spirits approaching from the north.

"Sir, something is coming up on us," warned Fester as he ducked under a fig tree near Blasphemy.

The demon yanked the binoculars away from his face. "Get over here, you dupe. They're on our side."

"Uh, yeah, I knew that, um..."

"Stop your rambling. Get up there and escort them to me."

Fester throttled into high gear and flew toward the swarm of demons. Blasphemy shook his head in disbelief. He despised dealing with amateurs, yet he didn't have a choice. When he won the war, he figured, he'd get rid of most of them anyway. Trash, he thought, pure trash.

Seconds later, several dozen demons were on the ground near Blasphemy, bickering and complaining about who was the greatest among them. Blasphemy's eagle-like wings stood up against his shoulders. They weren't flapping; they were just there, as if to dare anybody to mess with their owner. Every demon in the universe feared the sight.

"Shut up, you imbeciles, and listen to me!"

The demons obeyed, but only out of fear.

"There are three young felons in that camp," pointed Blasphemy, "and they are going to be ours."

One of the higher-ranking junior officers stepped forward.

"Sir, those camps haven't been penetrated by our forces since the Great Battle."

Blasphemy's wings began to flap as his sullied body lifted into the air.

"I haven't been around since the Great Battle," Blasphemy boasted. "Things will be different now."

Eight

A Wake-Up Call

Solomon lightly gripped the garden hoe, cursing under his breath. Painful blisters covered both hands from days of work in the seven-hundred-acre garden. The noon sun showed no mercy as it beat its unyielding rays down on the boys. Unfortunately, his heart was straying further from the Lord. He didn't even try to understand why he was here, and he certainly wasn't familiar with God's ways of getting one's attention.

"There's no way I'm here for life," vented Solomon as he slowed his work.

Denny ripped off his tee shirt and wrapped it around his right hand, which was raw with blisters. His venomous heart was contagious.

"I say we fight to the death." Denny's anger boiled as he winced in pain.

Cleveland groaned in frustration, the unyielding, dry ground not responding to his efforts. He was beginning to keep his distance from Denny, who had changed. To Cleveland, Denny was no longer a rebel with a cause, but a madman foaming at the mouth.

One of Grizzly's guards sneaked up behind them. He carried a bullwhip, more for effect than anything else.

"I want to see dirt flying," yelled the man, cracking the whip near Denny's feet.

Denny quickly lifted the hoe off the ground and threateningly waved it at the guard. He no longer cared about anything other than revenge and regaining his freedom.

161

"Don't even think it, boy." The guard grasped the handle of the whip in his hands, as if readying it for action. He would use it only to defend himself.

"Leave us alone," snapped Denny. "We'll do the work in our own way, and in our own good time." He tossed the tool toward the dirt and glared hatefully at the guard. He was hoping for a beating. He considered it an opportunity to escape, and any pain was secondary.

The guard flung the whip forward, sending dust flying.

Cleveland and Solomon began working faster as they slowly edged away from the confrontation. Neither wanted trouble; nor could they control Denny's temper. Denny picked up the hoe and slowly began to till the ground again, his heart racing with adrenaline.

The broad-shouldered guard pulled a small box from his pocket and began speaking into it.

"Grizzly, this is Hutch. Looks like we'll be out here until at least midnight." He sighed as he watched Denny's slow-moving hoe. "Got a boy out here who doesn't have much control over his emotions."

Solomon and Cleveland sighed in disgust as they looked at Denny. When he saw that he had lost their support, he suddenly exploded in rage, flinging the hoe toward the guard's head. The guard jumped backward, the metal part of the worn tool missing him by inches. Cleveland and Solomon backed away from Denny as he glared at the shaken guard.

"I have full control of my emotions!" he screamed, panting like two racehorses in a dead heat.

The guard cracked his whip at the ground in front of Denny. "Now take it easy, and nobody will get hurt."

Cleveland shouted, "Denny, don't be stupid. Back off, man."

Denny was hunched over, as if readying himself to spring toward the guard. Solomon wanted to say something, anything, to keep Denny from going berserk, but, helpless, he kept quiet as he watched Denny lunge at the guard. The guard jumped backward and swung the end of the whip against Denny's stomach. The bloodcurdling scream could be heard around the camp.

Dozens of candles dimly lit the Italian restaurant. Shadows of light danced among the dozen or so tables that were filled with gourmet food. A couple occupied each table, and intimate conversation and soft laughter added to the romantic ambience. An elderly man masterfully played a violin with a passion that could never be taught.

Ken gazed into Emily's eyes. He reached for her hand, lifted it to his lips, and gently kissed it. "I'm so glad I married you." He placed his hand on top of hers. He loved romance more than most men, yet he didn't always know how to show it.

"Ken, you're one of the strangest," she paused, "no, you're one of the most eclectic people I've ever known."

He smiled as he rubbed his fingers across her hand. "What do you mean by that?"

"Well," she paused, trying to come up with just the right words, "one minute you're like a county hick, with your 'Hey, babe, what's shakin'?' Then the next minute, you're a hopeless romantic with lots of class." She was trying to be honest without hurting his feelings.

In his deepest voice, Ken crooned suavely, "I'm a man of many talents."

Emily rolled her eyes and shook her head. "You're something else. I wasn't exactly complimenting you."

Ken appeared smug as he responded. He was smarter than he sometimes appeared and was clever at hiding his intelligence when it suited him. "You meant it as a compliment; you just didn't know it."

She leaned her chin against her hand. "If you know me so well, tell me what was going through my mind the day we got married."

His eyebrows lifted as he clasped his hands together. Ken loved a good challenge, especially when it entailed reading his wife's mind. He could never do it well, but it was always fun. Occasionally she would tell him he was

163

right when he was wrong, all in an attempt to promote good marital will. With the sun waning and the shadows growing, they began to reminisce about their wedding.

Ken began, "The first thing I remember is the setting. The sparkling silver lake, calm and inviting, and those trees were out of this world."

"Those trees were beautiful," began Emily. "Their multicolored leaves reminded me of a rainbow." She was glowing as the memories came to life, as clear and vibrant as the painting opposite their table.

"I've never seen grass so green and thick," remembered Ken. "And those leopards."

Emily's eyes lit up like a Christmas tree. "I think I counted twelve of them surrounding the stage. Back then, it was always so strange to pet something that once had been so fierce, when the earth was still under the curse."

Ken's heart began to burn with passion. "I'll never forget you in that gown." He leaned toward Emily and softly growled like a leopard. They didn't notice the couple near them giggling.

Emily blushed as Ken's eyes ignited with fervor.

"One hundred and forty-four diamonds, each one over a carat," said Ken, his hands beginning to perspire.

"Are you thinking about me or those diamonds?"

Ken looked at her in bewilderment. His years in politics during the Tribulation had served him well. "I'm thinking of you wearing those diamonds," retorted Ken.

Emily shot a skeptical glance his way. "Smooth answer, Ken Action." She could have gone for the kill, but she saw no reason to ruin the moment. Years of marriage helped her to pick her fights wisely.

Ken raised his eyebrows, attempting to appear innocent.

She continued, "I know all about your sordid past and your 'lady-killing' days."

Ken eyes widened as he shook his head back and forth. He hated when this conversation started, like he had the previous thousand times. "Every one of those rumors you heard from my so-called 'friends' is a vast distortion of the truth."

A Wake-Up Call

Emily placed a grape in her mouth and chewed it very slowly. Her body language was clear to Ken. "Come on, now. I'm telling you the truth." He edged closer to his wife. "You're the only woman for me." He reached over and kissed her. "I mean it."

Emily sighed as she thought about Allison.

"I'm afraid our son may turn out to be just like you—a lady-killer. Dump them at will." Her gestures were becoming dramatic. "Don't worry about their feelings. Just ruin another life, and be done with it."

Ken winced. He didn't know how it had happened, but he had lost total control of the conversation. Solomon and Allison were not supposed to be on their minds now. Desperate to recover the romantic mood, he knew they would have to finish this conversation first.

"Do you really think their relationship is over for good?"

"Ken, he's in detention camp for life. If she was in her right mind, she'd forget about him. I know I would. Besides, there's hardly any time left before Satan is released."

He stared at her for a long time before sipping his drink.

"But, Emily, we don't know how long Satan will be loose before Jesus destroys everything. They might have more time than you think."

"So let's get back to our wedding," Ken said as he tried to change the subject.

Hard as it was to put thoughts of Solomon and Allison aside, Emily acquiesced. She didn't want to ruin the evening, especially when Ken was trying so hard to make it special. Emily relaxed as she continued to recollect. "I've never felt closer to the Lord than on that day," beamed Emily. "Vice-Regent David's sermon on unconditional love was powerful."

"Ken Action," began David as several hundred guests listened, "I charge you today among this great crowd of witnesses to love Emily with all your heart, all your soul, and all your mind."

David was dressed in a simple white robe with golden threads woven into every twelfth stitch of the fabric. As he raised his hands, the robe glistened in the sunlight.

"Love is from God, and without the Lord's divine empowerment, it can never be achieved."

Ken and Emily's eyes were joined together as if moved by the same heart and mind. Their emotions were higher than the heavens and purer than the mountain streams.

"Emily, you must love your husband and respect him. You must be willing to give up the things that you want and think first about the needs of your husband." A broad smile covered her face as she agreed with the declaration of love.

The charming scent of roses, daffodils, and tulips filled the air. Thousands of flowers from every part of the world encircled the wedding stage.

"Ken," smiled David, "you must desire to love your wife, not out of necessity or brute force, but because it's the Lord's will for your life. Pray that our Great King shows you His mercy on a daily basis, and be sensitive and responsive to your wife's emotions."

Ken nodded at Vice-Regent David as his eyes feasted on his new wife. Emily was overwhelmed at the measure of Ken's devotion. David turned to Emily.

"Love is more than an emotion. It is an attitude of self-lessness. Love is displayed not only in words, but also in actions. It is a state of mind connected to the heart of Jesus and an attitude that always hopes, always trusts, and always provides. Love is easy during the tranquil times of life but is most prominently displayed during trials and tribulations."

Vice-Regent David reached for an orange that was lying on the gold podium. As he held it with both hands, he raised it into the air and turned toward the crowd.

"Love is always fruitful." David's expression turned serious. "During the church age, nearly fifty percent of Christian couples divorced. Their hearts were hardened by unforgiveness, which led to anger, bitterness, hatred, depression, and eventually divorce. Do not allow even a root of unforgiveness to spring up in your heart. Do not give evil a foothold in your spirit, or you and your mate will pay dearly in the future."

Ken and Emily were astonished by his wisdom, as well as a little taken aback by his tone. David began to squeeze the fruit. Soon drops of juice flowed through his fingers and onto his robe.

A Wake-Up Call

"True love will reveal itself during your darkest hours, during your most severe trials." He stared at the couple with a great intensity. *"When your marriage is up against a wall and squeezed in every direction, I ask you, what kind of fruit will flow from your heart? Just as I squeezed this fruit and its juices came forth, your true heart and the fruit it contains will be evident only when you are pressured by life's unexpected complications."* David placed the crushed orange on the podium. *"Will the fruit be loving, good, and pleasing; or will it be sour, bitter, and poisonous?"*

Ken tightly gripped Emily's hands. A handsome smile emerged. He knew that with the Lord's help, he would be up to the task. Emily cherished this moment in her heart. She would never forget it, never. She returned Ken's smile before returning her focus to David, whose face was glowing with righteousness.

"You will have a child, and his name will be Solomon. Train him in the love and fear of our great Lord, Jesus Christ. Your love for him must never be greater than your love for your Lord or for your spouse. My prayer is that one day he will grow up to live a life worthy of his divine calling."

Ken was jolted by the sound of his weeping wife.

"What's wrong?" asked Ken as he smiled reassuringly at a nearby couple dining in the restaurant.

Trying to regain control of her emotions, Emily asked, "Did we do something wrong in our marriage to lead Solomon astray?" She fumbled for some tissues in her purse, while Ken remained mute and confused. He felt helpless. "Did I not love the Lord and you enough, and now we're all paying the price for it?" she wondered aloud.

Ken sighed. His stomach churned as he considered her question and wondered if he had been at fault.

Emily continued, "I was so looking forward to seeing Solomon and Allison's wedding. I feel like my dreams have been shattered."

Ken hated not having the answers. He wanted to help, but he couldn't. He had no choice but to seek the Lord in a way that he had never sought Him before.

Solomon and Cleveland slowly walked toward the small chapel. Their bodies were aflame with pain. Every muscle throbbed; every joint ached. They glanced toward the field. Hours earlier, several hundred young men had been sweating from their labor, but now there was only one.

"Why was he so foolish?" asked Solomon as he forced himself to look away from Denny.

Cleveland answered in a sad monotone. "We've been best friends since we were five years old, but I have no idea what's gotten into him. He knows the limits and what he can get away with, but now it's like he doesn't care anymore."

Each of the wooden steps creaked as they entered the church. The pews were nearly full, so they slid into one in the back. Cleveland was beginning to bond with Solomon. Both were misled, lost, and rebellious, yet they had a spark of hope in their lives. The spark was small, but it was alive, and, seemingly, growing day by day.

The chapel was small but comfortable. Several dozen rows of wooden pews were lined up back to back, fully filling the modest sanctuary. The walls were bare; the altar unadorned. A single wooden cross was nailed to the front wall, a testimony to the King most of them had shunned.

Solomon glanced around this house of worship. A few eyes darted away at his look. It reminded him of his home church and the days he had sat in the pew listening to Allison sing like an angel. Solomon lightly elbowed Cleveland.

"You've been here before. What's going to happen?"

Cleveland looked toward the front of the church as he whispered softly, "Don't talk; they'll make you pay if you..." Catching the eye of the preacher, he lowered his head, hoping the preacher wouldn't embarrass him.

Pastor Paul moved toward the wooden podium, his Bible in his right hand, his face aglow. He gently put the Bible down; his reverence for the Book was obvious. He cleared his throat as he studied the rough crowd. Solomon stared at the preacher, his mind yearning for answers that his heart was unprepared to accept.

"Some of you have grown weary of hearing about hell. Some of you are here for the first time and are relatively new to the message of the Cross. You may be nearly ready to accept Christ as your Savior and commit yourselves to a lifetime of service."

His speech was not smooth or silky; his demeanor was anything but flashy. He was a simple preacher who believed what he preached.

"You are one step away from the fires of hell. Oh, yes, young men, hell is not here. But hell is as real as the hand in front of your face."

Solomon looked at his hand, which was swollen with numerous blisters. He had almost forgotten about the pain. This is hell, he thought. How could it be worse than this?

"The pain of hell is unbearable, yet you will have to bear it because you will have made your choice, and it will last forever. There will be no second chances, no opportunity for repentance once you reach the flames." Beads of sweat began to slide down the pastor's face as he lifted the Bible into the air. "This is God's Word. It's His mind. It's how He thinks and what He wants from you. Oh, you say, 'I've heard Him in Jerusalem, and I've read the Bible several times.'"

Solomon's face turned red as he gripped the pew with both hands. He didn't notice Cleveland's tears, his broken heart, or his shaking hands.

"Boys, you are here because of your lack of faith. Oh, you say, 'I have faith,' yet your deeds speak louder than your fruitless words of deception. If you love God, you will obey God! Repent, and be baptized for the forgiveness of your sins, and go and sin no more." Pastor Paul began to pace the floor in the front of the sanctuary. "Why do you refuse to believe and be saved? Your hearts are wicked and deceptive. You cannot know the depravity that lurks in the shadows of your soul."

Solomon's heart felt as if it were being jolted by surge after surge of electricity. His conscience began to ache as the preacher jabbed him with the Word of God.

The preacher stood on his toes as he peered at Solomon and Cleveland. "I see we have two new boys here tonight."

He left the platform and walked down the aisle toward them. Cleveland's heart nearly dropped out of his chest as the preacher neared. Solomon's hands began to shake, so he stuck them under his thighs.

"It's so good for you boys to make it tonight," began Pastor Paul as he smiled warmly at them. "Would you both introduce yourselves and tell us why you are here?"

Neither boy moved a muscle; each stared at his feet, hoping the other would make the first move. The pastor touched Solomon on the shoulder and nodded. Solomon wanted to die.

"Why don't you go first, son?"

Solomon slowly stood to his feet. His knees were about to give out. Solomon swallowed hard and tried to speak.

"My name is Sss...Sss...Solomon Action."

Paul cupped his hand to his ear as he looked around the church. "Son, you will have to speak up so those in the front can hear you."

"My name is Solomon Action." His breathing became erratic. "I, uh," he paused as he looked around the room, then at Cleveland. "I did something really dumb." He was having a lot of trouble breathing. He closed his eyes and tried to calm his nerves. "I really wanted this gravity machine, so I decided to steal it because my parents refused to buy it for me." He took a deep breath as he looked at the preacher.

"Is there anything else?" Pastor Paul's heart went out to Solomon. It was a difficult thing for the young man to confess, but the pastor knew it had to be done.

Solomon blankly stared at the preacher, wishing he could ignore that question. He took a deep breath and then said, "Nope, there's nothing else." He quickly sat down and hoped the pastor would move on to Cleveland.

Cleveland looked at the preacher, who was still staring at Solomon. Pastor Paul pulled a piece of paper from the inside lining of his robe and opened it. Cleveland knew what was coming and felt kind of sorry for Solomon.

"Stealing," began Paul. His voice raised as he continued reading, "assault, lying to authorities, resisting arrest, fleeing

170

from the police, attempting to deceive a judge, lying to yourself, and faking repentance."

Paul placed the rap sheet back into his pocket and stared with righteous indignation at Solomon. Solomon felt about an inch tall as the pastor began pacing the aisle in front of him.

"A person can never see the kingdom of heaven unless he turns from his evil ways. He cannot turn from his evil ways until he admits he has done wrong. Until you confess all of your sins, Solomon, you continue to lie—to yourself, to me, to those in this church, and most importantly, to God Himself."

Solomon slouched in his seat and closed his eyes in shame. Cleveland shook his head and rubbed his tired hands across his face.

"This is not your average church, Mr. Action." Pastor Paul quickly moved to the front of the church. "What is done in darkness will come out in the light. I will call you publicly on your transgressions. My Lord demands that I expose the evil within your heart. If you thought church would be hearing a message every evening and then going home to laugh and carry on, you are sorely mistaken. Jesus demands a change in your heart and actions. His demands are not too hard, if, and only if, you allow Him to work inside you."

Solomon couldn't handle the chiding any longer. He jumped out of his seat and ran toward the door. Cleveland reached out to stop him, but it was too late. Pastor Paul frowned as Solomon reached the exit. One could hear a loud thump as the boy collided with Grizzly. Solomon literally bounced off the giant of a man and landed on his back, dizzy and shaken. Grizzly reached under the back pew and snatched up some chains.

"Very foolish," growled the warden as he placed them on Solomon's hands and feet.

Pastor Paul walked to the back of the church and said to Solomon, "Son, that was an easy word from me. I pray that you never have to deal with a hard word from the throne of our Lord and King."

Grizzly then told him, "Get up off the floor, sit down, and keep your mouth closed." He smiled before adding, "And your heart open."

Paul turned to Cleveland. "You have a little more experience with God's style of justice during the Millennium. Many in the audience already know you from your previous time with us." Paul's serious tone began to make Cleveland uneasy. "Of course, there are some new folks here who need to know something about you. Please do a better job than Solomon did in telling his story."

Cleveland stood and focused his eyes on the front wall. He wasn't shy, but he was embarrassed. "My name is Cleveland Combs, and my initial sin was not going to church with my family." He looked at the preacher for approval. Instead, he saw disappointment.

"The real problem," continued Cleveland, "was not so much the church thing as it was not wanting to worship or obey Jesus."

"Keep going, son," encouraged Paul.

"So the deal was, since I didn't want to obey the King, it made me not want to go to church."

The pastor interrupted. "That's right, Cleveland. You were not punished for not going to church as much as not loving our Lord." The pastor moved toward the front of the church again. "Your disdain for church was a symptom of a much deeper, more grievous sin that, unless you repent, will keep you from inheriting heaven. None of you can possibly imagine the wonderful things God has prepared for you in the new heaven and new earth. A prerequisite for these gifts and responsibilities is a devotion and love for Jesus. God has a plan that we know only a little about for the future. I believe we will be used to do mighty things for Him, but if we are not on His team, we cannot be of any use to Him."

Cleveland started to sit down, hoping the spotlight would avoid him for the rest of the service. His heart was feeling heavier by the second, though he didn't understand why.

"Tell us why you are back with us," spoke the pastor from the pulpit.

Cleveland quickly straightened up and cleared his throat. He looked around the church without making any eye contact. "Well, pretty much everything Solomon has been charged with." He glanced at Solomon, who appeared strangely void of life. "Denny and myself were the ones who initiated the assault on the Lord's officer. Solomon just came along for the ride, probably my fault, some peer pressure, you know."

Cleveland's frank responses encouraged Paul. He interrupted him. "Thank you, son, for your honesty. Many of you claim that I am brutally honest, and I am for a reason." He looked around at the boys in the congregation with an authentic expression of concern. Not all of them knew it yet, but he loved each of them. "The truth always hurts. This earth is now like the former Garden of Eden, perfect in all its ways. But imperfect man still dwells here, and when the imperfect meets the perfect, something has to give."

His language confused many of the boys.

"Oh, your hearts are hard, and your necks are stiff. You do not understand because your eyes are blind and your ears are deaf. If only you would repent, change your ways, ask Jesus into your heart and mean it, then He would come and eat with you, and you with Him."

Most of the boys in the church knew what was coming next. When the Holy Spirit energized Pastor Paul, there was no stopping him.

"Cleveland, your answers are correct, but your heart doesn't believe them. For two years you heard the Lord's messages, yet you chose to sin anyway. You do not fear the Lord. You do not believe deep down that you will be punished in an afterlife. The fear of God is the beginning of wisdom. You have no fear and no wisdom, and you do not have salvation. Faith without deeds is dead. You have no true deeds; therefore, you have no faith. You are dead spiritually and are fooled by your own selfish pride."

The pastor's fiery message was slowly chipping away at Cleveland's heart. A week ago, those words would have incited Cleveland to fight; but not this evening. No, something deep inside him was changing. He raised his hand to speak, surprising Pastor Paul.

"Yes, Cleveland," acknowledged the pastor, taking the opportunity to catch his breath.

"I'm not dead spiritually as you say. I'm making mistakes, but I want to change."

He avoided eye contact with the other boys, looking only at the pastor. Pastor Paul clasped his hands together in joy. The Holy Spirit was getting to Cleveland. Paul felt energized by Cleveland's confession. He knew that the change in Cleveland's attitude could spark a revival.

"Why don't you just drive one of those?" asked Daniel, pointing toward a gravity vehicle.

Timothy shook his head as he walked toward the north. "Great idea, but I don't own one, and even if I did, I don't know how to drive one of those contraptions. Cut me some slack; I've just learned to walk."

Daniel's patience was waning. His wings fluttered as he flew at a measly three miles an hour.

"Well, we've got to do something. It will take us months to get to their house at this pace."

"If you have ideas, I'm all ears, but for now, this is the only thing I can do," reasoned Timothy.

A pack of demons suddenly flew overhead. The angels could hear the cursing from miles away. Timothy ran toward a thick bush and huddled beneath its large leaves. Suddenly, he desired his wings and his pointed sword. He wanted to fight for the Lord!

"Whoa," called Daniel, crouching near the bush. "I haven't seen that many demons together in a millennia."

Timothy's mind was working overtime as he stared at his angelic companion. The end of the age was nearing, and all he could do was to hide like a sniveling coward. Once the demons were out of range, he poked his head out from under the shrub.

"No doubt about it. It can mean only one thing," figured Timothy as he resumed his northward trek, trying to forget about his predicament.

Daniel looked at him with apprehension in his eyes. "What is it?"

"Someone has persuaded the demons to assemble again." He peered into the distance as he picked up his speed. "We can expect the first shot to be fired any day now."

The angels were silent as they continued moving northward. It was critical for them to meet up with Ken and Emily. Timothy wished he could fly again, and Daniel wished he could walk. A small town appeared on the horizon.

"Let's stop there for the night," said Timothy, his legs beginning to tire.

"What for?" asked Daniel without thinking.

Timothy stopped and pointed to his feet. He began to rub the muscles in his thighs. "I'll never whine at another human about not being in shape. These bodies can only do so much before they need rest."

Daniel exhaled loudly.

"Have some patience," responded Timothy. "I'll need a couple of days to get my act together."

A heart-stopping shriek exploded overhead.

Timothy and Daniel, who were in the middle of a large pasture, hit the dirt. Several thousand demons were traveling in the same direction as the previous group. They appeared to stop and go haphazardly, with no apparent reason—an obvious gesture of contempt for the angelic authorities monitoring them from a safe distance. Daniel's wings began to tightly vibrate in place. Timothy had seen Daniel do this hundreds of times before. Timothy crawled toward him and grabbed him by the neck.

"Don't do it," ordered Timothy. "It would be suicide, and I need your help here."

"I've got to take a stand for righteousness," vented Daniel, his eyes burning with desire. He began to overcome Timothy's grip.

Timothy nearly bit his tongue as he stiffened his hold on the angel. "Have some smarts doing it," he panted as he tried to crawl on top of the spirit's body. Daniel's body abruptly gave up the fight. Timothy lay sprawled out on the ground panting and wheezing as a fearful Daniel tried to slither further underneath him.

"What's gotten into you?" questioned Timothy.

Daniel said nothing, as he dug into the dirt.

"One minute, you're going to save the world single-handedly, and the next, you're cowering in fear. What gives?"

"I give," thundered an intruder from a not-so-comfortable distance.

Timothy took a deep gulp and slowly turned on his side. The foreboding voice was familiar, yet he couldn't place it.

Daniel continued to hide as Timothy spotted the shadow on the ground. The size of the shadow was disheartening, yet Timothy bravely turned to face the haunting voice.

"We've never gotten the chance to meet formally," began the voice as it moved into Timothy's line of sight.

Timothy's jaw dropped as the monster's face came into full view. It was pure evil, undiluted sin in its rawest form, and it was eyeing him as if he were dinner.

"Blasphemy!"

The demon fired off a mocking smile as he pulled Daniel out of the dust. It was good to be back, thought Blasphemy. Scaring angels out of their wings was a pastime he had dearly missed.

"It's always good to know angels don't forget, even after a thousand years." Blasphemy politely awaited their response, but he was sorely disappointed by their silence. "Well, I wouldn't waste my valuable time on you two low-ranking amateurs unless I had a good reason."

Without moving their heads and risking a violent reaction, both angels occasionally peeked toward the sky, hoping for a miracle.

"No, no, this is not a social visit, but a fact-finding adventure," mumbled the demon with a casual attitude. "And stop hoping for a miracle from above, because I can promise, it ain't goin' to happen."

He believed he was so superior to Daniel and Timothy that he could afford to be nonchalant.

"Two simple questions that even you simpletons can answer," began Blasphemy. He sat on the ground and turned away from them. It was an obvious attempt to humiliate them.

Daniel and Timothy were wise enough to know their own strength—or lack thereof. They dared not move or provoke a demonic reaction, which could be as unpredictable as the weather.

"Question number one. What purpose can the 'Big Guy Upstairs,'" he coughed in contempt, "what purpose can He have in changing one of you fellows into a sniveling, useless human?" The obnoxiously proud demon stared at his perfectly manicured black nails. "And number two, where is Ken Action and that oh-so-lovely wife of his?"

The angels looked at each other in anguish. They were in way over their heads and needed help, badly.

The pastor rubbed his hands together as if he were trying to keep warm in the middle of a raging blizzard.

"Cleveland, I heard you say one thing that could change your life and the lives of every young man in this audience tonight if you and each of them takes it to heart."

The audience, including Cleveland and Solomon, appeared perplexed by the preacher. He smiled at their reaction.

"Exactly what I expected. You just don't understand the things of God, nor can you because you are not spiritually discerning. And why? Because you do not have the Spirit of God to help you."

Cleveland glanced at his watch, a movement that caught the pastor's eye.

"Church is dismissed."

Pastor Paul appeared to slouch somewhat as he disappeared behind the small handmade pulpit. He was hoping for more response. He knew it took time, yet time was something they didn't have. How could he get through to them? Were they really listening, or were they all clever little demons in training?

"What was that about?" asked Solomon as he contended with the chains.

Cleveland hardly heard Solomon as he walked toward the door well in front of his struggling friend. He regretted looking at his watch at the end of the service. Pastor Paul's heartbroken reaction wouldn't leave his mind. He walked toward the dorm, his spirit downcast and lonely. He needed a friend badly, a perfect friend, one who would never let him down. He knew he wouldn't find it in any human.

"Hey, wait up and help me out," shouted Solomon as the other boys filed past him, also ignoring his pleas.

Solomon plopped down onto a hard seat until the church emptied. He was angry at Cleveland but knew they both needed time to think. He remembered the time his father had taught him to ride a bike. He violently shook his head at the memory. He needed to be forward thinking; that was the only way he could survive.

I'm a man now, thought Solomon as he stood and shuffled toward the door.

Grizzly was standing at the steps waiting for him. He was rubbing his chin.

"Let me help you get those chains off." Grizzly spoke with an almost fatherly attitude. Solomon watched as the warden showed him some undeserved compassion.

"I don't get it," said the boy in a soft, confused tone. "Why are you being," he thought about his choice of words, "civil, now?"

Grizzly looked him in the eyes as he unlocked the boy's feet first. "Son, I'm not a bad man. I have a job to do."

"And what is that?" inquired Solomon with a slightly mordant tone.

Grizzly ignored his attitude.

"The Word of God, written thousands of years ago, says that Jesus will rule His millennial kingdom with an iron rod. He knows the frailty of each and every human being and his urge to do wrong. Our fear of Him must overcome our desire to sin, or we will be left to our own devices, lost to our own sinful behavior."

The warden patted Solomon on the back as he led him to his dormitory. "My job is to make your life miserable."

Solomon shook his head in disbelief. "I just don't get it. Why would a loving God treat me this way?"

Grizzly stopped as they neared the dorm. He placed his bear-like hands on Solomon's shoulders.

"It's the question of the ages." He forced eye contact with Solomon. "A loving God is simply trying to get your attention before it's too late. Maybe this will help you to understand. It's almost like a game, and we are part of it. The Maker of the game gives us this set of rules, and we start to play. Suddenly, we decide that we don't like the rules, and we change them to suit our own wants. Then we think we're going to win this game every time because now it's easy, but, in reality, we have fooled ourselves. The game is still going on as originally established. The rules haven't and won't change, and you're losing, Solomon, and losing badly. God is trying to show you that He makes the rules, and you must agree to follow them. You cannot conveniently change them to suit your whims or desires."

Solomon's head was spinning. Grizzly was going way too fast for the youngster. Solomon tried to pull away from him, but Grizzly bucked him.

"One last thing, son. The game that you are playing is not an easy one. Life is much more complicated than getting your way, and that's the end of the matter. I promise to make your life as miserable as possible in order to smack you out of your spiritual slumber and help you see that hell is real and that you are on the highway that leads to it right now."

The truth hurt Solomon deeply. He thought about the words Allison had spoken the day before he had ended their engagement.

"Solomon, do you really love Jesus?" Those stinging words had circled around his head hundreds of times. He hated them with all his heart. He glared at Grizzly with an iron stare.

"That's your interpretation. That's your opinion."

Grizzly shook his head in grief, releasing Solomon to bunk for the night.

"Son, your fight is not with me. Your fight is with the Lord Himself." He paused as Solomon turned away. "Jesus is the way, the truth, and the life. No man will see heaven without surrendering himself to Him."

Solomon opened the door and then slammed it shut. He was fighting something he didn't understand, and it was getting to him more than he thought. Grizzly turned toward his quarters and smiled. The Spirit of the Lord was getting to Solomon, he thought. But was there enough time for him to respond?

Blasphemy casually glanced at the muscles protruding from his hairy arms. Daniel and Timothy stared at each other, trying to silently communicate a game plan.

"Hey, you peons. I don't have all day. There's a world out there to be conquered."

Timothy slowly stood upright and brushed the dirt from his clothes. "We are very low-ranking members of Jesus' army. We don't—"

"Quit blubbering and answer the question," spit Blasphemy, turning around and facing the two. "You will appease me or suffer greatly for your sins."

Blasphemy turned away from them. He lifted his fur-lined foot into the air and grunted. He loathed this kind of work. It was beneath him, yet he had little choice.

Daniel watched as Timothy moved around to make eye contact with the king of the demons. His hope began to grow once he noticed several dozen angels flying in from the south.

"Sir," began Timothy as he watched Daniel come to his feet, "I believe Satan is going to be loosed shortly, and Jehovah God wants us on the earth."

Blasphemy clenched his fists as he slowly stood to his feet. The black stare of evil seemed to drain some life out of

Timothy. "I know that, you imbecile. Why does He want *you* on the earth?"

Timothy closely tracked Daniel without moving his eyes and inviting Blasphemy's wrath. Daniel cautiously removed his sword from its holster.

"Sir, He did not tell us all of His plan," responded Timothy as he lifted his finger in the air, hoping to buy a couple more seconds. "But I do know where Ken Action is."

Blasphemy's dark eyes lit up in delight. He edged closer to Timothy as Daniel firmly gripped his sword.

"Where?" demanded Blasphemy in a deep, haunting tone.

"He's," Timothy edged closer to the demon, more for drama than for wisdom's sake, "located in a deep, dark place," he paused, hoping to brand this moment in his mind for eternity, "and the name of it is..." Blasphemy nearly fell over in anticipation. "The name of it is HELL," screamed Timothy as Daniel muscled his sword deep into the back of the demon. "Or was that your master?"

Blasphemy bent over in agony, roaring curses into the heavens. Daniel paused to kick the demon squarely in the gut before jetting away. Timothy sprinted toward some tall wheat and quickly dove in for camouflage. Blasphemy opened his eyes and immediately circled the landscape. He spotted Daniel fleeing into a cloud and swiftly sliced through the air, making up the lost time almost instantly.

"You will die," belched the dark angel as Daniel sang praise songs to his Creator.

Daniel stopped on the top of a cirrus cloud and faced the approaching demon as he sang to God.

"I lift Your name on high; I live to sing Your praises. I'll serve You with my life. Your worthiness is ageless!"

The sound forced Blasphemy to vomit. He slowed his speed and faced the small angel. He reached around and pulled the dagger from his back. He was so humiliated by the angel's attack that what wisdom he had was suddenly lost in his fury.

"You fool," vented the demon as he cracked each of his knuckles, one at a time. "You think you can mess with me and get away with it? Never has an angel of your low rank ever attempted such a foolish, asinine thing."

Blasphemy howled ferociously as he dove headfirst toward Daniel. The angel screamed as Blasphemy's paws wrapped themselves around his fragile neck. Suddenly, dozens of highly trained fighting angels stuck their swords into Blasphemy's back. The frightening, surprised look on the demon's face thrilled Daniel. He backed away from the demon's loosened grasp, still singing his praise song. The battle was over before it had hardly begun.

"I've been swindled," moaned the demon, struggling to take a breath.

The angels retrieved their daggers and encircled their comrade. The demon's dizzying eyes blurred, and his wings failed as he dropped from the cloud.

"You'll pay for..." muttered Blasphemy, hitting the ground with a thump.

Timothy jumped to his feet and ran toward the fallen angel. The unconscious demon lay on his back, his eyes sealed shut. Timothy bent down and stared into the face of a devil. The putrid odor made him queasy. In contrast, he thought about the goodness of the Lord. One day, there would be no more evil, no more temptation, and no more demons. He stood and walked away, smiling at the thought of heaven.

Nine

Chasing the Wind

The demon Fester glared at the fading sun. He looked toward Solomon's barracks and then to the west.

"Where is he?" asked Fester, obviously getting somewhat nervous about Blasphemy's disappearance. He tried to recall Blasphemy's exact words before he left. "I'll be twenty or thirty minutes. Don't move."

He kicked a rock with his foot and blasphemed God as he spoke to himself. "I know he said twenty or thirty minutes, so what do I do now?"

Fester ducked at the sight of several dozen angels flying overhead. He covered his ears to block out the annoying sounds of their singing. Once they had passed, he cursed to himself again. To a demon, cursing was as natural as a baby suckling its mother's milk. Naturally, he wanted to disobey Blasphemy, yet fear overruled that impulse.

Fester surveyed the camp one more time. Absolutely nothing was happening that interested him. He would have a good excuse for his disobedience, he thought, since Blasphemy hadn't returned, so he flew toward Jerusalem. Maybe he would find Blasphemy there.

Several minutes passed uneventfully as he traveled. Fester maintained a very low flight level of one thousand feet, far below the average angel's flight altitude. The demon scanned the valley floor below for clues to his boss's disappearance. Suddenly, Fester gasped at the sight of the fallen dark warrior. He recklessly plunged toward the ground.

"Blasphemy, what happened?" hollered Fester, landing within inches of the demon.

Blasphemy didn't move. Fester stared at his master's dark chest.

"It's moving," he panted as he circled the body. "What do I do?" He heard a noise behind him, causing his heart to skip several beats. Fester dug into the five-foot-tall grass and began to hyperventilate. "Come on, demon, think, think."

Several minutes seemed like several hours. Phantom sounds caused him to jerk his head to the left, then to the right. The imaginary appeared real as fear imprisoned his heart. He glanced toward Blasphemy's body, wondering what would happen if Blasphemy awoke to find him slouching in the grass like a coward. A burst of energy surged through his veins. He jumped up and hovered over Blasphemy.

"Blasphemy!"

There was no response.

He shouted louder. "Blasphemy!"

The demon's body remained limp and unresponsive. Maybe he should try to kill the general. It was a thought, but Blasphemy was his key to fame and success. Fester knew he couldn't succeed on his own. He took his paw and lightly tapped him on the cheek.

"Wake up."

His attempts to awaken the sleeping giant failed. When he spotted several rather large angels flying toward him, he lifted his paw and walloped Blasphemy squarely on the head. Blasphemy suddenly rocketed into the air and drew his sword. He stared at Fester as his mind cleared.

"You two-timing yellow demon," hissed Blasphemy.

Fester slowly backed away, shaking his head violently in all directions.

"Sir, it's not as it appears."

Just then, Blasphemy noticed the angels flying overhead. He screamed at them, "Get out of here, and go worship your pathetic God!" He returned his glare to Fester. "This had better be good."

"Sir, I found you passed out...and...I...I tried to wake you up, but...but you wouldn't respond." Fester had never been so scared in his life.

A lie naturally popped into Blasphemy's depraved mind. "I wasn't passed out, you fool. I was sleeping."

Fester stared at him in disbelief. "But, sir—"

"But what?" shouted Blasphemy as he began to file the nails on his paws into razor-sharp points.

Fester wisely let the point drop. "Sir, what's our next move?"

"Get back to the camp and get into those boys' minds. The last thing I want is for one of them to genuinely repent, especially that Action boy."

Fester's eyes widened. "All by myself, sir?"

Blasphemy stepped toward him. "You got a problem with that?"

"Uh," fumbled the demon, "no, but," he paused to gauge his boss's mood, "what are you going to do? How will I be able to find you?"

Blasphemy snickered as he tested his pointed claw on his arm. "I have to visit a once close friend of mine. Don't expect me for supper!"

Fester gulped as he thought back to the camp and the angels protecting it. It was an impossible job. What was he to do?

———

A rooster crowed before the first light of day. Solomon's eyes instantly opened. He looked around the rugged dormitory room and sighed. It would have been nice to wake up in his own bed, get up, and look out the window to see Allison walking in her yard. He could almost smell the delicious breakfast aromas of his mom's cooking—crispy bacon, scrambled eggs, melt-in-your-mouth cinnamon rolls.... It was too painful to continue the memory.

"Wake up, Cleveland," bellowed Solomon in a voice louder than needed or appreciated.

"Shut up, and go back to sleep," moaned Denny as he turned over onto his stomach.

Cleveland sat up in his undersized bunk bed and looked at Solomon. "What happened with Grizzly last night?"

Solomon stared through the dusty window opposite him. "He tried to play Mister Nice Guy with me, and then," he groaned as he stretched out the kinks in his spine, "he told me how much of a sinner I was and that I was going to end up in hell if I didn't see things his way."

"I'd rather be in hell with you guys," interrupted Denny from under his warm sheets, "than in heaven with a bunch of do-gooders."

Neither boy responded. They no longer paid much attention to Denny's remarks. He was the outsider, and he knew it, which caused him to rebel even more.

Solomon said, "This bed used to be uncomfortable, but now it's the only joy I have." He sighed as he pulled his uniform over his head. "I can't believe that I'm saying this, but sleep is the greatest pleasure left in my life."

Denny agreed. "Yeah, the day they can take my dreams away is the day I commit suicide."

Cleveland appeared irritated by Denny's words. "Stop with that suicide crap. Don't you have any fear of God at all?"

Grimacing from yesterday's whipping, Denny asked, "What did you say?"

Cleveland shrugged his shoulders as he sat on the bed to put on his work boots. "I'm so tired I don't even know what I said." He knew full well what he had said, but he feared Denny's reaction.

Solomon quickly reminded him. "Cleveland, you said he should fear God!"

Denny jumped out of bed and towered over his longtime friend. He shoved his finger into Cleveland's chest. "Warn me now if you are going to wimp out and give in to their mind games." He glared into Cleveland's eyes. "Don't get soft on us now. Fear is a weakness, and I can see it in your eyes."

Cleveland shot to his feet and shoved Denny in the chest. Denny fell on the bed and began to laugh.

Cleveland said, "The day I fear you, little man, is the day *I* commit suicide."

Solomon shook his head and laughed. "You guys are like two peas in a pod."

Denny picked himself up and quickly dressed. It was refreshing to see Cleveland stand up to him. He considered it progress. Minutes later, the three boys were lined up outside the barracks. Grizzly appeared a minute later, cleanly shaven, and with a freshly pressed uniform. He smiled as he walked past the boys.

"Good to see you three ready for some wholesome, hard work."

Abruptly, he stopped just yards past them and did a 180-degree turn. His eyes connected with Solomon's.

"It seems to me, Solomon, that you have an attitude problem similar to your buddy Denny's." His smile was calculated and cunning, devised to elicit a response. "You also seem to have an overabundance of energy." He hated taking this route, but Solomon had left him no choice.

Solomon's face reddened with anger.

"I believe this could be a problem in the future, so," he stopped for a moment as if to carefully deliver each word for maximum impact, "you, Solomon, will work until midnight each night until I inform you otherwise."

Solomon's angry face froze.

"Also, I think it would be wise to fast during your dinner hour, until further notice."

Solomon stared blankly. His anger had grown into full-fledged bitterness.

"You see," began Grizzly, "you have this idea that I'm unreasonable and wrong about pretty much everything. I don't see it your way, and since I'm the boss in these parts, I figure I *will* be unreasonable, without compassion, and downright disagreeable in every way humanly possible."

The warden nodded his head, as if he were quite happy with his wise conclusions. Solomon's heart crashed at the words. Cleveland knew what was coming and wisely stayed out of the limelight.

"Maybe you will begin to see things my way after a little time in the fire." He walked toward Solomon and faced him man to man. "My way is God's way, and until you see the light, you will suffer." He didn't come across as a dictator. Even though the sentence was harsh, Solomon couldn't help but hear the compassion in Grizzly's voice.

Solomon closed his eyes tightly. A single tear formed in his eye duct. He rubbed his eyebrow and then quickly passed his finger over his eye, wiping the wetness away before anybody could see it.

Denny walked over to Solomon and placed his hand on his shoulder as Cleveland looked on from several yards away.

"The day they break your will is the day you lose your real salvation." With a defiant glower, he said, "Salvation is the freedom to do what you want. Don't ever forget that."

Denny marched toward the field alone. Cleveland grabbed Solomon by the shoulder, and they slowly followed in Denny's tracks.

"Grizzly did the same thing to me the first go-around."

Solomon's mind was working overtime as he tried to make sense of it all.

"I don't get it, man," sighed Solomon with a blank look on his face. "He wants me to 'come to the Lord,' yet he does things that peeve me off to high heaven."

Cleveland answered, "There's a Bible verse that Pastor Paul likes to quote. Somewhere in the book of Romans, it says," he stopped a second to think, "well, it says something like 'we rejoice in our suffering, because suffering produces perseverance; perseverance, character; and character, hope.' Pastor Paul claims it's that 'hope' that gives you the faith you need to trust in Jesus."

Solomon peered at Cleveland uneasily. "Cleveland, something is going on with you, and I don't think you even know it."

"What are you talking about?"

"It's like, your attitude, the way you talk." Solomon struggled for the right words. "It's like you're starting to believe some of this junk. You remind me of a girl back..."

Solomon's face fell blank as he silently muttered the rest of the sentence.

"You mean Allison?"

Solomon looked as if he had seen a ghost.

"How do you know about her?"

Cleveland snickered and shook his head.

"You don't even know it, do you?"

"Know what?" shot back Solomon.

"You're constantly whispering her name in your sleep, Solomon."

Solomon closed his eyes. Anger was building inside him as he thought about Jesus and Allison. It was then, at that very moment, that he realized he was angrier at himself than at them.

"I broke up with her, and that's that. And you're dreaming if you think I'm whispering her name at night."

Cleveland rolled his eyes. "Whatever. You're in a total state of denial." He eyed him with a knowing grin. "You still love her, don't you?"

"Don't try to change the subject. We're talking about you, Cleveland. I want to know if you are going to convert. You're certainly beginning to act like it."

Poker-faced, Cleveland responded. "Maybe Jesus is trying to get to you through Allison."

They approached Denny, who was already chopping away at some weeds.

"Hey, preacher boy," Denny called.

Solomon and Denny both watched for Cleveland's reaction. Cleveland bit his lip as he hastily grabbed his hoe. He raised it over his head and held it there for several seconds as he glanced at his friends. Then he slammed it into the dirt with all his might.

———

Allison smiled out of politeness. She grabbed a French fry and bit into it, struggling to pay attention to what Brad was saying.

"Being one of the top quarterbacks in the conference, I'm hoping to get in to one of the prestigious schools near Jerusalem."

She avoided any meaningful eye contact.

"Uh, that's great, Brad. How's your mother doing?"

"Why do you want to talk about my mother? Don't you like football?"

Allison stared at the self-glorifying jock and sighed. The date her mother had arranged was not going as planned. If anything, their total lack of shared interests made her miss Solomon all the more.

She tried her best to smile. "Brad, football is okay, but you seem to be preoccupied with it. For the past hour and a half, you haven't been able to talk about anything else."

The look on his face said, "Yeah, so what's the problem?"

"Our mothers are good friends, and I was just hoping to change the subject. But since we've established that football is all-important to you, would you like to know what's the most important thing in my life?

Brad popped a carrot stick in his mouth and began chewing on it. Saying a quick prayer, Allison plunged ahead.

"The most important thing is my life is a person; it is Jesus Christ and my relationship to Him."

"Hey, I go to church three times a week," rationalized Brad.

Allison shook her head as she wiped her mouth with a napkin.

"Brad, that's good, but why do you go? Do you go to church because you have to, because you want to be seen, because you want to get a date, or because you know you won't get a decent job in Christ's economy if you don't go? Brad, have you ever been truly converted? Do you know Jesus as your Savior and Friend?"

Brad threw his napkin on the table and stood up. He gave Allison a disgusted look.

"Who gave you the right to judge me? This date is over. I'm out of here. Find your own way home, Ms. Perfect."

As Brad stormed out of the restaurant, Allison felt the Holy Spirit comfort her. Things hadn't gone the way she had hoped, but she knew she had been faithful in trying to share her faith. The waitress walked over to the table and smiled.

"That was a complete disaster, huh? Looks like he wasn't interested in what you were selling."

Allison looked at her with puzzlement.

"No, I'm afraid he didn't want to hear what I had to say. He's not saved, and I'm going to take every opportunity I have to witness. Satan will be released soon, you know."

A glazed expression greeted her. People were becoming very strange, very quickly.

"Are you a born-again Christian?" Allison asked.

The young lady turned and walked toward the counter.

"I'm a Christian, but I wouldn't say I'm born again. You people are extremists."

Allison's face wilted at her words.

Blasphemy shot across the sky like a runaway meteor. He approached the southern tip of Israel and began to descend rapidly. The Dead Sea came into view. He cursed at the sight of this rejuvenated body of water.

"That's just like Christ," huffed Blasphemy. "Always trying to show off. If that's not pride, then I don't know what is."

He slowed as he searched for a small hole in the side of the mountain. What once had been barren was now lush with every kind of plant and tree.

"Where is that hole?" grumbled Blasphemy, carefully examining the mountain. He exhaled noisily as he searched over the same landscape repeatedly. "It was so much easier to see when it was rock," griped the demon. Several minutes and curses later, he spotted the opening under a towering, aged fig tree.

The demon plunged headfirst into the cramped opening and began descending into a black wormhole. In less than a minute, he was deep in the bowels of the earth. The hole widened as he traveled downward. Complete darkness filled the cavity, which gave Blasphemy a warm, fuzzy feeling inside. He exited into a mammoth cavern the size of New York

City. Below him bright lava bubbled at his feet; above him was a ceiling of coal. Traveling horizontally to the east, he came to a thin, steep mountain six hundred and sixty-six feet high. His heart thumped against his chest as he flew toward the top of the peak.

"I don't believe it," stammered Blasphemy, staring at pieces of precious metal scattered around a platform.

He rushed toward the top of the dark mountain and quickly landed among the strewn rubble. He picked up a chunk of gold and stared at it.

"I did it," spoke a soft voice.

Blasphemy yanked his head around as he drew his sword in front of him.

"Michael!" muttered Blasphemy, raising himself on his hind legs.

"Satan's kingdom has been destroyed," said the archangel as he placed his hand on his weapon.

Blasphemy began laughing uncontrollably. Michael tilted his head in confusion.

"Your reaction is quite," he thought for a moment, "remarkable."

The demon put his sword away and tossed the broken jewel into the boiling lava below.

"Are you on my team?" asked Blasphemy in a condescending way.

"Far from it." The angel kept his hand on his sword.

"Look at this place. Satan's throne has been decimated, and you don't understand why I am overjoyed."

The archangel stared at the demon.

"You have done my dirty work for me," snorted Blasphemy.

Michael nodded his head in understanding. "Ah, what you don't comprehend, demon, is that you were part of that kingdom."

The stiff, black hair on Blasphemy's back stood on end. "Were?"

"I did not come here to debate the accuracy of prophecy," announced Michael. His wings lifted him off the ground. "If you're looking for your fearless leader, you will

192

find him down that way," pointed the archangel as he flew toward the exit.

"I will see you in hell!" shouted Blasphemy as he picked up a piece of gold and threw it at the angel.

The archangel quickly turned around and caught the projectile with his thumb and forefinger. "No, Blasphemy. I will see you there—sooner than you expect."

"Go bow to your loving Creator," mocked Blasphemy as Michael disappeared from sight, but not from mind.

He screamed violently, kicking the silver and gold nuggets off the cliff. He panted as he stared at the hole Michael had pointed toward. The drool inside his mouth started to boil.

"So much revenge, so little time."

Ken reached for the light sensor on the edge of the bed. The bedroom light flickered off. A few streaks of dim light brightened the darkness of the hotel room.

"So, what are you saying?" asked Ken, his hands propping his head against the pillow.

"Ken," began Emily with more than a hint of irritation in her voice, "sometimes you don't listen very well."

"Honey, try me again." He stared at the ceiling.

"Why don't you start by looking at me," chided Emily as she lay on her side, staring into his ear.

Ken uttered his "not this again" grunt, and begrudgingly turned toward her.

"I don't think we took an active enough role in Solomon's spiritual growth," she began, peering in his half-closed eyes.

"We've been through this a hundred times, Emily. I think your emotions are talking, not the facts." He knew she didn't like to hear that, but he thought it was true.

"Cut it with that emotional woman stuff!" She turned on her back and huffed. She didn't want to hear that, although she knew it was partially true.

Ken moved closer to her as he spoke. "Come on, honey. I'm just saying, give me some examples. You say this is the problem, but you don't have anything to support your point."

Emily puckered her lips as she thought. A smug grin slowly emerged on Ken's face as silence filled the room. As time passed, his grin grew. Through the corner of her eyes, she could see his face brighten. She elbowed him in the side. She was human and didn't like to be wrong, especially when it made Ken right.

"What was that for?" he groaned, folding up into a tight ball.

"That was for being right, but having a rotten attitude about it. Remember, pride comes before a fall."

Ken tried to talk, but couldn't. He scooted his body off the bed and carefully walked toward the bathroom.

"Cat got your tongue," smirked Emily.

"No...your elbow has it."

With Ken in the bathroom, Emily began to think about what Solomon was going through. The workings of Jesus' detention camps were required reading in the millennial kingdom. The Lord wanted everyone to understand that sin wasn't worth its price tag.

She pictured her son bent over a hoe, blisters covering his body. She gasped at the thought of his wasting away to a skeleton, covered only by a thin layer of sunburned skin. She turned on her stomach and buried her face in the pillow, hoping to erase the nightmarish images. It didn't work. There was her son, his head drooping to his chest, his hands barely able to grasp the tool.

Then the scene shifted to slow motion. Solomon was handed a scrap of bread and a cup of filthy water. The moldy crust teetered on the edge of his lips. Then, it suddenly plunged toward the roach-infested floor. Solomon didn't have the energy to respond as his half-tilted head rocked back and forth under the cruel noontime sun. Several roaches fought over the crumbs as they crawled over his calloused feet.

A security guard smiled cruelly at Solomon. His hand held a bullwhip. "Pick up that bread and stop littering our fine restaurant," he screamed as he smacked Solomon's back over and over again.

Emily rolled over and hit the light sensor. Breathing heavily, she looked at the closed bathroom door, assuring herself that what she had been thinking was not real. She took a few moments to try to obliterate her terrifying thoughts.

"Ken, what are you doing in there? Reading the entire English dictionary?"

A second later, the door opened, and Ken appeared. He walked slowly toward the bed, emotional exhaustion etched on his face.

"How bad are those camps, really?" Her eyes were moist.

He didn't want to hurt her any more than she was already hurting, but he had little choice. "I'm not going to lie to you, Emily. It's a lot of hard work with absolutely no downtime at all. I can assure you there is no fun or joy there."

Emily gulped as she stared sadly at her husband. "They're going to kill him in there."

"Come on, Emily. They're not going to kill him. A little bit of hard work never hurt anybody. It will make him grow up and become a man, and, God willing, a righteous man."

Words meant for comfort enflamed her anxieties.

"Ken, he's not used to that kind of work." She sat up in the bed, then slumped over in thought. "I'm afraid the work will just make him angrier and push him further from God, not closer."

Ken sat down beside her and took her hand.

"You may be right, Emily." Ken placed his hand under her chin, gently raising her face to meet his. "Think about it for a moment, though. Does Jesus know what He is doing?"

"Well, uh, yes."

The hesitation in her voice bothered Ken.

"If you trust Jesus, then why are you second-guessing Him?"

Emily shook her head in protest. "I'm not second-guessing Him. I'm just frustrated by not having my boy with me."

"Emily, you said a second ago that you were afraid. Now, I don't want to preach to you or overspiritualize the situation, but being afraid is fear." He looked at her, hoping she would finish his thought, but she didn't. "And fear is not from God."

Emily punched the light sensor off.

"Don't preach to me, Ken; just love me."

He took her in his arms. "I only preach to you because I love you."

———————

Three maple trees, six large tropical bushes, and some overgrown desert grass camouflaged Fester. His bravery was evident only when Blasphemy was by his side. Alone, he was a sniveling coward who often jumped at his own shadow.

Fester was lying comfortably on the ground, watching occasional groups of spirits pass overhead. Suddenly, a deafening scream jerked him to his senses. The demon pushed through the brush and flew to examine the camp surroundings. Several dozen boys were standing in a circle, staring at someone on the ground. The little sense Fester possessed was tossed aside. He raced toward the camp and hovered over the scene.

"I need a shirt—now," screamed a frantic boy.

Solomon ripped off his shirt and tossed it to him.

"Everybody stand back so he can breathe," yelled Cleveland as he wrapped the shirt around the boy's severed foot.

"Wrap it as tight as you can and push hard against the vein," added Solomon, who was now crouched next to Denny.

"I'm going to die, oh, God, no," he moaned.

Grizzly ran toward the scene with a loudspeaker in tow.

"Everybody back up and clear the area. Medical help is on the way."

The circle slowly expanded as the boys obeyed.

"What happened?" asked Grizzly as he grabbed the tourniquet and tightened it as hard as he could.

"He chopped part of his foot off with his own hoe," Cleveland said.

"If he had been getting some sleep lately," said Solomon in an ugly tone, "this never would have happened."

Denny was breaking down. "Oh, no, just kill me now."

The medics arrived on an air vehicle and quickly assessed the situation.

"Load him on board, now!" directed the senior technician.

Grizzly backed away and spoke sharply to Solomon. "Not another word from you," he ordered.

Grizzly turned around and started to head back to his office. His parting words were, "Everybody back to work."

The sight of blood hypnotized Fester. He hovered over the gruesome scene until Denny was lifted away in the ambulance. He looked at Solomon and began to salivate. He wondered where the angels were. Where was this boy's protection? He laughed as he thought of the possibilities. They had surely seen him, and they were scared away! He edged closer to the boy and whispered something in his ear. Solomon's face turned bitter at the words. Solomon moved toward Cleveland.

"This is Grizzly's fault, and he will pay!"

Cleveland stared at Solomon for a moment.

"If Denny had kept his nose clean, it wouldn't have been bloodied."

Fester laughed as he flew toward his hideaway. As he dropped into the grass, something grabbed him by the neck and stole his sword.

"He's mine," said Timothy, tightening his grip with each word. "What did you say to him?"

Fester struggled to get free, but Timothy had both his arms behind his back and was pressing his torso against Fester's wings. Fester twisted to look him in the face.

"I told him he should worship Jesus because He's worthy of honor, and glory, and—"

Timothy pushed with all his muscle, sending waves of pain down the demon's back.

"Try again."

"Ouch! All right! Calm down, angel." Fester's shoulders were on fire. "I told him to be careful out there. He could get hurt."

Timothy glanced at Daniel, who was keeping lookout twenty yards away on the edge of the field. Daniel shook his head.

"My friend over there doesn't seem to believe you, and I don't think I do either."

Fester smiled, taking his words as a compliment.

Timothy added, "I have this recording I made of you about fifteen minutes ago, when you were lying in the grass watching the clouds float by."

The demon's face turned pale.

"Wouldn't it be interesting to see Blasphemy's reaction when he hears about your total disdain for him?"

Fester muttered an incoherent curse word. "I told Solomon that the warden was responsible for that boy's accident."

Timothy slung Fester's sword toward the middle of the camp. It landed on the roof of the church. "I would think twice before fetching it. The angels inside that church aren't nearly as polite as I." Timothy slowly released his hold on the demon, then suddenly whacked him squarely on top of the head. The shot knocked him out cold.

Back in the field, Solomon grabbed the bloodied hoe away from one of the departing medics.

"He was my best friend. I would like to keep it."

The medic nodded and ran toward the vehicle. Cleveland looked at Solomon with a measure of distrust in his eyes.

"He's your best friend?" questioned Cleveland.

"Yeah, we're blood brothers now. We had the ceremony last night while you were reading your Bible."

"It was an assignment that happens to be mandatory," countered Cleveland.

Solomon scoffed. "I think you're starting to enjoy reading that hate book." He heard himself speak, but his heart wasn't in it. He looked away, attempting to mask his confusion.

Cleveland shook his head as he began tilling the ground. He glanced at Solomon, who was standing over Denny's pool of blood. He didn't believe Solomon either. They were both changing, and it felt kind of good.

Blasphemy flew through the hole at lightning speed, clutching the tattered pieces of Satan's throne in each hand. The glittering metal seemed to energize the demon as he traveled toward Satan's cell. Blasphemy had already formulated a script in his head, which he was replaying repeatedly. He knew this moment occurred only once in a lifetime, and he wasn't about to leave the outcome to chance.

The black hole narrowed to a size that could barely accommodate Blasphemy. His eyes picked up flashes of purple light in the distance. This is it, thought the demon as he flung a piece of gold toward the light. Seconds later, he heard a loud scream echo from in front of him. Blasphemy had to slow down as he delicately maneuvered his sleek body through the last of the rocks. As the light grew brighter, his heart beat faster. Suddenly, he got his first glimpse of the Dragon in nearly a thousand years. Goose bumps sent shivers throughout his body as he came face-to-face with Satan. The Devil appeared emotionless as he stared at Blasphemy. A lump of gold was stuck in his left thigh.

"Master," began Blasphemy, "it's so good to see you in one piece."

Satan continued to display his poker face.

Blasphemy bowed in a mocking manner. "My apologies about that rock. I didn't know you were down here."

A vile expression surfaced on the Dragon's face. "Where did you get that gold?"

Blasphemy laughed as he began tossing the rest of the rocks at Satan, several of them hitting him in the head.

"Oh, these. Well, this was your throne." A cockeyed smile filled his face as he rested his body against the force field encapsulating Satan. "I destroyed it because," he paused, "because it reminded me of an overbearing, self-centered demon that I would rather forget about."

Searing steam flowed from Satan's nostrils.

"From your actions, Blasphemy, one must assume you don't believe I will be getting out, at least not in your life-time."

Blasphemy angled his ear toward the Dragon. "Get out of here? I don't think so, considering I was the one respon-sible for jailing you in the first place."

A haunting laugh shook the chamber. "I think one of those rocks has done permanent damage to that ugly, de-mented skull of yours."

Blasphemy's face went blank. "The world is now mine to rule as I see fit, and there's nothing you can do to stop me!"

Satan was uncharacteristically at a loss for words. His humiliating position left him fuming in silent rage.

"I'll give your best to my troops," mocked Blasphemy as he turned to leave. "I'm sure they will be saddened by the report of your death."

Blasphemy enjoyed one last look at his trembling nemesis, then quickly disappeared through the hole. Sec-onds later, an earsplitting squeal shot from the hole.

"Whoa, ouch, what's happening?" cried Blasphemy as something transported him back toward Satan. The total darkness prevented the demon from recognizing the in-truder; he could see only the eyes.

"Who...who are you?" bleated Blasphemy as the angel held both of the demon's arms behind his back.

The angel remained mute as they approached Satan's hole. Blasphemy tried to kick, bite, squirm, and talk his way to freedom.

"I'll give you half my kingdom if you will only identify yourself," spouted the demon.

As the ricocheting rays of lightning struck the dark-ness, the angel spoke.

"I'm the archangel Michael," announced the angel in a deep, authoritative tone. Blasphemy gasped. "Since you have no kingdom, I'll assume your generous offer is quite worthless."

The archangel threw Blasphemy against a half-melted boulder only yards from Satan. The demon had never experienced such brute force in his life, so he wisely stayed low, nursing his wounds.

"I can actually say it's good to see you," Satan said as he glared at the archangel and then at Blasphemy.

The demons had never seen Michael in this mode before. His eyes were filled with fire, his muscles pulsing with power.

"In twenty-four hours, Satan," began Michael, "you will be released for a short time."

Blasphemy gulped deeply and then began to hyperventilate. Satan smirked at them both.

"You call it releasing; I call it breaking free," bragged the Devil.

"Your ability to lie has never been in question," responded Michael, "and those who are perishing with you will believe the lie."

Satan didn't try to free himself from the force field. He knew that words were more powerful than swords.

"It is you, Michael, who believe the lies of Jehovah God. Truth is relative, and more than anyone, you know that!"

Blasphemy said nothing, knowing deep down that he was out of his league. He watched in amazement as they continued to banter.

"Truth is relative, Satan," the archangel paused to watch the Devil's reaction, "to those who don't believe in absolute truth."

Satan retorted, "You play with words eloquently, but words are meaningless without underlying ideas to support them."

"Then I might assume that it wasn't a lie when Blasphemy claimed to destroy your throne, when, in fact, it was I."

Satan hissed like a snake as he eyed Blasphemy and then Michael.

"You will pay for your sins!"

The archangel ignored Satan's response, turning toward the dribbling demon on the ground.

"If I were you, I would hide from the wrath of the Devil. You can flee from him, but not from the coming wrath of the Holy One."

Solomon inhaled his lunch as if it were his last. Cleveland looked at him with disgust.

"You're acting like a pig."

Solomon stopped to breathe. "If you missed dinner every day, you would be pigging out, too."

Cleveland toyed with his lima beans as he thought. "You know, Solomon, the warden is not that bad of a guy if you obey his rules."

Solomon was chewing on a large piece of beef when he responded. "That's my problem; I don't like his rules!"

"The sooner you learn who's boss, the better life will be for you."

Solomon swallowed the beef prematurely, almost choking in the process. Cleveland was beginning to get to him in a big way. He didn't realize that it wasn't Cleveland at all, but God.

"I thought we just had this conversation, and you know what, I don't want to hear it anymore. Got it?" Solomon aggressively stabbed a fist-sized piece of beef. "Why don't you go bunk with him since you seem to love him so much?" Solomon grumbled.

Cleveland shook his head. "Come on, man. I want to be your friend. I'm just trying to tell you the way it is."

Solomon grunted, choosing food over conversation. Cleveland picked up his half-empty tray and walked toward the kitchen.

"Have it your way, and see where it gets you."

The door to the mess hall swung open. Grizzly walked in like a gunfighter in a western movie.

"Solomon, swallow what's in your mouth, and get to church," Grizzly commanded.

Solomon stuffed his mouth as quickly as he could. The warden walked toward him and, in a booming voice that everyone could hear, ordered, "Spit it out, and get moving!"

Solomon looked up from his plate. He angrily muttered, "I'm still hungry."

Grizzly stood over him like a vulture ready for dinner. "Let's hope that voracious appetite extends to the things of God." He looked around the room as the boys filed past the kitchen garbage can. "No more work today, gentlemen. We are going to have an old-fashioned revival."

Solomon quickly trashed his food and caught up with Cleveland outside the hall. "What's this all about?"

"When somebody gets hurt, which is often around here, Grizzly always calls a revival. It's his way of trying to use a negative and turn it into a positive."

Solomon was more confused than ever. "I don't get it."

"Some of the guys may think that they are next, that they could get hurt or even killed out there. It makes you think about death and what's going to happen."

Solomon sighed as he stared at the wooden cross on the church. "How long are we going to be in there?"

Cleveland seemed to smile. "Last revival went right till midnight. Man, did my butt hurt."

"Great," Solomon huffed. "I think I'd rather be in the fields."

"One wrong move in there, and you will be," warned Cleveland.

Solomon glanced toward the barren field, his heart aching within. His eyes fell on the steeple of the church. He sighed as his heart strayed to happier days—to times with Allison, walking toward their hometown church, hand in hand, heart to heart.

Ten

Red Sky in the Morning

The rambunctious boys quickly settled down when Pastor Paul appeared. Solomon turned around and looked at Grizzly who was eyeing him from the back row. He whispered to Cleveland.

"Why are we so close to the front?"

Cleveland whispered back, "Who would you rather be close to—the pastor or the warden?"

Solomon waved at the warden and returned his eyes to the front. Pastor Paul's eyes looked red and swollen. He stared at the boys for what seemed like an eternity. Occasionally, he would take his handkerchief out and wipe his face. Solomon started to say something again, but Cleveland squeezed his knee and gave a slight shake of his head.

"A quick report from the doctors about Denny's condition would be appropriate," began the pastor as he focused particularly on Solomon and Cleveland. "They have been able to reattach his foot, and I'm glad to report that he will make a full recovery, though he may have a slight limp for a time."

Solomon was relieved to hear the news, but Cleveland seemed disinterested, as if he were lost in his thoughts. Solomon nudged him back to earth and then scribbled a note. "Denny's going to be fine!" Cleveland grinned and gave him a "thumbs-up."

"I want to start this revival with a bit of information about me that I hope you will use to the glory of God." The pastor placed his Bible on the pulpit and walked around the other side. "Several boys across the years have inquired about my past, and this afternoon, I would like to tell you my story, which may shock some of you."

Solomon wiggled around in the pew like a cat trying to settle itself in for the night. He thought about the revivals he and Allison had attended when they were younger. Cleveland stared at the pastor without batting an eye.

"In my sordid past, I did things that would make the worst of you seem to be saints. I would hunt down Christians and would approve their executions, often, in the most cruel and inhuman ways imaginable."

Every eye was glued to Paul as he continued his confession.

"You see, I used to think that I was on the highway to heaven. I believed that it was my way, or no way. I grew up in a deeply religious household just like everyone of you boys, and I was taught right from wrong at an early age. Now, I'm speaking of a time that most of you consider ancient history, and that some even believe didn't exist at all."

The pastor seemed to be struggling. He closed his eyes and prayed silently for a moment, then resumed his story. Solomon glanced at Cleveland, who was sitting on the edge of the seat, gripping the pew in front of him.

"Years ago, when I told people that I had heard the audible voice of Jesus, they often mocked me and laughed at me. But hearing Him speak to me changed my life forever.

"Today, I'm at a loss how you, each of you, not only can hear His voice anytime you choose, but also see His face, and His nail-scarred hands and feet, but somehow not believe."

Pastor Paul sensed that he was losing some of his audience, so he cut to the grand revelation.

"I am the 'Paul' who wrote much of the New Testament."

Grizzly smiled at these words. He had always thought that the pastor might be the real McCoy, but he could never gather the courage to ask. Cleveland's jaw fell open. Solomon looked around the room. Half of the audience seemed in awe; the other half appeared to be bored, including Solomon.

"I reveal this truth for one reason only. My prayer is that this revelation would open your heart to God. I've never told a soul before because I didn't want people to look up to me as if I were some great man. The truth is, I was one of the worst sinners, saved only by God's grace, and that grace is freely available to each of you today."

Pastor Paul moved behind the pulpit and lifted the Bible as he said, "The time to choose is at hand. It's right at the door. Each of you must decide whom you will follow. That decision will determine what path you take. There are two roads. One is wide and leads to death and destruction; the other is narrow and leads to life and joy beyond your wildest dreams. The words in this Book," he waved it overhead, "are true and holy. You have seen the Author of this book your entire lives, yet most of you refuse to believe He is your Messiah."

Solomon sneaked a look at Cleveland, whose face was wet with tears.

"This Book tells us that Satan will be released at the end of the thousand-year period in which we now live." Paul slowly walked up the aisle, making eye contact with many of the boys, including Cleveland and Solomon. "Though you will not be able to see him with your naked eyes, the Devil himself will be freely roaming this planet tomorrow afternoon."

Several of the boys near the back of the sanctuary chuckled. Grizzly quickly stood up and eyed them. The pastor immediately rushed to the back of the church.

"Warden, hold the guns for a second," the pastor said as he nudged his way in between two of the louder renegades and sat down. "I used to snicker at the claims of the Bible, too."

The two boys were about sixteen. Their thin faces didn't hide their animosity for the Lord or the pastor.

"I assume you don't believe my words?" tested Pastor Paul.

"Nope," responded Billy, the larger of the two.

"Not in your lifetime," said the other, named Todd.

Paul didn't appear to be shocked by their faithlessness; if anything, he seemed energized.

"If you saw the Devil with your own eyes, would you believe me then?"

"The Devil is a figment of your religion," joked Todd. "He doesn't exist." The other nodded in agreement.

Paul retorted. "But you didn't answer my question. If you could see the Devil, would you believe me?"

"I would fall down and worship your Jesus if that happened," blurted Billy in a condescending manner.

Grizzly quickly moved toward them. "You will show respect for the pastor. Do you two understand me?"

The boys nodded sheepishly. Paul waved Grizzly back.

"For thousands of years, nobody could see Jesus. He was sitting at the right hand of God Almighty, and many like you said the same thing about the Lord. Yet today, in this current age, you can see Jesus with your own eyes, but you still refuse to believe in your heart. I hope you boys see that your position is not logical."

"We're not talking about Jesus," said Todd. "We're talking about the Devil."

Pastor Paul stood and walked toward the pulpit.

"Isn't it sad, folks, when we refuse the Lord to His face, yet make grand statements about loving Him if we could see His adversary, the Devil."

Several in the church began to mumble to themselves.

"You have all heard the term 'doubting Thomas.' This phrase originated during Christ's first visit to planet Earth. After He had risen from the dead, several of the apostles, including Thomas, hadn't seen Him yet. When the others reported their sightings of the Lord, they told Thomas the good news. He said, and I quote, 'Unless I see in His hands the print of the nails, and put my finger into the print of the nails, and put my hand into His side, I will not believe.' Then the Bible continues with the story and miraculously, Jesus does appear and He says to Thomas, 'Reach your finger here, and look at My hands; and reach your hand here, and put it into My side. Do not be unbelieving, but believing.'"

Pastor Paul stared at Todd and Billy and then frowned.

"You two won't believe even if you do see the Devil. But I promise you and everybody in this church today that you will see the Devil one day if you do not repent of your wicked ways and commit your lives to Jesus and His authority." His face turned white as a ghost as his eyes dropped to the ground. His voice began to tremble as he softly muttered, "In fact, you will see much more of him than you could possibly imagine."

Allison frowned.

"Honey, I'm sorry it didn't go well," her mother said as she sat on the edge of Allison's bed.

Allison stared at the ceiling as she lay under the covers.

"He was so conceited, Mom. All he could talk about was how amazing he was at football."

Gail shook her head. "I've been friends with his mother for a long time. It's so surprising."

Allison looked sadly at her mother. "No matter what I try to do, I can't seem to get Solomon out of my heart." She started to cry.

Gail hugged her long and hard.

"Maybe Jesus doesn't want you to let go of him."

Allison calmed herself a bit.

"What do you mean?"

Gail edged closer to her daughter.

"Just food for thought, but maybe God wants you to love Solomon so you will pray for him constantly, until he gives his heart to the Lord."

"You think so?" Allison said, drying her eyes.

"Prayer can't hurt, and we know it can help."

Allison sat up in bed as the start of a smile emerged on her face.

"You're the best, Mom."

Allison reached out and hugged her mother.

Gail said, "Has Solomon answered your letter yet?"

"No!" she vented. "He'd better, if he knows what's good for him."

Gail looked at her daughter compassionately.

"Be patient with him."

"I'll try, Mom."

"And keep praying."

"I will. You can count on that!"

General Ruse hunkered down behind a boulder the size of a small house. He had one eye on a hole in the side of the mountain and the other on a group of angels circling overhead.

"Blasted vultures," griped the demon.

He had been in hiding, devising a plan to get even with Blasphemy. Ever since that humiliating moment when Blasphemy threatened him in front of the troops, he could think of nothing but revenge.

"Oh, Blasphemy," muttered Ruse to himself, "it's going to be sweet, so very sweet to see you suffer and be humiliated in front of the whole world."

Suddenly, Blasphemy exploded out of the mountain at full throttle. General Ruse darted after him, cursing Blasphemy and the Lord in the same breath. Blasphemy didn't notice the demon trailing him. He was panting heavily as he shot into the sky, flying on nothing but fear and a surge of power after his encounter with Michael and Satan. General Ruse tailed him as Blasphemy jetted toward the sun.

"They will pay!" screamed Blasphemy as he fed on the light of the sun.

Ruse was within a sword's distance when he grabbed his dagger and steadied it. He imagined slicing Blasphemy into a million pieces and casually tossing the remains into space. He pictured himself in front of the demons, proclaiming his own greatness and leading them into a successful war against Jehovah God. Then, a second, more despicable thought suddenly came to his mind. His wings slowed as he put his sword back.

"That would be too easy, wouldn't it, Blasphemy?" he prattled to himself. He watched Blasphemy speed toward the sun. Laughing loudly as a brilliant idea flashed into his mind, he murmured under his breath, "Enjoy the vacation, my dear Blasphemy. It will be your last!"

"No way! Forget it; don't even think it—not in this lifetime!"

"I see there may be some wiggle room in there, right?"

Emily pushed Ken against a palm tree and held him there by her own body. A radiant yet firm smile adorned her face as she kissed him quickly.

"Ken Action, I'm not doing it. You've always been the one with the wild streak, not me, and I'm not starting now. Got it?"

Ken studied the fifteen-foot wings of a hang glider. "I understand where you're coming from, Emily." Ken was hopping around with excitement. He grabbed her hands and gave her his best puppy-dog look. "Come on, honey. This isn't dangerous, and it will help take your mind off all the worries of the world."

Emily shot back, "My greatest worry is going up in that thing." She pointed at the hang glider, fear filling her eyes. "I don't like heights, Ken, and you can't make me do it."

Ken sighed heavily and walked away at a snail's pace. "You've got to learn to face your fears head-on."

Emily countered, "And you have to learn to respect my feelings and learn what the word no means."

"Just forget about it," he mumbled to himself as he walked toward the hang glider. The sight of the machine generated an enthusiasm he hadn't felt since childhood. As he drew closer, his eyes inspected every inch of it. The atomic motor, the size of a grapefruit, was located at the rear of the contraption, underneath the captain's seat. The wings were bright orange, light, and maneuverable, and they had the capacity to react to the smallest shifts in wind or motor power.

He placed his hand against the seat and turned toward Emily, who was a good fifty yards away.

Ken squinted and raised his hands into the air. "So are you coming?"

Emily shook her head but walked toward Ken. She stared at him as if he were a child.

"Ken Action, this had better be good. What's the difference between this thing and an air vehicle?"

Emily watched his hand caressing the leather seat as he admired the beauty of the machine. "It would be nice if you were that gentle with me."

Ken jumped away from the aircraft and cuddled Emily in his arms.

"How's that?"

A distrusting look appeared on her face. "Will the real Ken Action please stand up?"

Ken seemed taken aback by her response. "Come on, Emily. Just one ride." He moved his eyebrows up and down and smiled hard. "Do this one thing for me, and I guarantee—"

She interrupted, "And you guarantee what, Mr. Macho? Let me count the past promises that you left at the altar." She paused to think as Ken began squirming. "Promise number one, I will stop forgetting to close the clothes hamper. Promise number two, I'll never drive like a maniac when you're with me. Promise number three, I will always listen to you when you speak."

"Hey, hey, now, just wait a minute. I keep those promises," he paused and frowned, "at least most of the time."

"Yeah, your definition of *most* is when you think about it, which barely exceeds fifty percent of the time." He stared at her, speechless. "And that's on a good week," Emily added. "Promise number four, I will remember to feed the fish before they starve to death." Ken looked exasperated, but guilty. "Promise number five, I will not mistake plant food for the bird's food."

Ken threw his hands in the air. "Ah, just forget about it." He walked past Emily with his hands shoved in his pants pockets.

Emily smiled; she knew she had him. "Just one ride, and only for a minute."

Life surged back into Ken. "Yes," he purred loudly as he turned around and sprinted toward Emily. He quickly hugged her and jumped into the pilot's seat.

Emily stared at Ken; he stared at the motorized glider. "One minute," she slowed her words so he would hear her, "which equals sixty seconds."

His eyes were darting in all directions as he punched a few buttons. "Gotcha, dear," he said.

She carefully sat down beside him, placed a seatbelt across her chest, and strapped on a helmet. A cunning grin greeted Ken as she tugged on his arm. "So, what did I just say?"

A blank stare gripped Ken's face. His hands and fingers suddenly stopped so his brain could work. The extended pause didn't surprise Emily. Life suddenly returned to Ken as he responded.

"You said to be careful and don't do anything crazy."

Emily closed her eyes and shook her head. She patted him on the back as she spoke. "Good try, honey."

Ken ignored her as the hang glider's engine started humming. His hands tightly gripped the airplane-like control stick. He adjusted his sunglasses as he said, "Hold on tight."

"Don't worry about that," she sighed as she watched the crazed expression on her husband's face.

The hang glider started taxiing down the beach. It took only a few seconds for it to break free from gravity's hold. The wind against Ken's face invigorated him. Emily watched him instead of the ground. The glider reached an altitude of twenty-five hundred feet within a few seconds. Ken pushed a button, which instantly turned off the engine.

"What did you do that for?" Emily asked as she glanced fearfully toward the ocean.

Ken looked at her and smiled. "Honey, this is a glider. Once you get up where you want to be, you *glide* back down to the ground like an eagle."

"Oh," she said confused. "I thought this was one of those machines all the teenagers were talking about. You know, the ones where you nosedive toward the ground like a crazy person."

Ken appeared surprised. "Oh, come on, honey. You're talking about the 'radar vipers' that just hit the market." He studied the dashboard for several seconds and began to fidget in his seat. "I didn't think this was one of them, but guess what?"

"Oh, let me guess," said Emily as she tried to act shocked, "this is a," she stuttered thinking of the name, "a 'radar viper.'"

"How did you know?" he shot back as he started tilting the wings downward.

Emily took one last look at the ocean. "Just a wild guess." She shrugged her shoulders and closed her eyes.

"When you start your nosedive," began Ken in his best instructor's voice, "the onboard radar calculates how far you are from land, or for us, the ocean."

The viper started angling downward as he continued the science lesson to his unresponsive and disinterested wife.

"Just as you reach the moment of no return, or when you get too close to the ground, it suddenly turns at the very last millisecond and you're saved from certain death." Ken glanced at his wife as the aircraft increased its downward descent. "Do you think we could try it just once?"

Emily didn't respond. Her long life with Ken had trained her to "ride it out" and try to make him happy.

Ken excitedly tapped her on the shoulder. "Was that a yes?" Emily closed her eyes even harder and tensed her whole body. "I'll take that as a yes."

As the nosedive began, both of them screamed—one out of sheer panic and the other from pure joy. The sound of the wind increased to a screech as the small white caps of the ocean came into view.

"You will pay," shouted Emily over the sound of the wind.

Ken could barely hear her. "You like?"

Gravity pushed hard against their bodies as the point of no return drew near. Their faces crinkled against the force as the nosedive reached maximum impact.

"Yes!" bellowed Ken.

"No!" shrieked Emily.

They were only a hundred feet above the water when the glider suddenly yanked its nose upward. It was traveling at over two hundred miles per hour as it skimmed within a few feet of the water's surface. Emily cautiously opened her eyes and thanked God she wasn't dead. Ken thanked God, too, but for a different reason. He looped the glider around the edge of the water and onto the beach. Emily was shaking as she uncoiled her body from its grip of fear. She glared at Ken.

"No! I don't want to go again."

"Honey, that was the coolest thing we've ever done together. I didn't know you had it in you."

She unlatched her helmet as she spoke, "I *don't* have it in me." She was having a hard time looking at him. "You ever try that kind of stunt again, and you might end up a widower!"

Ken laughed nervously as he jumped out of the seat and ran around to her side of the machine. He reached his hand out to help her down, but she knocked it away.

"You treat me like a delicate flower one moment, and the next you act like I'm John Glenn."

Sensing his words had fallen on hard ground, Pastor Paul made his way toward the pulpit. He gripped his Bible, confident in the power of its words.

"I could have chosen to live in the New Jerusalem with the other resurrected saints, but my heart has always been to convert the coldhearted. In my previous life on Earth, I was killed for my faith, for believing that Jesus Christ is the only way to heaven. Back then, there were many religions that claimed to point toward the one, true God; yet, sadly, those who believed those myths died in their sins. They were dedicated, but dead; they were religious, but dead; they were moral, but dead."

Solomon's heart was aching. He didn't want to believe a word of what Paul was saying, yet the Spirit of God was slowly chipping away at the stone encapsulating his heart. Allison's and his parents' prayers were beginning to have an effect.

"Today, the great lie that has captured your souls is nothing new. The Bible says that 'there is nothing new under the sun.' The Devil's age-old lie has been around since the very moment Satan decided that he wanted to be like God. He was the first liar, and he and his forces seek to devour you with their lies."

He opened his Bible and began thumbing through the pages of the Old Testament. Several seconds later, he found his spot and began to speak.

"The book of Jeremiah, chapter five, starting with verse thirty, says, 'An astonishing and horrible thing has been committed in the land: The prophets prophesy falsely, and the priests rule by their own power; and My people love to have it so. But what will you do in the end?'"

He placed the Bible on the pulpit and sighed deeply. He slowly shook his head as he steadied his hands against the podium, gripping it firmly.

"These verses are relevant to you today. Your hometown preachers are telling you the truth, yes. But there are a select few, self-appointed leaders in this group who are spreading lies about God. You are convinced that you are right, and Jesus is wrong. You attempt to influence as many as you can so that you can feel good about yourself. Your form of peer pressure will be responsible for sending your followers into the fiery pit of hell."

A picture of Denny immediately came to Cleveland's mind. Solomon glanced at him with the same thought.

"Those of you who refuse to acknowledge Jesus as your Lord love to surround yourselves with those who would tell you otherwise. As it says in Second Timothy, 'For the time will come when they will not endure sound doctrine, but according to their own desires, because they have itching ears, they will heap up for themselves teachers; and they will turn their ears away from the truth, and be turned aside to fables.'"

The pastor banged his hand against the pulpit.

"You want to hear lies because your father was a liar from the beginning. You know the truth hurts, that it demands a change in your lifestyle. You don't embrace the truth, so you surround yourselves with like-minded rebels who make you feel good. Too many people feel good throughout life, but sadly, at the moment of death, misery and judgment await. Don't make that mistake, young men."

Cleveland could feel the blood pumping through his veins. Every thought pointed toward Jesus, whose truth he had rejected repeatedly.

"As the Scripture from Jeremiah asks, 'What will you do in the end?' What will you do when you are standing in front of a holy, jealous God whom you have denied? At that moment, you will not have the luxury of choosing Him, as you do today. The Bible says, 'Let God be true but every man a liar.' If your buddies want to go to hell, please, I beg you, do not accompany them to this place of no return."

Paul paused as he flipped forward a few pages in the Bible. He found the fourteenth chapter of Jeremiah, then said to the boys, "There was a time thousands of years ago when the nation of Israel was deeply religious, yet the people were deeply in sin. Enemies all around them wanted to destroy them, and the people were fearful that they would lose their homes, families, and country. God was going to destroy them for their hypocrisy, yet the prophets of the day refused to give the Israelites this most unpopular message. Here's what the passage says. 'Then the LORD said to me, "Do not pray for this people, for their good. When they fast, I will not hear their cry; and when they offer burnt offering and grain offering, I will not accept them. But I will consume them by the sword, by the famine, and by the pestilence." Then I said, "Ah, Lord GOD! Behold, the prophets say to them, 'You shall not see the sword, nor shall you have famine, but I will give you assured peace in this place.'" And the LORD said to me, "The prophets prophesy lies in My name. I have not sent them, commanded them, nor spoken to them; they prophesy to you a false vision, divination, a worthless thing, and the deceit of their heart. Therefore, thus says the LORD concerning the prophets who prophesy in My name, whom I did not send, and who say, 'Sword and famine shall not be in this land'; 'By sword and famine those prophets shall be consumed.'"'"

His words cut their hearts. Cleveland was weeping, and Solomon was on the brink of tears. Grizzly had never been so moved by the Spirit of God. Tears began steaming down Paul's face as God's Spirit filled the room.

"Do you really want to be destroyed?"

He paused for a full minute to let the message sink in. He stared at the boys with a heart void of judgment.

"Do you really believe what your friends are telling you? Do you trust them more than your parents, who raised you to know right from wrong? Do you really want to chance going to hell?"

Pastor Paul placed his Bible on the podium and meekly walked down the aisle. He stared at them without speaking. Words were unnecessary when God was at work. Paul looked at Solomon squarely in the eyes. Solomon quickly looked away.

Pastor Paul sighed, yet the Holy Spirit pushed him forward. "I began my message this afternoon informing you that Satan will be released tomorrow. The lies that I have been speaking about will grow stronger every day that he roams this earth. His demons want to eat you alive, and for many of you, they will. Today will be your greatest opportunity to fall in love with Jesus. After today, it will be all the harder to see through Satan's delusions."

The sound of crying boys filled the sanctuary. Cleveland stood to his feet and brushed by Solomon as he moved to the aisle of the church. Solomon's heart was moved, but not broken. He lowered his face behind the pew and tried not to think.

"That's right, come out of that pew and leave your former life behind. Receive the gift of eternal life," Paul urged as he met Cleveland halfway up the aisle. When their eyes met, Cleveland collapsed in the pastor's arms and wept. "God can do nothing with a hard vessel, but a broken vessel, a soft pot, He can mold into something great, something that will last for eternity."

Every eye in the church was fixed on Cleveland and Paul.

Paul said, "Look at me, son."

Cleveland immediately obeyed.

"Why have you come forward today?"

"Because," he sniffled, "I'm so tired of fighting God."

A charged hush filled the church.

"Are you prepared to follow God through sickness and health, through good and bad, until death unites you forever?"

Cleveland nodded his head.

"That's not good enough, son. I need to hear it from your heart."

Cleveland gulped. "Yes, I will follow God no matter what happens."

"Cleveland," Paul stared at him as if he were the teen's father, "I hope you understand that you are better off to sit down and not walk down this aisle if you don't mean it."

"I know, Pastor. I've faked coming to the altar many times in my childhood."

"Then you know that what you are doing today is not just making an emotional decision to follow Christ; you are choosing to make a lifetime commitment to the Lord."

Cleveland glanced at several of his hoodlum friends from the corner of his eyes. He sensed his fear of them was waning.

"Yes, sir. I'm choosing the Lord today because I love Him, and I know one hundred percent that He is who He claims He is."

Paul clutched Cleveland's hand and led him to the front of the church. Several of the militant boys began to loudly whisper from their seats. Pastor Paul jerked his body around and quoted Scripture to the vipers.

"The Bible says in the book of Luke, 'There was a certain rich man who was clothed in purple and fine linen and fared sumptuously every day. But there was a certain beggar named Lazarus, full of sores, who was laid at his gate, desiring to be fed with the crumbs which fell from the rich man's table. Moreover the dogs came and licked his sores.

So it was that the beggar died, and was carried by the angels to Abraham's bosom. The rich man also died and was buried. And being in torments in Hades, he lifted up his eyes and saw Abraham afar off, and Lazarus in his bosom. Then he cried and said, "Father Abraham, have mercy on me, and send Lazarus that he may dip the tip of his finger in water and cool my tongue; for I am tormented in this flame." But Abraham said, "Son, remember that in your lifetime you received your good things, and likewise Lazarus evil things; but now he is comforted and you are tormented. And besides all this, between us and you there is a great gulf fixed, so that those who want to pass from here to you cannot, nor can those from there pass to us." Then he said, "I beg you therefore, father, that you would send him to my father's house, for I have five brothers, that he may testify to them, lest they also come to this place of torment." Abraham said to him, "They have Moses and the prophets; let them hear them." And he said, "No, father Abraham; but if one goes to them from the dead, they will repent." But he said to him, "If they do not hear Moses and the prophets, neither will they be persuaded though one rise from the dead."'"

Paul continued to tightly grip Cleveland's hand as he preached to the skeptics. "One day soon, you who mock my brother Cleveland will be in that rich man's hell. You will see Cleveland in paradise, and your greatest wish will be that he would come and wet the tip of your burnt, smoking tongue."

The biblical imagery ripped away layers of pride in Solomon's heart. He wanted to run far away, live on a deserted island, and never see anybody again—not even Allison. Life wasn't as simple as he would have liked to believe.

Fire filled Paul's eyes. "As the Scriptures say, even if someone came from the dead to preach to you about hell, you wouldn't believe. Jesus died and came back to life, yet you mock Him and deride Him as a self-righteous, narrow-minded imposter. Hell was made for zealots like you. Let me assure you that Cleveland will not be looking down on you. Scripture doesn't say that. But part of your hell will be to see into heaven and its glories and all those you mocked, and know that you will never taste it, never."

Several boys stood to their feet and made a beeline for the altar. Pastor Paul clutched his hands against his heart as the joy of the Lord moved him.

"This can be the greatest day of your lives if only you will come to the Lord and repent of your waywardness. Repent, and be saved from the fires of hell. Yes, that's right. Come and walk down this aisle; kneel before this altar. Pray that God would save you from the Great White Throne Judgment that will soon come upon this world."

Dozens more left their seats and walked toward the pastor, many weeping bitterly. Cleveland dried his eyes. He whispered something in Paul's ear, and the pastor nodded. Cleveland, now full of the Holy Spirit, began to speak.

"I cannot describe to you the immense joy that I feel. It's as if a huge load has just been taken off my back." He looked at Solomon with a passion Solomon couldn't comprehend. "I feel this power inside me that words cannot explain. How I wish I had made my commitment to the Lord sooner, to spare myself, my parents, my friends, and each of you the ugliness of a life bent on harming others." He didn't take his eyes off Solomon, who was slouching low in his pew. "Solomon, I love you as a brother. But I must tell you that you are not my brother anymore. Oh, yes, I love you and I always will, but we have different fathers now, different minds and hearts, and different ways of thinking. Solomon, won't you join me here, right now, and give your life over to the Lord? Think how happy that would make your parents and Allison."

Nearly a third of the boys were on their knees at the altar, repenting of their sins and committing their lives to the Lord. Pastor Paul sensed Solomon's heart, and said, "Cleveland, persuasive words and emotionalism do not bring one into God's kingdom. Only the power of the Spirit can do that. It's up to Solomon to respond to the Holy Spirit."

The pastor's words were like a knife stabbing Solomon in the heart. He jumped to his feet and ran toward the front. He fell on his knees and began praying to himself. Solomon's mind was preoccupied not with God, but with the letter from Allison. He had read it a hundred times, yet he somehow missed the spirit of her message. Cleveland smiled, yet Pastor Paul did not return the smile. He turned away from Solomon and addressed the others.

"The altar is open for anyone who wants a relationship with the Lord. Your condemnation on Judgment Day will be even greater if you walk this aisle without the proper attitude."

Solomon prayed even harder as the words pierced him. He could see Allison's smile, feel her touch, and sense the distance between the two of them. Her image suddenly faded. He opened his eyes and looked around. Dozens of boys were huddled around the altar, crying out of brokenness of spirit. He felt out of place as his stomach churned. Cleveland, moved by the Holy Spirit, walked to him and placed his hands on his shoulders.

He whispered gently in his ear, "Go."

Solomon stared at him for a moment. Cleveland continued, "You want acceptance. You want Allison, but you don't want Jesus."

"Who do you think you are?"

Cleveland sighed, then gently smiled. "I'm a child of the one and only living God."

Eleven

The Spirit of Judas

The next morning, Grizzly walked into the mess hall at the beginning of breakfast. He moved to the center of the room and began looking around. Each of the boys who had been saved the previous day, including Cleveland, were gathering on the right side of the room. As they sat down, each bowed his head and prayed for his food. Their faces were glowing with the joy of the Lord. Grizzly turned his attention to the other side of the hall. About one hundred and thirty of the boys were glaring angrily at their former friends.

Cleveland jumped out of his seat and rushed to the warden's side, reaching out his hand in friendship.

"Warden, I want to thank you for the tough love you showed me and my friends."

Grizzly shook his hand and smiled.

"Cleveland, what you did yesterday took courage. I'm proud of you, son."

The warden patted him on the back and looked over at Solomon.

"I see you're not sitting with your friend Solomon to-day."

Cleveland nodded and glanced toward his new brothers.

"Solomon is a big boy, and he makes his own decisions. I need to surround myself with those who are going to build me up, not tear me down."

Grizzly nodded. "Very wise."

Cleveland walked back to his seat and began eating his breakfast. As he looked up, Solomon caught his eye. Although it was difficult to discern if Solomon was angry or sad, it wasn't hard to tell that he didn't know the Lord.

The difference between the two groups of boys was like night and day. The boys to Grizzly's right were happy and content, laughing together as if they were of one heart and mind. Darkness and gloom seemed to hover over the group on the left.

Grizzly reached for a piece of paper from his shirt pocket. When he cleared his throat, the voices in the room quickly quieted.

"Yesterday was quite a day for many of you, and for me personally," he said, looking mainly at the boys to his right. "I have a brief statement to read to you that has come from Jerusalem." He paused as he placed the sheet of paper in front of him. "Today marks the thousand-year anniversary of Christ's reign on the earth. On this date one thousand years ago, Jesus fulfilled the prophecies spoken of through His Holy Word. Today, another prophecy will come to fruition. It is from the book of Revelation, chapter twenty. It states, 'When the thousand years have expired, Satan will be released from his prison—'"

Solomon rolled his eyes at the words. "You're dreaming, old man," he said loudly enough to make Grizzly pause. Several of the boys laughed underneath their breath. Solomon glanced around the table, returning their contemptuous gestures.

Grizzly continued, "'Satan will be released from his prison and will go out to deceive the nations which are in the four corners of the earth, Gog and Magog, to gather them together to battle, whose number is as the sand of the sea. They went up on the breadth of the earth and surrounded the camp of the saints and the beloved city. And fire came down from God out of heaven and devoured them. The devil, who deceived them, was cast into the lake of fire and brimstone where the beast and the false prophet are. And they will be tormented day and night forever and ever.' Effective immediately," Grizzly paused to fight back his emotions, "this camp is closed, and you are free to leave."

The Spirit of Judas

A loud roar erupted. Solomon couldn't believe it. He was free! No more work, no more Grizzly, no more church! He was free to.... Solomon's mind suddenly fell numb. He watched as the boys stood and waved their hands in the air, hooting and hollering as loudly as they could. Those to his right were tranquil and subdued.

Cleveland stood to his feet and raised his hand. Grizzly motioned for him to speak.

"Quiet," shouted the warden. "Cleveland wants to speak, and he deserves our undivided attention." The room grew silent.

"Thank you, warden. I'm sure that I'm speaking for all my new friends when I say that we are also excited about our freedom. But I do not understand why our Lord is doing this."

Grizzly nodded for a moment. "Son, Jesus is preparing to judge the world. You've heard Pastor Paul speak many times about the Great White Throne Judgment. This day is coming in the near future, and I emphasize, very near future, when God's final judgment will fall on the earth."

Pastor Paul appeared at the door. He walked to Grizzly's side and placed his hand on the warden's large shoulder.

"Grizzly is correct, young men," began Paul as his eyes canvassed the mess hall. "The Bible does not tell us how long Satan will roam the earth, but rest assured that God's Word will come to pass. The day that Satan persuades many of you to march against Jerusalem," he paused, looking straight at Solomon, "that will be the last day of planet Earth as we know it."

The pastor focused on the rebels to his left.

"Many of you sitting here today will take part in this rebellion. It breaks my heart to know that you will be condemned to spend eternity with the Devil, in flames that are never quenched, forever and ever."

Suddenly, the door to the mess hall opened. Pastor Paul, Grizzly, and all the boys watched as a young man hobbled in on a cane. A hateful look filled Denny's face as he passed near Grizzly and Paul. He stopped for a long while and stared them down. Silence permeated the hall as every eye looked on.

Pastor Paul smiled at him and said, "It's good to see you, Denny. We have been praying for you."

Denny ignored him as he gawked at the warden.

"You did this to me, and I promise with every inch of my being that I will get you back, someday, somehow."

Grizzly frowned at Denny. Cleveland couldn't help but speak up.

"Grizzly didn't do that to you, Denny. You did it to yourself."

Denny twisted his head, his eyes violently flashing at Cleveland.

Cleveland continued, "It's time you started to take responsibility for your own foolish actions and stopped blaming others."

Denny steadied himself on his cane. To him, there was something different, foreign, and unlikable about Cleveland. His blood boiled as his spirit suddenly recognized the light exuding from his former partner in crime.

In a ghostly tone, he asked, "What have they done to you, Cleveland?"

Pastor Paul wanted to rush to Cleveland's side and give him a big pat on the back. Instead, he remained silent as the boys sparred.

"If I were you," began Cleveland, "I would get my life right with the Lord before something much worse happens."

Denny gripped his cane so tightly that his knuckles turned white.

"It looks like you went off the deep end and became a born-again bigot."

"Well, once again, Denny, you're batting only one for three. I am born again, but I'm not a bigot, and I haven't gone off the deep end. I'm afraid, my friend, that you have."

Denny looked to the guys sitting on the left for help. Several stood up and began walking toward Cleveland. Paul and Grizzly quickly took control while they could.

"Hold your horses," yelled Grizzly, his hand reaching for his laser gun. "If you boys want to duke it out, feel free to, but not until after you leave this camp."

Everybody froze in place. Denny glanced at the warden's hand.

"Yeah, right. I have a life sentence in this dump."

Solomon started to laugh loudly. "Hey, bro, we're free."

Denny swung his head toward Solomon. "What did you say?"

Solomon smirked. "They said the Devil's loose now on the earth." He shrugged his shoulders. "We're free to go follow him."

Cleveland closed his eyes and prayed while an arrogant smile surfaced on Denny's face. He turned toward Grizzly. "If we're free to go, then why are you going for your gun?"

Grizzly placed his hand on the weapon, but he didn't attempt to take it out of its holster.

"There will be peace as you young men leave. What you do off this property is in your own hands."

Pastor Paul glanced at the warden and then at Denny.

"I care what you do when you leave, and so does Jesus. My prayer is that all the years of preaching you have heard have touched you in some way." He swiped at a renegade tear. "You boys are being released for the same reason Satan is being released. The Devil wants to prove his case to God that he deserves the freedom to live his life the way he chooses. Well, each of you here today will also be given that opportunity. Gentlemen, please, I beg you, do not squander your last chance to worship the King."

Grizzly nodded in agreement. He was expecting a long-drawn-out sermon, but he didn't question Paul's wisdom.

Grizzly hugged the preacher and then turned to the boys.

"Many of you hate me for the hard work I put you through, and that is understandable."

Denny snorted loudly in agreement. Grizzly ignored the theatrics.

"My orders came straight from the top. Jesus Himself told me to rule you with an iron rod, and I obeyed Him completely. Go in peace, and be aware that Satan and his demons will do everything they can to capture your allegiance and your hearts." He bit his lip as he held his emotions in check. "You're released." Solomon excitedly looked at Denny. As Denny's demon eyes penetrated his defenses, Solomon's enthusiasm wilted.

———————

"You wanted to see me, Master?" said the archangel Michael, bowing at the feet of the King.

Jesus responded, "The time is at hand."

The archangel nodded. He noticed the beauty of the throne as the light from the noontime sun reflected off the white stone. Far more worthy of praise, however, was his Master.

"My instructions?"

Jesus spoke tenderly, "Tell Satan how long he has, and do everything you can not to engage him in battle. I will take care of him shortly."

"Master, is there any way to avoid this war?"

"If he repents, of course; but we know that he will not, and evil must be destroyed before My kingdom can become eternal and universal." Jesus rose to His feet. He held a golden key in His scarred hand. As He stepped down from His throne, He placed the key in the angel's hand. "Your reward will be great in the heavenly Jerusalem."

Michael bowed again. "Thank You for allowing me to serve You."

Michael jetted off toward the south. Seconds later, he reached the lake formerly called the Dead Sea. He plowed his way into Satan's hole, past the Devil's throne, and into his jail cell. As he approached the Evil One, the archangel noticed that Satan's eyes were closed.

"I'm not sleeping, Michael," he said as he slowly opened his eyes. "I'm calling my troops together."

The archangel reached for the hand-sized key. "You are not God, Satan; you do not have the ability to do that."

Satan's laugh echoed in the dark chamber. "Oh, you know so little of my abilities."

The Devil slavered as the golden key appeared from Michael's robe. His eyes followed it as Michael slowly moved it toward a slit in the rocks.

228

"You have six days and no more," Michael sighed, "and then you, along with your troops, will be destroyed by the King."

"That's your interpretation," scorned Satan, his eyes brightening as the key neared its destination.

The archangel suddenly stopped his hand. He glared at the Dragon with an intensity he had never felt before.

Satan egged him on. "Don't play with me, you imbecile. Obey your Jesus; that's what you love to spew off your mouth about."

The archangel didn't move as he stared at the source of evil. "You don't have the authority to order me to do anything." He grabbed his sword with his empty hand. "You are not trustworthy, and I will defend myself."

Satan hissed, "You're not as dumb as I thought. Now go bless your God by obeying Him."

The archangel fit the key inside the incision in the wall. Once the key touched the back of the lock, a low humming sound flowed from Satan's invisible barrier. The Dragon reached for his sword, but the years of inactivity made him appear clumsy and disoriented. He began hobbling around in circles and cursing under his breath. Michael chuckled.

"You think this is funny?" spouted the Devil.

"No, I think it's pitiful." The archangel tossed the key near Satan's paws and flew toward the exit. "I recommend you stay here and regain your senses. Your followers may look down on you if they see you in this condition."

Satan had to have the last word. "Tell Jesus I will see Him in Jerusalem. I'm looking forward to sitting on His throne."

Emily blew the hair from her eyes. She breathed heavily as she looked around the room.

"There is no way I can pack all this stuff in ten minutes," she announced as Ken buzzed around like a bee in search of honey.

From ten feet away, he tossed his shoes into his suitcase.

"He shoots," he watched as the shoes bounced against some shirts, "and scores!"

"Your packing skills are pathetic."

Ken grabbed one of her blouses and raised it over his head.

"I will pack myself, thank you." She sprinted across the room and clutched her shirt with both hands.

"You're pretty fast when you want to be." Ken grinned and then turned toward the television. "You heard Jesus' announcement. He wants all Christians to come to Jerusalem immediately. The last thing I want to do is be late for that."

"We're not going to be late as long as you don't hold me up by annoying me to all get out."

Ken quickly finished packing and scanned the suite. He turned his attention to Emily, who appeared frustrated by something, but he didn't think it was him. At least, not this time.

"Come on, Emily. Spit it out. What's bugging you?"

Emily's eyes were fixated on her luggage, but her mind was elsewhere.

"Can't you be a little more gentle? I'm not one of your buddies where conversation is limited to caveman antics and one-syllable words."

Ken couldn't help but laugh. He moved to her side and hugged her from behind.

"It's Solomon again, isn't it?"

Emily stopped packing. Her eyes filled with emotion.

"Of course it is. We're heading for Jerusalem to worship, and you know that every believer will be there."

Ken squeezed her.

"What if we don't see him there?" she cried.

"It's a big place, honey."

"But if he is saved, I know Jesus will make sure we see him."

Ken couldn't argue with her logic. He pulled her around to face him. He looked at her with rare compassion and kissed her tenderly on the nose.

"You're right, Emily. Let's think positively."

Her gloomy expression brightened.

"I'll be ready in fifteen minutes," she said.

"Five."

"Ten," she countered.

"Seven, and not a minute longer."

She squeezed him tightly. "Do you always have to be so competitive?"

"Huh?"

"Never mind."

Timothy paced to and fro like a father waiting for the birth of his child. "This is big, real big." He was watching the detention camp. Hundreds of boys were running in all directions. "Do you see Solomon yet?"

Daniel, who was hovering a few hundred feet above the ground, called down his answer. "Not yet."

"Let me know the second you see him."

"Gotcha," replied Daniel.

Timothy was frantically running through the different scenarios in his mind. If Solomon were a Christian, they would immediately head to Jerusalem. He sighed at the other possibility. With Satan being loosed, and Solomon not saved, it would mean a tough road for them and their human.

"There he is," shouted Daniel.

"Does he look happy?"

"Uh, yeah, really happy."

Timothy's heart began to race. "Does it look like he's happy because he's free or joyful because he's saved?"

Daniel squinted. "I don't know; do I look like God?"

Timothy was frustrated. His inability to fly kept him from the action he so enjoyed taking part in. Hearing moaning sounds to his left, he ran toward Fester.

"At least I can still see spirits," Timothy consoled himself as he bent down over the demon.

"How was the trip?"

Fester placed his paw on his head and whined. "What happened?"

Timothy smirked. "You met up with a force more powerful than yourself."

Fester yanked his eyes open. "Where's Blasphemy?"

"Rumor has it that he's in a very hot place."

"Hell?" asked the dizzy demon.

"No, that's next week. He's hiding out near the sun from the wrath of Satan."

"Satan's loose?"

Timothy left the demon lying in the grass. As he started running toward the camp, he called back to Fester, "Do I look like your agent? Get your own information."

Daniel saw Timothy moving fast—at least for a "human." "What are you doing?" he called to him.

"Well, the whole idea in Jesus' giving us human form was so that we could encourage and evangelize people. I thought I'd better get started."

"I want to help, too," Daniel responded. "I'm getting a better look at Solomon, but I still can't tell a lot about his spiritual condition." He slowly hovered above his comrade as Timothy ran toward the camp.

"Can you tell who's he with? Is it Denny or Cleveland?"

"That's easy," answered Daniel. "It's Denny."

Timothy sighed heavily, slowing down to barely a crawl. He looked toward heaven, then toward Solomon and Denny.

"Come on down from there, Daniel. I think we have our answer."

———————

Cleveland was with his new friends in Christ. All the unsaved boys were gone, leaving only the remnant behind. Grizzly and Paul had left the building, too, but the boys didn't know where the men were going. Cleveland sensed an attachment to his new friends that he had never felt before.

"I'm real excited about our new freedom, but I think we need to temper that with the realization that we are in a war we know little about."

Somebody he didn't know spoke up. His name was Andrew.

"I think we should travel to Jerusalem. Jesus will give us our instructions from there."

Pastor Paul appeared from the outside. "That's right, Andrew. Every Christian has been ordered to the Holy City." He stared at the boys and smiled. "I'm glad to see you fine gentlemen did not scatter to the four winds as the foolish have done. You need to stick together, and each of you is invited to come with me. We have enough vehicles to get us there."

Cleveland interrupted, "Shouldn't we be trying to evangelize the lost, especially our brothers who are leaving?"

The pastor shook his head and sighed deeply. "Forget about them for now. My hunch is that we will have opportunity to do that soon. Our immediate concern is to go to Jerusalem to worship our King."

Cleveland said, "May I offer a prayer before we leave?"

Paul chuckled. "That's a silly question. Of course you can."

Cleveland clasped his hands together and closed his eyes. "Lord Jesus, first we want to thank You for saving us from ourselves. Bless our lives and expand our territories so we can save others from their sins." His voice was filled with passion. "Keep each of us pure as we seek to follow You wholeheartedly. Protect us from the Evil One. Amen."

Just as the prayer ended, the door opened. A man nobody recognized greeted them with a smile.

"Who are you?" asked Paul as he eyed the newcomer somewhat suspiciously.

The man brushed some dust from his pants and scanned the room.

"Did Solomon Action get saved?"

Cleveland walked toward the stranger. "No, he didn't, but I was his best friend, and I did."

The visitor's eyes moistened. "That's what I thought. Thank you." He turned toward the door.

"Whoa, now. Wait just a minute," started Paul. "I asked you who you were, and I would appreciate a straight answer."

With his back to them he said, "You wouldn't believe me if I told you."

Cleveland moved closer to the man. "Try us."

The man turned around. He looked toward the ceiling and spoke, "Do you think I should tell them?"

Seconds later, he seemed to get a reply. The eerie scene bothered some of the boys, but it intrigued Paul.

"Who were you talking to?" asked the pastor.

"A friend of mine. His name is Daniel."

Cleveland backed away from the unfamiliar person. "We don't pray to anyone but Jesus around here. Are you a demon?"

The stranger laughed as he sat down on an unoccupied bench. "I wasn't praying. I was talking."

Pastor Paul walked over to him and raised his hands into the air. "Lord Jesus, is this a satanic trick? What do we do?"

"No, no, stop it," responded the man.

Paul opened his eyes without getting a response. "Who are you?"

"My name is Timothy. Up until several days ago, I was an angel in the Lord's army." Everybody stared at him as if he were out of his mind. "Jesus transformed many of us into humans so that we could encourage Christians and evangelize sinners. I was just speaking to my partner, an angel named Daniel."

Cleveland rushed toward him, reaching out to touch his arm. "So we know that you are real, but how do we know that you are not a spy?"

Paul interrupted, "The Bible doesn't mention this event, though that doesn't mean he is lying. One question for you. Who is the only King of the universe?"

Timothy figured it wouldn't be easy to convince them. He made sure his answer didn't leave anybody guessing.

"Jesus is the only King of the universe. His Word is true to the core, and in six days, He will judge the unrepentant of this earth." He looked at Pastor Paul. "I was Ken Action's guardian angel during the Great Tribulation. Of course, you know that Solomon is his son, and we are doing everything to get him to repent." He sighed. "But up to this point, our efforts have shown little fruit."

The pastor patted him on the back and smiled. "Trust me, I know the feeling. Just remember, don't weary in doing good. I've preached for months at a time with no apparent response from these boys." His words encouraged the angel. "Do you need a ride to Jerusalem?"

"You bet I do," responded Timothy.

Demons from around the globe were gathering at the entrance to the wormhole. Word of Satan's release had spread faster than wildfire. Millions upon millions of demons of every rank, shape, and size were anxiously awaiting a mere glimpse of their king.

Suddenly, a black figure exploded out of the hole. It shot toward the evening sky, then plunged toward the lake below. The shape was moving so fast, nobody could tell who or what it was. Seconds later, Lucifer surfaced from the exact center of the lake. His black wings smoothly carried him over the mass of dark spirits, then dropped him in the middle of the crowd.

A thunderous shrill of screaming demons greeted him. He jutted his paws high toward heaven and surveyed his troops.

"I have risen from the dead!" belched Satan to the glee of the demons. His mocking reference to Jesus sent shivers through the crowd. "I have left you for this thousand-year period to prove a point." The spirits were spellbound, listening as his lies increased exponentially. "For one thousand years, I have been in hiding to prove to you that you cannot fight the good fight without me. In years past, we've had bickering, backsliding, and disloyalty in the ranks, which left me no option but to leave you leaderless until you came to your senses."

General Ruse, who was hiding near the flank of the horde, shook his head in disgust. He was jealous of Satan's ability to lie so convincingly.

"He actually believes this dung," he mumbled to himself.

Satan scrutinized the crowd, looking for even a hint of rebellion. He found none.

"In the past, you did not appreciate my leadership; you only feared it. Today, you not only fear me, but also appreciate me."

"We love you, Satan," screamed one.

"Give it to us straight," yelled another.

Satan's chest bulged with pride. He had been coveting this day for a thousand years.

"There's a madman on the loose who wants to destroy this kingdom. He has taken over this land that we hold so dear. His ways are not our ways, and I will go to the grave fighting if I must—fighting for your right to be your own demon, to rule your life the way you see fit."

A deafening cheer shook the foundations of the earth as the demons vented a thousand years of frustration.

"To be successful in the upcoming days and weeks that lie before us, I have instituted a new set of commandments. These orders from on high are not meant to shackle you, but to free you to win our next holy war."

An eerie silence gripped the pack. The Devil's evil heart was soaking up their attention like desert sand absorbs water.

"Edict number one: You will have no other ruler or loyalty other than me. I am the final authority. Edict number two: You will help your fellow demons in every way possible to further the kingdom of darkness. Edict number three: You will be fearless in the face of battle. You will fight to the end to win the great battle that lies before us. Edict number four: You will respect the chain of command that I have wisely established. When your senior officer orders you to accomplish a mission, understand that his orders are my orders."

Satan paused to gauge the reaction of the crowd. The demons appeared to be worshipping him as if he were a rock star. He didn't notice General Ruse.

"Edict number five: You will make every attempt to break every one of the Ten Commandments from our adversary. Not one is good—no, not one. Edict number six: Any demon not wholeheartedly obeying any of the words from my mouth today will be immediately put to death and thrown to the angels."

General Ruse wanted to vomit. He knew Satan didn't have the power to kill spirits. "He wished he did," murmured the demon scornfully.

The demons were hypnotized by Satan's words. The Devil threw his paws over his head, absorbing the delicious praise he so needed to survive. Only a few renegade demons questioned his commands, but they surely didn't do it now. Logic was strangely absent here. Any rational individual could see that the Devil was demanding nearly the same loyalty as Jehovah God. Satan could get away with being unreasonable, because the light of God was foreign to them.

"Our next battle will be bloody, but we will come out the victors," Satan promised. "Jesus has His throne in Jerusalem. Ninety-five percent of the angels occupy this holy land we once called home. My strategy is simple. First, we will take over every inch of land outside Jerusalem. This will be quite easy with the lack of firepower outside the city. Once we capture the hearts of the people away from the city, we will then march on Jerusalem and plunge a stake straight into the heart of the beast!"

Thunder and lightning filled the sky. For a moment, fear gripped Satan's heart. He knew that Jesus was signaling His disapproval. Satan pulled his sword and pointed it toward Jerusalem.

"I have all power to do as I please," lied Satan as the masses stared at the billowing black clouds overhead.

A lightning bolt suddenly shook the ground only a few feet from him. The pack of spirits gasped as Satan jumped backward. The Devil had to think quickly. The last thing he needed was to be seen as a coward. They had to believe he was all-powerful and totally in control.

"You will not upstage me, Jesus," muttered Satan. He smiled as he watched the clouds darken. "Your Word says I will be marching on Jerusalem, so You can't kill me now."

Several hundred demons began to break rank and run. The Devil threw his sword at the highest-ranking demon. It plunged into his back and came out the other side. The spirit fell to the ground, writhing in pain.

"I have created this storm to test your loyalty." Satan was an expert at manufacturing lies. "And many of you have failed."

The deserters were quickly rounded up by Satan's commanders and tied hand and foot. They were placed at the Devil's feet, all of them shaking in fear.

"Consider yourselves to be martyrs for the cause," spoke the Devil, placing his paws behind his back, as if he were their judge. "You have failed the simplest of tests." The severe thunderstorm began to slowly die. "Obviously, you do not trust me with all your heart, all your soul, and all your spirit. It is clear that you believe the thunderstorm I created was from our enemy, and that He has control over the weather, instead of me. You are a disgrace to my fine army and will now pay the final price for your lack of obedience."

Satan growled viciously at the faithless. "Throw them into the sun."

———————

The crowd was more numerous than grains of sand on a seashore. Every saved human and every angel was there to worship the King of the universe. Jerusalem had never seen anything like this before. Daniel, Timothy, and Pastor Paul, along with his group of seventy, were several hundred yards to the right of Jesus. Ken and Emily arrived in the nick of time and were standing nearly a mile to Jesus' left.

Vice-Regent David marched toward Jesus' throne and bowed at His feet. Jesus nodded His approval. David seated himself on the right hand of Jesus. Seven hundred and seventy-seven trumpeters blasted their trumpets, filling the air with a majestic sound that no one would ever forget.

"People of Jerusalem, and those from the four corners of My good earth, welcome to the Holy City." Jesus looked on His people with compassion. "For one thousand years, you have lived in peace and safety, as I promised in My Word. I love you with an unending, eternal love."

Millions wept at His words. Pastor Paul placed his arm around Cleveland and whispered in his ear.

"Aren't you glad you made the right decision?"

Cleveland smiled at him and nodded.

Ken was hugging Emily from behind as the two watched the proceedings from a distance.

Allison and her parents were huddled together near the front of the stage. While Bill and Gail were focused on Jesus, Allison occasionally scanned the crowd, hoping to see Solomon.

"As most of you know," began Jesus, "Satan has been loosed from his prison in the bowels of the earth. The peace and security that I promised you can no longer exist with the Devil roaming freely around the earth. He will come to you like a wolf in sheep's clothing, wanting to devour you and your household. Right now to our south, he is mobilizing his army of devils."

Emily scanned the crowd, hopelessly looking for her son. Ken gently directed her attention toward Jesus.

"I have given him six days of freedom. He will do everything to make your life a living hell. My people," voiced Jesus, smiling warmly at them, "do not give in to him. Fight the good fight, and pray that you do not fall into temptation."

Jesus looked toward the southern horizon. His face registered His displeasure as He watched millions of demons jetting off in all directions. "Right now, I see them going off to attack the peace-loving communities outside My city. I say, do not fear them or what they can do to you. My peace I give to you. Fear God alone, because only He has the power and the keys over the second death."

Pastor Paul raised his hands toward the throne and cheered. Hundreds of millions of Jesus' followers did the same. The applause from the saints nearly knocked a number of demons out of the sky.

"Pray without ceasing for your children. Many of them have not accepted Me as their Savior, and with Satan now free to do his evil, many will fall into even greater temptations. You are welcome to stay here in Jerusalem where your safety will not be compromised. Many of you will choose to go home and ride out the storm—and to be witnesses to your loved ones who have gone astray. Rest assured, I will be with you forever and ever."

Jesus rose from His throne and disappeared behind a large, white curtain. As the crowd began to disperse, Emily turned to her husband.

"What should we do?"

Ken pondered her question as he surveyed the crowd.

"Let's stay here for a while and try to find Solomon." He sighed. "If he's not here, we need to go home and wait for him there. It might be our last chance to lead him to the Lord."

Ken grabbed Emily's hand as they slowly maneuvered their way through the multitude of people. They headed for Jesus' throne, smiling at many as they walked. Emily's eyes began to ache as she desperately tried to find her son.

"It's no use. We're never going to find him in this size crowd."

"You're probably right," responded Ken, "but we've got to hold out hope where there is no hope. That's what Jesus would want us to do."

Emily managed a brief smile. She knew he was right.

As they neared the throne, someone began shouting Emily's name from a distance.

"Oh, my goodness," she said as she looked for a face. "It might be Solomon."

Ken winced. "It doesn't sound like him."

"Ken! Emily!" hollered the voice.

Ken pointed at a stranger running toward them. "Who in the world is that?"

Emily stood on her toes to get a better view. "I've never seen him before."

The man was somehow sprinting toward them through the massive crowd, without touching a soul. Ken tightened his grip on Emily as the stranger came upon them.

"Who are you?" asked Ken, with a touch of nervousness in his voice.

The unfamiliar person was grinning wildly at them.

"Do we know you?" posed Emily, taking a cautious step backward.

"Oh, guys, I'm so sorry. You don't know me personally, but you do know me, at least in a way, I guess."

The man appeared to be in his thirties. He was good-looking and quite excited. He stared at Ken for a moment.

"Hey, Ken, do you remember the time during the Great Tribulation when you were in that warehouse in Jerusalem?"

Ken was taken aback by his words.

"How in the world would you know something like that?"

"Don't you remember? You were meeting with those people who were the 'evil' Bible smugglers," he chuckled to himself, then turned serious. "I hope you know that hundreds were saved by Tina's and your efforts."

Ken swallowed hard.

"Did you get saved after reading one of those Bibles?"

The stranger laughed as he hit his thigh with his hand.

"No way, man. I can't get saved like you."

Emily looked at Ken.

"Honey, this is too much for me."

Ken turned his back to the man and hurried Emily away from him.

"Wait, Ken. Please."

Ken stopped, but he didn't turn around.

"Do you remember that noise in the warehouse? You know, the one that pulled the hate police off your tail? That was me and my partner. We did it."

Ken quickly turned around. "I didn't see you there. Where were you?"

The stranger smiled. "You couldn't have seen me or my partner. My name is Timothy, and I am your guardian angel!"

Jesus' peace steamrolled Ken. He stared into Timothy's bright eyes. A second later, he plowed into Timothy's arms. Emily watched with joy as the men hugged for a full minute. Timothy pulled away and looked behind him.

"There's someone else I want you to meet."

"Solomon!" exclaimed Emily.

Timothy's joy momentarily lessened. "No."

Emily's face drooped.

Timothy continued, "I want you to meet a young man named Cleveland. He was Solomon's close friend, and he did get saved."

Cleveland slowly walked toward the couple. Ken instantly recognized him from the police photos.

"You were one of the boys who ran off with our son after attacking our neighbor."

Cleveland looked remorseful. "Yes, sir, but that was the old Cleveland."

Emily stepped toward the boy. "Where's Solomon? Where's my son?"

"Mrs. Action, I don't know where he is, but I can tell you that he's not here in Jerusalem."

Emily collapsed in Ken's arms. Her worst nightmare was now real. Swallowing hard, Ken asked, "How's his heart right now?"

"Sir, I can't lie to you. Solomon is mad, and he's hanging out with one bad apple." Cleveland dropped his head in sorrow. "I know the guy's bad, because he used to be my best friend."

Timothy managed to place his arms around the three of them. "This is a time to stick together and formulate a plan of action. I still believe that Solomon is going to get saved."

Emily mumbled through her tears, "Why don't you two come home with us? We could use the company."

Cleveland and Timothy nodded their approval. The group slowly walked toward the parking lot, which was several miles away. Ken watched the sun as it inched its way below the mountaintop. The blazing orange star reminded him of a time during the Great Tribulation, a time when hope seemed far away, a time when only faith could see him through.

———————

Allison sat on the corner of the marble curb; her heart was sad and lonely. With her elbows on her knees, she rested her chin in her hands. She was bleary-eyed from looking for Solomon. Bill patted her on the back.

"Honey, do you want to stay and keep looking?"

Allison sighed, "No, I can read the writing on the wall."

Gail flinched. She couldn't stand to see her daughter go through such pain, but she felt powerless to help.

"We know he's out of prison now, so maybe he will come home," suggested Gail.

"Yeah, right, Mom," cried Allison. "He's a convicted felon who refuses to repent. With Satan lose and influencing him, he may try to kill us!"

Bill responded, "Come on, honey. Let's not go overboard here. Let's go home and wait it out."

As they began walking toward the parking lot, a man quickly approached them from behind.

"Wait a second," he shouted, apparently winded by the run.

Allison was the first to turn and recognize him.

"Oh, goodness! It's the apostle Peter."

Gail latched onto Bill's hand as Peter neared them.

"Folks, I want to encourage you to continue to pray for Solomon. We all know he's one hardheaded boy, but I still hold out hope that he will repent." He looked at Allison. "Your many prayers have been heard by our Lord. Keep up the good fight."

The apostle walked away and disappeared in the crowd. Allison's faith was renewed; she looked at her parents and smiled.

"Yes!"

Twelve

A Heart of Stone

That stupid rock," yelled Denny as he stumbled. His foot was healing but still caused him to be unsteady. "How far is your house from here?"

"It can't be more than five, maybe ten miles," figured Solomon.

"I can't believe that blasted machine conked out on us," Denny vented.

Solomon sighed from the pain in his aching leg muscles. He glanced at Kevin and then at Larry.

"How are you guys feeling?"

Kevin was the youngest in the group. He was tall and thin, but he had a huge temper.

"Just peachy," shot back Kevin.

"And I'm starving," announced Larry. Larry was the oldest in the group, but certainly not the wisest. He was short and plump and had an insatiable appetite.

Denny, who was in the front of the pack and the self-appointed leader, suddenly stopped in his tracks.

"Stop all your petty whining, or I'll do it for you." He glared at Solomon. "You'd better be right about your house."

"Of course I'm right. It's my house, and I know what we have in it."

Denny said, "We need supplies to last us for months. How can you be sure that your parents are just going to hand them over?"

"They're pushovers when it comes to me," responded Solomon in a cocky tone. "They'll do whatever I want."

Allison sat at her desk, staring out her bedroom window. Her eyes canvassed the rolling hills surrounding Solomon's house. She imagined him running over the hill to her house, whisking her off her feet, and proclaiming his love for her and the Lord. She sighed as she watched a doe and its buck amble along the top of the hill.

"Allison," called her mother from the other side of the door.

Allison's eyes remained frozen on the deer. "What is it, Mom?"

"May I come in?"

"Sure."

Gail opened the door and walked over to her daughter. Allison pulled herself away from her daydream.

"Allison, your father just received a phone call." She leaned forward, her eyes suddenly coming to life. "There's a group of boys only a few miles away."

Allison hopped off her seat. "It's Solomon, isn't it?"

Gail tried to remain cool. "Yes, honey—"

Allison couldn't contain her excitement. "Oh, Mom, I knew he'd come home. I can't wait to see him."

"Allison, hold on a minute." The look on her mother's face was enough to burst her balloon. "Honey, he's with several other boys who have criminal records. I don't want you leaving this house."

"But, Mom!"

Gail lifted her finger and pointed it at Allison, a signal that she meant business. "This is directly from your father, honey. These boys are bad news. If Solomon has repented, he's sure got a funny way of showing it. We'll have to wait and see why he's come home."

Gail turned toward the door and stopped to look at her only child. She spoke lovingly but firmly, "If Solomon wants to speak with you, he can come to our house, but not with those hoodlums."

Allison fell back on her chair and stared out the window. This wasn't the way it was supposed to happen. Her white knight was a dream, a vapor, a thorn, even a demon.

A Heart of Stone

After the meeting, Satan rushed to his throne room. As he looked around at the shattered pieces of metal and rock, hatred boiled up inside him. He lifted his head toward the ceiling as venom oozed from the corners of his mouth.

"If this is my ending, I promise You a battle that You'll never forget!"

He kicked a large chunk of gold off the side of the tall cliff. Seconds later, it disappeared in the molten lava. Satan dove headfirst toward the boiling, bright liquid. He swam in the lava as if it were a tropical Caribbean pool.

"This feels good," he muttered as he swam underneath the thick fluid. His regained freedom had invigorated him. It was good to be back in action.

A shadow appeared at the entrance to the cavern. A demon poked his head through the opening and inspected the area. "I know I saw him go in here," he said as he tiptoed along the ledge leading to the base of the throne.

As Satan surfaced, he caught sight of the figure out of the corner of his eye. He snickered as he plunged his body deep into the lava abyss. He wormed his way through several secret underground passages and suddenly appeared in a small hole at the top of the cavern. Lava dripped from his body as he howled with all his power. The demon fell on his stomach in fear and looked around the room. Satan dove from the ceiling and landed hard on the demon's back.

"What do you want?" shrieked Lucifer, pounding his paws against the back of the demon's head.

"Whoa, stop," panted the demon. "It's me, General Ruse."

Satan gave him one last kick and then laughed loudly.

"General Ruse, what brings you here? It had better be good."

The general slowly pulled himself off the rocks, straightened his bruised wings, and cleared his smoky throat.

"I have a nice surprise for you, O deceitful one."

Satan glared at him with disdain. "Compliments will get you nowhere, you fool."

Ruse cleared his throat again, and said, "Of course, your honor. I thought you would want to know where Blasphemy is spending his time, no?"

Satan rubbed his long, black nails against themselves, making the irritating sound of chalk screeching down a blackboard.

"I already know where that coward is hiding. Don't you remember?" seethed the Devil. "I'm God!"

"Of course, your majesty." Ruse's pandering attitude made Satan's skin crawl.

Satan grabbed him by the throat. "Why is it that the highest-ranking officers of mine give me the most grief?"

General Ruse wanted to tell him the truth—that they were wise enough to see through his lies. Wisdom, along with his survival instinct, kept him from revealing that.

"Sir, my most humble apologies for misjudging your powers. Rest assured that I want to succeed in your new kingdom." He turned toward the exit. "Since you already know where he is, I'll go rally the troops."

"Stop!" screamed Satan.

General Ruse immediately obeyed. He turned and faced the Dragon.

"Yes?"

"Since I already know where he is, I want to know if you really do. I wouldn't put it past you to come here with a wild tale."

The general expected this from his master. "I saw him fleeing from this very room. He was heading for the sun." The truthful reply bothered the general's conscience.

Satan growled as he said, "Get out of here, and I'd better never catch you in my house uninvited again."

Cleveland, Timothy, Ken, and Emily were seated around the dining room table.

"Do you think his heart is softening at all?" asked Emily, her voice cracking with emotion.

Cleveland thought about it for a minute.

"Mrs. Action, sometimes I saw sparks of righteousness in Solomon, but for the most part, he seemed to want to be like Denny."

"Did he give you any indication why he was acting out?" inquired Ken, sounding like an anguished father.

"Not really. He just seemed angry, very angry, about being in that camp." Cleveland paused for a moment to gather his thoughts. "I know he was mad because he got caught stealing that bike, but I think something bigger than that was bothering him."

Emily's heartbreak was apparent as she looked to Ken for comfort. Timothy saw their sadness and wanted to help.

"Mrs. Action, I was here, along with my friend Daniel," he pointed toward the corner of the room. Daniel waved at them, but they couldn't see him. "You and Ken did everything in your power to be godly parents."

Emily reached for his hand and squeezed it. "Thank you, Timothy, for that. With everything that is happening, it's so easy to question our own faithfulness."

"Ken and Emily," began Timothy, "do you think we could stay here for a while? When Jesus transformed some of the angels into humans, He wanted us to be here to encourage His saints."

Ken and Emily looked at each other. Ken said, "It would be our privilege to house you and Cleveland as long as you two can put up with us."

They laughed. Their bond of friendship was rapidly cementing.

Cleveland spoke up, "I believe Solomon is going to come back here. We need to be prepared for anything."

"What do you mean by that?" asked Emily, with a slightly worried look.

"I believe he is traveling with Denny, and probably a couple of other boys. Solomon has made some bad choices, but they are wicked to the core."

"Do you think they would try to harm us?" questioned Ken, grabbing Emily's hand.

Timothy chimed in, "I don't think Solomon would hurt you for the world. I'm sure he wants to see you both, and I'm positive he wants to see Allison, but the question is, What would Denny do?"

Daniel nearly jumped out of his skin. The screams of demons suddenly wakened him from his slumber. Timothy quickly jumped out of his seat and placed his hand in the air. Nobody said a word as Timothy watched Daniel like a hawk.

"What is it?" he whispered to Daniel.

"Several loud-mouthed demons, not more than a mile away. Should I investigate?"

They heard Timothy's question, but not Daniel's response.

"Yeah, check it out, but stay low, and don't do anything dumb."

The others were taken aback by his words. Timothy looked around the table and smiled.

"It's okay. My partner Daniel sometimes gets overly excited when it comes to battle. I'm the senior partner, so I feel the need to remind him to play it smart. He'd pick a fight with the Devil himself if he thought he could get away with it."

Emily smiled at the angel, her heart warmed by his presence. "Thank you for thinking of us. You're the best." Timothy blushed.

"How many are with me?" asked Paul as he looked for a show of hands.

Several quickly shot up, then a dozen more, then another dozen.

"It's your choice. I wouldn't think any less of you if you decided to stay in Jerusalem where it's going to be safe."

About half of the boys were waving their hands in the air, while the other half were looking at each other in fear. Pastor Paul read their faces and decided for them.

"You thirty-five stay here and worship Jesus. It will be an experience that you'll never forget. Just promise us one thing," his voice was earnest as he looked at the boys. "Promise us that you will pray for us day and night."

Once they had agreed to his request, Paul turned to the others.

A Heart of Stone

"The Bible says that Satan will gather his renegades from the four corners of the earth. But it seems to indicate that the majority will come from the north, from its references to Gog and Magog in the Old and New Testaments."

"Are you sure about that being to our north?" asked Andrew, one of the brighter of the boys.

"No, I'm not certain, but it's a good place to start, and anyway, Solomon's parents live up there. I'm almost positive that Cleveland is already on his way there."

Pastor Paul grabbed a large stick and started walking toward the north. The others marched in file behind him. Andrew chuckled out loud as he watched the pastor walking with the stick.

"You remind me of Moses."

Paul turned around as he walked. "The Bible doesn't tell you this, but when one of the younger brethren got on his nerves, he would use his rod to hit them upside the head."

Everybody laughed as they trekked northward. For several minutes, nobody said a thing. The gravity of the situation was starting to sink in. Inspired by the Holy Spirit, Paul began to preach to them.

"Young men, you are heading into the wolf's den. Be as wise as serpents but as gentle as doves. This opportunity comes only once in a lifetime. Hundreds of young people could get saved if we allow the Lord to lead us."

"Preach it, Brother Paul," encouraged Andrew.

"Listen, boys. We need to model Christ in and out of season. What I mean is that you will be tested in the upcoming days. It will be very easy to obey Jesus when people want to hear your message, but there will be times when they will want to kill you. Don't fight back, but let the battle be the Lord's."

"I was reading the book of Acts last night, Pastor," said Andrew, "and I had no idea what you went through when you were younger."

Paul didn't like to recall those times, but for their sake, he did.

"They tried to kill me by stoning me. They threw me in jail and tried to starve me to death. They did everything you could imagine to deter me from doing God's work. Remember, young men, that the Devil was behind it all, and with him now loose, he will do everything in his power not only to destroy your faith, but also to destroy your very life. If people don't want to hear what we have to say, simply turn around and walk away. Let their blood be on their own heads. You are totally absolved of any responsibility."

Hours later, as the group traveled further away from the safe confines of Jerusalem, they came upon a small town. Since the meeting in Jerusalem, the population had dwindled from several thousand to several hundred. Paul cautiously walked down the main street, his eyes expecting trouble at any second.

"Don't trust anybody until he has proven himself worthy of it. Understand?"

The boys nodded. The town was quiet, too quiet. Suddenly, several young teenagers ran out of a building toward them. They had knives in their hands and death in their hearts.

Pastor Paul gestured for his companions to stop. "Don't move, boys. Every one of you start praying like your life depends on it. I will try to reason with them."

"Everyone take cover, now!" shouted Timothy.

Ken, Emily, and Cleveland rushed downstairs to the basement, where there was a hidden room.

"Daniel, how close are they?" asked Timothy, who was uncharacteristically fidgety.

"The demons appear to be within a hundred yards or so of the house, and it looks like one of them is that Fester character that we beat to a pulp."

Timothy said, "I'm sure he's the weak link in their chain. Don't mess with them. We need you, Daniel, more than you think."

A Heart of Stone

Daniel jumped into the kitchen garbage can, the last place he figured they would look for him. After all, demons don't use trash cans; they litter, in more ways than one.

"Did you see any humans behind them?"

Daniel spit out a chicken nugget that had become lodged in his throat.

"Oh, yes. There's three, maybe four of them not far behind. But I couldn't make out who they were."

Timothy ran toward the steps. "Remember, Daniel, don't engage them in battle. Use your sword as the last resort."

Allison suddenly spotted the boys approaching Solomon's house.

"Mom, Dad, I see him," she yelled, pressing her face against the window.

Bill grabbed his gun.

"What are you doing?" asked Gail as she pulled the living room curtain slightly to the side.

"That Denny character is with them. He's the one who attacked me."

Allison stared at the gun, fear clawing at her. "Dad! Solomon is with him." Bill silently nodded his head and turned toward the window.

Timothy's words spiraled in Daniel's head as he dug deeper into the trash. Seconds later, the door opened. He heard voices, but he couldn't place them. Denny was the first inside the house, followed by Solomon and the others. Denny motioned to Solomon to speak.

"Mom, Dad, I'm home."

There was no response; nobody was around.

"I was freed from camp," Solomon shouted as the boys inspected the house. He glanced out the window facing Allison's house.

"They're not home," whispered Denny.

Solomon shook his head. "My record is clean! Mom, Dad, where are you?"

Denny stared at him as Solomon shook his head. Denny pointed toward the refrigerator. Solomon ignored him and headed for the living room.

"Hey, guys, I'm home. I know you're here; your vehicle is parked outside."

Emily's eyes widened as she stared at her husband. Ken didn't know what to do. They looked at Cleveland for direction.

"Don't put that on me," whispered Cleveland.

"We don't know the other boys, Cleveland," responded Ken, "so it's your call."

"I say we do it. Maybe we can be a witness to them after all."

Emily appeared fearful, but determined.

"He's right, Ken. Solomon knows we're here."

Cleveland slowly turned the doorknob as he stared at the others.

"I'm going to check downstairs," announced Solomon as Denny and the others raided the refrigerator.

He opened the door to the finished basement and slowly descended the steps. Emily's heart skipped a beat each time she heard his foot land on another step. How she wanted to hold him and never let him go. She dreamed of Solomon's hugging her and telling her how much he loved them, and how he had given his heart to the Lord. Her greatest fear was that first look, that first expression on his face. It would tell her all that she needed to know.

"Mom, Dad, are you down here?" called Solomon as he neared the bottom of the steps. He glanced toward the pool table, then by the half-bath near the laundry room.

"Solomon, is that you?" mumbled a voice from the other side of the room.

"Dad!" Relieved, Solomon ran toward the couch. "What are you doing?"

"Uh, we must have fallen asleep." Ken pulled himself off the couch without disturbing Emily. "Don't wake Mom yet. It's been a long day."

A Heart of Stone

Solomon's eyes widened as he looked at Cleveland, who was curled up on the loveseat. "What's he doing here?"

Cleveland pretended to slowly wake up. He stretched his arms and opened his eyes. "Solomon, it's good to see you." He jumped off the couch as if he hadn't slept a wink. The one-sided hug revealed Solomon's heart.

Emily kept her eyes closed. Ken's last-minute idea didn't sit well with her. She didn't like having to deliberately deceive anyone—let alone her son. She wanted to see him, to feel his hands on hers, and to share in his experiences, no matter how horrible they might be. She honored Ken, though, by feigning sleep. Ken and Cleveland both agreed they should check out the situation before involving her. If she heard any fighting, she had promised to hide in the secret closet. Even Solomon did not know it was there.

Solomon politely pulled away from Cleveland and reached out his hand to Ken.

"Not in this lifetime," rebuked Ken as he grabbed Solomon with all his strength. "You're never too old to hug your pop."

Solomon nearly lost his breath; a rare smile emerged from his troubled face.

"It really is good to see you, Dad." He looked at his mom. "What's the deal with Mom? Let's wake her up. I know she's itching to see me."

"Let's go upstairs and talk for a little bit first. She's had a traumatic time with you in that camp."

Cleveland punched Solomon in the arm. "Maybe we can do a little punch boxing in the yard. I was the champ at my high school."

Solomon ignored his comments. "So what are you doing at my parents' house?"

Ken glanced at Cleveland.

"Uh, it's a long story." Cleveland evaded telling him any more details.

Ken put his arm around Solomon and guided him toward the stairs. He heard voices coming from the kitchen.

"Do you have friends with you?" asked Ken, acting surprised.

"Yeah, they're really cool guys, especially my best friend, Denny."

Ken and Cleveland sighed as they climbed the steps. Emily opened her eyes and stared at the ceiling. She didn't want to hear Denny's name, especially the way Solomon said it, with enthusiasm and even reverence.

Demons were flooding the planet with hellish lies and smooth flattery. Satan had commanded that groups of six demons each be given small parcels of land. These communes dotted the globe like measles on a child. Their mission was clear: Persuade the humans occupying the area that Jesus is a fake. Each group had a leader, who had at least a minimal officer's ranking. He was the boss, answerable only to Satan or his chain of command.

Since most of the angels had converged on Jerusalem, vast areas of the globe were left undefended from demonic attack. Many of the angels were anxious to see their humans, hoping that they would pass the spiritual test. The war was on! Good versus bad, angels against demons, Jesus against Satan.

Pastor Paul glared at the razor-sharp knife staring at him. He could feel the demons possessing these boys. Six boys, six knives, but probably six hundred demons, thought Paul.

"Why do you want to kill us?" asked Paul in a kind, non-threatening tone.

"You're one of those Jesus freaks, aren't you?" hissed the largest of the boys.

Paul glanced back to make sure his friends were praying. "We are not freaks, young man; we are saints."

The six stopped their forward movement. All their knives pointed at Paul's head.

"We don't believe in your God! And we're tired of you weirdos preaching to us about hell."

"Jesus gave you the choice, the free will to decide what you want to do with Him. If you don't want to hear about Him, that is your prerogative."

The boy lowered his knife, and the others followed suit. Paul smiled at them, clasping his hands together in joy.

"I'm so glad we have that resolved," voiced the pastor. "We are heading north. You boys are welcome to join us."

Several of Paul's young friends nearly fainted. What was Paul doing inviting the enemy along on their crusade?

The leader of the pack eyed Paul suspiciously. "I don't think you guys have the guts to hang out with us. Plus," he smirked, "you guys just look," he stuttered as he searched for the right words, "well, you look too happy for my taste."

Paul reached his hand out in friendship. The young hoodlum stared at him for several seconds before returning the handshake.

"It was nice meeting you, boys," said Paul, motioning for his disciples to following him. "You guys stay out of trouble."

Several of them grunted loudly at his suggestion.

Once they were a safe distance away, Andrew questioned Pastor Paul.

"What were you doing back there? You could have gotten us killed." Paul listened politely. "It just takes the cake." Andrew threw his hands in the air. "Inviting them to come witness with us? Are you sure you don't have a demon attacking you?"

Paul's joyful mood remained steady against the verbal hurricane.

"Andrew, please, son, you are young, excitable, and very inexperienced. I didn't invite them along so they could witness with us. They were the ones needing the Good News. If they had agreed, we would have been doing the witnessing to them. They didn't accept the invitation because their hearts are closed. It was a sign from God for us to move on to a more receptive audience."

Andrew felt as tall as a grasshopper. "I, uh, I don't know what got into me. I'm sorry, Pastor."

Paul put his arm around him as the group continued to walk.

"I'll tell you what got into you: It was a demon taunting you." He looked at the sky. "If you could see the spiritual realm at this moment, it would scare the pants off you. There are demons everywhere, circling around like vultures."

Andrew and a few others looked at him like he was an old kook.

"Come on, Pastor. Don't you think that might be a little exaggerated?" reasoned Andrew.

Paul stopped.

"You don't believe me. Maybe we should pray that God would show it to us."

Everybody stared at Paul. The mere thought of seeing the demons was quite inviting. Andrew's response was eager—too eager. "Let's go for it."

Having second thoughts, Paul wondered about the wisdom of his suggestion. "Curiosity killed the cat, you know." Paul looked at them; it was obvious that they wanted to see something supernatural. "Gentlemen, I have fought enough demons in my life. I have no interest in this whatsoever, but if this will help out your walk with the Lord, I'll go along, this time." He closed his eyes and prayed. "Father of the universe, I pray that You would let us see the battleground in the sky. May You use this to strengthen our faith. Amen."

Everybody opened his eyes and jerked his head toward the sky. All they saw were blue skies and a few puffy white clouds.

"Real scary stuff," responded Andrew as he looked all around him.

Paul said, "God's timing may not be our timing."

Suddenly, a blast of light shot down from the sky. The landscape turned dark, as shrieks and screams from drunken demons assaulted their senses. Hundreds of hideous spirits hovered directly over their heads. Every few seconds, several spirits would swoop down toward them. They were the size of burly men, with black wings, oversized paws, and sharp claws. One of the largest of the demons cursed repeatedly as he plunged from the sky toward Andrew. Andrew hit the ground screaming. The demon collided with some kind of invisible barrier only a few feet above Andrew's head and bounced back into the air.

"Get him off me," shrieked Andrew as he lay on the ground, crying.

Everybody but Paul closed his eyes in fear. Pastor Paul looked boldly toward the polluted sky and shouted, "You have no power over us. I rebuke you in the name of God's Son, Jesus Christ. Now, be off!"

The demons squealed when they heard Jesus' name come from Paul's lips. Within seconds, they were gone, chased away by a blinding flood of divine light. The sky quickly returned to its blue color, and the clouds reappeared as they had been before.

Paul turned to the frightened disciples. "You of little faith, get up and follow me."

The boys slowly uncovered their faces and looked around. Andrew was the last to open his eyes.

"Be careful what you pray for, young men; you might just get it."

Solomon called to his friends, as his dad, Cleveland, and he reached the tops of the steps. "Hey, guys, straighten up and act right. You're going to meet my dad."

Ken could hear the boys laughing as he walked through the door. Cleveland patted him reassuringly on the back. When Ken saw them, his heart fluttered with anxiety. They were rough-looking boys with wild, sadistic expressions.

Solomon introduced them, "Dad, this is Denny. He's the leader of our little club."

Denny's mouth was overstuffed with food. He sneered at Ken.

"It's good to meet the man of the house," he said with a discernibly mocking tone. "You have a fine son here." Denny pointed toward Solomon as he laughed.

Ken didn't know what to do. Cleveland helped him the best he could. He nudged him toward Denny.

"Uh, I'm glad to see you're getting some food." He glanced at the open refrigerator. "Help yourself."

Denny's expression turned tart. "We did." He looked at Solomon. "You didn't tell me your father was so," he glanced at Ken, "so average."

Ken wanted to pick him up by the neck and kick him in the rear, out the door, off his property, and out of his son's life.

"Well, thank you, Denny, for that," he paused to find the right word, "observation."

"Oh, come on, Dad. He's just joking," laughed Solomon as he motioned toward Larry and Kevin. "This is Larry and Kevin, and they're a lot more, uh, socialized than Denny."

As Larry and Kevin shook Ken's hand, Denny punched Solomon on the shoulder. "Watch it, bro. You're expendable, you know."

"Just kidding," smiled Solomon, patting Denny forcefully on the back.

Seeing Cleveland, Denny turned pale and ghostly. "What is this two-timing, Jesus-loving loser doing here?"

Ken immediately stepped in between the two. "I will have no fighting in *my* house, Denny." His tone was authoritative, which irked Denny. "I invited him to *my* house, and I will not have you or any of your buddies bad-mouthing *my* Lord. Do you understand?"

Denny glared at him with animosity. Suddenly, he started to laugh uncontrollably. Solomon looked at his dad with an apologetic expression.

"Solomon," started Ken, "I do not approve of this ill-mannered person you call your friend. You have a choice: stay home and lose him, or go with him out of this house without our blessing."

Emily struggled to hear the conversation. She felt helpless as she silently stared at Timothy.

Solomon looked at his dad for a long while, then at Denny.

Denny couldn't help but shoot off his mouth. "Sounds like your old man is expressing some of that 'Christian love' he likes to preach about."

"Get out of my house now!" yelled Ken as he pointed toward the door.

Denny clenched his fists and spit on the kitchen floor.

"Nobody speaks to me that way!"

"The same goes for me, buddy!" Ken retorted.

Ken and Denny moved toward each other. Solomon jumped in between them.

"Whoa, guys, come on. Cool your engines." He looked at Denny. "Just chill out for a second, man." He looked at his dad. "I can't stay here, Dad. Something is telling me to go and live my own life."

Ken sighed, "Yes, I know who's telling you that, and I know that I can't change your mind. Only God can."

Denny smirked. "In our gang, I'm God."

Downstairs, Timothy begged Emily not to do it. "Ken told you to stay down here. It might get violent," pleaded Timothy.

"I just want to see his face," she said as she inched her way up the stairs.

Once at the top, she noticed the door was not completely closed. She cautiously nudged it a millimeter or two and peeked out of the crack.

"I've heard enough," announced Denny as he glared crossly at Ken. "Look, Solomon, are you with us or against us?"

"I'm with you, dude!" Solomon spoke proudly.

Emily began to whimper softly at her son's words.

Denny smiled victoriously at Ken. "Hope you don't mind if we 'borrow' some supplies for the road." He motioned for Kevin and Larry to pack as much food as they could carry.

Ken turned toward Solomon, who appeared unemotional and distant.

"Take what you want."

Emily burst through the door, running toward Solomon. "Don't leave, honey." As she hugged him, she quickly sensed his coldness. She pulled away and stared into his eyes. "You're making the biggest mistake of your life."

Solomon gently pushed her away as he turned to the door. "I'll be outside waiting for you guys. I can't handle this stuff in here."

"Wait, Solomon," she cried.

Solomon stopped with his back to her. Emily fought back her emotions as she stared at the back of her son's head.

"Allison's home."

Solomon closed his eyes without saying a word. Seconds later, he moved toward the door.

"Is her dad home?" he asked.

"I believe so," responded Ken.

"I'll be out on the front porch, guys."

Allison's heart sputtered as she watched Solomon sit down on the porch. She could see him looking toward her house, but she couldn't make out his expression. Bill walked into her room without knocking.

"Are you okay?"

Still staring at Solomon, she spoke. "I'm stronger than you think, Dad."

Thirteen

Evil of the Worst Kind

You've got a problem with me?" mouthed Denny.

"They're my parents, man! They gave you food, and you spat on their floor!" berated Solomon.

"We would have taken it if they hadn't."

Solomon was following Denny, but he suddenly stopped. Kevin and Larry walked past him, hurling ugly looks in his direction.

"We might need their help in the future, Denny. It's not wise to burn bridges, you know."

Denny stopped walking, did a 180-degree turn, and scowled at Solomon.

"Tearing down decrepit, useless bridges *is* wise when you don't plan to cross them anymore." He studied Solomon intently. "Maybe your problem is that you want to stay at home." His tone turned childish. "Why don't you go back to Mommy and Daddy? They miss you so much."

Kevin and Larry joined in, and the three of them ridiculed Solomon relentlessly. Solomon took a deep breath. His temper boiled higher, and his patience thinned.

"You guys are not going to get to me," Solomon huffed as he turned and walked away.

"Tell Mommy we said hi," teased Denny as the others laughed. "Oh, and tell choirgirl Allison that she sings like an angel."

Solomon stirred up the dust as he stomped off. Denny laughed as he looked at Kevin and Larry.

"He'll be back," smirked Denny.

"Do you think he's headed back home?" asked Kevin.

"No doubt, man. But it's not his parents he's after."

Larry appeared confused. "What do you mean?"

"It's that girl," responded Denny as he glowered at the sun.

The master of evil streaked across the horizon. All he could think about was Blasphemy and settling the score. Satan left Earth's atmosphere and within seconds was in the bowels of outer space. He stared at the boiling star and howled with all his fury. Minutes later, the heat from the sun began to turn Satan's black wings dark orange. His spirit body didn't feel pain; on the contrary, he felt invigorated by the unbridled energy flowing from the star.

As he neared the core of the sun, he scrutinized every inch of the exploding plasma. His bionic-like eyes peered through the blinding light with remarkable ease. He was at home in the intense heat.

"Blasphemy!" barked the Devil.

There was no response.

"Blasphemy!" He waited a few seconds. "Better to respond now and get some mercy than make me find you."

He heard nothing but electromagnetic explosions. He moved toward the lower end of the sun.

"Blasphemy!"

Suddenly, a sunspot the size of Earth detonated in his angry face. The atomic discharge blasted him millions of miles backward, all in the blink of an eye. The explosion knocked Satan unconscious. His limp body floated harmlessly near a belt of meteors on the outskirts of the sun's magnetic pull.

Blasphemy, who saw the blast from the other side of the sun, raced toward Satan's body.

"Divine intervention!" hissed Blasphemy as he approached the Devil's unconscious body. He inspected Satan closely, looking for any signs of consciousness. Blasphemy took his sword and raised it over his head with the sharpened end pointing at Satan. He stood over the king of the demons and froze in place. He wanted to cherish this memory.

"My whole life I have waited for this moment," he said as if Satan could hear him. "You have done everything in your power to humiliate me, or as you call it, put me in my place." His lowered his nose to within inches of Satan's face. "You might have been the first liar and the first to rebel, but I'm the best demon for the job." He jammed his finger in Satan's chest. "And you know it!" He straightened up.

Closing his eyes, Blasphemy savored the moment. He readied his sword. "Die!" screamed Blasphemy.

As he lifted his sword higher, the Devil suddenly opened his eyes. Just as Blasphemy was ready to plunge the weapon into Satan, the Devil rolled away from the sword's tip, jumped up, and caught hold of the weapon in mid-air. Blasphemy came eye to eye with Satan.

"You're alive!" he gasped in a shaken tone.

Satan smiled as his right hand easily pulled the sword away. Terror filled Blasphemy; he tried to escape from the evil giant's hold, but his efforts were futile.

"Satan, it was a joke, just a stupid joke." Blasphemy's eyes grew wide as he contemplated his fate.

"And you're dead," Satan smirked as he hurled Blasphemy's sword away, sending it rocketing toward the sun. He turned his scorching stare back to the infidel.

"It would be too easy to kill you here," reasoned Satan.

"Do it!" yelled Blasphemy, hoping to end his own misery.

"A simple, quick death would be such an injustice," thought Satan out loud. "To die when nobody is watching, when you are alone. No, no, that's not my style, Blasphemy." Fire filled the Devil's eyes as he tightened his grip on his prey. "You will die in complete humiliation, in front of every demon and angel, in front of Jesus Himself!"

———

Allison's eyes were full of tears; her heart was filled with pain. She wanted to forget, but it was impossible to erase the memory from her mind. Five minutes ago, she had watched Solomon walk over that hill, laughing and kicking it up with the boys. Allison knew Satan had six days, which meant that Solomon had six days, too.

Her eyes were fixed on the hill over which he had disappeared. Sliding her clammy palms down her dress, she sighed. "I can't wait for the new heaven."

Suddenly, something, or maybe someone, appeared over the horizon. She moved to get a better look.

"Solomon!" she whispered.

Solomon was walking toward home, his feet moving toward his house, his heart moving toward Allison. He stopped near a grand oak tree and sat down underneath its shade. He needed a quiet place to think before he faced his loved ones. He rubbed his hands hard on his face, massaging his temple.

"Come on, Solomon!" Allison opened the window and stuck her head outside. She was about to call out to him when she suddenly stopped herself. He's got to come to me freely, she thought, trying to rein in her desperate heart.

Solomon glanced toward Allison's house. He wanted to run to her and profess his love, but his pride was holding him hostage. He looked behind him, knowing he could still catch up to Denny and his buddies. His divided heart was hopelessly lost.

"What do I do now?" wondered Solomon, his head against his knees.

Allison stood by the window, praying for a miracle. Her hands quivered as she waited for him to make a move.

"Do something, Solomon," she urged.

Solomon leaned his head back against the tree. A protruding piece of bark pushed against his ear. He turned around and tried to pull it off the tree. Something caught his eye just above his head. It was writing of some type, but it was old and hard to make out. He got up for a closer look, and the letters became clear.

"S," he whispered, wiping at the bark. "I don't believe it." He smiled as the words resurrected old, good memories. "Solomon loves Allison," he read. He stood there, reading the message repeatedly.

Allison suddenly realized what he was doing. "He's reading the tree!" she cried out. Gail heard her from the kitchen. She ran upstairs and into her daughter's room.

"What's wrong, Allison?"

Allison couldn't contain her enthusiastic smile. "Mom, he's reading the tree. He's just standing there, looking at it. I think he's breaking."

Gail rushed to the window.

"Honey, don't get too excited." Allison didn't hear the advice above the pounding of her heart.

Solomon began to frown, not at the memories, but at his predicament. He turned toward Allison's house, then glanced at his. He took a long breath and sat back down against the tree.

That night, Pastor Paul and the thirty-five boys found a large cave forty miles north of Jerusalem. They sat around the campfire listening to Paul talk about his New Testament journeys.

"Weren't you afraid of being killed?" asked one of the boys.

Paul chuckled to himself. "The human side of me was, but to be honest with you, I learned not to listen to that sinful side. To be absent from the body is to be present with the Lord. I concentrated on that truth."

"How?" inquired Andrew, Paul's favorite convert.

"We humans make some things way too difficult. Faith is a very simple thing. If one truly believes that death is the only thing that separates him from seeing Jesus and being with Him in heaven, he won't fear it; on the contrary, he will look forward to it."

The boys nodded in agreement.

"Tomorrow," stated Paul, "we're going to cover a lot of ground. Let's get a good night's sleep."

Paul lay down on the hard floor of the cave. The others did the same, all except Andrew, who sat upright watching the fire fade.

"Pastor, everybody was too afraid to ask you this, but I've got to."

"What is it?" responded Paul, lifting his head off the ground.

"Why didn't we get rooms at that hotel in town? I mean, it was practically empty, and we know you have the money for it."

The sound of the crackling fire filled the crisp night air. Nobody said a word as they watched the pastor apparently struggle for an answer.

"I was hoping you guys would have figured that one out on your own." He looked around at the teenagers, but he saw only blank expressions. "The people that we need to reach are roaming the streets and countryside. Most are young and don't have any money at all. They can't afford hotels. If we are going to make a difference for Christ, we need to meet them on their level, where they are living. During the church age before the Great Tribulation, the body of Christ really fumbled the ball on this point."

Just as Paul finished speaking, four uncouth-looking boys walked into the cave. Paul turned toward them and smiled.

"Can we join you?" spoke the tallest of the bunch. "It's getting cold out there."

The pastor looked at his boys as he spoke, "Absolutely, gentlemen. We're glad for your company. Come on in and warm yourselves by the fire."

The four looked somewhat suspiciously at Paul and the others as they found some open spaces close to the flames. Paul didn't recognize them.

"Where are you boys from?" he asked.

The apparent leader of the group, Billy, responded, "We asked if we could share your fire. What's with the interrogation?"

Paul nodded his head. "My apologies. I was trying to be friendly. That's all."

"No problem," responded Billy, a bit taken aback by Paul's humility.

Several minutes passed without further words. Many of Paul's team were falling asleep, but Paul, Andrew and a few others remained alert, praying for an opportunity to witness to the strangers.

Andrew turned to Billy. "Did you go to Southern High School?"

"Yeah, I dropped out a couple of days ago with my buddies. Did you go there?" A friendlier expression filled Billy's face.

"You bet, but I got kicked out last year for some wicked stuff!" revealed Andrew. He looked at Paul for permission to continue.

"Cool. What did you do?" asked Billy.

"The question is, what didn't I do." Andrew didn't want to appear braggadocios or to condone his sin, but he certainly had the attention of the newcomers. "Unfortunately, I got caught up with the drug crowd. I refused to listen to my parents or my teachers. I punched out several of the high school athletes." Andrew stopped and stared at the four. They were smiling at the thought of bruising the class jocks. "You know what? I'm not proud of it, and it's in my past. It's under the blood of Jesus now."

Paul smiled as he read the boys' faces. Stubborn, negative expressions surfaced when they heard Jesus' name.

Several dozen demons of varying ranks were attached to the boys like leeches. The senior demon barked out orders when he heard *that* name.

"I knew these guys were trouble," barked the demon to his cohorts. "I want you ten to guard the cave, you ten to shut that boy's mouth, and you ten to keep talking about self-righteousness and the ugliness of those Christians."

Everybody was sleeping now, except for the four strangers and Paul and Andrew, who continued to engage the four in conversation. Some of it was casual chatter; some of it was deep and engaging. Paul prayed for their souls when Andrew spoke, and Andrew prayed for their souls when Paul spoke. Waves of angels attacked the demons with each successive prayer, demoralizing the evil spirits until they were beaten, bruised, exhausted, then finally gone.

The light from the sun awoke the boys. Andrew, Paul, and the four guests continued to sleep as the others got up and went outside. Minutes later, Andrew slowly opened his eyes. Much of the night was a blur to him. He shook Paul, immediately awakening him.

"I fell asleep in the middle of the conversation. What happened?"

The pastor stretched his arms and smiled broadly.

"We have thirty-nine boys on our team now."

———————————

It was the worst night of Allison's life. She had sat at her window for hours, waiting for Solomon. She called Ken and Emily, but they refused to go out to him.

"He's got to make up his own mind without our influence," they told her. "He's listened to us for years; it's time for him to be still and hear from the Lord."

Allison opened her eyes and looked around. She had fallen asleep at the desk. She bent her neck as far back as it would go, trying to work out a muscle spasm. She rubbed her eyes and peered out the window. She couldn't see Solomon. She ran to the window and looked more closely. Nothing.

Allison ran downstairs in a tizzy.

Bill and Gail were eating breakfast when they heard their daughter frantically call out to them.

"Mom, Dad, have you heard anything about Solomon?"

Gail responded, "Not a word, honey."

"All I know is that he isn't out by the tree anymore," her father told her as he swallowed a sip of coffee.

"I wonder where he could be." She rushed toward the phone. "I'm going to call Mrs. Action. If anyone knows, she will."

Bill quickly stood up and moved toward her as she dialed the numbers. He gently took the phone from her hands before she could finish and set it down.

"That's not wise, honey." He looked at her compassionately.

"Why?" she questioned anxiously.

"Because if he is there, he's hopefully repairing the damage he's done with his parents. He'll be no good to you or the Lord if he doesn't right those wrongs first."

Allison looked at her father with a blank expression, considering his words. Realizing his wisdom, she nodded her head and said, "You're right, Dad, as usual."

Several hundred yards away, Solomon leaned against the corner of his family's garage, camouflaged by large bushes. His head was spinning, his heart aching, and his mind racing. A few hours earlier, before sunrise, he had decided to go home, rush into his house, and announce that he was a changed man. But something happened as he crossed that short distance from the tree to the house. He couldn't explain it, but something told him not to do it, to stay away. He could hear voices, audible voices, taunting him to leave home and never return. And now, he was back where he had started, this time hidden away. Everybody would think that he had left with Denny and his hoodlum friends.

Suddenly, the voices returned. This time, they were louder and meaner.

"Be your own man! Do your own thing!" shouted a plump demon with an obnoxious attitude.

"You go back now, and they will think you are a sissy!" advised another.

Solomon tightly squinted his eyes and clamped his hands over his ears, but neither action offered any relief.

"If you go back and admit you were wrong, you'll never live it down. A man would never, ever do that!" barked a third demon, who was balancing himself on the bush directly over Solomon's head.

Inside the house, Ken, Emily, Cleveland, and Timothy were just opening their eyes after a long night of fellowship. Timothy immediately picked up the demon voices and rocketed out of bed.

"Daniel! Do you hear that?"

There was no response. Timothy threw on his clothes and began running around the house yelling Daniel's name.

Ken and Emily heard the ruckus and rushed out of their bedroom.

"What's going on?" Ken asked as he rubbed his eyes.

Timothy stopped and looked at him, saying nothing.

"Come on, Timothy. Is it Solomon?"

"Uh," he stuttered, hesitating a moment as he wondered how to tell him. "There are demonic voices coming from somewhere inside or just outside the house. I think they're taunting Solomon, but I can't seem to find Daniel."

He ran down the hallway. "Daniel, it's an emergency! Where are you?"

Daniel was in the attic, dreaming of his fighting days during the Great Tribulation. He heard Timothy calling from downstairs.

"Here I am!" he yelled as he flew through the floor and into Timothy's sight.

Timothy tried to remain calm.

"There are demons attacking Solomon. Where have you been?"

"I, uh, well, you see," he stammered as Timothy eyed him angrily. "Oh, just forget it."

Timothy shook his head. "I think they came from near the garage. Go check it out!"

Solomon was depressed. He just couldn't seem to make sense of his life. He loved Allison, but even she couldn't fill the emptiness in his heart. Breaking up with her had only made things worse. Even the wild ride with Denny had left him miserable. Nothing seemed to satisfy. He didn't know what he should do next.

"Do some drugs!" tempted the fat demon.

As Solomon considered the idea, Daniel charged into the area with his and Timothy's swords waving wildly in all directions. He had caught the demonic swine completely off guard.

"Get out of here!" he screamed as the demons ducked the swords.

He slashed one of the demon's wings and nearly severed another's arm. The third spirit fled in terror.

"I must be going crazy," sighed Solomon, looking around at the trees and bushes. He saw nothing but the gentle breeze dancing in the branches of a fig tree.

Daniel blew on his swords, acting as if he were a gunfighter in the Wild West of America.

"Next time I won't be so easy on you!" he shouted, watching the demons rising like missiles.

He rushed inside the house and announced, "Solomon is outside the garage!"

Timothy was elated. "Yes!" he shouted as the others looked on.

Emily sent a scolding look his way.

"Don't play games with me, Timothy. What is it?"

"Solomon is still here. He's behind the garage."

Emily's eyes sparkled with life. "I knew my boy would make the right decision."

Ken squeezed her shoulder. "It's a start, honey. It doesn't mean he's accepted Christ."

Emily stared fiercely into her husband's eyes. Although his words hurt, she knew they could be true.

"You guys looking for me?" voiced Solomon with a sheepish grin. He hurried toward his mother and hugged her before she could even reach out for him.

Vice-Regent David meekly approached Jesus' throne. He bowed for several seconds, then stood and looked at his King.

"Master, reports are surfacing all over the earth. The younger generation is running mad. Many cities are reporting riots in the streets."

Jesus looked lovingly at David. He smiled and tilted His head. "David, My son, I know."

David nodded. A worried expression still coated his face.

"Of course, Jesus. But what are You going to do?"

"I'm going to win the war." His piercing eyes turned toward the sky. "My Father in heaven knows what's best. We are in control of the situation, David."

"People are going to be assaulted, raped, and killed if we don't do something quickly, Master."

"No, David. People are safe; they need only to believe."

———————

Denny was testier than normal. It was noon, and Kevin and Larry were getting on his nerves. Everything was getting on his nerves. The boys didn't realize the number of demons following their every move.

"I don't want to hear another word about Solomon," vented Denny as he led the pack southward.

"This food is getting heavy," complained Larry, trying to realign the load on his back.

"Yeah," added Kevin, eyeing Denny resentfully. "Why aren't you helping us with this stuff?"

Denny stopped, turned around, and solidly punched Kevin in the shoulder.

"Because I'm the leader, you fool, and I make the rules."

Kevin held his ground. "Who made you the leader?"

Denny shoved Kevin with his body. "I did." He lifted his fist near Kevin's face. "You want a piece of this?"

Kevin gulped, lowered his head to the ground, and mumbled, "Just forget about it."

Denny laughed and walked away.

Larry interrupted, "You keep it up, and you will lose us—just like you lost Solomon."

Denny ignored him. Several demons were belching orders in his ear.

"Solomon must pay for his sin! Nobody crosses you and lives to tell about it. You must save face or risk losing your pride. It's all a matter of principle."

Denny looked at the midday sun. He was tired of being on the move. A decision about where to go could wait until tomorrow.

"Let's camp out here," ordered Denny. He glanced around the barren landscape. He didn't see a cave, but he did spot a dead spruce tree a couple hundred yards away. "Come on, guys. Let's go chop up some of that wood so we can make a fire tonight."

"Whoa, man," started Kevin, acting as if he had just seen a miracle. "Your majesty is actually going to do some of his slaves' work."

Larry dropped the food on the ground and softly laughed.

Denny ignored them as he led the way toward the tree. He needed them, he knew, but he didn't want them to know it. Larry and Kevin followed him to the decaying tree.

Kevin said, "So what is it with you, Denny?" Denny turned around and glared at him. "I mean, I have my own beef with Jesus, but you, man, you have this hatred that even I don't get."

Denny didn't respond. He turned away and started breaking up pieces of wood. A couple of minutes passed before Denny spoke. "When I was thirteen years old, I visited Jerusalem with my family." He stopped for a moment, his anger building as the memory became more vivid. "I was really excited about seeing Jesus."

Kevin and Larry listened intently as they gathered the wood, surprised by Denny's openness. Denny started working faster as adrenaline pumped into him. "When we got to the center of town, there were these kids in foot and wrist chains, leaving Jesus' throne. I overheard them say that Jesus had sentenced them to years of hard labor for stealing a candy bar! That blew me away."

At his young age, Denny never even considered that the boys were lying about their crime.

"Was that your first trip to Jerusalem?" asked Kevin, who had stopped working to hear the story.

"Nah, we would go up three, maybe four times a year. But I had never met anybody who had ever gotten into trouble before. I didn't know Jesus was so controlling, so vindictive. I don't think He understands real justice at all. I mean, come on, the punishment should fit the crime."

Kevin looked at Denny, somewhat confused.

"Is that it?"

Denny appeared annoyed. "What do you mean, 'Is that it?' Come on, guys. Put two and two together. The only reason Jesus is that harsh with people is because He wants to have power over you. The older I've gotten, the more I believe we should go back to the way life was before the Great Tribulation. We studied a lot about it in history class."

"He's right, Kevin," added Larry. "I've talked to a lot of my friends about it. Jesus is great, unless you disobey Him. Then He turns on you and makes you pay until you bleed."

The boys carried the wood back to their makeshift camp. They talked through the evening about their families, their friends, and their lives during the Millennium. They didn't understand Jesus at all. It had taken years for evil to infiltrate their lives, but it had taken root, and the sour fruit was blossoming faster than a well-watered weed. They didn't understand the seductiveness of sin, that, given time and the wrong attitude, the smallest of sins can turn the most righteous of individuals into the worst of sinners. If they had considered that one drop of a concentrated poison could contaminate an entire city's water supply, they would have recognized that there is no such thing as a small sin.

Blasphemy had been gagged, tied up, and tossed into a small room next to Satan's throne. He could hear voices outside his makeshift prison, but he couldn't make out what they were saying.

"General Ruse, we are only a few days away from attacking Jerusalem, and we are way behind schedule!" shouted Satan.

The general cunningly smiled. "Why not change the date of the invasion?"

General Ruse knew it was God's timetable and that Satan couldn't change it even if he wanted. Satan ignored Ruse's gibe.

"My timetable will not change. It's you, Ruse, who needs to change." He poked his finger into the general's hard chest. "Your organizational skills stink, and your deficiencies are showing on the battlefield."

Satan paused, hoping to hear the general's retort. Ruse didn't take the bait.

"We need fresh, creative ideas to hit them with. They're not going to march on the city with what we are feeding them."

Satan sat down on his reconstructed throne. It enraged him that it was only half the size of his old one. He watched the stewing lava bubble beneath his feet.

"Calling Jesus a tyrant is old. We must feed the younger generation new ideas to get them excited, to get them pumped up for war. Tell your commanders to spread this new propaganda: Jesus isn't just a tyrant; He's a fake. He claims to have the power of the universe in His nail-scarred hands." Satan choked at the thought of the scars. "The truth is He doesn't have that power. That's why He punishes people as harshly as He does. He's afraid that they will find out the truth and take His kingdom away from Him."

General Ruse nodded his approval. He was impressed with Satan's logic and knew it would work well.

"Also, tell the kids that their parents are part of this vast conspiracy. That's why they've forced them to attend His hate-mongering churches. Make sure the teenagers and young adults understand that anybody who lived through the Great Tribulation would choose this Imposter over their own flesh and blood. Remember, that Bible of His says that He's more important than any family member."

Satan moved his eyes from the hot lake to his prime general. Ruse appeared delighted by his wisdom, which pleased Satan greatly.

"Last, General, we must appeal to them as a group. They need to gather as one—you know, be of one heart, one mind, and one spirit. We can't have our kingdom divided."

"How would you like me to implement this plan, O great one?" General Ruse's poker face was brilliant. He hated

Satan with a passion, but he loved the power the Devil dispersed to him.

"A rally," voiced the Devil, in a deep, dark, dreary tone.

"A rally?" repeated General Ruse.

"Yes." Satan glanced toward the room imprisoning Blasphemy. He rubbed his sharp nails against the armrest of the makeshift throne. "It will have to be spread by word of mouth since we can't penetrate the media. Three days from now, I want every person who is disillusioned with Jesus Christ to meet outside the city limits."

"Brilliant," muttered Ruse as he bowed and backed away.

"Yes, it is."

As Ruse neared the exit, Satan barked, "Oh, tell them the god that created Jesus is fed up with Him and will speak to them in person about His overthrow."

Emily didn't want to let go of Solomon. She held him so tightly that he nearly lost his breath. He looked at his father and smiled.

"I guess she missed me, huh?"

"We all missed you, son. Are you home for good?"

Emily released Solomon so that she could look him directly in the eyes.

Solomon glanced at the floor for second, not sure what to say. His heart was still divided, but at least now he was leaning in their direction.

"Guys, I'm still confused by a lot of stuff, but for now, I plan on hanging out here for a while."

Cleveland stepped toward him and shook his hand.

"I'm glad you're home. Your parents love you like crazy, and they've really missed you."

Solomon sighed and looked out the window.

"Allison's missed you, too," added Emily, knowing where he was looking.

Cleveland glanced at Ken, eyeing him as if to say, "Are you going to, or should I?"

Ken's smile lessened somewhat as he said, "Solomon, you know Satan's been loosed, and the time is short. We need to talk about it."

Timothy chimed in. "It's your future."

Solomon noticed Timothy for the first time. "Who are you?"

"I'm your guardian angel."

Solomon wondered if the guy was crazy. Bewildered, he looked at his dad.

"Dad, who is he really?"

Ken smiled. "He's this family's guardian angel. He can prove it to you quite easily."

"Oh, yeah. How?" Solomon tilted his head back and watched Timothy suspiciously.

Emily said, "Just ask him any detail of your life, things or events nobody would know about, not even us, and he will tell you."

Solomon thought about the darker side of his life, then decided it was safer not to try that test. Instead he said, "I trust you, guys."

Solomon sat down on the living room couch and took a deep breath. He kept looking at Timothy, wondering what to think about this miracle from God.

"Son," began Ken as he and the others sat down, "you know that you were released at the end of the Millennium."

Solomon seemed bored with the subject. "Yeah, so what?"

"The Bible says that Satan will be released at the end of the thousand years, which was three days ago."

Solomon sat forward on the couch, still not understanding his dad's point.

"That's the problem with this stuff. So Satan has been loosed. I can't see him, so number one, it's already hard to believe. Even so, what's the big deal?"

"The book of Revelation doesn't tell us how long the Devil will roam the earth," explained Cleveland, "but it says that Satan will gather people from all over the earth and bring them against Jerusalem."

Solomon grimaced at the theology. He surprised everybody by standing up and walking toward the door.

"Guys, I need some air. I'll be back in a while."

Emily stood up and followed him to the door, her downcast face revealing her fears. Solomon took one look at her expression and sighed.

"Mom, I promise. I'll be back. I need some time to think." He looked into her eyes. "No fooling."

Emily smiled and patted him on the back.

"Take your time, honey, I'll go make your favorite breakfast."

Solomon walked out the door and headed for his favorite spot, under the tree on top of the hill. As he approached the shade of the tree, his eyes were drawn to the words he and Allison had carved long ago.

"Solomon and Allison," he whispered to himself as he sat down and placed his hands behind his head.

He tilted his head toward the sky and watched a few sparse clouds moving slowly along. Suddenly, a fast-moving gray shadow flashed across the sky. He shook his head and closed his eyes. He opened them again and looked back at the blue sky. Nothing unusual here, he thought. Solomon took a deep breath and closed his eyes again. He thought about the good things his parents had done for him over the years and the times Allison and he had sipped milkshakes at the local hangout.

"They're part of the conspiracy!" shouted a spirit at the top of its tar-filled lungs.

Solomon instantly opened his eyes, looking directly in the spot where he had just seen the shadow.

"It's time to take back the earth!" yelled another demon.

He couldn't see anybody, but he knew the voices were real. He could hear them, and they scared him. Goose bumps popped up all over him as his eyes darted all over the place, hoping that the sounds were human.

"Meet in Jerusalem in three days, at high noon, and prepare to meet the real god!" The demon repeated the message several times before zooming off toward town.

Solomon began to shake. For the first time in a long while, the puzzle was coming together. He had been wrong, badly wrong. The voice was trying to get him to go to Jerusalem, just as the Bible, his parents, Allison, and Cleveland had told him.

Allison watched from her window. She saw Solomon stand and face the tree, placing his quivering hand on her engraved name.

"I'm so sorry," he mumbled. "Jesus, please forgive me."

Solomon started walking toward his house, then began to jog. Soon, he was in a full sprint. Allison didn't know what to think or do, so she prayed like she had never prayed before. Solomon burst through the front door of his house and collapsed on the floor. His breathing was fast and sporadic.

"Solomon!" shouted Ken, running to his side. "What happened to you?"

He was lying on his back, desperately trying to slow his breathing and his racing heart. Emily heard the commotion from the kitchen and rushed into the living room.

"Solomon!" she cried, bending over and touching his forehead.

He looked at his mother and started to cry.

Fourteen

Hurricane Watch

Pastor Paul raised his hand, signaling for the group of boys following him to stop.

"Hand me the binoculars," he told Andrew, who was standing directly behind him.

"What is it?" Andrew asked.

"I'm not sure, but I don't like it," Paul responded, peering through the lenses.

It appeared that a group of forty or fifty young people were headed directly toward Paul and his followers. As the pastor watched them approach, he began humming a hymn. Then he handed the glasses back to Andrew.

"Looks like big trouble is coming our way. They must be going to Jerusalem, too."

"Are we going to stop and witness to them?" asked Andrew, a hint of nervousness coloring his voice.

Pastor Paul seemed to ignore the question, but in reality, he was praying for guidance. He took a deep breath before answering Andrew.

"These young people are filled with the Devil. They're headed for Jerusalem in hopes of destroying Jesus. We would most likely be just an appetizer for them."

Andrew stared at Paul, unsure of what to think or feel.

"So...?" Andrew waited for Paul to continue.

"So we engage them with the strong arm of the Lord on our side!" Paul enthusiastically lifted his fist in the air. He looked at his spiritual warriors and told them, "There are young men and women approaching us who want to kill our

Lord. We, however, want to save their lives. We can't do it in our own strength. Let's pray and ask God to help us."

Paul dropped on both knees and lowered his head. The boys quickly followed Paul's example of humility and joined him in prayer.

Several hundred demons attached to the Jerusalem-bound group were partying and celebrating with despicable antics not fit to describe. Their influence over the young people was powerful. When the leader of the teenage group saw Paul and the boys praying, intense hatred welled up in his heart, which was now fully controlled by a demon.

He began running in their direction, followed by the others, screaming, "Down with Jesus! Down with Jesus! Down with Jesus!" When they were about a hundred yards from Paul and the boys, a towering thunderhead suddenly formed between the two groups. Although the rough gang screamed demonic threats from across the field, Paul and the boys didn't flinch. Their eyes remained closed in prayer, begging the Lord for a miracle.

"Hear their threats, Lord, and protect the righteous," shouted Paul above the sound of the increasingly violent thunderstorm.

Suddenly, a flurry of lightning bolts struck the dirt in between the groups. The thunder shook the ground and the rebels' hearts. They glared at the ever-darkening sky as their screaming obscenities were silenced. They had never seen or even imagined a storm like this one. Lightning continuously rained down from heaven as hail began to pound the rebel group, while leaving the righteous unscathed. Paul raised his hands to heaven and cried, "Jesus is Lord." Paul's companions opened their eyes just as a thin tornado dropped down from the black cloud. Not a hair was blown out of place on Paul's head, while the evil youth opposite them were pushed back by the powerful wind moving in their direction. Several were swept into the sky by the violent whirlwind.

Moments later, the sun was shining, the birds were chirping, and the revolutionaries were gone. Paul looked toward the area that had just been occupied by the enemy.

As he turned to his companions, his face radiated with the Lord's light.

"We must move forward, men. Pray for their souls, that God would have mercy on them."

Solomon's eyes darted back and forth. His hands were trembling, and his heart was beating dangerously fast.

"Daniel, get out there and see what's happening," Timothy ordered. Timothy remained by Ken and Emily as they attended to their son.

Immediately, Daniel zoomed through the roof and into the air. He searched the airspace surrounding the homestead. He could smell the foul odor of the demons, but he couldn't see any of them. He put his sword away and dropped down onto the roof. Glancing at the cedar shingles, he spotted a bloodred inscription that was scribbled on the roof.

"Leave or die!" it read. He examined the letters, looking for clues to its origin.

He quickly yanked his sword out, bent over, and placed his finger on the letters. Daniel brought the red liquid to his nose and quickly pulled his hand back, choking from the stench. He raced inside.

"Timothy!" he yelled, with a serious expression that Timothy hadn't seen since the Tribulation. "They're threatening to kill everybody."

Timothy glanced at Solomon, then motioned for Daniel to follow him into the kitchen. He didn't want to alarm anybody.

"What did you find?" inquired Timothy.

Daniel was nearly hyperventilating as he tried to speak. "There was a note, written in blood." His eyes widened. "It said, 'Leave or die!'"

Timothy paced the kitchen floor, his mind filled with questions but no answers.

Daniel said what was on Timothy's mind. "We need reinforcements!"

Timothy nodded as he eyed the angel. Moments later, a bright idea came to him.

"No, Daniel. We're not going to die; they are, and they know it. Their weapon of choice is no longer the sword," he paused as he stared at his friend, "but fear!"

The words seemed to settle Daniel down a bit, but he looked out the window and shook his head.

"I can't defend this entire house on my own. I need help!"

Timothy smiled and assured him, "Jesus will take care of it."

"It would be nice," Daniel mumbled to himself, but loudly enough for his friend to hear, "if I could see some of this 'help' with my own eyes."

The truth suddenly hit Daniel. He wasn't trusting in Jesus; he was trusting in what he could see—not in what he knew. He looked at Timothy for a moment, then he slowly flew toward the ceiling.

"Don't start with me. I know," he grimaced, not able to look Timothy in the eyes. "I'll be outside standing guard."

Timothy smiled at the angel, then hurried back into the living room to check on Solomon. Ken and Emily were by his side, softly talking to him.

"What did you see?" asked Ken as Emily stroked Solomon's brow.

"I, I'm...not sure." He was obviously in pain and having difficulty talking. "I saw these shadows, but, but it wasn't the shadows that scared me as much as..." His face turned ghostly white, and he began to shiver.

Ken gently shook his son, who appeared to be fading into some kind of self-induced stupor. Solomon's eyes suddenly opened wide.

Solomon whispered, "It was the voices." He looked back and forth at his parents repeatedly.

Cleveland, who was watching from the corner of the room, started to pray silently for Solomon.

"What voices, Solomon?" asked Emily, visibly shaken by her son's condition.

Solomon looked at his mother, the fear in his face slowly beginning to disappear.

"They were real, and they were telling me to go to Jerusalem for a big rally."

His eyes filled with tears. Ken nodded his head; it all began to make sense now. He turned toward Cleveland and Timothy.

"It's starting."

The doorbell rang. Timothy rushed to answer it, hoping not to distract Solomon or his parents.

Solomon sat up on the couch, and the color in his face started to return to normal.

"You guys told me this stuff was coming. Jesus warned me, too, but I didn't believe any of you. Then when I heard those voices and knew they were demons, I realized that everything you've ever taught me is true."

Emily wrapped her arms around her son, and Ken enfolded himself around the two. Timothy, followed by Allison and her parents, stopped at the doorway of the living room. They didn't want to interrupt the moment.

Solomon lowered his eyes. He swallowed hard before looking back at them. "I've been so wrong. When you didn't want me to have that bike, I acted like a spoiled brat. I should have known that you just wanted what was best for me." He paused, thinking about what he had done. "I can't believe how my life turned around that night. Yielding to the temptation to steal that bike led me down a road I never thought I would travel. I'm so sorry, Mom and Dad. Can you ever forgive me?"

Allison couldn't believe her ears. Solomon was sounding like a real Christian—being humble, willing to admit when he was wrong, and asking for forgiveness. She crossed her hands and placed them over her heart. She wanted to let Solomon know that she was there, but it wasn't time, not just yet. Her father placed his arm around her and smiled. Prayers were being answered.

"Oh, honey, don't be too hard on yourself," said Emily, caressing his face with her hands.

Ken interjected, "Son, I'm proud of you for what you've said, but the most important thing you can do right now is give your life to the Lord."

Solomon looked at his father without saying a word. There was still a struggle in his heart, but things were becoming clearer by the moment.

"Jesus doesn't want you to make just a decision for Him; He wants a full commitment. Solomon, do you know the difference?" his father asked.

Ken suddenly realized that Allison and her parents were in the hallway, but he didn't react, in hopes that Solomon would not be distracted.

"Yeah, Dad, I know the difference." He appeared embarrassed as he spoke. "I've made plenty of decisions for Christ, walking the aisle of our church and saying that I would accept Him." He sighed as his memory convicted him. "It seemed that nothing ever changed after those times. I guess I didn't mean it."

Ken was invigorated by his son's openness and honesty.

"Solomon, Jesus wants you to love Him with all you've got. You've been giving Him lip service for years. Outwardly, you'd been a good boy up until you stole that bike, but I bet inwardly you have been fighting a lot of bad stuff you don't even want to talk about."

Allison knew that side of Solomon more than his parents did or could probably handle, but she loved him anyway.

As Timothy was relishing the tender scene in the living room, Daniel suddenly plowed into the room with his swords drawn.

"Timothy, there's a black cloud of demons just north of here." He was frantically waving the swords in all directions. "There must be thousands of them. We're dead!"

Timothy motioned for Cleveland to follow him to the other room. Then he grabbed Allison's hand and whispered to her parents, "Follow me. We've got an emergency."

Ken didn't notice that they had left.

Emily asked her son a question, point-blank. "Solomon, how sure are you that you will be going to the new heaven?"

Solomon stared at her for a good while.

"Fifty-fifty, I guess."

Ken closed his eyes and shook his head.

"That's not good enough, Solomon. When you give your heart to Jesus, you know you love Him. If I were to tell your mother that I'm only fifty percent sure that I love her, or worse, that I'm only fifty percent sure I want to be married to her, what do you think she would do?"

Before Solomon could answer, Emily blurted out, "I'd have you for breakfast." Ken nervously smiled at her reaction.

"Don't you see, Solomon?" continued Ken. "Not being sure is a sign that you are lost, only hoping against real hope that you might be let in if you are lucky." Ken's face turned tough. "This isn't about luck; it's about commitment."

Solomon was confused. One second, he was ready to commit; now he was unsure.

In the laundry room next to the kitchen, the others huddled in the small space as Timothy told them the news.

"Allison, Bill, Gail, listen to me. We don't have much time, but I'm the Actions' guardian angel." Allison's eyes lit up with excitement, as did Bill's and Gail's.

"There is a huge force of demons heading for this house. My fellow angel Daniel tells me this is big-time trouble." Timothy's voice was steady and to the point. "Solomon could make a huge commitment any moment." He looked at them, hoping that they understood the urgency of the situation. "These demons want him badly, and they will stop at nothing to take Solomon to hell with them. We need to pray like there is no tomorrow for Solomon." He paused, looking through the kitchen and into the living room. "I mean that literally."

Allison spoke up as he uttered his last syllable.

"I want to lead the prayer, if you don't mind."

Timothy smiled at her request.

"It would be a pleasure to be led in prayer by someone whom I've admired from a distance for years."

Allison smiled at Timothy's kind words, and they all bowed their heads. They prayed hard, and with a power that could move mountains.

Ken and Emily sensed Solomon's division. Neither said a word as their son struggled to surrender his life to his Creator. His decision was not about their persuasive words or theological arguments; it was about the power of God to invade a dark heart and make it fresh and new.

"They want you as a trophy, Solomon! Don't do it!" belched demonic voices from all around him.

Solomon jerked his head up, fear overtaking him instantaneously. Daniel, who was standing on guard, lunged upward when he heard the voices. He catapulted his body from one side of the room to the other, his sword flying in circles. He covered the room with enough firepower to finish off dozens of demons. What he didn't know was that there were hundreds of them, all closing in on Solomon.

"Take him out now!" barked the commanding devil, pointing toward Solomon. "He's going to do something stupid if we don't stop him."

The demons converged on Solomon, all of them spitting out their sadistic lies about Jesus.

"Solomon," shouted Ken, "what is it?"

Emily began to cry as Solomon started to go into seizures. His arms swung wildly in all directions, nearly knocking her and Ken to the ground. They tried to hold him down, but the power of the demons was too great. The demons knocked both of them across the room. Ken and Emily were badly bruised, lying helpless on their backs. As they struggled to their feet, they saw that Solomon was drooling profusely.

"He's possessed!" cried Emily. She tried to go to Solomon, but Ken held her back.

"No, honey, it's not Solomon. Pray, just pray," he cried.

Timothy and the others could hear the uproar from their spot in the laundry room. Allison clenched her fists and began shouting her prayer as loudly as she could. The demons laughed at her faith. Several demons grabbed Daniel by the hair and wings and carried him to Solomon's tree on the hill. The angel's wings were badly injured. A demon laughed at the inscription, "Solomon loves Allison," and spat on it.

"Solomon loves Solomon!" the fiends shouted as they threw Daniel into the branches.

In a moment, in a twinkling of an eye, a light brighter than a thousand suns lit up the sky. The demons assaulting Daniel fainted with fear as the force of Jesus' fury hurled them miles to the east. Daniel covered his eyes as the light brightened around him.

"Daniel, get up. You can fly now," thundered Jesus, picking up the angel in His arms and gently tossing him into the air.

"Jesus, thank, thank...," uttered Daniel, emotion overtaking his tongue.

Jesus smiled at the young angel before He flew to the house.

"Thank you for your service!" called out the King.

Meanwhile, a chorus of a hundred demons danced around Solomon, singing, "Jesus is dead!"

Solomon's body suddenly went limp. Emily looked at his chest, and cried, "Ken, he's not breathing."

Ken crawled along the floor, following his wife toward their son. Solomon was out cold, but they feared he was dead.

Suddenly, a radiant light filled the room, and the darkness of the demons was instantly neutralized by Christ's light. They disappeared before one of them could belch out an obscenity.

Ken and Emily covered their eyes as the glory of the Lord filled the house. They all dropped to their knees in reverence and praise.

"Ken, Emily," spoke the Lord. The light faded to an aura encompassing Him.

They opened their eyes. Their hearts were filled with joy. This was it, and they knew it. Allison and the others ran into the room. Christ greeted each of them with a holy kiss.

"I want to commend each of you for your faith. You have continued praying through this adversity and have continued seeking Me and My Father's will. You will be rewarded in the end."

Jesus sat down next to Solomon.

"He's not breathing, Lord," sobbed Emily through her tears.

"Have faith, Emily; he's only sleeping." Jesus touched Solomon's chest, and instantly, it began to move. "Arise, My son." Solomon immediately opened his eyes, sat up, then turned and stared at the Lord.

He whispered, "Jesus!"

Allison was muttering, "Praise God, praise God," as Jesus and Solomon stared at each other.

Jesus remained silent and waited for Solomon to fully regain his senses. He wanted him to make the first move. Solomon couldn't take his eyes off the Lord. Struggling to find the right words, he began, "I had this nightmare, Jesus. There were these animals, no, they were demons, devils, and they were trying to carry me away." Solomon stopped talking. His face turned pale and ghostlike. "I was going to hell."

Emily closed her eyes and started weeping again. Allison swallowed hard at the thought.

"Solomon, look around this room," Jesus said in a tender voice.

Solomon turned and smiled at his mother and father, then he saw her—Allison, his love. His eyes fastened on her as he realized just how much he loved her and how much she still loved him.

"Solomon!" she cried, her heart collapsing under the load of their rocky past.

Jesus interrupted the love scene.

"These people, Solomon, have been praying for you unceasingly. They love you, and you owe them much. I am here today because of their faith—not because of anything you have done. Do you understand, Solomon?"

Solomon nodded without uttering a word. There was something different about Jesus, something new, something his heart could connect to.

Jesus looked at Ken. "You have been faithful to My Father and to Me since your conversion, Ken. Talk to your son."

Jesus remained seated next to Solomon as Ken addressed his son.

"Solomon, we love you very much." He looked around the room at the others. "And we want the best for you."

Solomon interrupted his father. "Dad, you don't need to tell me that. You and Mom," smiling brightly, he turned his eyes to his mother, "have been teaching me the truth since I was crawling around this house getting into everything. It's not that I didn't know right from wrong. I was confused and thought that having freedom meant doing my own thing and turning my back on all that you had taught me." Solomon turned to Jesus. "You washed my feet, then I spat in Your face. I'm so sorry, Jesus, for rejecting You."

Emily tried to fight back her tears as she watched Solomon's confession through the eyes of a mother. With loving compassion, Jesus accepted Solomon's apology.

"Lord," began Solomon, his eyes fixed on Jesus, "please forgive me for what I've done." Solomon dropped to his knees. Everyone was crying. "Help me to change, Jesus. Help me to love You. Help me to be the Christian I should be."

Solomon wept. Jesus placed His right hand on top of Solomon's head and said, "Be filled with the Holy Spirit!" A tongue of fire streamed from the Lord's hand. It began to spin around Solomon's body, eventually coming to rest on his chest.

"Lord, I love You!" whispered Solomon. His energy was spent, just like a soldier coming to the end of an intense battle.

"Repent, My son, and be baptized in My name."

The ball of fire hovered outside Solomon's shirt, directly over his heart.

"I want to change, Jesus. Please help me to!"

The fire suddenly disappeared under Solomon's shirt. The energy invigorated Solomon. His spine suddenly straightened with renewed strength.

"Enter into My rest, Solomon."

The power of Jesus' smile mesmerized Solomon and the others. Solomon gazed at his Lord and Savior with overwhelming love and adoration.

"Thank You, Jesus," Ken said softly, his eyes never straying from the Lord.

"Do you love Me, Solomon?" asked Jesus.

"Yes, Lord," answered Solomon, a bit surprised by the question.

"Then obey My Word."

Solomon stared at Jesus as the Lord's words began to sink into his heart.

Jesus announced, "Soon, Solomon, you will be with Me in paradise."

The Lord stood to His feet and looked around the room. The love in His face was immeasurable. He slowly lifted off the ground, the light surrounding Him growing brighter by the second.

"Be faithful to the end, and great will be your reward!" The next second, Jesus was gone. Allison was the first to rush to Solomon's side.

"Solomon, I love you!" she sobbed, her arms shaking as she held him tightly.

Ken grabbed Emily as she made a move to her son.

"Wait a second," he whispered, pointing to the couple.

Emily stopped, a smile emerging on her face.

She spoke softly, "I've been praying for this for months."

Cleveland glanced at Timothy, who was staring at him. Having the same idea, they quickly tiptoed out of the room. Bill grabbed Gail's hand and tried to lead her into the kitchen, but he was met with an iron grip that communicated, "Don't even think it!" Gail was not going to miss this moment for anything.

"Do you have any idea how hard I prayed for you, you hardheaded man!" Allison lightly punched him in the chest.

Solomon blushed. "I wasn't being hardheaded," he retorted as he tried to come up with something witty. "I was just being an independent thinker."

"Independent, maybe," responded Allison, firmly clutching his hand. "A thinker," she smiled one of those "gotcha" smiles, "no."

Solomon lifted his eyebrows. "I'm smart enough to know how stupid I was to break our engagement."

Allison spoke what the Holy Spirit had revealed to her. "You didn't dump me, Solomon; you dumped God first, and I was simply His representative. You were running from God, and that meant you had to break up with me as well."

Solomon started to speak, then stopped. He knew that Allison had assessed the situation perfectly. He dropped on his knees, took her hands in his, and gently pulled her close.

"Allison," he said as their parents looked on, "I know the time is short, but would you marry me?"

Allison didn't expect the proposal. She shook her head in disbelief, which Solomon immediately read as a no. He got off his knees and quickly turned away. Allison lunged toward him and shouted, "Yes, yes, yes," as she embraced and kissed him passionately.

Emily and Gail rushed to hug them.

"I've been dreaming of this day for years," cried Emily.

"Me, too," added Gail. "Whatever you two want to do is fine with your father and me. It's so good to see both of you happy again." Gail could barely contain her joy.

Then the reality of the situation hit Emily. Her happiness suddenly turned to sorrow. "Satan could march on Jerusalem any day now. You may not get to have your wedding!"

"Listen, guys," Ken said. "For years, Jesus has been counting down the time until Satan's release. But what we don't know is how long he will be free before he attacks Jerusalem. It could be today, next week, next month, or even longer. I say we plan the wedding for sometime next month and hope for the best."

Solomon read Allison like a book. Her face sealed his decision.

"You guys," began Solomon, "we know that you all want everything to be just right for this wedding. We are your only children, after all, and this is a big thing for you guys." He paused, careful to find the right words. "I think I can speak for Allison, though, that it's more important to us to get married now than it is to plan a huge wedding and not have time for it to happen." He watched Allison's face; she nodded in agreement. Solomon smacked the coffee table with the palm of his hand. "I say we get married tomorrow evening. What do you think, Allison?"

Allison's eyes twinkled at his words. She looked at her mother and father for their approval.

"Sounds good to me," said Gail, grabbing Bill's hand.

"Me, too," he responded.

Solomon looked at his mother. She said nothing for several seconds, which gave the couple the jitters.

"If you two want to be married tomorrow, I say, let's go for it!" smiled Emily, her mind already making plans for the big day.

There was no doubt as to who was in charge as Denny and a large group of guys sat around the campfire. The entourage had expanded during the day as several dozen young men had joined them. All of them were bent on getting even with Jesus and His followers. Denny stared at the flames with a hypnotic glower.

"I want to get to Jerusalem as fast as possible," he informed them. "It will take forever to get there by foot, so I have a plan that will make things a lot easier for all of us."

His smile was sadistic and frightening yet somehow charismatic. He knew his destiny and welcomed it with open arms. He was a rebel and proud of it.

Larry said, "There's not a town for a hundred miles or more between here and Jerusalem. Does your plan include sprouting wings and flying?"

Most of the boys laughed until they saw that Denny didn't.

"You want a piece of me, Larry?" He stood to his feet and rolled up his sleeves, pacing like a hungry hyena before dinner.

Larry didn't move. He contorted his face and responded, "Come on, Denny. Lighten up, man. I was just having some fun with you."

Every eye watched for Denny's response. Denny stared at Larry for a long while. He wasn't planning to take Larry on; he knew Larry was just kidding, but he coveted power and would do anything to secure his leadership with the others.

A smirk crept on Denny's face as he kicked some dirt toward Larry.

"The only one flying around here is going to be you when I kick you in the rear."

Kevin laughed first, followed by the others. Denny looked around at the teenagers, feeding on their attention. He started to laugh, too. Then he sat back down by the fire.

"Okay, guys, here's the deal. I had this dream last night that told me to get to Jerusalem by Friday." He looked around, making sure everybody was listening. "That's two days!"

A younger teenager raised his hand, hoping to be heard. Denny rolled his eyes and pointed to him.

"Yeah, what is it?"

The ruddy-looking boy appeared spooked.

"I had the same dream last night. It was intense." He stood up. "There were millions of us all gathering in Jerusalem for this huge rally. We were all protesting the stupid stuff that Jesus demands of us."

Kevin jumped up and said with excitement, "I had the same dream! Jesus was on His throne, acting all righteous and calm when we stormed the city and took over!"

Everybody started talking at the same time, sharing the same details from their dreams.

Denny glared at them with contempt, and they all got quiet.

"Well, it's obvious," began Denny, "that we all had the same dream, and I believe that this is not by chance. It's a miracle!" He became animated as he spoke. "This is a sign from the gods, the real gods, that it's going to happen. All the rules that bind us and keep us from having fun are going to end on Friday!"

He raised his hand in the air in the exact way that Hitler had done before the Great Tribulation.

"Are you with me, men?"

They returned the salute and shouted.

"Jerusalem! Jerusalem! Jerusalem!"

Denny stood boldly in their midst.

"We have one option, men, and that is to head north and pillage the town that Larry, Kevin, and I just left."

The rebels nodded their heads as Denny started counting them.

"There's almost a hundred of us, and I'm sure we can easily scrounge up fifty or more gravity machines." His face fell dark and cold. "I think it would be nice to get even with those who elected Jesus their King after the Great Tribulation. They should have to pay for their sins like many of us had to at those blasted camps!"

It was obvious that Denny didn't know his history, nor did he care to learn the truth. Whatever served his purposes and achieved his desires was fine with him.

"Gentlemen, our parents are part of this vast conspiracy to make us slaves to their way of life." A powerful demon suddenly entered Denny's body. He took a deep breath and closed his eyes. His chest began to bulge, and his fingers tightened and curled at the ends.

"Ah," moaned Denny. He opened his eyes. They began to dart nervously as he looked around at the crowd of boys. "We will get even with them, and the best way to do that is to kill their King!"

The demonic captain possessing Denny whistled loudly to his fellow spirits. Hundreds of demons stormed in, fighting over which young man they would possess. Some of the boys were screaming; others were laughing. Larry and Kevin howled at the moon as "something" took hold of them.

Denny and his spirit guide looked around at the chaos and smirked. Something strange was happening in Denny's head. It was like he was hooked into a powerful computer, and it was feeding him endless amounts of information. He thought it was great.

"Gentlemen, in the morning we head north. We take what is rightfully ours, inflict a little pain and suffering along the way, then we move on to Jerusalem and kill the King."

Larry looked at Denny. Denny knew what he was thinking. Larry walked toward him and spoke softly. "You know Solomon is probably home. He might have gone over to the enemy."

A sneer emerged on Denny's face.

"Treason is a terrible offense. Before the Great Tribulation, it was punishable by death. Back in the days of the great Babylonian Empire, they killed not only the guilty one, but his family as well."

Satan hovered above the Holy City, miles out of the range of the angelic army. He glared at the temple where Jesus resided. The hatred in his heart could power several nuclear generators. Occasionally, a stray demon or two would invade the city's airspace. The results were ugly. It was as if somebody had taken a newspaper and tossed it directly into the sun. The demons weren't just injured; they were annihilated.

General Ruse flew in from the south and saluted his master.

"Sir, everything is going as planned. The young humans are eating up your wisdom hook, line, and sinker."

Satan closed his eyes and nodded his head. Good news was pleasing to his soul. He didn't need another day like the Battle of Armageddon.

"How are the humans responding to my deadline?"

"Some are having trouble securing transportation, sir." He paused as he carefully worded his next statement, since it could easily be misinterpreted by Satan. "I took it upon myself, sir, to order those who cannot find a gravity machine to do anything in their power to find one, including lying, stealing, and even killing."

A smile formed on Satan's face.

"Well done, Ruse!"

"Sir, may I have the details on Friday's event? You've left me in the dark. Your success is contingent—"

Satan hissed violently at him.

"I know that, Ruse! You will get the orders when I decide to give them to you. I can't afford to allow that information to fall into the wrong hands, and I know your history!"

General Ruse appeared stunned by the accusation. He was about to defend his honor when Satan nixed the idea.

"Do you remember the day I told you my plan for Hitler and how we could finish off the United States?" Ruse said nothing. "You and I were the only ones with that knowledge, but somehow the Americans found out."

Satan turned his back to the general. The general's silence sealed his guilt.

Satan was a great liar. He was hiding knowledge from the general. The truth was that he had no idea how he was going to penetrate Jerusalem and kill Jesus. What the general didn't know was going to hurt him, but Satan didn't care. Revenge controlled him like drugs controlled an addict.

———————

Solomon and Allison leaned against their tree, talking about their past and future while gazing at the stars. They held hands, and Allison laid her head against Solomon's shoulder.

"What got into you in the first place?" she asked.

He took a deep breath.

"I don't know, honey. I was stupid. I couldn't get that gravity machine out of my head."

Allison kissed him lightly on the cheek.

"Solomon, I'm talking about us. Why did you really break things off with me?"

He gazed into the night sky, not wanting to look into her eyes.

"Honestly, I started getting really scared. I knew that I wasn't a Christian, and I knew I couldn't be the husband

that you wanted and needed me to be. You deserved someone far better."

She squeezed his hand tightly.

"You've always been the one for me, Solomon." She
placed her hand on his face and turned him in her direction. "I was at fault, too. I knew you weren't serious about
your relationship with God, Solomon. I disobeyed Him by
continuing to date you."

"I know, and I'm sorry I led you, for even a moment, to
do anything that God didn't want you to do." Solomon
smiled tenderly at her. "I'm glad you stuck it out with me,
though. God is so merciful for finally putting us together."

"How do you feel now that you are truly saved?" Allison
asked.

Solomon shook his head.

"It's so different from faking it. It actually feels good to
obey God, and it's already easier than it was before."

Allison nuzzled closer to Solomon as she dreamed
about the future.

"I hope we get to have our honeymoon before Satan attacks. I've always dreamed of being married since I was a
young girl."

Solomon nodded. "It's going to happen." He stared into
her eyes. "Did you ever think about going out with somebody else?"

Allison instantly looked away. She hesitated for a moment, which aroused Solomon's jealousy.

"You did go out with somebody else. Who was it?"

She avoided looking at Solomon.

"It was no big deal." She tried to cuddle up to him, but
he was not going to be so easily appeased.

"No way, girl!" responded Solomon, placing her directly
in front of him. "Don't tell me it was that egotistical quar-
terback with the—"

Allison quickly interrupted him. "Solomon Action, I
went out with him one time, and that's all. I didn't even
want to go, and the only reason I did was because my
mother arranged it. She thought it would be a good idea."
Allison looked at him with righteous indignation. "She

thought it would help me get my mind off the guy who had dumped me and ended up in a detention camp!"

The truth hurt. With a pained expression, Solomon forced a weak smile. He laughed nervously as he said, "I was just testing your loyalty, dear."

Allison had him exactly where she wanted him. She ran her fingers through his hair. She said nothing, waiting to see if this conversation was over for good. A couple of minutes passed before she changed the subject.

"Where are we going to go for our honeymoon?"

Solomon had been thinking of that all night, but sighed when he heard the question. With Satan free and morality crumbling all around them, the only safe place to go to was Jerusalem. Solomon did what any good politician would do; he answered an easier question that hadn't been asked.

The young couple talked into the wee hours of the morning as they sat under the light of the stars. Heaven smiled on them as their love grew brighter than the coming dawn.

"I love you," she said. "This is a dream come true."

The vision slowly faded, then suddenly reappeared again, more vivid than the first time.

"I now pronounce you, husband and wife!" declared the preacher.

He didn't recognize anybody as his eyes scanned the crowd. There were flowers and a church and lots of well-dressed people. The dream turned hazy again.

"Go, Paul!" thundered a voice from heaven.

"Wait!" called the pastor in his sleep. "Where do I go, Lord? Who are these people?"

Paul awoke suddenly. Sweat was dripping from his body. He looked around the campsite and sighed. Most of the young men were up, while he, their leader, had still been sleeping! He remembered the dream again and quickly looked toward heaven.

"Lord, I don't understand. You didn't tell me who they were. You want me and my men to attend a wedding when we are trying to save the lost?"

Andrew walked over to Paul and sat down, a worried look filling his face.

"Pastor, I had a dream last night." The pastor raised his eyebrows. "There was a wedding, and Solomon was in trouble."

The hair on Paul's arms stood on end as the Holy Spirit spoke to him. He suddenly realized that, with Solomon marrying, the young man must have given his life over to the Lord. Paul's face came alive.

"Solomon—in trouble on his wedding day?" Paul jumped up and shouted, "We're breaking camp in ten minutes. We've got to get to Solomon!"

The group quickly packed the few things they had to carry and marched toward the north at an uncomfortably speedy pace. Then Paul spotted a huge mansion, built on the top of a hill.

"Go to that house, now!" whispered the Holy Spirit. "Solomon needs you!"

Pastor Paul waved his arms and shouted.

"Let's take that hill! Something big is going down!"

Paul looked toward the sky, somewhat confused by the command. "Lord, Solomon isn't up there. I don't get it."

"Go!" shouted the Spirit.

It didn't make sense to Paul, but he didn't question the prompting of the Lord any further. That was what faith was all about, thought the pastor. Don't ask how, why, or what. Just say yes.

The group hurried toward the large house. Fifteen minutes later, they reached the mansion. Paul knocked on the door. Seconds later, a man, dressed in a white robe, opened the door.

"Sir, the Lord has called us to come here, but I do not know why."

The man smiled, then stated, "Follow me to the back of the house." Paul and the young men followed him around the house. A monstrous garage the size of two or three houses was built behind the mansion.

"What's that for?" asked Paul.

"It's for you," answered the stranger.

"Why do I need a garage?"

The man smiled, "You don't. You need what's inside."

The stranger spoke in a commanding tone. "Open!" The door lifted in response to his voice.

As Paul saw what was inside, he did a double take. Inside the garage, at least forty or fifty gravity vehicles were lined up.

He smiled and said, "God is good!"

The boys raced inside the garage, acting like a bunch of teenagers going for the front car of a super roller coaster. Paul tried to give directions above the ruckus.

"Gentlemen, it's a long trip to Solomon's house. Take it easy and follow me, and no hot dogging!"

Fifteen

Hurricane Warning!

Ken and Bill were frantically running around town rushing through last-minute errands. They hadn't wanted their wives to do the shopping because they were concerned for their safety. The number of crimes had dramatically increased over the past few days. Many shops remained closed after several robberies and assaults had occurred. Ken and Bill walked quickly down the street, looking for a flower shop that was still open.

"Shouldn't you be working, Bill? I'm surprised that everyone at the police station isn't pulling overtime now."

Bill shook his head as he watched three apparent hoodlums approaching them.

"No, Jesus shut us down last week."

Ken appeared surprised.

"Why did He do that?"

"For the same reason He let Solomon out. With Satan on the loose, it's obvious that He's allowing evil to go unpunished. He wants everybody to see what happens when evil finally has its way."

Both men closely observed the young troublemakers. As they passed by, Bill reached for the laser gun hidden in his jacket. Ken's eyes widened as he realized what Bill was doing.

"You trying to cause trouble?" Ken asked, as the boys suddenly stopped behind the men.

"No, I'm trying to prevent it."

As Bill and Ken continued walking, they could hear the sound of the boys' steps coming back toward them. Bill turned around and pulled out his weapon, pointing it in the air.

"Stop right there!" he shouted. The thugs stopped immediately when they saw the gun. In spite of their fear, they were still belligerent.

"What do you think you are, a cop or something?" yelled the oldest and meanest of the boys.

"That's exactly what I am," Bill answered, pulling out his badge and holding it out for them to see. "You boys get out of here!" Bill commanded, keeping his gun in full view.

The hooligans sprinted away, shouting obscenities.

Ken shook his head.

"I just don't get the rebellion brewing out there. It's like these kids were reared by wild animals."

"Ken," began Bill, somewhat surprised by his friend's statement, "you know that's not true. Think of Solomon!"

Ken nodded, feeling bad about his insensitive remark.

Bill continued as they reached an open florist's shop. "Most couples have to be tearing their hearts out over the decisions that some of these young brutes are making. I guess we're extra blessed."

Ken grimaced at the thought of Solomon's not repenting, yet thanked God for His grace.

They walked into the flower shop and looked around, somewhat surprised by the lack of merchandise. A plump but jolly-looking man with a notable mustache greeted them from behind the counter.

"Welcome, gentlemen." His smile was friendly although his hands fidgeted at his sides.

"Are you okay?" asked Bill.

The man took a long gulp.

"Yeah, I'm sorry. I guess I'm just a little nervous." He kept looking out the large window. "I've been robbed twice in the last two days. The only reason I've stayed open is to have a chance to witness to these youngsters." He shrugged his shoulders. "I could care less about the money."

Ken looked around the shop, disappointed by what he saw. Five less-than-appealing arrangements were on display. He knew the ladies would understand their predicament, but he had hoped that there was something better than this available.

"My son and his daughter," he said, pointing to Bill, "are getting married today, and we were hoping to get some flowers for the ceremony."

Bill swallowed hard. "And it's in two hours."

The florist smiled. "And you fine gentlemen want to make the bride and your wives happy." He looked around the store and laughed. Ken and Bill looked at each other.

"What's so funny?" asked Bill.

"Well, I'm picturing you men coming back with that junk on the shelves." The florist motioned to them. "Follow me to the back. I've been trying to keep the good stuff out of sight." He grimaced. "Some kids came in here yesterday and pulled all the flowers out of the arrangements. They tossed them on the floor and pounced on them, just to be mean!"

Bill and Ken followed the florist through an empty room into what appeared to be a broom closet.

He looked at Bill and Ken and smiled. "I hope you like these." He opened the door and stepped out of the way. They walked into a back storage room, their eyes popping out at what greeted them.

"Wow! I think we hit the end of the rainbow!" smiled Ken.

––––––––––

Satan was slouching on his fixed-up throne, staring mindlessly at the rock wall across from him. The faint sounds of boiling lava beneath his feet eased his anxiety. He tried to ignore the constant moaning sounds from Blasphemy, who was still tied up in the adjacent room. Satan had it all by the world's standards: fame, power, and respect; yet, he wanted more. He had to have more! More of what, he wasn't sure, but he would get it!

The Great Dragon rubbed his elongated chin. He was in deep thought. How could he penetrate Jerusalem? How could he destroy the Son of God? How could he get away with it and not be caught? He grunted to himself, realigned his aged body against the hard throne, then spit into the liquid fire at the bottom of the cavern.

"You can't win!" he mumbled, his fists clenching in anger. "I can't be wrong!" he yelled, his body stiffening with rage. Satan stood up and lifted his paws defiantly toward heaven. His spine curved backward, like a snake readying to attack its prey. "You will pay!" shrieked the Devil at a pitch Blasphemy had never heard before.

Blasphemy smirked.

Ah, divine justice, thought Blasphemy. He's not all-powerful! He's all-pitiful.

Suddenly, a loud, frightening scream rocked the cavern, nearly knocking Blasphemy out of his demonic skin. A second later, dead silence filled the chamber, the kind of silence that often followed tragedy or a once-in-a-lifetime storm. Blasphemy mustered all his energy to bend over and peer under the rock door into Satan's throne room. Patches of lava covered the floor of the cavern. Blasphemy's eyes widened as he watched the puddles of lava miraculously move uphill, then into the river below.

The Devil lay on the floor inches from his throne. The smell of burning flesh filled the room. As Satan looked at the burns covering nearly half his body, his heart filled with terror. He replayed the cataclysmic event in his mind—lava exploding toward the ceiling, covering him and the entire cavern. His normally immune spirit flesh reacted as if it were human flesh. Satan crawled across the rock floor, panting like a deer that had just been sideswiped by a truck. He looked toward heaven, mumbling an expletive before everything turned black.

———

"Yee-haw!" barked Denny at the top of his lungs, his gravity vehicle recklessly weaving through the heart of town. He glanced down at the rest of the boys. "You fools go to the north end of town. That's where all the rich people live."

Larry and Kevin led the group across town. Just for the fun of it, they took off their tee shirts, lit them, and tossed them into the downtown businesses. Scared business owners ran out on the street, fleeing for their lives. None of them dared to confront the violent teenagers who seemed to be possessed.

Minutes later, the angry group reached the edge of the peaceful neighborhood. They spread out across the quiet community, looking for gravity vehicles.

Larry and Kevin sprinted toward a rather large ranch house. When they reached the driveway, lined with blooming tulips and daffodils, Larry squashed the flowers while Kevin knocked over a bike.

"Let's head for the garage," shouted Larry as he watched several of their comrades eyeing the houses on either side.

When they reached the garage door, Larry tried to pull the handle upward, hoping that the owners had left it open. He pulled and then cursed loudly when it didn't respond.

"We're going to have to kick it in," decided Kevin, backing up.

Larry looked into the living room window.

"Forget that. Let's just break the window and go through the house."

Larry picked up a decorative rock near a small fountain in the yard and tossed it through the window. From inside the house, a woman screamed.

The boys laughed as they cleared the glass away from the window. They could see people running out the back door.

Kevin sneered, "Let's smack some of those Jesus lovers around before getting the machine."

Larry looked behind him.

"No time, man. We've got to help the other guys find vehicles."

Kevin carefully climbed through the window, followed by Larry. They ran through the living room, knocking over lamps and chairs. They made their way through a hallway that led to the garage. Kevin suddenly stopped, causing Larry to run into him. Both of them fell on the floor.

"You fool!" yelled Kevin as he tried to push Larry off him.

"What did you stop for?" said Larry, more than irritated.

As Kevin turned around to scold Larry, he saw a small bathroom off the hallway. A young teenager's head was visible behind a cabinet. He silently pointed toward it. Larry squinted for a moment, then nodded his head.

"Let's check it out," Kevin suggested deviously.

Slowly, silently, they walked into the bathroom. They couldn't see the boy's head anymore, which seemed to excite them all the more.

"Let's take him hostage," smirked Larry. "I'd love to see his parents squirm!"

Kevin appeared delighted by the suggestion. They were eager to have some fun. Demons completely possessed them, but they didn't know it. They wanted to get even with everybody who had survived the Great Tribulation, because it was those people who, in their minds, had established Jesus as King.

Larry was the first to approach the cabinet, the only available hiding place in the bathroom. He stopped and reached for the knobs to open the cupboard doors. Kevin stood directly behind him. Both boys hoped to scare the daylights out of the boy. Larry flung open the doors, then started to curse loudly.

"He's gone!" he yelled, punching Kevin roughly in the chest.

Kevin had to inspect the area for himself. He shook his head in anger, "Where could he be? He couldn't have just disappeared." He looked out the window but saw nothing. He checked the window, and it was evident that it was securely locked. He checked the cabinet again, the bathtub, and even the trash can, but he still found nothing. Larry walked toward the garage, ignoring Kevin's desperate attempt to prove his credibility. Kevin followed him seconds later. "I'm not stupid or blind. That kid disappeared!"

Frustrated, Larry said, "Forget about it!" as he opened the door leading into the garage.

Two beautiful gravity machines were theirs for the taking. They were some of the best on the market, and the boys knew it.

"Yeah, baby!" yelped Kevin as he jumped on the snazziest one.

"I'll race you," challenged Larry as he boarded the other high-octane machine.

"You go look for your ghost!" laughed Kevin.

He started the engine and instantly hit the throttle, sending him and the machine right through the garage door, splintering it into hundreds of pieces. Kevin was thrown twenty yards in the air. He hit the pavement with tremendous force. Larry jumped off his machine and ran to his side.

"Kevin, you okay?" he called, touching him lightly on the back.

Kevin, who was lying on his stomach in the middle of the street, didn't respond. Larry grabbed him by his pants and rolled him over. He gasped at the sight. Several large pieces of the garage door were lodged in Kevin's chest, stomach, and face. Blood dripped from the wounds. He tried to turn away, but his eyes were drawn toward Kevin's face, and in particular, to his eyes. They were open, but lifeless. Larry slowly backed away from his best friend, his eyes hypnotized by the look of death. He started to stammer and turn away.

His heart felt like it was going to burst. Leaning against a tree, he wrapped his quivering arms around it. He took a deep breath, then howled toward heaven, "Nooo!"

The shrieking scream echoed, catching Denny's ear from a quarter of a mile away.

"What was that?" he wondered as he turned toward the sound.

He didn't see Larry or Kevin, but what he did see sent shivers down his spine. A crowd of people was gathering around a rather small building with a steeple on top. He maneuvered the machine a safe distance away, not wanting

311

to be spotted yet. Denny grabbed a pair of binoculars from a compartment on the machine and looked through them. A monstrous smile filled his face.

"Traitor!" he murmured under his breath.

———————

Allison recalled the feelings she had experienced just days ago when she had stared into the mirror. Was she pretty enough? Was her personality too—whatever? Had she done something wrong? Was God mad at her? She sighed happily at the different feelings she had today. She was content, excited, and looking forward to the future. Her dark hair was pinned up, with curls escaping on each side. Her face was partially hidden by her bridal veil, yet no one could miss seeing her enormous smile. The white, silk wedding gown flowed delicately down her petite frame.

"Do you think it's too much?" she asked.

Emily and Gail smiled.

"Too much?" laughed her mother. "You can't be too beautiful, honey."

Gail hugged her and began to cry.

"Solomon is so blessed," his mother said. She was trying to hold back the tears, too, but was doing a miserable job.

A look of panic hit Allison.

"Is Solomon here?"

The mothers rolled their eyes.

"No," began Gail, "last time I saw him, he was off to the mountains to do some hiking."

Allison half laughed and half cried.

"That's not funny." Her roller-coaster emotions were getting the best of her. A serious look suddenly overtook her face. "Is he ready? He can't be late, you know."

Emily placed her hand on her future daughter-in-law's shoulder.

"I just came from his room. He's as nervous as you are, and he looks as handsome as his father."

———————

On the other side of the church, Solomon was rearranging his white bow tie for the nineteenth time. He was sporting a white tuxedo with gleaming white shoes. Ken and Bill were sitting nearby, now able to laugh together and put behind them the night that Solomon had been caught stealing.

It was strange, but the pain of the past was gone now that Solomon' s future was secure in Christ. The men enjoyed the moment as they realized what God had done in all of their lives—especially in Solomon's.

Ken stood next to his son and stared at him in the full-length mirror.

"I'm proud of you, son." He placed his hands on Solomon's shoulders. "You've been a wonderful son, and I know that you're going to be one fine husband, even if it's only for a few days."

Solomon shot off a smile. "I've heard that the honeymoon is the best part of the marriage."

They laughed.

Bill said, "Maybe so, Solomon, but in reality, it's the years of life and the trust and companionship that really matter," he looked around the room, "even for us men."

Ken agreed. "Allison's one special girl, son!"

"She sure is," added Bill, "and you'd better treat her right, or I'll come and arrest you for blatant stupidity."

"I will, too," came a familiar voice from the other side of the half-closed door.

Solomon instantly recognized it.

"Pastor Paul!" He ran to the door and hugged Paul, nearly knocking the air from the poor man's lungs. "It's so good to see you. How did you know I was getting married today?"

The difference in Solomon's demeanor was obvious. As Paul looked into his eyes, a huge smile spread across Paul's face.

"You really did get saved, didn't you, son?"

Solomon grinned, "You bet, sir, and a lot of it had to do with that mean preaching you did."

"I just obeyed the Lord. I wasn't sure any of it was getting into that thick skull of yours."

Ken couldn't wait to meet Paul. "I'm Ken, Solomon's father. I can't thank you enough for all that you did for my son, my wife, and me."

Paul latched onto Ken's hand.

"I only reinforced something you and your wife taught him through blood, sweat, and tears. You owe me nothing!"

Solomon placed his hand on Paul's elbow. "Thank you, Pastor, for what you did for me. I will be eternally grateful. Now, please tell me how you knew I was getting married today."

Paul pointed toward the ceiling.

"The Holy Spirit led me here, but to be honest with you, I don't know why."

Solomon frowned a bit.

"Oh, son, don't take that wrong," Paul quickly interjected with a tender tone. "With Satan marching on Jerusalem any day now, I've been evangelizing the lost," he looked out the door, "along with my army of seventy."

Solomon gulped, "Uh, we don't have room for seventy—"

Paul interrupted him, "No, Solomon. They're standing guard outside. I don't want anything to interrupt your big day."

"Well, you're going to stay, aren't you? We want you to be our honored guest."

The pastor nodded. "I wouldn't miss it for the world!"

The sound of the organ playing in the background caused butterflies to attack Solomon's stomach.

"This is it!" announced Ken.

Bill laughed. "Looks like your son has a case of the jitters." Bill walked toward the door and placed his arm around the pastor as they went toward the sanctuary.

"I think I feel sick."

"Only natural," assured Ken. "Just remember: Listen to the preacher. Allison's quite sensitive, and a miscue from you could really upset her."

This was it. As Solomon's friends and family talked among themselves, he started thinking about Denny. He squinted and shook his head. Why in the world was he thinking about Denny? This was his wedding day. Suddenly, the Spirit softly spoke to him, "Pray for him, Solomon. I had mercy on you, and you must now show mercy to him."

Daniel was resting comfortably near the bottom of the steeple as several dozen angels circled the church.

"I'm glad you angels agreed to help," he called out. " I could never do this on my own." He was tossing his sword into the air, then catching it by the handle as it came back down.

Timothy stepped out of the church and looked around. He hadn't grown accustomed to seeing hundreds of demons circling the town, like vultures waiting for their victim to die. He saw Daniel haphazardly tossing his sword.

"Daniel!" he shouted loud enough for the angel to hear, but still out of the demons' range of hearing. "They could attack at any minute. What are you doing?"

Daniel grabbed his sword out of the air and quickly put it away. He cleared his throat and sat down, as if he hadn't heard the rebuke.

"Don't ignore me!" yelled Timothy.

Daniel bobbed his head as if surprised and looked down.

"What did you say?"

Timothy shook his head and sighed.

"I said to be careful up there! You might have some hefty angels at your disposal, but if all those demons decide to attack at once, you might end up as demon stew meat."

Daniel saluted without saying a word.

Inside the church, Cleveland was two rows from the front, squirming in the pew. He was acting like a father whose son was about to be married. Cleveland felt a little

315

like Solomon's spiritual father. Even though Cleveland had become a Christian so recently himself and had had so little time to plant seeds of faith in Solomon, God miraculously had made them grow in record time!

Emily and Gail sat side by side in the front row as tears of joy flowed down their cheeks. They had talked about this day since Allison and Solomon had been in diapers. It was a day of victory and of hope.

A door in the church creaked open. Solomon and Ken walked to the platform. Their hands were folded in front of them. It was hard to tell that Solomon was nervous unless you watched his eyes, which were darting all over the room. He was facing the crowd and bouncing up and down on his heels. Ken, who was standing next to him, whispered, "Calm down, son. She's not even in the room yet."

Seconds later, at full volume, the organ sounded out its octaves, indicating the bride's arrival. The congregation stood to their feet and turned to look toward the back of the church. Allison tightly clutched her father's arm as she appeared from the vestibule. Her radiant smile lit up the church. Solomon had trouble breathing at the sight of the jewel he knew he didn't deserve. His eyes fastened on hers as she slowly made her way toward him. Every eye was on the bride as her father escorted her to Solomon's side.

"Who gives this woman to be married to this man?" questioned the preacher.

Bill answered, "Her mother and I do." He placed her hand in Solomon's hand and slowly walked toward his seat, choking back the tears. Solomon squeezed her delicate hand and whispered, "I love you, Allison."

The preacher looked to the congregation.

"Is there anyone here today who knows any reason why Allison and Solomon should not be joined together in holy matrimony? If so, speak now or forever hold your peace."

———

Above the church, the black cloud of demons seemed to be growing denser. Daniel started getting scared as the horde began moving toward the church.

"Man your stations!" he shouted to the other angels. With swords drawn, they instantly encircled the church.

Before Daniel could finish his words, the demons raced toward him like a tsunami. Thousands of evil spirits attacked all at once. Daniel ducked several dozen swords before getting kicked in the head by a demon's paw. The other angels were knocked unconscious before they knew what had hit them.

———————

As the preacher waited for any objections from the crowd, the noise of gravity machines filled the sanctuary.

Bill turned to Gail and whispered, "I don't like what I hear, but try to stay calm." Gail's face crumbled at his words. He tightened his hold on Gail's hand as the sound quickly escalated.

Timothy didn't know what to do. Should he run outside and see what was happening and disrupt the wedding? Pastor Paul was wondering the same thing, but their decision was quickly made for them when they heard shouting just outside the door.

Allison's face dropped. Solomon grabbed her other hand and whispered into her ear, "It's going to be fine. My pastor at the detention camp, who happens to be the Paul from the Bible, has seventy guys out there protecting us!"

The words seemed to soothe her mind, but her heart was a wreck. Her eyes followed Timothy and Paul as they quickly made their way up the aisle and out the back door.

"Folks, please remain calm!" announced the preacher. "We all know the times that we are living in. Let us pray."

Outside the church, Pastor Paul's boys were on their knees, praying in front of the church's entrance. Paul looked at the motorcade of empty gravity machines parked across the street. Fifty boys or more were walking across the street, wearing black clothes and visibly wicked attitudes. Paul's heart dropped when he recognized their leader.

"Denny!" he exclaimed. Paul looked at the Christian young men, who were in the midst of deep intercession. "Keep praying, guys—no matter what happens!"

Timothy couldn't believe his eyes. Daniel and the other angels were seriously injured, incapable of defending the church. He didn't know what to do, so he dropped on his knees and pleaded with God to save them.

Denny led the group onto the church property. He had a baseball bat resting on one shoulder and a chip twice its size on the other. He recognized Paul from across the court-yard.

"Lookie here. If it isn't Pastor Paul, the great and wonderful author of the New Testament."

Paul said nothing as he stood in front of the church door. He couldn't see the demons who were surrounding the building and spitting their vile denunciations of Jesus. He couldn't see the angels lying on the ground, completely bulldozed by the enemy. He could, though, see Jesus, and he trusted in Him completely.

As Denny and his gang neared the church, they took turns punching and kicking Paul's converts. Not a single young man raised a hand against them. They remained on their knees praying. When they were knocked over, they got back up and continued to pray. Paul couldn't have been more proud of them, yet righteous anger surfaced in the man of God.

"Denny, you and your mob are a stench to the Lord. Renounce your sins before it's too late!"

Denny spit at the ground near Paul's feet and cursed incessantly.

"You've got some gall, preacher!"

Denny walked onto the steps of the church and stopped directly in front of Paul. His followers behind him were still beating Christ's disciples.

Denny continued spewing his venom as he gently tapped the end of the bat against his palm. "You insult me and my men and then tell me to repent." He jumped in Paul's face, but the pastor didn't yield an inch. "Repent of what? We do what we want to, when we want to. We believe in the freedom of choice. You guys are the slaves!"

Paul took a deep breath before responding. "You have the freedom, Denny, to choose Jesus or to spit in His face. You have the choice to go to heaven or to burn in an everlasting hell!"

The swarm of demons filling Denny howled in protest. He took the baseball bat and readied it behind his shoulders. Timothy jumped up from his kneeling position and dove toward the bat, catching it just as Denny started to swing it. Denny cursed loudly and turned around. He saw Timothy on the ground, crouching with the bat under his body. Denny nodded at several of his followers, and they ran over and started to beat Timothy. The former angel uttered one final prayer as he looked toward the demon-filled sky.

"God, help Denny to repent and—"

Without hesitating, Denny hit Paul squarely on the jaw, knocking the faithful preacher off the steps and into a bed of flowers. Then Denny shoved the doors open, panting heavily as he led the charge into the sanctuary of the Lord Almighty. As he marched forward, his abhorrence for the Christian faith overcame him. Everybody was on his or her knees, praying loudly for the boys' salvation and their own safety.

Allison and Solomon were kneeling at the altar, holding each other tightly and praying with all their hearts. Allison sneaked a look at the gang of criminals and tightened her grip on Solomon. Her reaction caused him to look up, and his eyes met Denny's. Solomon stood to his feet, against the wishes of Allison, who tried to hold him back.

"Denny!" he shouted as the preacher and the congregation continued to pray. "This is my wedding, and I would appreciate it if you would leave in peace."

Denny laughed long and hard, as did the other unregenerate boys. He slowly walked toward the couple, his cheeks twitching from demonic possession.

"Solomon, we're blood brothers. Don't you remember the oath you took when we were in camp?"

Cleveland stood up and ran to Solomon's side.

"You leave Solomon and Allison alone! We're blood brothers with Jesus Christ now."

Denny edged closer to them. The smile on his face was sarcastic and scary.

"Cleveland, I figured I would find you here. You took the same oath and must pay the price for your disobedience."

Denny watched Allison praying. "Solomon, looks like you've got yourself one sweet-looking babe there. I bet she's never been kissed by a real man before."

Solomon started to shake as his anger blossomed into action. He moved toward Denny, but Cleveland grabbed him and whispered, "Vengeance is for the Lord. Wait on Him." Solomon calmed down, but Denny did not.

"We subscribe to the old-world theology that treason is punishable by death. Before the Great Tribulation, family members of traitors were also executed to rid the land of evil." He looked at Allison, mouthing unspeakable words.

Suddenly, the preacher ended the prayer and quickly stood to his feet. He heard the threat and was prepared to act. Blood rushed to his face as righteous anger quickly took hold of the man of God.

"You will not disrupt this loving occasion and threaten the bride and groom. Get out before the fire of God falls on you and your demonic friends."

The demons surrounding the church were livid at the strong words of the preacher. Those outside the sanctuary immediately rocketed toward the building. Denny's group was bombarded with the blackest part of hell. Instead of one or two demons possessing each boy, dozens vied for position, causing the boys to stampede toward the pulpit.

Allison screamed as she ran toward the door. Solomon, Cleveland, and the preacher sprinted toward the legion, fed up with the threats and ready to fight. Gail and Emily ran toward the front of the church. Many of the men pushed toward the aisle, hoping to protect their families.

Denny screamed like a wild animal as he neared Solomon. Both boys were running low to the ground, like two bulls readying to lock horns in a bullfight. Solomon tensed his body as he prepared to tackle Denny. He closed his eyes and...

Solomon tripped and fell, landing in a patch of lush grass. With his eyes closed and his face against the ground, he slowly patted the grass under his hand. He could open his eyes, but he was afraid to. He knew grass didn't grow in churches. He heard nothing but a gentle breeze whispering a soothing message to his soul. Was he not getting married to Allison? Was he still in that detention camp? Did he even steal a gravity machine? How long had he been dreaming?

"Solomon!" called a familiar voice from nearby. "Can you believe it? It's a miracle!"

Solomon opened his eyes but kept his head buried in the grass. There was nothing right about this, nothing at all.

"Solomon!" called the same voice. "Open your eyes and see your salvation!"

Solomon recognized the voice. It was Pastor Paul! He peeked above the grass line and slowly looked around.

"Get up, Solomon." Pastor Paul began running around and shouting at the others. "It's a miracle, I tell you, a real miracle!"

Solomon took a deep breath and stood to his feet. To his right was a river of pure water, flowing peacefully. He glanced to his left and saw the city of Jerusalem in the distance.

"Solomon!" cried a feminine voice from just behind him.

He quickly turned and gasped, "Allison! What are you doing here?" He didn't wait for her answer; neither did he notice the anxiety on her face or the wedding gown she was wearing. He hugged her and said, "You wouldn't believe this dream I had. I, uh...I stole this machine and went off to this detention camp and..."

Solomon's brain suddenly came back to life. He pulled away from her and watched as friends and family appeared all around them. Solomon looked back at Allison. Their eyes locked as their hearts melded into one.

Denny slammed into the steps of the altar. His face landed just inches from the bottom of the pulpit. Obscenities gushed from his mouth as he bent over in anguish. The sound of screaming women and grunting men started to fade. Using all his strength, he yanked his head up. He looked around the church, and his jaw dropped. People were disappearing at the exact moment his men were attacking them!

Denny sighed at the miracle. His wicked heart refused to believe what his eyes confirmed. He saw a young teenaged girl hiding behind a flower arrangement, and he pulled himself to his feet. Something inside him craved death and destruction. He was completely possessed, and he knew it! The last semblance of goodness inside him had been squashed by the darkness. The girl didn't see him coming. She didn't see the satanic look on his face. She didn't see his fists clenched in rage. She didn't see the demons marching him to his destiny. She didn't hear or see anything, but God did!

As Denny lunged toward the helpless girl and screamed, "Die!" he hit the floor and crashed into a flower arrangement. "Where did you go?" he screeched as the other boys watched in horror.

He looked around the church and grimaced in pain. Everybody was looking at him for direction. They didn't know he was as lost, if not more so, than they.

"Obviously Jesus doesn't want to fight us. If He won't fight us on our turf, then we will go to His!" Denny yelled.

The boys responded like a pack of wolves howling at a full moon. They ran for their gravity machines with one singular purpose: to take out the old King and replace Him with theirs.

"To Jerusalem!" Denny shouted as he raised his fist against heaven.

Sixteen

The Eye of the Storm

Allison's face glowed as she stared at the stage. Hundreds of varieties of flowers and tropical plants decorated the wedding arena, splashing an eclectic array of colors. Solomon gripped Allison's hand as his eyes traced the mile-high rainbow that framed the wedding stage. Then he looked at Allison like a schoolboy with his first crush.

"You're my pot of gold!"

Allison watched him examine every inch of her face. She placed her hand on his cheek and gently caressed it.

"That's sweet, but I hope I'm worth more than that to you."

Solomon sighed and said softly, "I was just trying to be romantic."

"Solomon, you don't have to try to be romantic; just be yourself." She pulled his face toward hers. "This is a miracle! I couldn't have even dreamed of a wedding as magnificent as this." Looking around, she saw her pastor talking to someone who was dressed in a white robe. The person's back was toward her so she couldn't recognize who he was.

"Let's get things started," Solomon said as he pulled Allison toward the men.

"Honey, slow down, please. These shoes aren't made for track and field, you know."

Solomon slowed his pace and glanced at her feet. "Oh, sorry."

Their parents, along with Cleveland and Pastor Paul, walked toward the couple. Gail and Emily nearly knocked

323

Allison down with their hugs. The men gathered around Solomon and patted him on the back.

Pastor Paul said, "If this isn't a faith builder, then I don't know what is!"

Ken hugged Solomon, marveling at the outdoor wedding God had arranged. "You certainly are blessed, son!"

Cleveland smiled as he backed away from the men. He tried to slip away unnoticed. He didn't want to interfere with Solomon's special day.

Solomon spotted him and called, "Where do you think you're going?"

Cleveland looked down. His voice quivered with emotion as he explained, "I didn't want to get in the way."

Solomon went over and grabbed him by the arm.

"You know, Cleveland, you are family to me. Flesh and blood is important, but my spiritual family is who I'll be spending eternity with."

Pastor Paul hugged Cleveland and pulled him to his chest. Paul stared at Solomon for a moment, hoping that Solomon would read his mind. Solomon looked at Paul and squinted, trying to interpret Paul's message. A moment later, it became clear.

Solomon smiled at Cleveland and said, "This wedding was so haphazardly planned, I forgot to get a best man! Interested?"

Cleveland's eyes came to life.

"Uh, yeah." He shook his head. "I mean, sure. I'd be delighted—and honored."

Solomon grew serious. "If it wasn't for your Christian witness in that hellish hole, I would be with Denny right now."

Cleveland smiled but remained silent. He didn't want to take credit for Solomon's conversion.

As Solomon was thanking Cleveland, Emily and Gail excitedly talked with Allison.

"This is going to be the most spectacular wedding of the millennia," Gail exclaimed.

Allison's eyes scanned the area, taking in the whole scene. She smiled at the seven young doe that were nibbling the grass between the stage and the seats.

"I never would have thought of having baby deer at my wedding," Allison remarked.

Emily beamed. "Isn't it wonderful?"

Allison smiled. "But I wish we'd get started. I want to be married!"

A male voice reacted to her statement from several yards away.

"I think we should start right now!" spoke Vice-Regent David as he left her pastor's side.

The entire wedding party recognized David's voice. No one had known he was there.

"David!" Ken exclaimed. "What are you doing here?"

David smiled and answered, "I've asked your pastor to give me the honor of participating in your son's wedding."

Overcome with excitement, Allison clasped her hands to her chest.

"Thank you so much for saving us from those madmen!"

David shook his head.

"No, Allison, don't thank me; thank King Jesus for that. The entire world is being put through the fire as I speak. Jesus is testing His people's loyalty before bringing them into His new heaven."

Gail appeared perplexed by David's statement.

David quickly explained, "Peace and prosperity tend to make people complacent. Even the greatest saints can fall prey to this subtle sin. Unfortunately, millions of people, mainly the youth, are rebelling against Jesus. With Satan loose to tempt them, they are now showing their true colors. All who stand firm to the end and keep their faith in God will be saved from these thugs and transported to the safe haven here in Jerusalem."

Solomon walked over to David and dropped to one knee, his face cast to the ground.

"Thank you for your kindness, Vice-Regent David."

Allison closed her eyes as a tingling sensation filled her body. It was so good to see Solomon humble and contrite. She said a silent prayer, thanking the Holy Spirit for keeping His hand on Solomon.

David placed his right hand on Solomon's head.

"Father, bless this man for the decision that he has made. May his fruit be sweet and pure. Amen."

David glanced at the guests, who were quickly finding their seats. Looking at Allison and Solomon, he asked, "Are you two ready?"

Allison grabbed Solomon's hand and waited for him to respond.

"Yes, sir!"

"Excellent," said David as he started for the platform. The rest of the wedding party moved to their proper positions.

"Vice-Regent David," Solomon asked softly, "can you tell me just one thing?"

David stopped and turned toward him.

"Yes, Solomon?"

"Are we going to have time for our honeymoon before the great battle begins?"

David smiled. Gail and Bill didn't hear the exchange, but Ken and Emily had heard their son's question clearly.

Ken whispered in his wife's ear, "A chip off the old block, if you ask me."

A half-embarrassed grin filled Emily's face.

"You men are all alike!"

Ken's raised his eyebrows in protest, but he didn't say anything.

David thought for a moment before responding to Solomon's question. Deep emotion consumed his face before he quietly replied, "Solomon, there isn't going to be a battle in the traditional, historical sense." A deep sense of righteousness and holy indignation seemed to possess David.

"Satan will come against Jerusalem soon, very soon." David stared at the sky, as if he could see the armies taking their places. "Thank God for your faith, Solomon, and never take it for granted."

Vice-Regent David walked toward the altar, leaving Solomon and Allison alone. Solomon suddenly forgot about the honeymoon. He forgot about Allison, about the wedding, the rainbow, the flowers, the deer, and the guests. He looked toward heaven, closed his eyes, and breathed in deeply. He slowly exhaled and opened his eyes, turning to Allison.

"I love you, Allison, but I love God more!"

Allison embraced him, and with her head buried in his shoulder, she wept softly.

"I thank God for that, Solomon. I really do."

"That's the way it's supposed to be, right?" asked Solomon.

Allison nodded as she lifted her face to meet his.

"Yes, Solomon, it is. I didn't reveal that to you; Jesus did!"

As Satan's eyes opened, he stared at the ceiling of the cavern, oblivious to the events that had knocked him out earlier. Somehow he had ended up just inches away from the edge of the cliff. His paw hung over the side, immersed in the boiling lava. The Devil lifted his left paw and grimaced in pain.

The king of demons cursed as he examined the welts on his arm, which resembled baseball-sized blisters. He took a deep gulp of air, causing the lesions on his chest to bleed. Forcing himself to sit upright, the Devil glared at the lava stream. The sight of it helped to restore his memory.

"How could this have happened?" he wondered aloud, as the sting from the blistering sores clouded his thinking. "Who's responsible? To be attacked in the safety of one's abode is criminal," he griped.

Satan attempted to stand upright, but the pain prevented that. He knew he would heal, but it would take time, and time was his greatest enemy now. In spite of the lies and exaggerations he had told his troops and closest advisors, the Devil knew that God's timeline could not be altered.

A rush of wind suddenly gushed from the wormhole exit. Satan jerked his head toward the sound. His breathing was erratic, and his mind was restless. His eyes struggled to track the streaking shadow falling across the ceiling.

"Michael, is that you?"

The fear seizing the Dragon excited the stranger.

"Gabriel!" Satan shouted, his fingers twitching with every heartbeat.

The shadow seemed to have disappeared near the east edge of the cavern. A minute passed, then another, and another, until Satan couldn't take it anymore.

"What do you want with me?" he shrieked with a ferocity that could shake a mountain.

Satan's weary eyes scoured the cave. This was his worst nightmare. He was defenseless and out of control. Worse still, he was being toyed with like a rat in a testing chamber.

The Devil lowered his voice. "You fool, you spineless ingrate! Come out of the darkness and face me demon to angel, you coward!"

As Satan blinked, the shadow lunged. The dim, orange light from the lava suddenly flickered as the unknown spirit approached the Devil.

A diabolic voice screamed, "Die!"

As Satan turned toward the voice, a large rock fell on his head, breaking his neck in several places. Darkness wrapped its deadly grip around the Devil.

The spirit laughed vociferously.

"Revenge will be mine!" uttered General Ruse.

He snorted and grunted with glee as he placed his ear near Satan's open jaw. He sensed a sporadic, faint, hot breath.

"That should keep you out of the way for a while," said the general as a rush of adrenaline surged through his body.

Suddenly, a soft murmuring sound came from behind him. He turned to identify the sound, but he saw nothing. He slowly flew toward the soft squeals, his wings flapping against the stale air. The sound grew louder as he neared the rock wall. His eyes inspected every nook for a crevice or crack. Finally, he spotted the faint outline of a door.

"Identify yourself!" he ordered.

The indistinguishable voice grew in sound and intensity. General Ruse cautiously edged closer to the wall. He placed his claws in the crack and pulled it apart with increasing force.

"If this is some sort of game," he called, "you will pay a high price for it!"

The muffled whining from the other side of the rock wall vanished. The general glanced over his shoulder at Satan, who was still lying motionless on the floor of the cavern. He took a full breath, readied his feet, got a good grip between the crease in the rock, and pulled with all his might. The rock door swung open. He snickered as his eyes met Blasphemy's.

"Well, look at this," Ruse's belly laugh echoed throughout the dark cavern.

Blasphemy appeared drained by the incarceration. He bobbed his head back and forth in an effort to communicate.

Ruse nodded, "I see." He walked over to Blasphemy and lowered his head so that he could look Blasphemy in the eye. "May I assume that you want me to free you?"

Blasphemy stared at him without responding. He knew the other general well. He assumed a humble attitude as he dropped his eyes toward the ground.

"Yes, I know. You are helpless." Ruse watched the tied-up demon as he considered his next move. He knew he couldn't lead the troops on his own, but he didn't know if he could trust Blasphemy, either.

The general smirked. "I have an offer you cannot refuse!"

A small but quaint cottage was nestled near one of the scenic bends of the Jordan River. A white porch, fragrant with wild flowers, wrapped around the front. A stone fireplace rose above the wooden roof, and wisps of smoke steadily streamed from its chimney.

Inside the rustic cabin, Solomon and Allison were lying on a plush, king-sized bed, staring into each other's eyes.

"Being together is a dream come true," said Allison, her eyes blazing with love.

Solomon agreed and said tenderly, "You are my dream come true."

He moved closer and kissed her passionately. Several minutes later, Allison gently pulled away from his embrace.

"You've never kissed me like that before," she sighed happily.

Solomon's voice quivered with emotion.

"I've never loved you as I do now."

Allison smiled, then quickly sat up in the bed. She reached toward the deep maroon drapes that encircled the bed and pulled them aside.

"Let's go out on the porch!"

Solomon frowned. "Right now?"

Allison rolled her eyes. "Oh, come on, Solomon," she coaxed.

The new bride jumped out of bed and grabbed her husband's hand from beneath the downy comforter.

"I know what you're thinking, Solomon Action!" She stared at him with one of those looks Solomon couldn't resist. "How does sitting with me for a few minutes on that rocker sound? We can enjoy the full moon and listen to the night sounds."

Solomon quickly gave in.

"Sounds pretty romantic to me," he admitted, pulling his shirt over his head.

They walked barefoot onto the porch and sat down on the two-person glider that faced the river. Both of them were mesmerized by the moon's reflection on the water.

Allison snuggled against his chest. Safe, at last, in his arms, she asked, "What do you think heaven is going to be like?" Solomon breathed deeply and then slowly exhaled.

"I don't need to imagine it, Allison," he answered as he turned her face toward his. "I'm living it!"

His words melted Allison. She put her head back on his chest and stared at the gently flowing water. The delicate sounds of the river, combined with the intoxicating creak of the well-used rocker, created a dreamy moment neither wanted to come to an end. Hours seemed like minutes as they enjoyed this paradise. Deer, lions, leopards, and even bear walked past them, lapped up fresh water from the river, then quickly disappeared into the night. Several shooting stars lit up the night sky. Crickets chirped, but the most memorable moment was seeing the full moon set against the mountainous backdrop. As its light faded, their eyes became heavy, and they both fell asleep in their own heaven on earth.

Daniel, who was standing guard by the chimney, looked away from the lovebirds and saluted the angelic commanding general hovering over the river.

"Thanks for the help, commander!"

The general returned his salute.

"Anything to help, little guy!"

The heat from the rising sun beat down on Denny and his friends as they streaked across the desert plain north of Jerusalem. Denny's gravity machine was in front of the pack as they traveled toward their destiny. He looked back at the swarm of new vehicles that had joined the Devil's parade.

"What's going on back there?" he asked Larry through the satellite intercom.

From his position in the rear, Larry responded, "Looks like lots of guys had the same idea as you. Maybe that dream of yours wasn't a dream but a vision!"

Denny stuck his chest out as he boasted, "I'm a prophet!"

Moments later, a demon on his left shoulder prompted him to correct his self-proclamation.

"I'm God!" Denny announced.

As the stolen machine cut through the air at over two hundred miles an hour, Denny glanced over his shoulder. Pride filled his heart as thousands of air machines followed him toward the Holy City.

"Larry, how's the morale of the troops?"

Larry's heart was racing faster than the engine of the bike. The young men and women around him were hollering and yelling in glee.

"It's a big party back here! Lead us, messiah!"

Denny smiled as he tightly gripped the machine's controls. He glared at the sky above him, unable to see the swarm of demons accompanying him to his demise.

Hundreds of millions of fallen spirits were flocking toward Jesus' city, all bent on dethroning the King of the universe. Millions upon millions of humans were unwittingly following them in an effort to destroy the One who could pronounce them guilty of their sins. They reasoned that if they could kill the Judge, then they could make up the rules and relieve themselves of the responsibility and guilt for their actions. It was the Garden of Eden all over again, yet man refused to learn the lessons from history; hence, he was destined to repeat the mistakes of his past. Proverbs 26:11, "As a dog returns to his own vomit, so a fool repeats his folly," was being fulfilled again this day.

Allison squinted as the sunlight invaded her sleep. She opened her eyes and looked around the porch, unable to find Solomon. She jumped off the rocker and ran around to the other side of the house.

"Solomon, where are you?"

She could hear her voice echoing against the mountains but didn't hear any response.

"Solomon! Solomon!" She shuddered as fear pervaded her heart.

She ran back to the front of the house and shoved the door open, frantically running throughout the chalet.

"Solomon, where are you?" she kept calling.

She ran back outside and stood on the porch facing the river. Her heart raced faster than her mind. She fell on the glider and started to cry.

"Allison," called Solomon from the middle of the river.

"Solomon Action! You nearly scared me to death!"

She ran toward the Jordan River, tripping over her feet several times.

"Come on in." He splashed water in her direction. "It feels great, and there's nobody around."

She placed a foot in the sparkling water and looked at her husband.

"Solomon Action, you're skinny-dipping!"

Solomon looked around at the water with a puzzled expression on his face. "Yeah, so what?"

"I can't—" Allison began, but Solomon interrupted before she could finish.

"You can't what?" he asked. "We're married now, and Vice-Regent David told us we would have the entire area to ourselves."

Allison hesitated for a moment. She looked up and down the banks of the river and saw nothing but friendly animals. "I can't let you have this river all to yourself." Flinging her clothes aside, she jumped into the water.

Solomon grinned as his wife swam toward him.

"You're like a fish out here. I had no idea you were so talented."

She wrapped her arms around him and kissed her husband. Several minutes passed before they came up for air.

"Whoa!" Solomon was breathless, his face flushed with emotion. "Where did that come from?"

"You didn't know fish could kiss like that?" Allison teased.

Solomon turned away and caught his breath. As he glanced toward the mountain peaks, something captured his attention on the top of the crest. His passion quickly turned to anxiety. Allison saw the change immediately.

"What is it, Solomon?"

She turned toward the mountain and squinted through the sunlight. She could see something moving, but she couldn't make out what it was.

"There are hundreds if not thousands of people on gravity machines," he told her.

Allison bit her lip. It was her trademark, "I'm nervous," signal.

"What does it mean?" she asked, not sure if she wanted to know.

Solomon placed his hands on her shoulders, his eyes reading her every emotion.

"It means they're coming."

———————

General Ruse snickered as he looked at the rock stuck in Blasphemy's throat.

"Quite innovative, I must say. I bet that's very uncomfortable for you, Blasphemy."

Blasphemy stared angrily at the general. Ruse reached toward the well-lodged rock, then suddenly pulled back.

"I don't think I want to do it that way. It's very unwise to stick your hand in the mouth of a beast." He smiled. "One might get bit, you know."

Blasphemy watched as Ruse walked directly behind him. General Ruse was humming his favorite demonic chant, titled, "My Way or No Way." Ruse nonchalantly looked around, hoping to irritate Blasphemy.

"Well, you've gotten yourself in quite a dilemma here."

Ruse placed his paw in the center of Blasphemy's back and felt around his curved spine.

"Satan is quite the character, isn't he?"

Blasphemy tried to ignore Ruse's stalling, but patience was not a virtue he knew much about. He squirmed like an animal caught in a hunter's trap.

"Now, now, calm down, Blasphemy. If you want that rock out, you'll need to sit still and relax."

Blasphemy took a deep gulp of air and closed his eyes.

"Now, that's better." Ruse enjoyed dragging this out.

He placed his palm in the middle of Blasphemy's back.

"This might hurt just a little," he mouthed, punching Blasphemy as hard as he could.

Blasphemy was catapulted to the other side of the closet. His head hit the wall at forty miles an hour.

Ruse puckered his lips as he casually walked toward the demon. He kicked Blasphemy over onto his back and inspected him.

"Well, it looks like we got the rock out," he snickered. "Now what did you want to tell me?"

Blasphemy didn't respond; he was out cold. Ruse untied the demon and sat down on a rock next to him. Several minutes passed before he threw his black paws up in frustration.

"You do something nice for the ole fellow, Ruse, and look what you get for it. Now he wants to nap." He flew toward the exit. "Rude, if you ask me."

The twelve apostles circled Jesus' throne, their gold crowns lying on the marble floor in front of them. Vice-Regent David was seated on a smaller throne next to Jesus. David stood to his feet, then dropped to his knees in worship. The apostles followed his example. Thousands of angels formed an angelic wall around the throne, ready at a moment's notice for war of any kind.

Jesus placed His bronze-colored hand in the air as a tear trickled down His cheek.

"Today, evil will test My Father once again." He paused as He made eye contact with each of the apostles and David. "The time of judgment is near."

He looked toward the horizon, His eyes scanning the mountain peaks near Jerusalem.

"Millions of people are now surrounding the Camp of God." Jesus' face began to shine like the sun. "They want to kill Me and install their own king!"

The apostles shook their heads in disbelief. They knew this was coming, yet they had trouble comprehending how such absolute evil could thrive in the presence of a holy God.

Jesus lifted His head toward heaven. Lightning immediately shot down out of a clear sky toward the rebels closing in on Jerusalem.

Denny and his band of raiders were north of town when the miraculous lightning storm started.

"Take cover under those trees," Denny shouted above the claps of thunder.

Several dozen boys, including Larry, huddled under a large pine tree. Denny started running toward the group when a lone lightning bolt zapped the tree in half, electrocuting all of them beneath it. The force of the electricity knocked Denny to the ground. While he was lying on his back, struggling to breathe, his entire life flashed through his head. It ended with the emblazoned image of his small-town pastor pointing at him, saying, "Do you want to go to hell, Denny?" It seemed like an eternity, yet the experience lasted only a few seconds.

Daniel flew toward Timothy.

"Timothy! Did you hear that?"

Timothy, who was sitting on a bench talking with Pastor Paul and Cleveland, jumped up, too.

"Whoa, you bet I did," Timothy exclaimed. He looked at Paul and Cleveland before turning to Daniel.

"You know the drill, Daniel. Get to the front line immediately."

As Daniel shot off like a rocket, Timothy hugged Paul and Cleveland.

"This is it!"

Solomon and Allison were walking toward the porch when they noticed the lightning in the distance.

"What's happening?" Allison called as they started running toward the safety of the cabin.

"Jesus is probably giving them a warning to stay back," he shouted above the not-too-distant thunder.

Seconds later, Jesus lowered His head, and the lightning ceased. Denny opened his eyes and saw his friends dead by the tree. Allison and Solomon ran inside the chalet and held each other.

King Jesus took a deep breath and stood to His feet. Placing His hands high into the heavens, He shouted so that every living creature on earth and in heaven could hear His voice.

"Jerusalem is Mine!"

Denny shook off the smell of death and turned toward the remaining troops. Christ's words incited Him.

"If that tyrannical King wants a war, then He will have one!" he shrieked as he started the engine of the gravity machine.

Allison was glued to Solomon on the living room couch when they heard the voice of their Lord. She looked at Solomon. She was at peace. "I should be scared to death," she said as a smile formed on her lips, "but I'm not."

Solomon turned away from the window and stared at her for a moment before saying, "Allison, you're a gem. If anyone deserves heaven, you do."

She placed her hand into his and blushed. "We go into the fire together. Don't let go, Solomon."

———————————

General Ruse rushed out of the cave and saw the black cloud of demons surrounding the city.

"Not yet!" He cursed incessantly as he flew frantically toward the battle line.

Jesus' thunderous voice awakened Blasphemy in a hurry. He yanked his eyes open and looked around the closet in fear.

"Where are you?"

His paws started shaking violently as the fear of God consumed the angel of darkness. He crawled out of the closet and slowly made his way into Satan's abode. He saw the Devil on his back, still unconscious.

Blasphemy screamed loudly, "Satan!"

The Devil's chest began to heave; his paws started to tremble.

"Satan! Wake up!" roared Blasphemy, lightly slapping the Dragon's black cheeks.

Satan opened his eyes, then snatched Blasphemy's paw before it could strike him again.

"Get off me, you..."

Blasphemy jumped backward at the words. He watched Satan as he struggled to stand.

"Master, I heard Jesus claim the rights to Jerusalem."

Satan hissed, "My troops! They're attacking without me!"

The Devil grabbed the back of his neck and massaged the breaks in his armor.

"Master, we've been double-crossed by General Ruse. He's the one who attacked you, and he almost took me out as well."

Putrid drool bubbled from Satan's lips.

"I should have known," heaved the Devil. He stared closely at Blasphemy. "What makes you any different from that traitor?" Satan edged closer to the demon.

Blasphemy held his ground and said, "Revenge, my master. He nearly killed me in that closet. I want his head!"

Satan appeared to snicker.

"I was the one who put your sorry tail in there in the first place!"

Blasphemy responded wisely, "Master, I deserved that for my transgressions, but I did nothing to him."

Satan studied Blasphemy's face, which appeared honest and forthcoming. He looked toward the exit, knowing his time was severely limited. With his neck tilted, he lifted off the ground.

"Follow me, but be warned. I'm watching your every move."

Blasphemy followed Satan toward the exit. A smug grin leaped to the surface of his face.

He whispered under his breath, "Fool!"

Denny crept up the last mountain before the city limits. The engine of his air bike purred as the horde of rebels trailed him.

"What do you see?" he asked one of the boys.

"I don't see anything," the boy answered in a nervous tone. "Something isn't right. They know we're coming." He paused. "Maybe it's a trap."

Denny scoffed, "It's not a trap, you fool! We're dealing with cowards here, and the way I see it, they should die a coward's death."

Denny was the first to clear the top of the mountain. What he saw took his breath away. As far as the eye could see and in every direction around Jerusalem, millions of air bikes filled the sky.

Denny's face turned cold.

"We've got them surrounded!" he said over the intercom system to the other bikers. "They don't have a chance."

Solomon pulled away from Allison and ran toward the window.

"I've got to see what's happening."

Allison ran to his side.

"No, Solomon! It's too dangerous."

He looked at her and smiled.

"No, it's not, Allison. Don't you remember prophecy class?"

Allison gulped, "Well, yes, but—"

"No, Allison, there's no 'but' here. They'll never make it into the Lord's city."

She nodded nervously as she watched Solomon head toward the front door.

"Let's go to the bank of the river and pray for them."

Jesus remained silent as the apostles and David worshipped Him. He was standing, watching the troops encase Jerusalem. His face was shining brighter than a star as He watched millions of His angels circle around the perimeter of the city. Their swords were lifted toward heaven as they waited for their King's command.

General Ruse arrived on the front lines south of Jerusalem.

He yelped, "Field commanders, report."

Several dozen demons instantly flew to his side and bowed to the four-star general.

"What was your last command?"

The senior general answered, "Satan said to surround the city and await his orders."

Ruse's face turned glum.

"Satan is dead! You will now take your orders from me."

His lie was met with cold stares of disbelief. The senior general eyed him suspiciously.

"Yes, sir," he answered in a smooth, monotone voice. "I assume you plan on leading us into battle?"

General Ruse smacked the general across the face as he shouted, "Get that haughty smirk off your face!"

Ruse flew above the commanders and stared at his troops. The ranking demons raced back to their positions and listened for his command.

Satan raced northward toward Jerusalem with Blasphemy behind him. His flight speed had been severely reduced by his injuries. Blasphemy's sword hand was twitching madly, which made him more than nervous. The demons were less than a hundred miles away when they both spotted their troops.

The Devil hissed, "Ah, right on time. Revenge will be mine!"

Blasphemy slowly closed in on the Devil as he scanned the sky for witnesses. His shaking paw quietly moved toward his sword.

"Master, there it is!" said Blasphemy. "The fruit is ripe for the picking!"

Daniel was on the front line on the south side of Jerusalem. He was toe-to-toe, sword-to-sword with angels he had never met before, yet he felt at home. He was standing up for righteousness and was looking forward to his reward. He didn't fear the demons; on the contrary, he was pumped and ready for action. He felt like a kid at the entrance to the world's best amusement park.

General Ruse took a deep breath and tilted his head upward. He closed his coal-black eyes and bellowed, "Attack! Attack! Take no prisoners!"

The demons repeated his message to their humans, who instantly obeyed. Both the demons and their human cronies shot toward the Holy City. The angels held their positions, their silver swords flying defiantly over their heads.

Satan's eyes nearly popped out of their sockets when he saw his troops respond to Ruse's order.

"No!" roared Satan.

Blasphemy jerked his sword from his body and lunged toward Satan.

Allison dug her face into Solomon's shirt.

"I can't stand it!" she shouted above the roar of the approaching mob. Solomon held her in his arms as he watched the horde of humans quickly descend the mountain. His muscles tightened as Allison's sobs were drowned out by the revving engines.

Meanwhile, their parents and friends were focused not on the advancing hurricane, but on their Lord and King.

"My eyes have seen my salvation!" shouted Pastor Paul, his hands held high in praise and thanksgiving.

"Hold your ground!" yelled Timothy to Daniel.

"Come, Lord Jesus, come!" prayed Cleveland, his eyes wet with tears.

Ken and Emily said nothing as they held each other tightly. Bill and Gail were next to them. Gail glanced in the direction of the honeymoon cottage miles away. Her heart yearned to see her daughter and know that she was safe.

Jesus' face filled with righteous anger. He clenched His fists.

"Angels," He thundered, "put your swords away."

Daniel sighed heavily, his heart dropping into his stomach. He wanted to fight, yet he obeyed the command.

General Ruse couldn't believe what he saw. He soared through the sky and moved in front of the pack of demons approaching the city.

"Fire!" he screamed.

The demons shouted in triumph as they sped toward the angels.

Blasphemy's sword was inches from Satan's head when Satan ducked out of the way.

"Did you really think I would trust you?" the Devil laughed, grabbing Blasphemy by the wings.

The demon kicked and howled in pain and anger as Satan ripped Blasphemy's wings off his body.

"Die, you coward!" Satan hissed as he watched Blasphemy's flashing eyes turn blank.

Satan dropped him toward the ground and zoomed toward the city.

"Stop!" he bellowed with a ferocity the demons had never heard. Every demon obeyed except one.

General Ruse flapped his wings all the faster as he entered Jesus' city. Jesus turned toward the advancing demon and stuck His fist in the air.

"Away from Me, you evildoer!" roared the King.

General Ruse struck an invisible barrier at full speed; his body crumpled from the force of the impact.

Satan scanned the sky, his troops watching him with admiration. He heaved his fist toward Jesus.

"Your kingdom, Jesus, is finished!" barked Satan.

The Devil's troops cheered wildly.

Out of the hundreds of millions of people and angels in Jerusalem, nobody uttered a sound. Every eye was on Jesus.

Jesus stood before His throne like an iron statue. He sighed deeply as righteous indignation flooded His Spirit.

"Children of Jerusalem, today you will be with Me in paradise!"

The residents of the Holy City stood and worshipped their King. Satan lost control and rocketed toward Jesus.

"Charge!"

The demons followed his lead, racing toward the city limits with wild, hateful glares possessing them.

"Fire!" thundered the Lord.

Seventeen

The Great White Throne Judgment

Satan quickly drew his sword and rocketed toward Jesus. The demons didn't flinch as they watched their leader prepare to attack the Lord.

"Satan! Satan! Satan!" they chanted, their swords swaying to their mantra.

Daniel closed his eyes as Lucifer approached.

"Get him, Jesus," he muttered.

The Lord thrust His hand above His head and proclaimed, "Open the curtain!"

Suddenly, the humans could see the angels and demons. Many nearly fainted at the hideous sight.

Solomon yelled, "Allison, look!"

She took one peek, then buried her head deeper into his shirt.

Further away in the heart of Jerusalem, Emily nearly crushed Ken's hand when she saw the demons spread across the breadth of the heavens. Their nightmarish features and antics sent shivers down her spine.

"I can't believe it!" he shuddered.

Denny and his followers, along with all the other human intruders, pressed toward the Holy City, their faces wild with hatred.

The residents of Jerusalem watched in horror as Satan passed by the shield that had destroyed General Ruse. Pride flooded his spirit. "You can't hold the great one back!" he boasted. He kicked his wings into overdrive and recklessly dove toward Jesus.

The King lifted His hand into the air and shouted, "It is done!"

Jesus' fingers were rigid and curved inward. He clutched what appeared to be thin air and yanked His arm downward. In the blink of an eye, the sky was literally sucked into His hand. Instantly, Satan was motionless, as if a movie projector had caught on one frame. Jesus clutched His fingers downward, then yanked upward. All of creation—the land, oceans, and rivers—vanished in His outstretched palm.

There was complete silence as all humans and spirits were frozen in time. They were alive, but they were unable to move anything but their eyes. The light from the sun was gone, replaced by a divine light that radiated from Christ the King. Creation was literally hanging in His hand, unable to react unless He allowed it. The humans and spirits were levitating in the air, their eyes following every move of the King. Denny cursed the sight in his heart, unwilling to admit this was happening.

Jesus stared upward for several minutes, communicating with God the Father. Nobody except the apostles and David could hear what was said.

Satan's left arm was extended outward with his sword pointing toward the King. His eyes were full of fire as they stared at the One he hoped to pierce. A burning, acidic hatred possessed the Devil as Jesus turned to face the great Serpent.

"You, who have caused many to stumble, prepare for your final resting place!"

Solomon wanted to shout to the heavens, "Finish him off! Pay him back! Destroy him, Jesus!"

Satan watched in horror as a ball of purple light exploded from Jesus' hand. The spinning ball of energy divided in two, then broke into four pieces, then continued to split apart. Seconds later, millions of small spheres of light ricocheted off Christ and shot toward the demons. They appeared to target the lowest-ranking demons first, each one hitting an evil spirit and absorbing it into a cocoon of light. Satan helplessly watched Christ's revenge, knowing his attempt to deceive the nations had failed miserably. Admitting failure, though, was not an option.

Satan closed his eyes tightly. A ball of swirling light raced from Christ and ripped off the Devil's eyelashes.

Christ thundered, "You will watch the fruits of your wickedness!"

Allison wanted to yell, "He almost destroyed my life! Have no mercy on him, Jesus!"

Millions of demons were possessed with fear, encapsulated by the light of the Lord. The balls of fire started slamming into Satan's generals, each one hopelessly unable to resist. General Ruse, who had fallen to the ground, watched as a sphere of light zoomed toward him. His eyes nearly popped out of their sockets as the energy wrapped its icy grip around his injured body. Blasphemy cursed as judgment enveloped his broken body. The light was as powerful as a cross thrust in the face of a vampire. The light stung Blasphemy's skin like fire would scorch a human.

Solomon and Ken couldn't believe what they were seeing. They were cheering for judgment. After all, it was Judgment Day, a day like no other. The fiery light of Christ had consumed all creation. Nothing but Christ and those who could choose Him or reject Him were left.

Every demon except for Satan had been imprisoned in an eternal jail cell. Every eye watched the Lord confront the Master of Evil.

"Satan, I created you as the most beautiful of angels, perfect and holy." Jesus' eyes flamed. "You were to serve Me and My Father with all your heart, mind, and spirit. Instead, evil was found in you, Lucifer. Pride filled your heart and darkened you into the creature you have now become."

Jesus looked at the Serpent, an iron glare shooting from the Lord's face. There was so much to judge Satan for—the broken hearts and vanquished dreams that had all been torn asunder by this creature, this animal, this Devil!

"For the sake of the Christians who will be with Me and My Father in paradise, I will allow you to offer a defense."

Lightning flashed from the Lord's mouth, hitting Satan squarely on the head. Pretending to be unfazed, the Devil smiled cunningly.

"Quite gracious of You, O Master," he slurred in a vicious, sarcastic tone.

Jesus ignored his putrid attitude and continued, "As My people follow Me into paradise, I want them to understand the depth of evil that exists in any heart that becomes filled with pride and arrogance. In paradise," He paused as He looked over the crowd of saints, "they will follow Me with all their hearts, all their souls, and all their minds. They will be a testimony against you and all of your followers who have forsaken their first love."

Satan glared at Jesus, his face bursting with hatred. Jesus said nothing as He waited for an outburst from Lucifer. It didn't take long.

"You talk about arrogance!" shrieked the Devil, his lips trembling with fury. "You call me prideful because I have my own opinions on truth and justice. You say that I'm arrogant because I have my own mind and do with it what I please! You are a judgmental bigot!"

Satan wanted to say more but couldn't; he was starting to hyperventilate. His eyes didn't move off the Lord.

Jesus responded calmly, "If I weren't God the Son, you would be right. But I am; therefore, you are mistaken."

Satan hissed, "Your status and position have nothing to do with Your idiocy. You hide behind that name You call Yourself." He paused for a second. "The truth is, there is no truth, and You know it! You want it all Your way, or it's hit the road. I tell You...!"

Jesus lifted His hand into the air.

"Children of My kingdom, hear Me!" He shouted as He looked at them. "You are witnessing the last gasp of demonic thinking. There is absolute truth, and it is revealed through My Father in heaven. He has chosen Me, His only begotten Son, to share the secrets of the kingdom. Satan has been lying since the dawn of creation, and sadly, he will be lying until the moment of his judgment."

Jesus nodded toward Satan, giving him the opportunity to rebut.

"It's just like You," cried the Devil, "to cut people off in mid-sentence." His demeanor was snakelike as he vomited his words. "You stick people and spirits out on a string and hang it over a fire. That's sick, and You know it! To fear the so-called fires of hell is ludicrous."

Jesus showed no emotion as He stared at the Serpent.

Satan continued. "It's all a grand plan You have to take over the universe. Fear is a powerful motivator, and You are using it to the hilt." He paused to catch his breath. "Why don't You tell everybody here why You use the fear of hell to bring them into submission? Why don't You tell them the truth, that You don't have absolute control over the universe because You didn't create it in the first place? It evolved, and You are hiding that fact like the sniveling coward that You are."

Allison couldn't believe her ears. Right before Satan's eyes, Jesus held creation in His hands, yet Satan denied it. She wondered how this animal could have turned on his Creator the way he had. Her heart was shaking inside her, wanting, desiring, and even demanding vengeance against this beast.

Jesus countered, "I call heaven and earth as a witness against you today, Satan. Your words are treasonous, convoluted, and intentionally deceptive. If I chose to, I could exercise absolute control over the universe, but in My foresight, I have chosen not to."

Satan snorted, "Tell them why. Go ahead. Tell them why."

Jesus nodded. His manner was distinguished and forthright.

"I have chosen not to control everything because I desire love from the people and spirits of My creation. You cannot force people to love you; they must choose to love you. In the same way, I have given beings the free will to love Me or to hate Me."

The Devil ridiculed, "That's a blatant lie! You don't have the power to make people or spirits love You." Satan laughed. "That's the chink in Your armor, O mighty God." His voiced dripped with sarcasm. "You are powerless to control the wills of people, so You create these dreams to make Yourself look good and all-powerful."

Ken stared at Jesus, watching His every reaction. He couldn't believe the Lord's patience and His ability to control Himself in the face of the Devil. If Ken had his way,

Satan would already be in the oven with the setting turned to broil.

The light emanating from the Lord brightened.

"I am all-powerful and incapable of lying," responded Jesus. "I choose to use My power not to glorify Myself, but My Father in heaven. You, Satan, use your power to destroy and to glorify yourself."

The light continued to increase around the Lord. Satan didn't know how much longer he had, so he went for the grand slam.

"I have three simple questions that prove You are a fake. Will You allow me the chance to prove You wrong?"

Jesus glared at the Devil. Everybody was wondering what the demon was up to—everybody but the Lord. Jesus nodded His assent.

Satan smirked, but inside, he felt like a prisoner sitting in the electric chair, knowing the switch was going to be flipped at any second. Should he go out dignified or with a bang? One thing he would never admit was that he was wrong—that he knew all along he would be thrown into hell and ultimately lose the battle. No, he would never tell! Never! A billion years in hell was not enough time to extract that dark secret from him and give the victory to the Lord. In Satan's mind, hell was a small price to pay for the chance to get back at Jesus for kicking him out of heaven.

Satan began, "Question number one: If You are all-powerful, can You create a rock that You cannot pick up?"

Solomon was confused. Of all the questions the Devil could have asked the Creator of the universe, why had he asked that one?

Timothy sighed, knowing the question was foolish and shortsighted, but Jesus didn't flinch. The fire radiating from Him simmered a bit.

"Question number two: You claim to know the future. If that is so, then why did You create me in the first place, knowing I was going to be a thorn in Your side and become this 'terrible' Devil who would be the source of all suffering?"

Pastor Paul wasn't surprised by the Devil's obsessive desire to discredit the Lord. He knew the Devil's tactics well.

The Devil stared angrily at the Lord, hoping Jesus would lose His patience. Jesus waited for him to continue.

"Question number three: How could an all-loving God create a place so evil as hell for those who simply disagree with Him? Isn't love essentially tolerant?"

The fiery light surrounding Jesus shot toward Lucifer, cutting off the Devil's speech.

"I have given you the opportunity of your lifetime, Satan," began Jesus. "You have said your piece, unhindered by Me, in front of all of creation. Now I will have the final word."

Almost everyone knew how this encounter would end, but few realized that it would happen as it did: Jesus Christ and Satan in front of the creation, sparring like gunfighters before the whole town. It was the Battle of the Ages!

"Your first question, 'Can I create a rock that I cannot pick up?' is simply your attempt to question My power. The answer is, yes, I could if I chose to. Doing so, though, would then be used by you to question if I am all-powerful. You would say, 'Why can't You pick up that rock?' The answer is that I can't because I chose to create a rock that I couldn't pick up. The same logic follows that I can't lie because it is not in My nature, just as it is not in the nature of a thorn bush to produce grapes. Simply put, I would never do anything that would not bring glory to My Father in heaven!"

Satan knew he had been defeated. He was livid, but unable to show it.

"Question number two cuts Me deeply. At the dawn of creation, you were a sparkling jewel, radiating goodness and light to your fellow spirits. Oh, how you fell from grace! Yes, Satan, when I created you I knew you would turn into a traitor. I didn't make you do it; you chose to disobey out of your own free will. I desire true worshippers who love Me unconditionally. Satan, I have used your evil ways to test those who love Me. I have used your bad choices to strengthen the saints. The only reason you have been allowed to exist is so that My people would learn that suffering produces perseverance, and perseverance produces character, and character produces hope."

Jesus untied the golden sash around His waist. Sparkling gold dust drifted off the belt as He lifted it into the air.

"This belt is gold. Gold must be put through the fire before it is pure. In the same way, My saints must go through the fire, through life's adversities, through all the arrows that you throw at them, before they are ready to live with Me and My Father in heaven. True faith comes only through adversity."

Ken wanted to yell, "Amen." Instead, he glanced at Emily and smiled. They both knew what the other was thinking. God had used Solomon's backsliding to strengthen their faith in Him and their love for one another.

Satan sighed. He hated it when Jesus quoted Scripture.

"Question number three: Why does hell exist, and why am I not tolerant of sin?" Once again, Jesus used Scripture to answer the Devil. "'The fear of the LORD is the beginning of wisdom.' As the Creator of all spirits and humans, My desire is for people to love Me. People do not naturally love; they must be taught. They must understand that there are consequences for their actions. Discipline is vital when teaching a youngster to love and live life correctly. Those who go to everlasting punishment will be there because they have chosen to follow you. I am not unreasonable and do not desire anyone to be condemned. I long for all to come to a heart knowledge of Me. Hell is reserved for those who, by their actions, spit in My face."

Thunder sounded softly in the distance.

"Tolerance is a lie that you made up. You teach people to tolerate sin, to cover up wrong, to allow evil to go unpunished. You, Satan, push your evil agenda by accusing those who have standards to lower them or give them up altogether."

The fire in Jesus' eyes flashed toward Satan.

"Hell is for those who hurt others! Hell is for those who hate the Father, Son, and Holy Spirit. Hell is for the spirits who forsook their first love. Hell is for those who are not fit to live in My holy heaven." Jesus pointed toward the Devil and said, "Hell is reserved for you, Satan!"

The Great White Throne Judgment

A deafening blast of thunder shook the sky and the Devil's heart. Lightning rained down from heaven, lighting the sky as if it were day. The lightning streaks latched onto the balls of light surrounding the demons and slowly carried them downward.

"Guilty of trying to take over the heavens!"

Thunder pounded.

"Guilty of leading Adam and Eve astray!"

Lightning flashed.

"Guilty of treason and of sabotaging your fellow spirits!"

One could see the white of Satan's eyes.

"Guilty of murdering the saints!"

A dark orange cyclone, hundreds of miles in width, appeared. It had its own gravitational field, sucking the demons closest to it into the center. It was a black hole, and it was headed his way!

"Guilty of burning Bibles and misquoting My Word!"

Jesus' voice was like a thousand winds.

"Guilty of breaking all My commandments!"

The lava-like tornado edged closer to Satan.

"Guilty of trying to kill Me on the cross!"

The Devil was trembling in fear.

"Guilty of covering up My resurrection with lies!"

Satan started to slowly float toward the entrance to hell.

"Guilty of killing innocent children!"

The Devil could hear millions of demons screaming in anguish, gnashing their teeth at the intense heat of the hellish storm.

"Guilty of blasphemy, seduction, and betrayal."

Satan watched in horror as Blasphemy, howling in pain, disappeared into the center of the fiery tornado.

"Guilty of pride and arrogance!"

Satan tried to turn away as General Ruse followed Blasphemy into the flames of Hades. The image of the general kicking and screaming like a coward was immediately emblazoned in the Devil's mind.

"Guilty of killing My prophets!"

The Devil's black heart sputtered as he began to spin downward out of control. He made eye contact with Jesus one last time.

"Guilty of not loving the One who created you!"

Jesus turned His eyes toward the saints.

"Guilty of attempting to destroy My kingdom!"

The Devil screamed in anguish as the blackish orange whirlwind swallowed him whole.

Solomon wanted to fly to the stars and shout, "Hallelujah!" Satan was gone forever!

Jesus quoted a Scripture from Revelation 20:10: "'The devil, who deceived them, was cast into the lake of fire and brimstone where the beast and the false prophet are. And they will be tormented day and night forever and ever.'"

The hellish tornado began to slowly drop down and fade away. The cries of the demons suddenly stopped. Jesus' face was somber but steady.

"My children, never forget what you have seen. The price for evil is high, and the cost is more than any of you can bear."

The lightning suddenly disappeared from the sky. A colossal, pure white throne appeared behind the Lord. Jesus looked at the saints with compassion.

"What you are about to see will change your life forever," He thundered, His voice shaking the sky. "Your redemption is near, even right at the door!"

Jesus sat down and called the archangel Michael to His side. "Michael, bring them in one by one."

The archangel bowed at the Lord's feet.

"Yes, Master. As You wish."

Michael placed a golden trumpet—never before used, reserved for this moment in history—against his lips. As the trumpet blared, billions of people suddenly appeared to the Lord's left. They were standing in what appeared to be a sea of glass, sparkling and pure. The likeness of the firmament stretched out above them was the color of an awesome crystal. A rainbow encircled the throne, and four beasts appeared. Their legs were straight, and the soles of their feet were like the soles of calves' feet. They sparkled like burnished bronze. They had the hands of a man under their wings. Each one had four faces and four wings. Their faces resembled a man, a lion, an ox, and an eagle. Their appearance was like the appearance of torches or coals of fire. Fire was going back and forth among the living creatures; the fire was bright, and out of it went lightning. They softly sang a song of redemption.

The humans who stood in the sea of glass were those who had died without Christ. This crowd was amazed at the sight of what they thought was heaven. Many of them saw the Lord and ran toward the throne, falling on their faces as if dead. Jesus glanced at these people and wept.

Denny and his band of rebels were among this group. Their vile opinions about the Lord were suspiciously absent from their faces now.

Denny looked around at the majestic sight, and a sense of awe filled his face.

"So this is heaven," he whispered.

Larry and Kevin were directly behind him. Kevin nudged Denny in the back.

"I can't believe we made it to heaven," Kevin said, the astonishment evident in his voice.

Denny turned to face him.

"Blows me away, too, man. I knew Jesus was a forgiving guy, but..."

Staring at Jesus, Larry asked those around him, "What's He doing up there?"

A man behind Larry spoke softly in his ear. "He's assigning people's mansions to them."

Larry turned to look at the stranger and instantly recognized him. "Hey, aren't you that famous rock star?"

The man's smile was smug. "Yeah, dude, want an autograph?"

Larry began to speak, but stopped when Jesus started talking.

"People of the earth," announced Jesus, His voice filling the sky like light, "today is your Judgment Day!"

Denny's eyes glassed over. Kevin nudged him and asked, "What's Judgment Day mean?"

Denny shrugged his shoulders. "No clue!"

353

Solomon and Allison, along with all of the others who had lived through the Millennium, were directly above this glass sea and the throne of God. Nobody dared to speak as the archangels Michael and Gabriel stood beside the Lord.

A book suddenly appeared in each person's hands. Each book was generally an inch or two in thickness, depending on the length of the person's life. The covers of the books were all the same. They were gray, with the words "My Life" emblazoned in blood.

Denny slowly opened his book. He began to read, line by line, every one of his deeds, every one of his attitudes, and every one of his thoughts. He glanced at Kevin and Larry. They were babbling about the sights and sounds around them while ignoring the books in their hands. Denny's hands began to tremble as he suddenly realized that Jesus was who He claimed to be. Denny left Larry and Kevin and ran toward the front of the throne, joining the others in worshipping the King.

"What's he doing?" asked Larry.

Kevin shook his head as he glanced at his own book.

"There's something in that book that got to him in a big way," Kevin said, shaking his head in disgust as he glared at Denny.

Jesus appeared to ignore those who were worshipping Him. He turned toward the archangel Michael and said, "The Book of Life, please."

Michael nodded and handed Jesus the large book. Jesus placed it on His lap. The cover of the book resembled coal, but its pages were bloodred. Jesus looked out at the vast expanse in front of Him. Billions of people from every nation, rich and poor, famous and ordinary, from every ethnic background, were huddled together like goats without a goatherd. His penetrating eyes turned toward those on their knees; He saw that many of them were crying.

"When your name is called, step forward and face your Judge," Michael announced. The sea of glass suddenly turned bloodred as the first person was called.

"Elder Michael Martin Action," called Jesus.

Ken's heart jolted at the name. It was his father, the man who had single-handedly molded Ken into a God-hater for most of his life before the Millennium. Ken looked at Emily with tears streaming down his cheeks. Emily's face filled with compassion. She knew the story well. Ken's father was the head elder at his church and one of the biggest lukewarm, hypocritical churchgoers in the town.

Ken's father, Michael, was on his knees in front of the throne when he heard his name. He jumped to his feet and ran toward the blazing light.

Jesus stared at the man; a grave look filled the King's face. Michael saw Jesus' face and swallowed hard.

"Michael Martin Action," voiced the Lord with a stern tone. "Why should I let you into My heaven?"

Ken's father nervously smiled and answered, "I was an elder at my local church for forty years! I've tried to live a good life!"

Jesus looked at him sadly.

"Did you repent of your sins?"

Michael stared into the light emanating from the throne. He didn't really understand the question.

"I walked the aisle of my church when I was six years old."

Jesus shook His head. Again He asked, "Did you repent of your sins?"

Ken's father was speechless. Michael's soul was on the line, and he knew it. He dropped on his knees and bitterly cried, "Lord, Lord, did I not prophesy in Your name, and in Your name drive out demons and perform many miracles?"

A hushed reverence fell over the sea of people. Every eye was glued to the Lord. Ken's heart ached. His father, his flesh and bones, was standing in front of the King of the universe quoting from the seventh chapter of Matthew.

Jesus' fiery eyes penetrated Michael. The Lord looked in the Book of Life and then stared at Ken's father.

"I never knew you. Away from Me, you evildoer!"

Michael screamed, "No! No! Give me another chance! I'll make it right!"

Ken sobbed as he heard his father condemned to the fires of hell for eternity. Tears flooding his face, he felt as if his heart would break. Emily tried to console him, but the truth was too much for him to handle.

A bolt of divine light shot from the Lord, encapsulating Ken's father instantly. The ball of light holding him fell underneath the sea of glass and disappeared below their feet into the outer darkness.

"Denny Blanchard," roared the Lord.

Denny's heart leaped inside his chest. He wiped the tears from his eyes as he walked toward the Judge. His mind was racing as he formulated excuses for every sin he had ever committed.

"Why should I allow you into My heaven?" asked the Lord.

Denny began to shake.

"Master, I have made mistakes, and I'm truly sorry for them."

His voice was low and somber, his head staring at the ground before Jesus.

"Look at Me!" thundered Jesus.

Denny tried to look in His eyes, but his guilt overwhelmed him. Jesus opened the Book of Life and then frowned.

"Your name is not here."

Denny's heart dropped. Larry and Kevin wanted to run and hide from the wrath of the Lamb.

"Your sins are not pardoned! You are guilty!"

"Master!" cried Denny, his hands extending toward the light.

"I'm not your master! Your father is Satan! Away from Me, you evildoer!"

Denny jumped up and ran. Fire shot from the Lord, capturing the rebel in the blink of an eye. Denny cursed the light as it pulled him toward the blackness of hell. "No!" he screamed.

The sobering day of reckoning continued. It was becoming painfully clear to those standing in the sea of glass that they were all condemned by their actions and lack of faith. Many tried to claim that they had faith in the Lord and had asked Him into their hearts, yet their actions while on earth didn't corroborate their claims. There wasn't a dry eye among the saints or the angels. Many were looking toward the glass sea, wondering if their friends and loved ones were among the condemned. One after one, each person stood before the Judge of the world and pleaded his or her case. Each time the standard was the same. Did they have a personal relationship with the Lord that was manifested by righteousness in their lives? Lies were exposed; excuses were like stubble.

Bill and Gail were both searching among the vast numbers of people, both of them looking for their parents. They hoped for the best, but they feared the worst. Bill's father had talked the talk but never walked the walk. Gail's mother called herself a good Christian, but she had lived a life of sin and had refused to repent.

Bill spotted his father and closed his eyes. Heartbroken, Bill cried, "No, Dad, no! No, Dad, no!"

Gail was trying to comfort her husband when she recognized her mother in the middle of the crowd. She placed her hand over her mouth, choking back her sobs.

Jesus called Kevin's name and looked in the Book of Life.

Kevin tried to hide behind several larger men, but Jesus pointed at him and shouted, "Come!"

Kevin miraculously appeared at Jesus' feet. The Lord didn't allow him to speak.

"You have lived in paradise your entire life and have refused to worship Me as King. You have fallen short of the glory of God. Away from Me, you evildoer!"

"You can't do—" shouted Kevin before the Lord cut him off.

Solomon sighed, and Allison squeezed his hand. Kevin disappeared like all the others before him.

"Larry Brock," announced Jesus.

Larry had a plan as he walked toward the throne of glory. He cleared his throat and glared into the intense light.

"Jesus, I did live a righteous life up until the age of fourteen, then I backslid, Lord. Please forgive me for my mistakes. I love You!"

Jesus stared right through his heart, dissecting every thought and intention. He turned through the pages of the Book of Life, then looked at Larry.

"Your righteousness did not come by Me! You tried to do it on your own. You did not take up your cross and follow Me."

Larry's face looked flush.

"You didn't continue to the end in your righteousness because you didn't know Me. My power was not working within you. If you had loved Me, you would have obeyed Me. I never knew you. Away from Me, you evildoer!"

Larry said nothing. An angry glare controlled him as the light tied him up and dropped him into hell.

Jesus called a Pharisee's name, which Pastor Paul instantly recognized. He glanced toward the righteous-looking man as he knelt before the Lord.

"Why should I allow you into glory?" asked Jesus, recognizing the man who had contributed to His death on the cross.

The Pharisee stared at Jesus for a long while before speaking. "I've obviously made a mistake. I pursued my father's religion, and his father's religion, and so on."

Jesus opened the Book without saying a word. He shook His head.

"I do not see your name in My Book of Life. Pride sent the Devil to his final destination; sadly, it has captured your heart as well. Away from Me, you evildoer."

The Pharisee dropped to his knees and tried to repent, but it was too late. Seconds later, he was gone.

Jesus knew that His death on the cross brought hope and salvation, whereas Judgment Day brought only misery and death. How He wished He could have persuaded all these people to follow Him while they had lived. He glanced toward the saints, compassion and joy filling His face. Then He closed His eyes as He steadied His heart. Although He had done everything He could to provide salvation for all, some had chosen to reject His gift. Jesus knew that a one-sided love affair was not enough. He loved them, but they did not return His love. This choice had closed heaven's door to them. Now eternal doom was their reward.

Eighteen

Paradise

$\mathscr{J}$esus' voice filled the sky like the sound of a thousand freight trains as the final Judgment came to an end. "People of My kingdom, behold the glory of God!"

Like a sparkling diamond, a planet appeared in the sky above Jesus. It grew larger and brighter as it came closer.

The voice of the Father rumbled from heaven, saying, "'Behold, the tabernacle of God is with men, and He will dwell with them, and they shall be His people, and God Himself will be with them and be their God.'"

Ken stared in awe at the new heaven, yet his heart was still heavy. He tried to stop crying but was unable to control his emotions. Although his eyes were seeing the heavenly city, his heart could not forget the spiritual death of his loved ones and all the others who were forever lost. Emily tried to comfort him, but his pain was too great. He couldn't imagine bearing this memory throughout eternity.

As the new heaven neared them, Jesus raised His hands into the air. The Lord couldn't bear the sounds of sorrow any longer.

"It is done!" He proclaimed.

The light surrounding Him suddenly exploded in all directions. The blinding rays of light purified the saints as a summer thunderstorm cleanses the polluted sky. As the light faded, they were filled with joy. The Spirit of God had renewed their hearts, removing all scars and hurts from the past and any sadness caused by the Great White Throne Judgment.

Ken slowly raised his hands toward his face. They were the same hands, but somehow, they felt different, new, invigorated. He was exceedingly joyful. He stared at Jesus as the divine energy of the Spirit throbbed deep inside him. His mind was cleansed, swept clean by the Spirit of God.

"I have wiped away all tears from your eyes. There will be no more death or sorrow or crying; there will be no more pain, for the former things have passed away."

Jesus pointed toward the heavenly planet and said, "Behold, I make all things new. Since you have thirsted for Me and for My Father, you may now drink freely from the fountain of the water of life!"

The light from the new heaven resembled a jasper stone, clear as crystal. It sparkled in Allison's eyes as she gazed at her future home. Unable to take her eyes from its beauty, she whispered to Solomon, "Can you believe this?"

Solomon smiled. The heavenly planet mesmerized him, too.

"Thank you, Allison, for praying for me." The look on his face was priceless. She didn't need him to say what he was thinking; the peace on his face said it all.

A brilliant light encircled the planet. Heavenly fireworks exploded around them as Jesus uttered in a loud voice, "Blessed are you because you have kept My Word! Come! Enjoy the paradise I have prepared for you." Immediately, the Holy Spirit led the saints as they followed Jesus to their heavenly home.

"Oh, my!" cried Allison. The presence of the Lord and His words left her breathless. "I can't believe this is happening, Solomon. I can feel the presence of God as never before!"

An enormous grin spread across Solomon's face. For just a moment, he thought about the gravity bike and how it had almost kept him from this divine experience. How in the world could he ever have considered trading all of this glory for a foolish bike?

As they neared the God-made planet, the fantastic view was awe-inspiring. Every kind of jewel and precious metal known to man sparkled in the light radiating from Jesus.

Pastor Paul's heart leaped inside him. How he had yearned to see God's kingdom, the Lord's handiwork. He had longed to see the New Jerusalem and the Father's face. Now, all his faith and hard work were being rewarded. To finally finish the race of life and see his reward was better than he could ever have imagined.

As the saints drew closer to their eternal home, the landscape grew even more luxuriant. Daniel, Timothy, and the rest of the angels were behind the saints as they approached the new heaven. The angel had memorized the prophecies and descriptions of heaven by heart, yet to actually see it brought an indescribable joy. God had created something beyond even the angels' imagination.

Jesus was the first to touch down on heavenly ground. As He did, every tree and flower bent toward Him in allegiance. He turned toward the saints and angels, His eyes blazing with unconditional love and acceptance, and said, "Welcome to your new home!"

Trumpets blared hallelujah praises as the Holy Spirit guided the Christians to the ground. As Solomon and Allison landed, their eyes were drawn toward the gate at the east entrance to the New Jerusalem.

"Solomon," began Allison, her voice quivering at the spectacle, "would you look at that!"

Solomon followed her eyes. His mouth dropped open in disbelief. "I...I don't believe it," he stuttered. "What is it?"

Allison shook her head. "I think it's a gigantic pearl!" The magnificent sight was overwhelming.

The pure white pearl was over two hundred feet high and one hundred feet wide. Once everyone landed, more trumpets sounded from inside the city. The pearl suddenly split open as if it were a door.

Emily looked toward the striking aquamarine sky. "Where's the sun?" she wondered aloud.

Ken smiled, looking toward Jesus. "We don't need the sun when God is inside."

Emily smiled at his words. Every time her eyes wandered toward the beauty of the New Jerusalem, the Lord's Spirit led her thoughts back to Him. Jesus wanted everyone to worship Him, not His creation.

His radiance saturated the sky. Inside the gates, another light also shone, infusing the city with a color never before seen by human eyes.

Jesus walked toward the open gate. The saints and angels followed Him, and the angels began singing a song of praise.

"You are worthy, Lord, to receive glory and honor and power; for You have created all things, and for Your pleasure they are and were created."

The saints joined in the angelic song of praise as they neared the pearly gate. The heavenly hymn gave Emily goose bumps. The light emanating from Jesus appeared to brighten as their voices grew louder and more passionate.

Emily looked across the crowd to Solomon, overjoyed to see him in heaven. As she turned toward Jesus, she whispered, "Thank You, Lord." Jesus instantly turned His gaze on her. He nodded slightly and mouthed, "You're welcome." Emily nearly fainted.

Ken slowly, delicately touched Emily's hand, carefully intertwining his fingers with hers. Years of sometimes difficult parenting and lots of prayer had truly paid off.

Allison stared in awe at the pure jasper wall that surrounded the city. It was over two hundred feet high and extended as far as the eye could see. Beneath the wall lay a foundation with twelve layers, each one glowing with its own unique color of stone. The bottom layer resembled a diamond sparkling in the sunshine. The next was opaque blue with gold specks. The third stone was sky blue with a rainbow of colors running through it. The next layer looked like an emerald, bright green and striking. The fifth was white with layers of red swirled inside. On top of that was a fiery red stone, and above that lay a transparent golden yellow gem.

Struck by the wall's indescribable beauty, Allison inspected each layer. The eighth one was sea green and the ninth a transparent golden green color. Above that, a blue-green stone glowed brightly, and the eleventh layer was violet in color. The top one was amethyst, a flashing purple stone.

As they walked by the foundation of priceless gems, Allison noticed that names were written inside the stones.

"Look at that, Solomon," she said.

"Amazing, isn't it?" he responded.

"Do you see that? The names of the twelve apostles are etched inside those crystals."

Solomon smiled, but his attention was diverted by the street in front of them.

"Wow!" He rubbed his eyes in amazement. "I thought the Bible was being symbolic when it talked about streets of gold!"

They followed Jesus onto the golden boulevard. When Allison placed her foot on the glittering street inside the gate, a lump formed in her throat.

"This is it! This is heaven! Streets of gold, walls of precious stones, and a feeling that denies description." She continued to count her blessings—"God the Father and Jesus together, the angels from heaven, being with my loved ones for eternity, and..."

She caught a glimpse of a river flowing from a huge white throne set on top of a hill. Along the banks of the glistening river were the most beautiful trees she had ever seen.

"Solomon, look!" She pointed toward the fruit-bearing trees.

Solomon's skin began to tingle. "The Tree of Life!" he exclaimed, his eyes feasting on the sight.

What appeared to be thousands of fruit trees lined the banks of the river. Each tree bore the same fruit, yet each had a different colored leaf. It was like imagining the richest fall colors possible, then multiplying the picture a million times over and then some.

Then, Allison and Solomon saw God the Father. His awesome presence filled their souls with a passion they had never experienced while on earth. Sitting on His throne, He was overlooking His world. His garment was snow-white, and the hair of His head was like pure wool. A bright white light streamed from the throne, splashing the sky with a soul-soothing canvas of colors. The Lord Jesus stood in front of Him.

As the saints approached the Father, they collapsed to their knees in awe. The Holy Spirit of the Living God hovered over them all.

Timothy and Daniel, reunited again, joined the other angels entering the gates of heaven. They could sense the presence of Father God. Feeling at home again, they joined in worship. Timothy sighed softly. His heart was at peace. There was no more evil to fight, no more demons to worry about. Satan had been destroyed once and for all. The curse was history, the war was won, and now, the spoils of victory were theirs to enjoy throughout eternity.

Jesus approached the Ancient of Days, God the Father, and bowed at the steps of the throne. They had separate bodies, yet they were intricately connected in mind and Spirit. The Father stood up and lovingly gazed at His Son. The silence was electrifying; the moment, extraordinary.

A wind of light gushed from the throne as the Father spoke. "Well done, Son! You have not lost one of Your sheep."

God's voice was like a raging river; its tone was deep and full. Jesus began to walk up the steps toward the Father. Pastor Paul watched the meeting of the Godhead with a sense of awe and wonder. He had never gotten used to living on the same earth with Jesus, and now, he would be spending eternity in the presence of the Father! He thought a moment about the pain he had endured for the sake of the Cross, the humiliation and stonings, the shipwrecks and chains. He smiled and said softly, "It was worth it all and then some."

White and purple clouds with swirling silver dots appeared in the sky above the Godhead. Lightning and peals of thunder flashed around them as the Father and Son embraced in front of the creation. Joy spontaneously flooded the hearts of everyone as the Father looked into the Son's eyes.

"This is My Son in whom I am well pleased. Listen to Him, My people!" The Father lifted His hands outward.

Paradise

"Paradise is won!" He thundered as the clouds spiraled upward and then to the four corners of heaven.

Mansions suddenly appeared on the surrounding hills. Made of every kind of precious stone and gem, they had been fashioned by the Creator Himself.

Jesus turned toward the saints. His eyes filled with compassion. "Today is the moment I have yearned for since the dawn of creation." He raised His nail-scarred hands into the air and shouted, "Evil is dead!" A blast of light shot out from the Father's eyes and landed on Jesus' hands. Seconds later, the scars were gone.

The angels jumped to their feet. "Hallelujah!" they exclaimed as they thrust their swords skyward. The mystical-looking clouds floated toward the spirits. As the multicolored vapor moved over them, tongues of mist drew the swords upward.

Jesus announced, "There is no need for weapons in heaven!"

Daniel watched excitedly as his sword floated away. This is it! he thought. No more pain, no more suffering, no more smelly demons with an attitude.

Allison closed her eyes. She felt like she couldn't handle any more joy, yet her heart kept expanding to receive more. Heaven was beyond what she could have imagined, more than she could have hoped for. She recalled the verse from First Corinthians 2:9: "Eye has not seen, nor ear heard, nor have entered into the heart of man the things which God has prepared for those who love Him."

The purplish-white clouds floated away against the deep blue horizon. They disappeared with the swords—and with the past. Bill and Gail watched the clouds fade from sight.

Gail turned to her husband and whispered, "How big is this place, anyway?"

Bill's eyes sparkled as he spoke. "Nearly fifteen hundred miles wide, long, and deep. I know what you're thinking, Gail. There's billions of people and angels waiting for homes, but don't worry, honey. I did the math, and God's got it covered. We'll have plenty of room!"

They turned toward the throne when they heard a trumpet blare. Jesus faced His people. A glowing aura surrounded Him as He spoke.

"Saints, receive My reward to you for being faithful and true to your calling! Blessed are you for not denying Me. Blessed are you because you have kept the faith until the end. My reward is with Me, and today, I am giving to you according to what you have done. I am the Alpha and the Omega, the First and the Last, the Beginning and the End. Blessed are you, for you have washed your robes. You now have the right to the Tree of Life."

Jesus floated above the crowd of Christians and hovered over the river that flowed from the Father's throne. He pointed toward the trees lining the banks of the river.

"Adam and Eve disobeyed and lost the right to eat from the Tree of Life. I placed My strong angel at the gate of the Garden of Eden to prevent any humans from discovering this special tree."

Jesus picked a perfectly shaped apple from one of the trees and raised it above His head. "Every month a different fruit will bud on these trees. This is your food."

Plucking a leaf from one of the branches, He told them, "The leaves are for the healing of the saints. There will be no more sickness, no more pain, no more death, for the old order of things has passed away."

Solomon sighed, glad to know that the past was the past, and that the future offered only hope. Allison glanced at Solomon and silently mouthed, "Amen."

Jesus floated toward the Father's throne. The Holy Spirit could be felt by everyone. It was as if He was in the air they breathed. When Jesus' feet touched the ground, a deep rumbling sound could be heard in the distance.

Jesus said, "I have promised each of you a mansion in heaven. My peace I give you!"

A brilliant flash of light consumed the entire atmosphere, its intensity impossible to measure. As the light faded, Allison could hear birds singing and water splashing around her. She saw that she was standing beside a small waterfall with hundreds of trees dotting the rolling countryside. The birds were not just chirping; they were singing the tune of her favorite hymn. Suddenly she thought of Solomon and spoke his name. "Solomon?"

"I'm here, Allison," he said, his voice sweet and gentle.

She turned toward him. Her heart raced as her eyes met his. "Solomon!" The couple was now one. Their love was no longer an earthly love. Instead, they were experiencing the pure and perfect love of God. With their entire hearts, minds, and spirits open to one another, love no longer need to be expressed physically.

Solomon turned his head to the left and nodded. "Have you seen our new home?"

Allison looked toward a hill a short distance away. When she saw their eternal home, she cried, "It's the most beautiful mansion I could ever have imagined."

She ran toward it, nearly pulling Solomon's arm out of joint. Like exuberant children, they raced side by side toward the sprawling castle on the hill. Suddenly, Allison stopped and dropped to the ground. She stared at the incredibly blue sky, drinking in heaven's beauty.

"Allison," Solomon said in a surprised tone, "what are you doing?"

"I'm having some fun! Want to join me?"

Together, they rolled down the hill. Their playful laughter could be heard by their next-door neighbors, who walked toward them. When the young couple reached the bottom of the hill, Allison giggled as she sat up. "I've always wanted to do that!" Both she and Solomon were discovering what life untainted by sin could be. Even simple pleasures were better in heaven.

Allison heard the sound of familiar voices and glanced over her shoulder.

"Mom! Dad!" she yelled.

Allison ran to hug her mom and dad. She cried, "Can you believe this place!"

Her mother cupped her daughter's cheeks, and said, "It's great, honey. We've been through our house, and it's out of this world!"

Allison smiled. "Of course it is, Mom. It's an all-new world!"

"You're right, honey, and we'll have the rest of eternity to thank God for it."

Solomon's voice interrupted them as he came toward them with his parents.

"Hey, Allison, check out who our other new neighbors are."

Allison's smile broadened. "This is great!" she exclaimed as the three couples hugged.

Bill said, "I never imagined heaven could be so...uh...heavenly!" He rolled his eyes as he smiled at Allison. He had never been very good with words.

Allison smiled at her parents. "Thanks, guys, for all that you've done for me. I owe you so much."

Gail placed her arms around Allison. "Don't thank us, honey. We simply obeyed Jesus."

Allison looked at her dad. "Thank you, for..." she glanced at Solomon, emotion almost getting the best of her, "for everything!"

Bill hugged her and whispered, "I love you."

Minutes later Bill and Gail headed toward their heavenly home.

"We'll be over to visit soon," Allison called as her parents waved good-bye.

———————

Ken and Emily were getting ready to return to their own home when they heard voices whooping and hollering in the distance. The sound was coming from across the hill. They looked at each other, wondering what all the commotion was about.

"What in the world...?" questioned Ken as he strained to make out what he was hearing.

Two beings appeared over the hill. Ken recognized Timothy immediately, but he didn't know who the other one was.

"Timothy!" Ken shouted, sprinting off to meet him.

"Ken, it's so good to see you!" the angel yelled, running recklessly down the hill.

They hugged for a moment before Ken looked toward the stranger.

"Who's this?"

Timothy's smile was a mile wide.

"This is that angel I kept talking to." He patted Ken on the back. "See, I wasn't nuts. Here he is. This is Daniel."

Daniel tried to shake Ken's hand, but Ken reached out for him. "Not in this lifetime. Give me a hug, buddy."

"It's great to see you face-to-face," sighed Daniel.

"Is this that angel you kept conferring with?" asked Emily.

Timothy patted Daniel on the back.

"Yep, this is the one. He's a loose cannon, but he's my best friend."

Daniel raised a fuss. "What do you mean 'loose cannon'?"

Timothy responded, "Hey, don't get yourself in a tizzy. We'll let Ken be the judge of that."

Ken threw his hands in the air. "Hey, guys, don't get me involved."

The angels' faces turned serious. Their expressions made Ken curious. "What's going on?" he asked, grabbing Emily by the hand.

Timothy glanced at Daniel before he turned to Ken.

"We are here on a mission," announced Timothy.

Solomon and Allison made their way to the angels. The look on Ken's face was priceless. Ken wondered if the angels were going to reveal all those things he would just as soon forget.

Ken quickly stepped forward. "Why don't we talk about this stuff later?" He added quietly, "When we have a little more privacy."

Timothy shook his head.

"We can't do that, Ken."

Solomon interrupted, "Hey, Dad, why are you turning pale?"

Ken placed his hands on his face. "I am?"

Emily knew something was up. "Why are you guys really here?"

371

Timothy's poker face started to break down.

"Our mission is critical. We have been ordered by our Lord to come and..." He looked at Ken one last second. He was having too much fun. "Ken," the angel saluted him, "before we can receive our heavenly reward, we need to be judged." He paused for one last moment. "Judged by you!"

Ken's heartbeat returned to normal, but his face was puzzled.

"Judge you?"

Daniel interrupted, "Yes, sir. The Bible says in First Corinthians that you will be judging us." He looked around. "Where's your white throne?"

Ken didn't know how to respond. Deep in thought, he looked at the angels. Then something came to him.

"I don't see a throne here, and to be honest with you, I don't think I need one."

Timothy and Daniel sat down in the lush grass. Their eyes were focused on their friend and judge. It was one of the most exciting moments in their long lives, and they would relish it forever.

Ken stood in front of them and rubbed his hands together. Taking a deep breath, he said, "Well, okay. Why don't you two go through everything you need to say, then I'll let you know what I think."

Timothy began, "The first conflict I had when I was your guardian angel was—"

Solomon interrupted the angel and patted Ken on the back. "Dad, it looks like it's time for us to leave. You may be here for a while. Even though we have all of eternity, I don't want to waste any of it."

Solomon began to pull at Allison's arm. "Let's go, honey. We haven't even seen inside our new home yet. See you guys later," he told his mom and dad.

Over the next few hours, Ken, Timothy, and Daniel were in deep conversation. For the first time in his life, Ken realized the full blessing of having guardian angels. He began to see how God's loving hand had been upon him even when he had thought that he was all alone.

Paradise

As Timothy and Daniel finished their stories, the ground began to tremble. A rainbow burst through the clouds and Ken said, "Well done, good and faithful servants! Come now and enter into the Lord's joy!"

Timothy and Daniel zoomed into the sky like fire rockets. They followed the rainbow across the God-lit sky to their reward.

Ken placed his arm around Emily as they headed home. "What should we do first?"

Emily smiled, "We rest."

"Rest?" he countered.

"Yes, Ken, we rest. I can say with certainty that you have all the time in the world to do whatever you want."

"Yes, dear," he answered. As they walked home, Ken said, "So this is heaven." Ken glanced around their land and then stared into Emily's eyes. "God is so good!"

As they walked toward their mansion, a soothing hymn of redemption filled the sky around them. The song refreshed their souls. Emily closed her eyes and savored the moment. "Do you hear that, Ken?"

Ken appeared to be hypnotized by the heavenly music. He raised his hands toward God's throne, not meaning to ignore her question. He could feel the Spirit encompassing them as the sound of a multitude of angels praised God.

Solomon and Allison heard the angelic music as well. Solomon dropped to his knees in worship. Allison couldn't move as the Spirit-filled song ministered to her soul. The ecstasy of the music moved her in a way that she could never describe. It was as if the Spirit of the Living God had only partially dwelled within her in the past. Now He was filling her fully, imparting a peace that was beyond human description. "What's happening?" she murmured, bathed in the Spirit of God.

Solomon's mind was no longer on Allison, their mansion, or his parents. Nothing was significant apart from Jesus; only Jesus mattered. The soft music gradually grew louder, intensifying the bliss. Solomon began to sing.

"Holy, holy, holy, Lord God Almighty, who was and is and is to come!" Overwhelming joy filled Allison's heart as she joined her husband in singing praises to God. "Holy, holy, holy, Lord God Almighty, strength and honor and glory and blessing be unto You."

The God of the universe caressed their souls as tenderly as a mother comforts her child.

For just a moment, Allison wondered if she were dreaming. Could this be real? She opened her eyes and sighed as she saw Solomon caught up in the Spirit's presence. This was reality! This was paradise!

For most of her life, she had eagerly awaited this moment. Heaven wasn't about mansions, beautiful landscapes, or even about marriage. It was all about Jesus, adoring the Creator with all of one's being. And now, she was experiencing the completely all-encompassing presence of God.

Rhythmic trumpets blended with the angelic choir in heavenly harmony. Solomon opened his eyes and gazed toward the sparkling sky. The singing faded as the trumpets grew louder and more intense. Suddenly, Jesus' radiant face materialized against the horizon. Solomon's heart nearly leaped out of his chest as he beheld his Savior. All of creation focused on the Lord, their hearts filling with indescribable love and thanksgiving. When Solomon had become a Christian, the feeling of the Holy Spirit coming into his heart had been overwhelming, but this experience defied anything he had ever known before.

Allison and Solomon gazed upon their Salvation. A warm smile filled the Lord's face as all of creation worshipped Him. Church had begun, and it would last throughout the ages. For the first time in Allison's life, eternity became real for her. Her love for Jesus grew immeasurably as she fixed her eyes on the Author of Life.

A surge of life filled Solomon's being. Heaven was more than he had ever hoped for—it was beyond human description. He realized that it was impossible to describe the indescribable. Only those who experienced it would know this joy and peace.

Solomon took a deep breath and sighed in utter happiness. He thanked God that Jesus, his parents, and Allison had never given up on him. As he gratefully gazed into the face of his King, he recalled a verse from the Bible: "For now we see in a mirror, dimly, but then face to face. Now I know in part, but then I shall know just as I also am known." Just as a newborn baby smiles at his father, Solomon looked lovingly into Jesus' eyes. Finally, he understood what unconditional love was, and the best part was that he had all of eternity to enjoy it.

About the Author

Jonathan Cash, a meteorologist for one of the highest rated morning television newscasts in the country, is also a Bible teacher and popular speaker. Brought up in a traditionally religious home, Jonathan loved storms and the display of the power of nature. While he was in college studying atmospheric science, he became fascinated with the biblical accounts of climatic upheavals. As he read through Revelation seven times, Jonathan met the God behind the storms, the Creator of the universe and the Savior of the world. He was saved at the age of twenty-three.

Jonathan is a scientist who believes in creationism and the Bible as the inspired Word of God. As such, he brings a unique voice in reaching out to many who would not otherwise listen to the gospel message. Jonathan has established In the Sky Ministries to help fulfill his heart's desire to evangelize lost churchgoers. He lives in Chesapeake, Virginia, with his wife, Tina, and growing family.

OTHER POWERFUL BOOKS
from Whitaker House

Understanding the Purpose and Power of Woman
Dr. Myles Munroe

To live successfully in the world, women need to know who they are and what role they play today. They need a new awareness of who they are, and new skills to meet today's challenges. Myles Munroe helps women to discover who they are. Whether you are a woman or a man, married or single, this book will help you to understand the woman as she was meant to be.

ISBN: 0-88368-671-6   Trade   192 pages

Strong Medicine
Dr. Millicent Hunter

Life's traumas may seem like bitter pills to swallow. Yet God causes all things to work for our good. Here are God's prescriptions for healing the hurts and trials of life. Learn how to counteract the works of the adversary, understanding that God's strong medicine--the power of His presence--always shows up when we are at our weakest.

ISBN: 0-88368-660-0   Trade   224 pages

Loosed to Love
Dr. Rita Twiggs

You can be set free and walk right into the powerful things God has for you. Dr. Rita Twiggs shares how you can break free from the bondages that separate you from the Lover of your soul. You can be released to a new level of intimacy with the Father. Your God-given destiny awaits you. Discover a powerful purpose for your life.

ISBN: 0-88368-651-1   Trade   224 pages

ANOTHER POWERFUL BOOK
from Whitaker House

The Master Is Calling
Lynne Hammond

Lynne Hammond offers a powerful biblical perspective on prayer that takes you to the heart of meaningful, effective, an d joyful communion with God. She presents a victorious approach to worship, intercession, petition, and spiritual warfare that will revitalize your Christian life. Experience the joy of true fellowship with the Lord and be tremendously effective in prayer.

ISBN: 0-88368-634-1   Trade   208 pages